The Great Martian War

The Grand Alliance

By Scott Washburn

T0245930

ZMOK
BOOKS

The Great Martian War: The Grand Alliance by Scott Washburn
Cover Image by Michael Nigro
This edition published in 2023

Winged Hussar Publishing is an imprint of

Winged Hussar Publishing, LLC
1525 Hulse Rd, Unit 1
Point Pleasant, NJ 08742

Copyright © Winged Hussar Publishing
ISBN PB 978-1-958872-291
ISBN EB 978-1-958872-307
LCN 2023947536

Bibliographical References and Index
1. SciFi. 2. Alt-History. 3. Martians

Winged Hussar Publishing, LLC All rights reserved
For more information
visit us at www.whpsupplyroom.com

Twitter: WingHusPubLLC
Facebook: Winged Hussar Publishing LLC

Prologue

Excerpt from "The First Interplanetary War, Volume 2", by Winston Spencer Churchill, 1929. Reprinted with permission.

Although the smashing victories along the Dardanelles and Bosporus in the spring of 1913 had foiled the Martians' plans to join together their forces in Russia, Africa, and the Near East, the situation around the world was still very serious. The other great arm of the enemy offensive, the one coming out of Russia, reached the Danube in Romania. The German and Austro-Hungarian armies, which had rushed there, managed to halt the Martians along that great waterway, but unlike the force which had reached the Bosporus, this one did not retreat when its advance was halted. The battle there raged into the summer, drawing in more and more of the Kaiser's forces, the last great reserve of untapped military potential in the world.

The question facing the nations of the world was what to do next? Only a portion of the great international force which had come to the rescue of the Ottomans was needed to shore up Turkey's southern defenses once the Martians withdrew. The rest, including most of the naval forces, were free to be employed elsewhere. But where?

Every nation involved had an opinion, of course, and the debate quickly became fierce. I greatly feared that the coalition which I had labored so hard to create would splinter into its component parts, each going its separate way. The Germans and Austro-Hungarians wanted to reinforce their line on the Danube. The French and Italians wanted a major commitment in North Africa. The Americans wanted their small, but vital contingent of land ironclads sent back to North America. Even within the British Commonwealth, there was no consensus. Some wanted a greater commitment in Canada, others saw this as an opportunity to push the Martians out of the Levant and the Arabian peninsula entirely. Field Marshal Kitchener was eager to resume his interrupted offensive up the Nile to retake Khartoum. And there were the near continuous pleas for forces to retake the lost portions of our South African colony or to liberate the lost one in Australia.

Some of these proposals were completely beyond the ability of the forces available and others were too narrow to grab the imaginations of the many countries involved. I had a plan of my own, but it would take some time to organize and I was afraid there was no time. The grand alliance was on the brink of dissolution when I conceived of a smaller operation that could be put into effect at once. I convinced the allies this was not only within the capabilities of the forces at hand, but that it would yield results which all could see as beneficial...

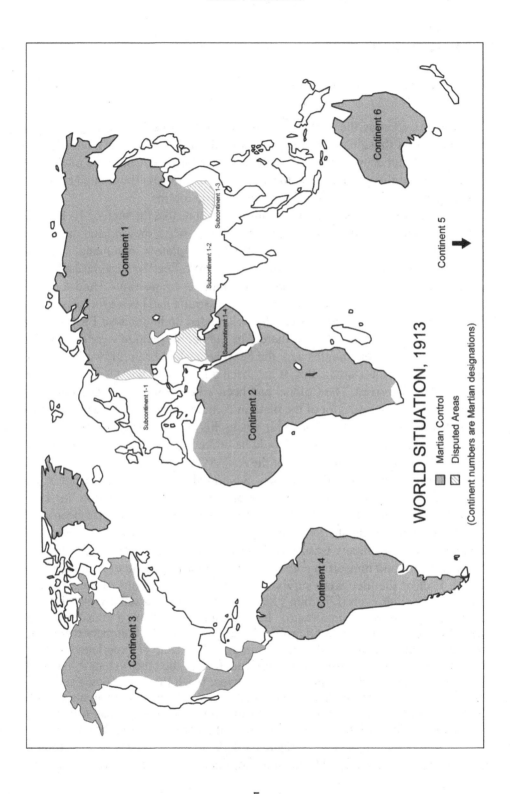

WORLD SITUATION, 1913

Martian Control
Disputed Areas

(Continent numbers are Martian designations)

Continent 1
Continent 2
Continent 3
Continent 4
Continent 5
Continent 6

Subcontinent 1-1
Subcontinent 1-2
Subcontinent 1-3
Subcontinent 1-4

Chapter One

"**O**kay! As soon as the artillery lets up, we go! No hesitation. Every second we delay gives those bastards time to get ready for us. Go on my whistle, understood?" Lieutenant Harry Calloway, commander of C Company of the 15th Newcastle Battalion, looked over the men of his command. They stared back and made affirmative gestures, or shouted enthusiastic replies.

Some of the faces were very familiar to him, like the men of 12 Platoon who had been with him since those long-ago days when they'd been defending Sydney back home in Australia. He'd just been a platoon commander then, a green-as-grass kid who had only been named an officer because he had some education and his dead father had had some political connections. He'd survived the siege and learned his job, and then when Australia had been evacuated in the face of overwhelming Martian strength, he'd ended up in the Near East with the other survivors, fighting Martians there. The men of his platoon were like family.

But then, a few months ago, the Newcastles had been thrown into a desperate fight near the Dardanelles. It had been a nightmare and less than half the battalion had survived. The Colonel had been killed, three out of the four company commanders, and a lot of the platoon commanders were left dead or badly wounded. Harry himself had been hit, losing his left eye. There had been fears that what was left of the battalion would be broken up to supply replacements to the other battered Australian units of the ANZAC Corps.

Fortunately, that didn't happen. Several shiploads of replacements had arrived from New Zealand where much of the evacuated population had been relocated. The men aboard, mostly boys not out of their teens, had been used to rebuild many of the shattered formations, including the 15th Newcastle. But replacing the lost officers wasn't as easy, and Harry, barely out of the hospital himself, had found himself in command of a company instead of a platoon.

Half of the men were survivors from the four platoons of the company and were familiar even if he didn't know each of them personally like the men from 12 Platoon. More importantly, he was familiar to them, a known quantity who they could follow with no problem. But the rest of the company were new; men of unknown qualities, sketchy training, and no combat experience whatsoever. In the two months since they'd arrived, he and the other veterans had done everything they could to whip them into shape; teach them the tactics and techniques they'd need to be effective and to stay alive. They had not arrived totally without training, but the parade ground stuff they'd been taught had little use on a real battlefield. Still, they were eager to fight and that counted for a lot.

Another salvo of shells screamed overhead like a passing express train to explode on and around the Martian positions about a mile away. He wasn't sure if the shells had come from the army's heavy guns or from a navy warship. Both services were joining in, trying to smash the Martian defenses before the Poor Bloody Infantry had to move out. The waters of the Red Sea, off to his right, were full of warships, but they had to keep their distance. The Martians had built dozens of positions mounting their new super heat rays near the narrow Strait of Bab el Mandab, creating a deadly killing zone that no ship, even the most heavily armored dreadnought, could survive.

It was up to the army to do the job. They'd been put ashore well to the north of the first emplacement and then moved south, taking out each heat ray position in turn. The Martians had tried to stop them, of course, using their standard tripod fighting machines and their fiendish little spider-machines. So far the enemy resistance had been surprisingly weak and the first dozen positions had been destroyed without heavy casualties. The optimists said that they'd taken the Martians by surprise, that the aliens hadn't expected this sudden shift of forces from northern Turkey to southern Arabia. The real optimists said that the Martians had been so badly hurt in the battles around the Dardanelles and Constantinople that they had no forces left to meet this new attack. Harry had stopped being an optimist years ago and simply felt that they had been lucky and there was no telling when that luck would run out.

The force that had been sent south was a powerful one, and up until now the Newcastles had been kept in reserve while other troops did the fighting. Not all of the men were from the Commonwealth, either; there was a French division, and an Italian one, and several brigades of Greek, Egyptian, and even some Belgian troops. But today the Australians would be leading the attack.

Another group of shells passed over and they had a slightly different sound than the others. Harry looked up and as he expected it was a group of star shells rather than explosive ones. Normally used at night to illuminate the landscape, they burst high overhead, and magnesium flares drifted slowly earthward on parachutes. So amazingly bright at night, the star shells didn't look like much in daylight, but they were distinctive enough that everyone could see them and that was the whole point. Rather than try to coordinate an attack by using unreliable pocket watches, the flares were the signal to launch the attack.

Harry put his whistle in his mouth and blew it as loudly as he could. Other officers to the right and left were doing the same thing, and the sergeants were bellowing at the top of their lungs: *Go! Go! Get moving!*

The men surged up from the shallow trenches they had scraped out of the rocky ground the evening before and went forward at a slow trot, the veterans crouching to make themselves the smallest possible target. Many of the new men were nearly erect, gawking at the spectacle around them.

And it was quite a spectacle. Thousands of infantry, supported by scores of tanks, were advancing across the arid ground. The line stretched for at least three or four miles. Hundreds of guns were still blasting away at the Martian positions, although if they followed their instructions, they would soon be shifting their aim to more distant targets to avoid hitting the attack wave as they went forward. Half a dozen aircraft were circling overhead to keep a lookout for local Martian counterattacks, and even higher, a German airship was watching for more distant threats.

Harry struggled to keep his footing on the uneven ground and cursed when he unexpectedly bumped into someone next to him and nearly fell. "Sorry, sir!" said a voice, but Harry knew that he was to blame. He still had trouble dealing with the blind spot on his left side due to the loss of his eye. He had to keep swiveling his head back and forth to make up for it.

Regaining his balance, he continued forward, glancing around at his men. His company seemed to be in good order; most men were carrying their SMLE rifles, although some also had the crazy crossbow contraptions which could toss modified Mills Bombs fifty or sixty yards with fair accuracy. The Lewis gunners had their awkward light machine guns on their shoulders while their assistants carried spare ammo magazines. Against the Martian tripods, only the Mills Bombs had any real chance of hurting them, but their rifles and machine guns, all now equipped with armor-piercing bullets, could bring down the spider machines with a bit of luck. Harry had his Webley revolver, but he knew it was nearly useless, so he always had at least two of the Mills Bombs. Today he carried four.

One other thing about his men caught his eye and he frowned. Nearly half of them had taken off their steel helmets and were wearing the distinctive Australian bush hats instead. He'd warned them about that again and again, and they were usually careful to wear the helmets during formations or inspections, but on the march—or in battle!—the damn bush hats seemed to be everywhere.

Too late to do anything about it now. He trotted forward, trying to keep his eye on the uneven ground and his men at the same time. They advanced a quarter mile without any problem. No enemy heat rays tore into them, no spider-machines emerged from hidden holes. Their objective was a smoke-obscured ridge which tumbled down from the higher hills to the east, nearly to the shore of the Red Sea. There was a super heat ray position tunneled into the rock that pointed out onto the water at the western end. It was their job to destroy it, so the fleet could come down a little bit farther and be able to support the next attack on the next position. Mile by mile and position by position, they would reclaim the whole strait. And that was the point of the whole offensive: to open up the straight. It lay at the southern end of the Red Sea and connected to the Indian Ocean beyond. In Martian hands—er, tentacles, the straight was impassible and ships headed from England to India or the Far East could not use the Suez Canal but instead had to take the much longer route around Africa. The Martians had seized the area the previous year and the Admiralty wanted it back.

At half a mile Harry was gasping and sweat ran down his face. Arabia in July! What the hell were the generals thinking? He resisted the urge to drink from his canteen and kept moving. Almost without his noticing, the barrage had shifted to targets farther south. The shells still screamed overhead, but the noise from the explosions were much fainter. The star shells had burned out and the smoke from the bombardment was slowly drifting away to the east on a gentle breeze.

His Company Sergeant Major, Arnie Breslin came up beside him. "Hot as blazes, sir," he said unnecessarily. Breslin had a habit of stating the obvious, but at least he had the sense to always approach Harry on his good side. "But the boys are doin' well. Eager to get at the blighters."

"Yeah, maybe too eager. Don't let any of the new ones get too far ahead."

"No, sir, I've warned the corporals to keep a tight rein on 'em."

Wiping the sweat away from his eye, he squinted toward the ridge. It was farther away than he'd thought. They still had a good two or maybe three miles to go. Without any orders being given, the pace of the advancing infantry lines slowed. The initial eager trot was now a more sensible walk. The sun, which had just been a pink glow on the horizon when the bombardment began, was fully up now, turning the clouds of dust and smoke into a golden haze.

Still no response from the Martians. Had the fights for the earlier emplacements used up all their reserves? Would this be an easy fight like the optimists said? Harry found that hard to believe and a moment later his skepticism was rewarded in the only way it could be.

"What's that?" cried someone. Harry glanced around expecting to see tripods or spiders, but then someone was pointing skyward, toward the ridge. Then he saw: tiny specks, dark against the azure sky. They rose up and up and then, when they were almost overhead, they began to fall.

"Cover!" he shouted. "Take cover!" He flung himself to the ground next to a sizeable rock. "Don't look! Close your eyes!"

He turned his face downward and covered his head with his hands. A moment later a series of heavy concussions shook the earth and he could see blue flashes seeping through his eyelid. The blasts seemed to punch the air out of his lungs and they left his ears ringing. He could dimly hear a few screams amid the explosions.

It was over in a moment and when no more came for a dozen quick breaths he gingerly opened his eye and looked around. The Martian barrage weapons, first encountered during the awful Dardanelles campaign, usually detonated just a few yards above the ground. They produced almost no shrapnel; they killed and maimed by an intense flash of heat and light and a massive concussion. But they produced very little smoke and didn't kick up much dust, so the visibility cleared very quickly. Harry could see a few of his men clustering around those who had been unlucky enough to have been hurt. More of the bombs were exploding further down the line, but overall, the barrage had not been nearly as intense as ones he'd seen before.

"Get them moving again, Harry," said a voice. He twisted around and saw Major Berwick, the battalion commander, only a few yards behind him with some of his staff. "Can't get stalled here. Move them out."

Scrambling to his feet, Harry replied: "Yes, sir." Turning to Sergeant Breslin he repeated the major's order. "Move them out, Sergeant."

Orders were shouted and whistles blown and soon the battalion was in motion again. Berwick had already moved on down the line. Up until the blood-bath in April, Berwick had been the commander of C Company. But Colonel Anderson had been killed and Major Stanford badly wounded and Berwick was the only company commander left, so he had inherited the Newcastles. Anderson had been a popular commander and the old timers still missed him, but Berwick was well-liked and seemed to be growing into his new position.

Just as Harry was.

Commanding a company was different from commanding a platoon. It wasn't only more men, it was more levels of command. He had four platoon commanders under him and he really didn't know any of them well. The relo-cated people of Australia could send the army bodies to fill the vacant ranks, but the men to lead them were harder to come by. Training schools had been set up in Bombay and Cairo to train junior officers, and Harry had to admit that some of these new lieutenants knew more about the regulations than he did; he never attended any formal training at all. But most were green as grass and terribly young. Three of the four platoon commanders in C Company were new to the battalion, new to the war. Only one, Lieutenant Griffin, was an older man who had come up through the ranks and was a veteran, but he wasn't from the New-castles, either.

Looking right and left, he could see those four men, leading their platoons, and doing a good job of it—so far. They plodded forward over the rough ground, under the merciless sun for a quarter-hour and neared the base of the ridge. More salvos of the Martian artillery rained down on parts of the advancing line, but the Newcastles were lucky and nothing fell near them.

A commotion off to his right caught his attention. There was a company of tanks over there and they appeared to have run into an obstacle, a ditch of some sort, and several of the large, armored vehicles seemed to have gotten stuck in it. He couldn't tell if it was a natural feature or something the enemy had contrived. The Martians had some very sophisticated tunneling machines and it wouldn't surprise him if this was something they had dug deliberately.

The infantry to either side of the tanks were pulling ahead and after a few moments, the ones that weren't stuck swung to their left and followed along be-hind the Newcastles. The ground started sloping up and they encountered craters and debris gouged out by the bombardment. There was no trace of any Mar-tian wreckage, though, so apparently the enormous expenditure of ordnance had done nothing but rearrange some rocks. Still, they were here and with only very light casualties. Once atop the ridge they could then advance down it to attack the heat ray position near the water. If the Martians were going to try to stop them, they ought to run into something soon.

The line slowed as it neared the top, a collective fear, perhaps, of what might be waiting out of sight on the other side. Harry glanced up at the circling aircraft. They had given no warning, no signal of anything waiting in ambush, but that meant nothing. The Martian tripods, and especially the small spider machines had grown very adept at concealing themselves in rough ground and then emerging to ambush advancing humans.

He reached the top and peered down into the valley that separated them from the next ridge that…and saw nothing. Wait… there was some movement. He took out his binoculars for a closer look. Peering through the right eyepiece he could see a half-dozen silvery shapes moving rapidly up the far slope—away from him. They didn't look like the standard tripods and he realized they were the artillery tripods, the ones that threw the bombardment shells. He rarely ever got a look at those since they would usually retreat if the humans got too close—just as they were doing now.

Whistles started blowing, and there was Major Berwick signaling a change of direction to the right. They had taken the ridge and now it was time to move down it to find and destroy the super heat ray positions that were supposed to be close to the water. The attack line swung around to face west, the Newcastles with them. The reserve line moved up to take their place on the ridge to deal with any counterattack that might develop from the south.

Harry and his men were near the outward part of the wheeling movement and had to double-quick it to get into their proper position, which left him gasping. Damn, it was hot! But at least the bloody Martians weren't using their black dust weapons today. They had short-range rockets which would explode into a cloud of tiny particles that were deadly. A grain on bare skin would burn into it like a bead of white-hot metal, and if inhaled, it was almost always fatal. As a result, the troops were forced to wear long sleeves and long trousers and always have their gloves and breathing masks close at hand. In heat like this, the masks were almost as likely to kill the men as the dust.

The line got itself sorted out and resumed the advance. The tank company was still right behind them, but the awkward machines were having trouble on the broken ground. The waters of the Red Sea sparkled invitingly a few miles ahead of them, and off to the north he could see the black shapes of the fleet. Some of them were still firing, vanishing briefly behind dark clouds of cordite smoke, but most were just waiting for the infantry to clear the way for them.

They were about a mile from the water when the spider machines hit them.

Harry had just turned around to look at one of the tanks that had thrown one of its tracks and slewed around sideways, when there were shouts and the sound of firing off to the right. He immediately shouted out the order to halt and find cover, but before his men could respond, a dozen nightmare shapes erupted from the ground all around them.

The Martian spider machines had egg-shaped bodies about the size of a cow with three spindly legs. They had two tentacle-like arms, one holding a miniature heat ray and the other a cutting blade. A glowing red 'eye', like the ones on the larger tripods, was set in one end of the body. Unlike the tripod machines, there was no one inside the spiders. They were controlled remotely somehow by Martians using some sort of wireless system.

The spiders had been hiding in shallow holes partially covered with dirt and rocks. As they stood up, the camouflage slid off them and their small heat rays began to claim victims. The full-size heat rays on the big tripods were so powerful that a man caught in the beam vanished instantly in a blast of flame and steam; nothing remained except a handful of ash. The small versions weren't nearly so powerful, but they could still burn a hole through a man in a few seconds.

And these were burning holes through Harry's men.

Six men fell in as many seconds, some dead and some wounded. The veteran Newcastles had taken cover at the first sign of trouble and blasted away at the spiders with rifles, machine guns, and their crossbow-launched Mills bombs. But far too many of the new men froze in place, or tried to shoot back while still standing, or fumbled with their hand-held Mills bombs while exposed in the open. They were easy targets and the spiders burned them down or sliced them up with their cutting blades.

In moments the whole area became a swirling mass of searing heat rays, roaring guns, screaming men and exploding bombs. Then the following tanks joined in with their cannons to complete the bedlam.

Men were dying, but the spiders weren't invulnerable, and one by one they were wrecked. Armor piercing bullets found weak spots and Mills bombs blew off arms and legs, and a lucky shot with a four-inch gun from a tank blew one to pieces. None of the nightmare devices had appeared very close to Harry, so he just found cover and watched his men, and the men of the other companies fight. He felt completely useless, but in a fight like this there was nothing he could do at all. It was entirely up to his men and any attempt at heroics on his part would only make things worse. He glanced aside and saw Sergeant Breslin watching him closely and knew full well the man would not hesitate to tackle him if he tried to do something stupid.

The fight was over in what seemed just a few moments. All twelve of the spiders were wrecked and a score of Newcastles—nine from Harry's company—were dead or wounded. Two of the wounded men were terribly burned and screamed horribly until the stretcher bearers carried them off to the rear.

The army was well-equipped with medical support and those men would soon find themselves in a tidy field hospital with professional doctors and nurses to tend to them. His special friend, Vera Brittain, was a nurse in one of them; he hoped she was all right.

Major Berwick appeared and got them all moving again. A couple of the new men who had lost buddies in the fight had to be pulled, pushed, or kicked back into motion by their sergeants and corporals. The veterans were not unsympathetic; they had gone through this themselves, but they weren't going to let anyone shirk their duty.

"Blimey, that was really something, wasn't it, sir?"

Harry looked and saw that it was Lieutenant Fenwick who had spoken. He was one of the new officers and he commanded C Company's 10 Platoon.

Harry didn't answer, but Fenwick kept gushing. "That wasn't nearly as bad as I expected. I mean nine men down and all, but we managed to wreck all of the bastards. The way some of the old-timers had been talking, I would have expected a dozen of 'em to have chopped the lot of us into chutney!"

Wait until you have to fight them in the dark, inside a ruined town. Your opinion might change a bit, Harry thought. Aloud he said: "We've got good men here who know how to fight the damn things. Look, listen, learn, and live, Lieutenant."

Only slightly daunted, Fenwick said: "Yes, sir."

They continued forward and the sea got closer and closer. A battalion a half mile to their right ran into another nest of spiders, and they watched from safety as they were dealt with. Shortly after that, there was noise from their rear. They halted in alarm, but apparently it was just a handful of the spider machines who had let the first line of troops pass, perhaps hoping to take the second by surprise. The fighting only lasted a few minutes.

And then they reached the top of a line of bluffs only a half-mile from the shore. There were a lot of craters from the navy guns in evidence. Their briefing had said that the Martian super-heat rays were mounted in caves and tunnels cut into the face of the bluffs, positioned to fire out to sea. Peering cautiously out from the edge, Harry thought he could see some openings to his right and left, but nothing immediately below him. They were told to hold their positions and wait.

They did so and watched the troops to either side begin to move down the bluffs toward those openings. They were joined by sapper companies with explosives to destroy the ray machines if they could get at them, or to seal up the caves if they couldn't. Harry let out a silent sigh of relief. He'd been in a Martian tunnel complex once, up north during the fight along the Dardanelles. That was where he'd lost his eye. It had been as frightening an experience as he'd ever had. He was glad he could stay above ground today.

Major Berwick put them in defensive positions and then let them relax a bit. Some of the men broke out their portable stoves and began brewing tea. Others munched on their rations. After about a half hour there was a loud rumble to the south and they could see a cloud of dust and smoke boiling out of one of the cave entrances they'd spotted.

"Is it just me, sir," asked Sergeant Breslin, "or is this too damn easy?"

"I know what you mean. They fought like the devil to hold the first couple of positions along the coast. But then the one two days ago was easier, or so I've heard. And now this. I have to wonder if they are luring us into a trap."

"Lovely thought, sir."

* * * * *

Secondary Base 14-3-1, Cycle 597,845.6

The being known as Lutnaptinav activated the communications device and contacted its progenitor, Kandanginar. The elder being responded at once, and Lutnaptinav reported: "The prey-creatures have destroyed ray positions, 8-1,

8-2, and 8-3."

"Acknowledged. What damage was done to the enemy?"

"Minimal. A hundred or so of them slain and a few vehicles. They are reorganizing to advance upon our next positions."

"Our losses?"

"Sixty-seven drones and the three heavy ray projectors. All personnel were evacuated in time."

"Good. The lost equipment is trivial, but we cannot afford to lose more of our people."

This was certainly true. The most critical need of the Race upon the Target World was people. When the first wave of the invasion arrived three cycles ago, there had been a mere six hundred of them, scattered across a planet far larger than the Homeworld. More had come in succeeding waves and those that were here created buds as quickly as their metabolisms would allow. Lutnaptinav, although only two cycles old, had a bud attached to its side which was nearing maturity. The memories Kandanginar had transferred to it during its own creation had told of a slowly dying Homeworld so desperately short of resources that the creation of a new individual was a rare thing. People would bud off replacement bodies and transfer their intellects to them when necessary achieving an immortality of sorts, but new individuals would only be needed if someone died through accident or violence.

Things were much different on the Target World. Here there were resources in abundance; the shortage was in people to use them. If the Race was attempting to colonize an empty planet, that would not be a problem. If it took thousands of cycles to build up the population, what did it matter? The Race had patience in plenty. But this planet was not empty. It was teeming with life and the intelligent species was fighting desperately to hold onto its home.

The prey-creatures—Lutnaptinav sometimes wondered what they called themselves?—were vastly inferior both biologically and technologically, but there were huge numbers of them. And they seemed able to adapt and change at a pace that was almost unbelievable. The Race was ancient and its knowledge immense. Its history reached back over a million cycles. But that antiquity had been bought at the price of a conservatism as solid as the core of the Homeworld. Change was difficult, innovation a rarity. The idea of attempting the conquest of the Target World had been so radical that it had nearly brought on a civil war.

The initial scouting expedition had reported the prey-creatures' technology as being so primitive that there would be no problem conquering them once precautions had been taken against the deadly indigenous microorganisms. But in the mere four cycles between the scouting expedition and the first wave of the invasion, the prey-creatures had improved their machines and their weapons and their techniques to an amazing degree. The first stage of the invasion had gone smoothly because the landings had been in areas far from the main population centers, but when advances had been attempted against the more populated regions, resistance had stiffened alarmingly. Setbacks and outright defeats had been suffered in many areas and in the last cycle a near-stalemate had developed.

Recently, the Colonial Conclave, the governing body on the Target World, had decreed a grand offensive to link together the Race's forces on several of the Target World's continents. It had not gone well. Clan Patralvus—

Lutnaptinav's clan—along with other nearby clans and reinforcements from the clans on Continent 2 off to the southwest had driven north to link up with forces coming south from the interior of the huge Continent 1. A great battle had been fought along a narrow waterway that blocked their path. Victory had appeared at hand, but then enemy reinforcements had shifted the balance and they had been forced to retreat with very heavy losses. Similar setbacks had been suffered on other fronts.

Now, after being driven back nearly to their starting point, the prey-creatures were threatening to retake the lands around the narrow waterway separating Subcontinent 1-3 from Continent 2. The very first part of the failed offensive had been to seize a small island in the midst of the strait and then construct a tunnel beneath it to allow the forces from Continent 2 to join them. If the prey-creatures were to take this area back, the connection would be severed.

"Progenitor," said Lutnaptinav to Kandanginar, "can we expect reinforcements? Without them I see little hope in holding this territory." Kandanginar was the third in line of command for Clan Patralvus on the Target World, so it should know the answer to that question, but the length of time it took to reply was surprising.

"No reinforcements will be coming," it said at last. "Begin preparations to withdraw all of our forces to Holdfast 14-3."

"Truly? We will abandon the tunnel? There are still substantial forces from Continent 2 in our territory, what will they have to say about this?"

"They will use the tunnel to return to their own territory starting immediately."

"But with their help we might possibly be able to hold this area. Is this a wise decision?"

"You dare question my orders, Lutnaptinav?"

"Never, Progenitor. But your manner indicates the decision came from higher up—and that you do not agree with it."

"And you dare disagree with your seniors?"

"Forgive me. I am young and ignorant."

"That excuse will not serve you much longer, Lutnaptinav. But as for the forces from Continent 2. They insist on returning to their territory. Their holdfasts are being threatened by more of the prey-creatures. They will not be dissuaded."

"We could deny them the use of the tunnel. They would have no choice but to help defend it."

"They have indicated they will accept no delay."

Meaning they would actually fight their way through? The idea was shocking. The Race did sometimes fight among themselves, but as far as Lutnaptinav knew that had not happened on the Target World. "We could threaten to destroy the tunnel..."

"Enough! You will obey your orders."

"Of course. I will make preparations at once."

Chapter Two

July 1913, New Castle-upon Tyne

"The delays are unacceptable, gentlemen. These vessels are of the utmost importance to the Navy and the Empire and they must be put into service at the earliest possible moment." Professor Frederich Lindemann looked around the meeting room in the Armstrong-Whitworth Head Office Building. It was a sumptuous space with fine wood paneling, a thick carpet, and several large windows letting in the morning light. Heavy drapes could be drawn over them to cut off the sight of the smoke-belching foundries, steel mills, machine shops, building slips, and warehouses of the vast enterprise that stretched for a mile or more along the Tyne River. Lindemann met the eyes of a half-dozen irritated men.

These men glanced at each other for a moment before one of them replied. "Mister... excuse me, *Professor* Lindemann, I don't believe that you—or His Majesty's government—fully appreciates the engineering challenges posed by these... devices. They are unlike anything that's ever been built before."

Lindemann flinched slightly at the misuse of his title. He was quite certain it had been deliberate, but there was nothing he could do about it. The speaker was Sir Andrew Noble, 1st Baronet and Chairman of the vast Armstrong-Whitworth conglomerate. Before he became the head of the biggest arms manufacturer in the Empire, Noble had been a scientist of considerable note in the field of explosives and had collected a fistful of exactly the sort of awards and commendations Lindemann dreamed of acquiring himself. Add in the fact that the bald, bewhiskered Scotsman was forty years his senior and the man outranked him professionally and socially by such a degree he could call Lindemann anything he liked.

Still, it rankled. Lindemann might have been young and with few famous accomplishments, but he was also the personal representative of Winston Churchill, First Lord of the Admiralty (and some said, the next prime minister), and the titular head of the project to design and build Britain's first land ironclads. That should have earned him some measure of respect. He cleared his throat and leaned over the table around which they were all standing. It was littered with papers and engineering drawings. He brushed a few aside, found what he was looking for, and then picked it up and slid it toward Noble. It was a photograph of a huge tracked vehicle which looked like a cross between an army tank and a navy warship.

"Unlike anything ever built *in England* before, you mean, Sir Andrew. The Americans seem to have managed it. Not just once, but over twenty times now, with more on the way. Are you saying the Americans can do something we cannot?"

Noble's face reddened, but before he could answer, the man standing next to him, Noble's son, John, broke in: "No one is saying we *can't* do it. But it took the Americans nearly two years to build the first one of theirs, and longer to work out all the problems. We have only been working on this for six months!"

"As I recall, the Navy managed to construct the *Dreadnought* in less than a year. And that was a ship just as revolutionary as the land ironclads."

"But it was still a *ship*, Professor," said Sir Andrew. "A ship, not this monstrous… crossbreed that Churchill is asking for. The ship part of it we *could* build in a year—much less, actually—but trying to mate it with the caterpillar tracks and then make it functional on both land and sea is the problem."

"The Americans did it."

"Aye, but they didna' do it vury well, mon!" Noble's Scottish accent, normally rather faint, often blazed out when he got irritated—and that seemed to annoy him even more. He calmed down before continuing. "The first American land ironclads couldn't even float on their own. They needed to have additional 'floatation modules' attached if they wanted to travel by water. These had to be jettisoned before they could go ashore. Their next batch could float—barely—but they were slow at sea and slow ashore and horribly prone to breakdowns. We've been tasked with creating a machine that can travel long distances at moderate speeds, both ashore and afloat, and with great reliability. Frankly, Professor, I'm surprised that he didn't demand that the thing could fly like an aeroplane, too! Churchill may be a great lord of the admiralty, but he is no engineer."

Lindemann frowned. "So you are saying Armstrong-Whitworth cannot fulfill this contract, Sir Andrew?"

Noble snorted. "Sir, there is no shipbuilding or construction firm in the world that could do so. You have to understand: any ship, any machine is a compromise. A compromise between size, weight, and the equipment you want to put into it. In the case of a warship you have the armament, the armor, the engines, the fuel bunkers, and a host of other items that all have to be crammed into a hull of a certain size. If you want more weapons, or more armor, or a higher speed, without increasing the size and weight, you can only get them by sacrificing one of the other things. More armament means less armor and less speed. More speed means less armor and armament, and so on."

"I understand that, sir," said Lindemann.

"Well, clearly Mr. Churchill doesn't! He wants everything on the list—power, protection, and speed—and doesn't want to sacrifice anything to get them. Add in the amphibious nature of this beast and it's simply impossible to give him what he wants. I'm sorry, Professor, but there it is."

Lindemann frowned, but he knew that in truth, Noble was almost certainly correct. In the early planning sessions at the Admiralty, Churchill and some of the admirals had taken the specifications for the American land ironclads and had simply made everything just a tiny bit larger. A thirteen-point-five inch main gun instead of a twelve, larger secondary guns, thicker armor, higher speed, more fuel capacity, the American design writ large. But they had given no thought to what that would do to the weight of the machine. The extra weight meant bigger engines, bigger caterpillar tracks. The larger size meant that the armor had to cover a greater area, so then that would weigh more—meaning even larger engines to keep the same speed. It was a vicious circle.

After a few moments Lindemann sorted through the papers on the table and found the one he wanted. It was a design proposed by the Armstrong-Whitworth engineers. At first glance it appeared to be an inferior version of not just Churchill's design, but the Americans', too. Smaller guns and less armor, although the Armstrong people claimed a better speed and more reliable mechanical system. Most importantly they claimed they could build the first one in nine months and the following ones in six.

"You're confident you can make this work?" asked Lindemann.

"Yes, Professor," said the elder Noble. "Just give us the word."

"And you're certain that a pair of eight-inch guns will do the job? The First Lord was set on the thirteen-point-five."

"Every report indicates that an eight-inch shell will destroy a Martian tripod just as thoroughly as a larger gun," said one of the engineers; Lindemann couldn't recall his name. "And the twin guns will have a much higher rate of fire and the reduced recoil will allow us to save weight on the structural support for the turret. Improved performance for less weight. That is the key to success, Professor."

"And the coil gun in the forward mount? Could it be swapped out with one of the American Tesla Cannons if and when they are available to us?"

"Assuming it's no larger than what we've seen, then yes, the mount should be large enough, and the electrical system should be able to power it."

"But what about the lesser amount of armor? The Martians are now employing more powerful heat rays. How will this design be able to survive them?"

"Less total *weight* in armor," said the younger Noble. "But with all due respect to our American cousins, they didn't give proper thought about how to best place the armor on their machines, or the location of their vital areas. For example, the magazines for their main, secondary, and tertiary batteries are in three separate locations, each one requiring armor. Our design concentrates all the magazine space in a central area and then similarly concentrates the armor. The result is thicker armor at the critical points but for less weight overall."

"Sort of putting all your eggs in one basket, aren't you?" asked Lindemann. "If an enemy ray does penetrate through the armor to the magazine, you'll lose the whole ship."

Noble frowned and shook his head. "In a vessel... ship of this size, if any one of the magazines exploded, the others would be sure to go up, too. I assure you, Professor, our design lessens the danger rather than increases it."

Lindemann sucked on his teeth and nervously tapped his finger on the table until he forced himself to stop. "And you are confident about the speed and endurance figures you have claimed here?"

"Yes. By extending the forward hull downward, we provide streamlining for the caterpillar tracks. In the American design they create an enormous drag in the water. No wonder they can barely move on their own and require a tow for any sort of long distance movement. We feel confident this will be able to do ten knots in calm seas. Land speed," Noble shrugged, "probably not much more than the Americans, but still enough to keep up with a ground advance. And we're using fuel oil instead of coal. Much quicker and easier to refuel and fewer crewmen needed. Professor, if you want an effective weapon in a short time, this is the route to follow."

Lindemann scowled but stared at the drawing before him. It was *not* what Churchill had asked for and he was used to getting what he wanted. But Lindemann was coming to believe the Armstrong men were right in what they were saying. And, they clearly believed in this design. If given the go-ahead they would throw themselves into it with a greater fervor than if they were forced to build something they didn't believe in. And right now speed of construction was the issue. Churchill had indicated he had some grand strategic plan in mind which required the land ironclads. He wanted them and he wanted them soon.

"Very well," he said at last. "I will recommend your design to the First Lord as soon as I can meet with him. If you can provide me with a set of these drawings, I'll be on my way."

The faces around the table all brightened significantly. A duplicate set of drawings in a leather valise appeared like magic and Lindemann tucked it under his arm.

"C-can I carry t-those for you, sir?" asked a hesitant voice from just behind him.

Lindemann turned to see a very young man wearing the uniform of a naval sub-lieutenant staring at him anxiously. Oh, yes, his new aide. The man had not uttered a word throughout the whole meeting and Lindemann had nearly forgotten he was even there. A few weeks earlier, Churchill had decided that his science advisor should have an aide and with the weight of his workload Lindemann had readily agreed.

He quickly came to regret the decision.

There was nothing wrong with the man himself; he was reasonably bright, attentive, and except for a distinct stutter, a pleasant enough assistant. The problem was his name.

His first name was Albert, nothing wrong with that, but his last name was Windsor. He had three middle names, too, but it was the Windsor that was the problem. And his title. He was the Duke of York and the second in line of succession to the Throne of England.

He'd graduated a few years ago from the Royal Naval College, Osborne, and after two years of seasoning as a midshipman, had been promoted and apparently landed in Churchill's lap. Considering his parentage, he obviously had to be handled with kid gloves, and with the losses the Royal Navy had been taking recently, a ship-board assignment was probably considered too risky. The First

Lord had to do something with him—and then he'd thought of Lindemann.

It wasn't that the lad wasn't eager to please, and even useful at times, but Lindemann found it very difficult to treat him as a subordinate. One false word might ruin his career permanently. It was like walking around with a time bomb.

"Ah, yes, thank you, Albert," he said, handing him the valise.

The Armstrong people escorted them out of the building and they soon found themselves in a carriage drawn by four fine horses being whisked to the railway station. Their route took them through the immense Armstrong complex filled with furnaces and foundries, smelters and workshops, factories and building slips. After only a short wait at the station, they boarded an express train of the North Eastern Railway. They had a first class compartment all to themselves, as was only proper. It had a fold-down table which Lindemann soon covered with the drawings and his own writing paper. As the train pulled out of the station, it moved along the river for a mile or so, before heading south. If there were no delays, they ought to be back in London before dinner.

To the rhythm of the train's clickety-clack he composed his report. This was for Churchill's eyes and it had to be as clear and concise as possible. The First Lord had no patience with sloppy writing or wasted words. The man was a superb writer himself, and struck right to the heart of a matter with an admirable directness. He expected the same from his subordinates—but rarely got it. So he had established a rule that limited any report—no matter how complicated—to a single sheet of paper. *One side* of a single sheet of paper. If you ran over, he wouldn't read it.

Lindemann had been working for Churchill for about a year and a half. He'd first met him by chance in November, 1911 when they were both taking flying lessons of all things. The First Lord, impatient at the slow pace of British developments in aircraft, had grabbed the steer by the horns in his usual fashion and created an air arm for the Royal Navy. But then, to the horror of both his wife and the instructors at the fledgling Navy flying school, he had decided that he wanted to learn to fly himself. Lindeman, at that time working part time for the Advisory Committee for Aeronautics, had also decided he wanted to learn to fly, but in his case to try to solve the usually-fatal phenomenon of aircraft spins.

Neither of them, as it turned out, had ever completed their training, other events having intervened, but Churchill decided that Lindemann, with a degree in physics, was exactly what he needed in a science advisor. And so, barely twenty-seven years old, he had found himself a close advisor to the First Lord and rubbing elbows with admirals and ministers of vastly greater experience and prestige.

He sometimes felt in over his head, but with Churchill's steady support— once he decided you were one of 'his men', he would stand by you like a rock— he had managed to do his job. Most of the time his job consisted of giving Churchill the scientific justification for doing things he had already decided to do. It *was* possible to change the man's mind if he was in the wrong, but you had to be ready for a ferocious argument before he finally gave way. Still, he would respect you for having the nerve to stand up to him.

Lindemann hoped that he would not have too hard a time to convince Churchill to go along with the Armstrong design for the land ironclads. He went through three drafts of the report before it said everything that needed to be said—and would hopefully fit on a single page once it was typed up.

He hesitated for a moment and then handed it to Albert, who had been sitting unspeaking—and nearly unmoving—this whole time on the other side of the compartment. "Here, what do you think?"

The young man read it through carefully and then looked up. "S-seems very clear, sir. It c-covers most of the main points that were discussed. B-but it's rather… short, isn't it?"

"Churchill likes short. He's a very busy man."

"Y-yes, that was the impression I got the few times I've seen him. D-do you think he'll go along with the Armstrong design, sir?"

"He won't be happy; he likes getting his own way. But he wants the ironclads as soon as humanly possible and I think he'll choose speed of delivery over getting the design he wants. He's working on some new strategic plan that requires these machines and he won't want any more delays." Albert handed the report back, and Lindemann folded away the drawings and the other documents and fit them carefully into the valise.

By that time the train had passed through Durham and Darlington and would be stopping for a short while in York. Lindemann leaned back in his seat and watched the countryside roll past. This region was quite flat and almost completely devoted to agriculture. Fields full of wheat, corn, barley, rye, and potatoes zipped past his window. Every square yard appeared to be under cultivation. Prior to the invasion, England imported a great deal of its food, but with large parts of Canada and the United States—the two biggest suppliers—under Martian occupation, there was little coming from there these days. England had been forced to become self-sufficient in food. During the first few years things had been very bad with malnutrition common and outright famine in some areas. A few imports from untouched parts of Europe had helped, and a massive program to increase local production of food had finally carried them through the crisis.

The fields he passed were dotted with women and children working in them. With most of the young men in the military, there was a serious shortage of labor, too. Some of the slack was being taken up by the refugees from the far-flung corners of the Empire which had been occupied by the Martians, but not enough. Factories and mines were going at full blast, working around the clock, seven days a week, and many women and children had been drawn to them. Many more were involved in agriculture. Schools only ran for a few months during the winter these days and the domestic life of the common Englishman was being transformed almost beyond recognition.

For the upper class—which Lindemann was very much a member of—things were not too bad. If you had money you could still get meat and eggs and white bread, cheese and wine and brandy and many other things that most people would consider luxuries. Lindemann felt no guilt over those luxuries. His class of people were the ones that kept the Empire running; surely they deserved these little amenities. He glanced at Albert and wondered what the food was like at Buckingham or Windsor.

The express train began to slow as it approached York. The tracks of the railway passed through a gap in the ring of fortifications which encircled the city. A pair of massive concrete redoubts sat on either side of the gap. There were many more of them spaced a quarter mile or so apart, all of them connected by thick earthen ramparts with deep ditches in front. Heavy guns were mounted in the redoubts and more were in revetments behind the walls.

After the first invasion, England had spent years preparing in case there would be a second attempt by the Martians. The strategy settled on by the military and the government had two main parts. First, there would be a number of mobile army forces that, at the first sighting of the enemy, could be rushed to any spot in the British Isles within a few hours to immediately assault any newly-landed cylinders. The first invasion had revealed that it took the Martians a day or more to assemble their fighting machines once they had landed. An immediate attack, it was hoped, could wipe out these landings before they were able to defend themselves. The other part of the strategy was to heavily fortify the major cities so that even if a few of the invaders eluded the Army's flying columns, they could do little serious damage before forces were brought to deal with them.

It seemed like a good plan, but sadly the Martians did not cooperate.

Clearly, they feared exactly the sort of defense which had been prepared by the English and most of the other civilized nations of the world. So instead of landing close to populated regions, their cylinders had landed all over the world in the most remote and difficult to reach places possible. By the time any military forces could reach the landing sites, the Martians had their machines assembled and were ready to fight. Not a single cylinder landed in England. Nor in all of Europe. The obvious conclusion was that the Martians had been observing Earth for some time, probably with larger and better telescopes than humanity yet possessed. They had been able to map out where all the major cities were located and selected landing sites far away from them.

So, despite all the plans and hopes of Earth's militaries, the Martians had been able to establish well defended strongholds on each of the planet's continents. Within these fortresses the aliens had set up automated factories which could produce their war machines at a frightening pace. Indeed, the size of the Martian armies appeared to be limited only by the number of Martians available to pilot the machines. Analysis of the bodies of the aliens found after the first invasion had revealed that they were asexual, reproducing by a budding process. But it was not until the second invasion that further studies had revealed that apparently the newly budded Martians reached maturity in an amazingly short amount of time and they were able to operate complex machinery at a stage where human babies were still struggling to turn over in their cribs. Still, there were very few Martians on Earth in absolute terms, and even with their great rate of reproduction, that would remain the case for the immediate future.

Looking out the window of the train, they noted that there was construction work going on around the York fortifications. "L-looks like they are f-fixing the place up," said Albert. "I wonder why?"

"There's another opposition coming up in January," said Lindemann.

The boy looked puzzled for a moment and then his eyebrows shot up. "Oh! Right. Another w-wave of those cylinders m-might be coming."

The other way the enemy could increase their numbers was through direct reinforcement from their home world. Enormous launching guns on the Red Planet could hurl these reinforcements across the gulf of space to land on Earth. The Martians launched their cylinders a few months before Earth and Mars reached their closest points in their respective orbits, and the cylinders arrived a few months afterwards. The oppositions occurred every twenty-six months, more or less, and each time they did, the aliens launched another wave. The numbers launched each time varied, but so far all the arriving cylinders had fallen inside territory already controlled by the Martians. Nevertheless, as each opposition approached, preparations were made because no one wanted to assume there would be no direct attack on England or other populated regions.

The train eased into the York station and came to a halt. There would be a quarter-hour delay while the engine was watered. Lindemann stepped down to stretch his legs along the mostly deserted platform. He sent Albert off to buy lunch for them at the station's tavern. Not many people were traveling these days. A special permit was needed for any non-essential travel. If you had money, or the right connections, it wasn't that hard to get one, but few common folk could manage it—not that there were many places to go. Most of the usual places of entertainment were shut down, although not drinking establishments, of course. Dance halls, race tracks, and most of the seaside resorts were closed. Many of the museums and theaters and operas were also shuttered. Some of the most exclusive ones were still open as well as places for the use of military men on leave, but for the most part England had become a grim and dreary place.

Albert returned with two box lunches but shook his head. "P-pretty sorry fare, sir, I-I'm afraid."

"It will have to do." Just then, the engine's whistle gave a short toot and they climbed back into their compartment and were soon off again. Albert was right about the lunch: sliced potatoes fried in grease, a piece of brown bread with no butter, and a slab of fish which defied identification. Two bottles of thin, watery ale rounded it off. He ate what he could stomach and put the rest aside. Albert ate all of his and then finished off what Lindemann had refused.

Lindemann leaned back in his seat, closed his eyes, and tried to nap. He would have to report directly to Churchill when he reached London, and for the First Lord of the Admiralty, working hours usually stretched well into the night. He would often keep working until two or even three in the morning and then go to bed and sleep until late morning. It drove the military men around him to distraction, but his servants and civilian staff had gotten used to it. Lindemann was still adapting.

He did manage to doze off for a while, but kept waking up when they would stop at a station or if there were any particularly strong jolts. Each time he woke, Albert was there staring at him, or out the window. At least he wasn't prone to chattering. Lindemann fell asleep again and when he woke, was surprised to see the sunlight streaming in the window at a considerable angle. He must have slept for several hours.

"Where are we?" he asked.

"J-just left Newark, sir," said Albert. "Peterborough is n-next and then London."

He rubbed his eyes and stared out at the landscape. Yes, he recognized where he was now. The train was coming down out of the midlands and heading into the valley of the Thames. London was still sixty miles away, but there were more and more factories to be seen. Ugly brick buildings with tall smokestacks belching black clouds into the sky, tinting the afternoon sunlight. Mounds of coal were piled ready to feed the insatiable furnaces; a black grime covered everything, even the trees. It was a gray, dismal landscape filled with gray, dismal people trudging to their next work shift.

It was depressing, but utterly necessary. The railroad sidings were clogged with flat cars carrying tanks and guns and box cars filled with ammunition. This was a new sort of war and it would not be won by men carrying rifles and bayonets—although those were needed in plenty—but by machines. The invaders, soft, weak creatures nearly helpless in Earth's powerful gravity, were totally dependent upon their machines. Mankind, if it was going to win, needed machines, too. Perhaps not as good as those of the Martians, but in numbers the aliens could not match.

"P-pretty impressive, isn't it, sir?" said Albert.

"What is?"

"All the s-stuff we're making." He gestured out the window. "I r-read we're producing near to five hundred tanks a week. Tanks, guns, aeroplanes, it—it's a lot of power, sir."

"Oh. Yes, it is impressive. But the trick seems to be bringing all that firepower to bear on an enemy thousands of miles away. Getting it there, keeping it supplied, keeping the machines running. It's all very complicated."

"Yes, sir."

They fell silent again. The train stopped in Peterborough and Lindemann had Albert dash off to send a telegram to the Admiralty requesting that a staff car meet them when they arrived. An hour later, they rolled into King's Cross Station, and somewhat to Lindemann's amazement, the car was waiting for them as requested. Fifteen more minutes saw them deposited in front of the Admiralty building.

It was a four-story structure of yellow brick built in the Georgian style. Three broad bays faced Whitehall, and the rear of the large structure was on the Horse Guards Parade, beyond which was Downing Street where the Prime Minister's home was situated. Marine sentries were on guard around the main entrance, but they did not challenge them as they strode past. They had seen Lindemann often enough and Albert's uniform assured them they had business there. At least one thing about fighting Martians: you didn't need to worry about spies slipping in.

They went up two flights of stairs and walked down several corridors to reach his small office. He dropped off his report with one of the typists and inquired about Churchill's whereabouts. He was in a meeting with the Prime Minister and wasn't expected back for at least an hour.

Sitting down at his desk, he went through a small pile of mail which had accumulated in the two days since he'd left. All of it was routine except for a letter from William Eccles at the National Physical Laboratory. The Laboratory was where Lindemann had his actual job, even though he almost never went there anymore since Churchill had drafted him as his science advisor. Eccles was his boss. Opening the letter, he saw that no, Eccles wasn't his boss any longer and he now had no 'real' job. *'Your lengthy absences have made us reluctantly conclude that we can no longer continue your employment here. We request that you take all necessary steps to turn over your responsibilities to James Chadwick and remove any personal effects at the earliest possible time.'*

He'd been expecting this; actually he was amazed that it had taken this long. He didn't really regret it since his responsibilities at the Laboratory had been routine and not terribly rewarding. There was, however, the matter of his salary. The position of science advisor to the First Lord of the Admiralty was not an official government position and he received no pay for the work he did. He'd been living on his NPL salary and the modest allowance his wealthy father granted him. His lifestyle was not especially lavish, but he could not get by on just his allowance. He supposed he'd have to talk to Churchill about this, but he was reluctant to, because Churchill, despite his glorious forebearers and his current exalted position, was clearly not a wealthy man, either. His lovely wife, Clementine, in private moments, would sometimes complain about Churchill's spendthrift ways and the extreme difficulties she had in making ends meet. The First Lord might not be terribly sympathetic towards Lindemann's financial worries.

Albert was sitting silently on a small chair across from the desk and Lindemann noticed that he was shuffling his feet and checking his watch. Checking his own watch, Lindemann saw it was after six. "I think you can go, Albert," he said. "Not likely to need you again tonight. See you in the morning."

"Yes, sir," he said, springing up. "Thank you, sir, good night." He was gone in an instant. Lindemann wasn't sure where the young man lived. He was a serving officer, but Buckingham Palace was only a short walk away. Did he stay there with his family?

Lindemann put Sub-lieutenant Windsor out of his mind and concentrated on the other correspondence on his desk. He briefly thought about getting some dinner, but the boxed lunch from York was still weighing heavily on his stomach and he thought better of it. He was nearly at the bottom of the pile when the typist came in and sheepishly informed him that his hand-written report did not *quite* fit onto one page. He snorted and quickly went through the document and managed to eliminate enough words so it would fit. He thrust it back into her hands and she hurried out to retype it.

A few minutes later she returned with the corrected report. "Oh, and pro-fessor, a messenger just came by to tell you that the First Lord is in his office and waiting to see you."

"Ah, good. Thank you," he replied. He looked at the document and then back at her, and feeling a bit embarrassed by his earlier snit added: "Well done, Miss Taylor." She blushed and stammered a thank-you of her own and fled back to her desk. Lindemann followed her out and then headed for Churchill's office.

He found the First Lord in a jubilant mood, sipping from a glass of whis-key and with a cigar clutched in his fist. He was talking with Prince Battenberg, the First Sea Lord, resplendent in his uniform, but immediately turned when he saw Lindemann. "Ah, there you are, Professor," he said. "Come in, come in."

"Good news, sir?" ventured Lindemann.

"Yes! Splendid news! We've re-taken the Bab el Mandab Strait! The route to the East has been reopened."

"That's wonderful, sir. Congratulations." Lindemann knew this had been weighing heavily on Churchill's mind ever since the Martians had seized the area and shut down the Strait the previous October. A hastily arranged attempt to retake the area had been repulsed with disastrous losses shortly afterwards and any further attempt had been postponed due to the extremely dangerous Martian drive against Constantinople. But with the defeat of that offensive, Churchill had resumed the drive to retake the Strait and it appeared to have succeeded. "Did the Martians put up much of a fight?"

"Not nearly as much as we were expecting," said Battenberg. The Prince, despite living in England for nearly fifty years, still had a trace of a German accent—just as Lindemann did. "They fought hard for the first dozen super heat ray positions, but then they just seemed to give up. They pulled out, leaving their base and quite a lot of equipment. Overall, our losses were very light."

"We've taken Perim Island and will fortify it and also a big area on the Arabian side to make sure they can't close it again," added Churchill. "We con-firmed our suspicions that the Martians had connected the island to both the Ara-bian and African sides with tunnels. That's almost certainly how they captured the island in the first place."

"Are the tunnels still usable?"

"We're not sure. No one wants to venture very far down them, and I can't say I blame them. They are starting to fill with water, though. The Martians must have had pumps going to keep them dry, but they seem to have been shut down.

Unless we want to install pumps of our own, they'll soon be unusable even if they are still intact."

"Probably safer to just destroy them and be done with it," said Battenberg.

"The one leading to Africa certainly, since we don't control the other end, but the one to the Arabian side might be worth keeping," said Churchill.

"If we can keep the sea out."

"But I understand you wanted to see me, Professor," said Churchill, taking a long draw on his cigar.

"Uh, yes, sir. I met with the Armstrong people about the land ironclads today and…" He took out the drawings he'd been given, spread them out on the table, and held out the report. Churchill took it, glanced at it briefly, turned it over to make sure it *was* just one side of a single sheet, and then set it on his desk.

"Pray give me a summary, if you will."

Lindeman swallowed and said: "Yes, sir." He had hoped that he could arrange to have Churchill read his report *first* and then follow it up with a discussion after the First Lord had gotten over his disappointment, but that was not to be. So, he gave a brief description of the conversation, emphasizing that to insist on the original design could lead to lengthy delays, and pointing out that the Armstrong design should be nearly as effective and they could produce it much more quickly.

Churchill was frowning and chewing on his cigar and flipping through the drawings Lindemann had brought. He snorted and looked to Battenburg. "What do you think, Louis?"

The First Sea Lord picked up one of the drawings and peered at it for a moment. "Looks potent enough," he said. "And if you really hope to go ahead with your new plan, we simply must have these things soon."

Churchill drained his glass and then stared hard at Lindemann. "Very well," he growled. "Order them to proceed. But let them know there will be Hell to pay if they can't stay on schedule."

"Yes, sir," replied Lindemann, relieved. He hesitated and then asked: "New plan, sir?"

Churchill brightened. "Yes. Now that we have the Strait back in our hands, we need a new goal to keep this alliance together. The Germans are insisting that we help them out along the Danube and in Poland. The Martians are shifting forces north and west now, apparently trying to outflank the Kaiser's line on the Danube."

"And we are going to help?"

"Yes, no choice that I can see. But I don't want to just feed our troops into that meat-grinder alongside the Germans and Austrians already there. I've thought of a better way to help out, something to change the whole situation. Instead of meeting the scoundrels head-on, we'll slip around them and hit them in their soft underbelly."

"Uh, where, sir?"

Churchill turned and went to one of the large wall maps that were everywhere in the Admiralty building. He put a pudgy finger on the Red Sea, where the operation to reopen the Strait had just concluded. He slid it up, into the Mediterranean, then through the Dardanelles into the Black Sea, and finally stopped on the Crimea.

"Right here!" he said triumphantly.

Chapter Three

July 1913, Near Bab el Mandab Strait

"To victory!"

Harry wasn't sure who had shouted, but he willingly raised his glass and joined in the toast. Around him, all the other officers of the 15th Newcastle did the same. The fighting had ended a few days ago when the Martians had up and high-tailed it off to the north, leaving their defenses inoperable and harmless. The battalion had gone into a bivouac on the shores of the Red Sea a few miles north of the small island that sat in the narrowest part of the strait. Their quartermaster units had caught up and supplied tents, food cooked in the field kitchens—and some beer. It was late afternoon and the sun, which had blazed down on them all day, was nearing the horizon.

The officers had all gathered by Major Berwick's tent, but the celebration extended to all the rank and file of the battalion, too, and beyond. Harry could hear other celebrations in the other camps that stretched along the shore. Some of the shouts were not in English and there was some unfamiliar music coming from various directions. But as he listened he became aware that the shouts and cheers were dying down.

"Just about time, sir," said Lieutenant Fenwick.

"What? Oh, right, the bomb." He took out his field glasses and directed them on an area to the right and beyond the island. A few ships were out there, but they appeared to be vacating the scene. The Martians had dug tunnels connecting the island to the Arabian and African shores. The commanders wanted to keep the one to Arabia, but had decided to destroy the one leading to Africa. A worthless old ship had been packed with explosives and was going to be sunk right over top of a part of the tunnel and then detonated. The explosion was expected to collapse a big section of the tunnel. The ship itself had disappeared beneath the waves about ten minutes ago.

"Why not just send the explosives into the tunnel from our end?" asked someone. "Why waste a ship?"

"I heard the tunnel is flooding pretty quickly," said Harry. "No one wants to go down into it. Would you?"

They watched and checked the time, but the designated hour for the explosion came and went. Harry was just about to give up and go back to his beer when there was a strange sort of... *burp* out on the water. A section of the sea seemed to rise up a trifle and then dissolve into a roil of white foam that quickly dispersed. A faint sound, nothing at all like an explosion, could be distantly heard. And that was it. The men shook their heads and went back to celebrating.

"So what's next for us, do you think?" asked Fenwick.

"I haven't heard anything," said Harry.

"Just so long as they don't keep us here," said Lieutenant Boyerton, leader of 9 Platoon. "Just too bleedin' hot."

The other officers agreed, although a few who had lived in the Outback made some extravagant claims about the heat out there. But that was the big question in the battalion: *what next?* They had heard that now that they had recaptured the strait, they were going to protect the Arabian shore so that the Martians couldn't take it back again. That would mean fortifications and a substantial garrison. And that garrison would be stuck here on a barren shore with absolutely nothing to do but sit and swelter and wait for an attack which might never come. None of the Newcastles wanted any part of that.

The celebration went on well into the night, but eventually Harry sought out his tent. As a company commander he rated his own tent. When he had his platoon, he shared one tent with the other three platoon commanders. That could be annoying at times—how MacDonald snored!—but he enjoyed the camaraderie. But those men were all gone. MacDonald blinded by one of the Martian bombs, Paul Miller killed by a spider machine in a ruined town on the Dardanelles, and Burford Sampson badly wounded in that desperate fight down in the tunnels. Sampson, at least, might be returning to the ranks soon, but the others were gone for good.

"Is there anything I can do for you, lord?" said a voice as he entered the tent. It was Abdo Makur, his servant, a man from Darfur or some such place in Africa, who they had rescued from a Martian 'farm' in Sudan last year. He'd attached himself to the company officers as a servant in gratitude. Their existing servant at the time, or 'dogrobber' as they were called, had been Corporal Ralph Scoggins, but he had been killed in the fighting up north, like so many others. Abdo was probably a more attentive servant than Scoggins, but he couldn't hold a candle to him in the scrounging department. Scoggins could get just about anything and had kept the officers well-supplied. Abdo tried, but he clearly didn't have the knack. With all the other platoon commanders gone and Harry promoted to company commander, Abdo had followed along. He'd spoken passable English when they'd found him, and it had improved markedly since then.

"No, I don't think so, thank you, Abdo. I'm just going to get some sleep."

"Your cot is all ready," said Abdo.

"Yes, I can see that, thank you." Harry started getting out of his uniform. Abdo waited to collect it. There wasn't enough fresh water available for laundry, but he would shake all the sand and as much of the dust out of it as he could.

"Where will they send us next, lord? Do you know?"

"Everyone's wondering, but no one's told us anything."

"Perhaps back to where you found me? Will the great Lord Kitchener resume his drive to Khartoum?"

"Maybe. There have been some rumors." Harry paused and looked more closely at Abdo. "Are you hoping to go home again?"

"That thought has been on my mind, lord. Just as I know the thought of returning to your homes is something you Australians think of often."

Harry sighed and lowered himself onto the creaking cot. Home. Australia. He tried *not* to think about it. Nearly two years had passed since he and Burford Sampson had waded out to the boat in Botany Bay and been among the very last of the men to escape from Sydney, the last significant human foothold in Australia. The sight of the burning city—his burning home—was the last glimpse he'd had of it. His family, and all of the rest of the people who'd managed to escape, were scattered now; New Zealand, Tasmania, India—or the ANZAC forces in the Near East.

Many still burned to return and take back what was theirs from the invaders, but month by month, as they saw just how large the world was, how vast the war was, that hope seemed less and less realistic. Oh, someday it would happen, Harry felt confident of that, but would he be alive to see it? Somehow he didn't think so. He took off his eye patch and laid it on the little folding table next to the cot and gently rubbed the scar where his eye used to be. "Good night, Abdo."

"Good night, lord." Abdo blew out the lantern and withdrew.

Several days passed with nothing more exciting than a huge sand storm that rolled out of the desert and blew down most of the tents in the camp and covered everything and everyone in a fine and persistent grit. It took nearly a day to get everything put right again and longer than that to get all the sand out of the weapons and equipment.

Everyone was getting heartily sick of the desert, so when they received orders to get packed up and board a ship which would be taking them to Cairo, the men were elated. It turned out that the entire ANZAC force was being withdrawn and loading took nearly a week as there was no significant port on that section of the coast. Men and equipment had to be taken out to the transports in boats—a slow process.

The troops who remained, French, Italian, Belgian and a few Indian units, looked on enviously. The engineers were already hard at work on the fortifications and they realized that they were probably going to be stuck defending this desolate spot for who knew how long? The Australians and New Zealanders were sympathetic, but did not feel the least bit guilty over their escape.

The voyage to Cairo was short and uneventful. They passed through the canal at Suez and reached the harbor at Alexandria in less time than it had taken to load the ships. Unloading was a lot faster in the well-equipped harbor. Everyone was expecting a short rest and then probably another voyage up the Nile to rejoin Kitchener's army.

They were driven in motorized lorries to an area outside the city that was set up with actual barracks, mess halls, showers, and a laundry. The men, already happy to be out of the cramped ships, were thrilled at their new accommodations. "Crikey! Will you look at this," said Fenwick as they toured the area the 15th Newcastle would occupy. The battalion had been given eighteen long, low tarpaper buildings, four for each company and two for the officers and staff.

There were additional buildings for the food services, washing and toilet facilities.

As with the tents, Harry had a room to himself. It was small, perhaps four paces square, with a bed, a desk, and a tall cabinet for his clothing and gear. There was a window with an actual insect screen in it and a glass casement that could be closed in the event of a sand or dust storm. After months of living in tents, it seemed like a luxury hotel. "Well, it's nice and that almost guarantees we won't be here long," he said aloud.

Abdo came bustling in, hauling Harry's gear. As usual, he'd carried everything in one load rather than two smaller ones. Abdo wasn't a large man and he wasn't a young one either. Harry didn't know exactly how old he was, but he guessed around forty. He deposited his burden on the floor and looked around the room, breathing hard. "This… this your room, lord?" he asked.

"Yes. You can put things away later. Have you found a spot for yourself yet?"

"There is little room at end of corridor. Mostly empty; I think I stay there." Harry nodded. There were a number of officers' servants in the battalion who were not soldiers and did not officially exist on the rolls. Old Scoggins had been a corporal so he could find a bed with the troops if he had to—although he usually managed to find better accommodations. But Abdo wouldn't be welcome in the barracks and had to make do with whatever he could find. Out in the field that usually meant a scrap of canvas rigged as a sun-shade, but here he'd have to settle for a storage closet. Harry had often invited him to sleep in his tent, but except during sandstorms the man had refused, saying it wasn't proper. But that reminded him…

"Here, this is for you," he said, dragging a few pound-notes out of his pocket and handing them to Abdo. The man looked at them a bit skeptically. He preferred hard coin, but then who didn't? Gold and silver coinage had all but disappeared in recent years. Even copper was becoming rare, and the paymasters were giving out paper notes for shillings now. Naturally, native servants did not receive any official pay, but thankfully they could be issued rations.

"Thank you, lord, you are most kind."

"You work very hard, Abdo. You've earned it. Try and buy something for *yourself* this time, eh?"

Abdo grinned and nodded and then began putting Harry's gear away, even though he'd said it could wait. It didn't take long to put his meager possessions where they belonged and Abdo quickly withdrew. Harry stared out the window for a bit, but there was nothing to see but the rows of other buildings, so eventually he lay down on the bed and took a nap.

At the evening parade Berwick announced that they would be staying here for a while and that they would be given passes to visit Cairo. This produced a huge cheer from the men. Between the interrupted drive up the Nile, the fight at the Dardanelles, and the campaign to reopen the straits, it had been a year or more since they'd been given any leave in a civilized spot.

The very next morning they began rotating companies into the city for two day periods. C Company had to wait a few days for its turn, but the men were very excited and could scarcely be made to concentrate on their duties. Part of their duty was to turn in their old uniforms and equipment. Their old uniforms were looking pretty ratty by this time, so they were happy enough to get new ones. The new equipment, however, was not welcomed so enthusiastically. Their Short Magazine Lee Enfield rifles were replaced with a new version that fired a much larger cartridge. Same .303 caliber bullets, but a larger propellant charge which they were told increased the ability to penetrate the metal skins of the Martian tripods and spider machines significantly. They were called Large Chamber Lee Enfield, or LCLE rifles. They weighed more than the old ones and they had a recoil like the kick of a mule. The ammunition pouches on their web gear were larger and heavier, too.

Their Lewis machine guns were taken away and replaced with a monstrous weapon produced by the Boys Company. It was a rifle, but it fired a 0.55 inch diameter bullet with a cartridge the size of a large carrot. The barrel was about four feet long and with the five-round magazine the contraption weighed over twenty pounds. They were told that it could punch through a spider's armor like it was paper and had a fair chance of piercing the thinner parts of a tripod. The Lewis teams were not at all happy with their new ordnance and Harry suspected that they had hidden away a number of the Lewis guns. The Vickers teams in the weapons company also got new and heavier weapons and the mortar crews received new ammunition that was also supposed to be better at hurting the enemy machines.

But the new weapon that got the greatest amount of attention could launch a modified Mills Bomb several hundred yards with fair accuracy. The 15th Newcastle had been told this was coming for a while because the idea for it had come from one of their own people. The last time they were in Alexandria, Private Greene had devised a thing that was like a medieval crossbow which could toss a Mills Bomb about a hundred yards. It wasn't terribly reliable, but it beat having to run right up to a Martian machine and stick the bomb on by hand all hollow. Greene had been one of Harry's men and once he showed off his device, the whole battalion had them by the time they reached the Dardanelles. More people saw them there, including some Ordnance Department officers, and they had now created their own version and were issuing it to the whole army. It was no longer a crossbow, but more like a mortar that could be fired from the shoulder. The bomb had its own propellant charge and a spring-loaded firing pin set it off. It was officially called the Launcher, Infantry, Anti-Tripod, or LIAT, but every man in the 15th Newcastle proudly called it a 'Greene Launcher'. There was one provided for each squad.

C Company did not have much time to play with their new toys before it was their turn to go to Cairo. The men and officers lined up early in the morning wearing their new uniforms to board the lorries that would take them to the train station in Alexandria to catch the train to Cairo. The men were in a rowdy mood and were talking loudly about the pubs and fleshpots they planned to visit. Lieutenants Fenwick and Boyerton were engaged in a conversation about the latter's facilities.

"I hear those oriental girls can do amazing things," said Fenwick, leering unpleasantly.

"Yeah, like give you all sorts of diseases," countered Boyerton, frowning.

"Well, y'got your rubber-johnny from the doc, didn't ya? Nothing to worry about if you're careful."

Boyerton turned to Harry. "You've been to Cairo before, ain't you, sir? You been to any of the places Fenwick is talking about?"

He tried not to blush. "I... uh, I only got there briefly, and didn't have time to visit any of those establishments. I'm afraid you'll have to do your own reconnaissance, gentlemen." In fact he'd been to Cairo several times but despite some serious cajolery from his fellow officers, Harry had not had the nerve to visit any of the brothels. He wasn't really planning to this time, either. He had to admit that he was tempted, but the thought of the nurse, Vera Brittain, left him too embarrassed to follow through. What if she found out? Vera was not his girlfriend, but she was his friend. He'd met her in a hospital on the earlier campaign up the Nile, and again at the Dardanelles. She was a lovely, brilliant, and talented woman—her poetry was divine—but her fiancé had been killed near Basra and she wasn't over him yet. Harry would have to bide his time.

The lories arrived and they piled in. The trip to the station was short and the train ride to Cairo was not much longer. The city was surrounded by a fortified line, but it was not terribly strong. It had been built in the early days of the war when it seemed the Martians were going to overrun all of Africa. Its main function these days was to keep out the sea of refugees which occupied crude encampments all around the city. Millions of people from the south had fled in front of the invaders, streaming down the Nile in search of safety. Five years later they were still there, even though thousands died every day of malnutrition or disease. The army camp at Alexandria was surrounded by a double ring of barbed wire fences to keep them out. Swarms of them lined the railroad tracks now calling out to the soldiers for food, money, anything. The Egyptian government could do little for the poor wretches and only aid from England and some of the European powers prevented a complete disaster.

"Bloody awful, ain't it? said Boyerton, staring out the window.

"Why can't they put these blokes to work?" asked Fenwick. "Or in the army? Look at that fellow there, he could fill a uniform. Just lazy if you ask me."

"They have been moving people out as we liberate more land along the Nile," said Harry. "Rebuilding the farms along the river to help feed all of the rest. And the Egyptians are raising new regiments, but it's a slow process. Hard to equip them with no industry of their own. I bet all of our old gear and weapons we turned in eventually will be used for that."

The train passed into the city and soon stopped at the main station. The troops got out and quickly dispersed to find whatever diversions they pleased.

Their sergeants bellowed to remind them they were due back in camp in forty-eight hours. Harry stayed with Fenwick and Boyerton for a while, but they became separated in one of the innumerable bazaars that filled the city and he did not see them again until they returned to camp.

Harry was a bit surprised at the quantity and variety of goods for sale in the little stalls that lined the streets. Nearly all industry on the whole planet was devoted to making armaments and there were shortages of everything from what he'd heard. But all this stuff was handicrafts, probably made right here in the city by individual workers. He spotted a beautiful beaten-copper tea set and was tempted to get it as a gift for his mother and sisters. They'd had to leave everything behind when they'd been evacuated to New Zealand and would probably appreciate it. But he wasn't sure how he could get it to them. Service for letters had become pretty reliable, but there were no provisions for packages. He reluctantly moved on.

Several stalls were selling items, mostly wood carvings, that were in a distinctly different style from most of the other things he'd seen. Not Egyptian at all. He suddenly realized that they reminded him of a little carving that Abdo wore around his neck on a leather thong. Items from farther south, in Martian controlled territory? His initial thought was that refugees had settled in Cairo and were carrying on their art here. Maybe. But it was far more likely that shrewd locals were buying up this stuff—the few prized possessions the refugees had been able to carry with them—from desperate, starving people in exchange for a few scraps of food and then reselling it here to people like Harry. Frowning, he bought nothing.

He left the bazaars behind and went into the central part of the city. Government buildings, hotels, and some grand mansions lined wide boulevards. He spent the rest of the morning in the Egyptian Museum looking at antiquities. It was interesting stuff and he wished Vera was there with him. She loved that sort of thing and he fondly remembered a tour the two of them had taken of some of the ruins at Aswan during last year's campaign up the Nile when they'd first met. The last letter he'd gotten from her, just the other day, had said her hospital unit was being ordered out from the area north of the Strait, but she didn't know where they were going.

After the museum he was hungry and he managed to get a meal at one of the hotels. Not one of the better ones, those were all reserved for generals and staff officers and high-ranking government officials, but at a place that wasn't too bad. His officer's uniform got him reasonably good service. The menu claimed the meat was duck, but he suspected it was some other sort of water fowl from the Nile delta. No matter, it was a welcome change from the usual mess hall fare. It was at meal time when they all really missed Scoggins. He always managed to find better stuff. Abdo hadn't developed the knack.

Afterwards he just wandered the streets for a while savoring the fact that he wasn't surrounded by soldiers. Not that there weren't a lot of soldiers on the streets, but the civilians outnumbered them significantly. Later in the afternoon he noticed a queue of soldiers lined up at one of the buildings. It was the wrong part of town to find a brothel, and looking closer he saw it was a theater. A play? How long had it been since he's seen a play? Since before the war, surely, and the theater scene in Sydney hadn't been exactly brilliant. Why not? He went over and joined the queue.

But as he neared the ticket booth and started reading the bills plastered near the entrance he realized that it wasn't going to be a play at all, but instead one of those new motion pictures! He'd heard about them, but never seen one and was having a hard time visualizing how they worked. He grew excited at the prospect and didn't begrudge the ticket price. Inside, the place looked like any other theater with rows of seats, an orchestra pit in front, and a stage with curtains drawn. He found a spot next to a pair of rowdy corporals and waited.

Eventually, a man appeared and went into the pit and sat down at a piano and started playing lively tunes. Shortly after that, the lights dimmed and the curtains drew back revealing a blank white screen about thirty feet wide and twenty tall. There was another delay, but then there was a mechanical noise from behind him and a square of projected light appeared on the screen. A moment later this was replaced with an official-looking crest and printed words announcing that what was to follow was approved by the British Information Bureau. Harry had never heard of them.

What followed was a sort of newspaper with a number of articles about current events. Except they weren't just words printed on a page, they were pictures—pictures that moved! People hurrying down city streets, horses pulling carriages, locomotives hurtling toward the screen so convincingly that Harry cringed a bit. Ships at sea, even an aeroplane circling in the sky. It was amazing.

There were some words thrown up on the screen explaining what they were seeing since the only sound was the piano, the machine behind them, and the excited comments of the audience. The articles themselves were interesting; a new dreadnought battleship being launched, happy people (too happy, really) working in factories or in fields 'doing their bit' against the Martians, trains loaded with tanks and guns heading off to war. One scene showed a group of important-looking men milling about. The printed explanation said they were the leaders of the Commonwealth nations in London for a meeting with the King and the prime minister. From there things got more serious. There were some confusing and blurry pictures of the battles going on along the Danube, then some better quality pictures from America showing wrecked tripods and what was claimed to be a captured Martian fortress, and the ruins of a city which had been liberated near the Rocky Mountains. Harry and quite a few of the others in the audience were delighted when there was news of the recent operation to recapture the *Bab el Mandab* Strait! Many of the men cheered and waved their hats. The pictures showed some men walking around a destroyed Martian heat ray site and then a line of ships steaming through the strait.

From there the program became one of entertainment. There were scenes of pretty girls dancing (quite popular) and then a few scenes from famous Shakespeare plays with all the dialogue written out (bring back the girls!) and some shots of horses and dogs and children for no particular reason that Harry could see.

The program concluded with a shot of marching soldiers and flags flying and the King on a reviewing stand saluting. The pianist began to hammer out 'God Save the King' and after some hesitation, the audience stood up and joined in. After that the pictures turned off and the lights came up and the pianist hurried off. The audience—almost entirely soldiers or sailors—slowly made their way out to the street, chattering about what they had seen.

It was late afternoon by then and Harry spent some time finding a place to eat dinner and somewhere to spend the night. All the decent hotels were filled, but the army had set up dormitory-like facilities specifically for soldiers on leave in a number of spots. He found a pretty decent one where he only had to share a room with three other officers, and two of them didn't get back from whatever they were doing until very late. Harry had definitely slept in worse places.

The next day he wandered around, found a good vantage point to see the Pyramids from a distance (they were completely surrounded by refugee camps, so a close-up visit was out of the question), and visited a few other historical sites inside the city. In the afternoon he went back to the motion picture theater and saw the show again. It was the same as before except the machine projecting the pictures broke down for a quarter hour before it could be fixed. He visited the bazaars again and bought a pretty little necklace for Vera in case he saw her again. That evening he found a sort of music hall with live entertainment and stayed there for a few hours before catching a train back to camp. Technically he didn't have to be back until eight the next morning, but he didn't see any point in staying in the city just to sleep. He was back in his own room in his own bed before midnight.

At morning roll call there were quite a few men missing from the ranks, but they all drifted in over the next few hours. Major Berwick had spread the word that the late-comers should receive a tongue-lashing but no other punishment. Then it was back to the same routine: drilling and trying out the new equipment. There were firing ranges at the edge of camp and they got a chance to try their new weapons, even the LIATs, which even Private Greene had to admit were easier to use than his crossbow.

The day after D Company finished its time in the city it was announced that there would be a special parade that evening with a few important guests and that they should all be scrubbed and polished for it. That afternoon while he and Abdo were laying out his best uniform, they heard a commotion in the corridor and a moment later Lieutenants Fenwick, Boyerton, and O'Reilly burst into his room. "Lieutenant Calloway! Lieutenant Calloway! Have you heard?" gasped Fenwick, a large grin on his face.

"Heard what?" asked Harry.

"The parade tonight! Have you heard what's going to happen?"

"No, but the Major said there would be important guests, so I assume we're going to be inspected by some general. He'll pat us on our heads and tell us what good boys we are and go about his business."

"No sir!" said Fenwick. "We were hanging around headquarters and we heard the Major talking and..."

"You're getting a medal sir!" blurted out Boyerton, earning a frown from Fenwick for stealing his thunder.

"What?"

"S'true, sir," said O'Reilly, commander of 11 Platoon. "And they're promptin' ya to captain!"

Harry reared back. "Nonsense," he muttered.

"No, sir!" said Fenwick, "It's true! For what you did up there at the Dardanelles. Blowin' up the Martian base and saving the whole fleet and all."

Harry scowled. "Now that *is* nonsense. I was one man among hundreds and we all did the job together. I don't know what rubbish you've been told, but that's the truth."

"But we heard the *Major* talking," insisted Boyerton.

Harry shook his head. "Well, it must be some mistake. Now you fellows get along and make sure your platoons are all spic and span for the parade." The grinning officers gave him exaggerated salutes and withdrew.

"This is a good thing, yes?" asked Abdo.

"If it's true, yes, I guess so. A company is normally commanded by a captain, so the promotion won't change my job. More money, though."

"And this medal they spoke of? What is that, lord?"

"Oh, it's just a little badge you wear on your uniform. It tells people you did something important."

"You do not seem pleased."

Harry shrugged and sighed. "I'm guessing that they are giving it to me—if they really *are* giving me one—because I was the one that fired the rocket that cut off the power to the Martian super heat rays. But I only did it because the man who was supposed to do it got killed and dropped the launcher right next to me. A hundred other men could have done it. Hundreds of other men had already gotten killed or wounded just getting us to that spot. Doesn't seem fair that I'm the one to get rewarded when so many all had a hand in it."

"I see," said Abdo. "Could you refuse the honor? Or give it to another?"

Harry blinked. "That's... not done. It would be disrespectful to the ones giving it to me."

"Ah. Then we must make sure you look your best," He picked up Harry's dress tunic and gave it another brushing.

As they were assembling for the parade Major Berwick pulled Harry aside. "Has the rumor mill caught up with you about this?"

"Uh, yes, sir, I think so. Something about a medal and a promotion?"

"Yes, the brass has seen fit to get our rank structure up to where it belongs," said Berwick. Harry just then spotted the new pip on Berwick's shoulder straps, just below the crown which had always been there.

"Oh, congratulations… Colonel."

"Thanks. So you and several others will be getting bumped up. As for your medals…"

"*Medals?*"

"Yes, General Legge will be awarding you the DSO, and there's some French admiral here, can't even pronounce his name, but he'll be giving you a medal, too."

"Uh… why?"

Berwick shrugged. "There were French ships in the fleet. Guess they figure your actions saved some of them, too. And the French love to give out medals. Prepare to have your cheeks kissed."

"Sir, I didn't…!"

"Yes, yes, I know, we all had a hand in it and it isn't fair to the others, but that's the way things are in the army so you'll just have to carry on. Smile, shake hands, and be done with it, eh?"

"Yes, sir."

"Good. Oh, looks like the guests have arrived, let's form up."

The parade went smoothly. Speeches were made, the promotions were announced, several other men were awarded lesser medals, and then Harry was called forward. Lieutenant General James Gordon Legge, commander of the Australian-New Zealand Army Corps, pinned the Distinguished Service Order medal onto Harry's tunic. Then the Frenchman, a very short man with a white mustache, came up to him and said something unintelligible, pinned another medal on him, and then grabbed him by the collar to pull him down far enough that he could kiss him on both cheeks. Harry blushed a bright pink.

But finally he was released to rejoin his company and the battalion passed in review. As they swung around the parade ground he saw that quite a crowd of spectators had gathered. They were mostly soldiers from other units, but there were a few civilians, apparently newspaper reporters, and there was a woman in a nurse's uniform standing next to an officer…

Vera! Burf!

Harry nearly tripped over his feet. Vera Brittain and Burford Sampson, probably his two best friends in the world, were right there watching him! Vera had a faint smile and Burford a huge grin. Harry was so transfixed he almost missed the wheeling point for his company and only a prompt from Sergeant Breslin saved him from disaster.

The Newcastles swung back into line and were dismissed, Colonel Berwick announcing that there was an officers meeting in ten minutes. As they broke ranks, Harry looked for Vera and Burf, but they were right there, walking toward him. He almost threw his arms around both of them, but stopped short with his arms apart, grinning like a loon. "Vera! Burf! What are you doing here?"

"Well, I'm here reporting back for duty…" began Sampson.

"You're back with the battalion? Wonderful!" interrupted Harry. "How's your back? All healed up?"

"Mostly," said Sampson. "Just released yesterday. And when I heard about this little party," he waved his hand at the rapidly dispersing parade, "I figured I would attend. I happened to notice Miss Brittain's hospital company was right next door to where I was staying and I invited her to come along."

"Oh, I'm so glad you did! Both of you!"

"Congratulations, Harry," said Vera quietly. "Your promotion and the medals are well-earned."

"Thank you," he replied, feeling warmer inside than the late afternoon Egyptian sun could account for. "Is your hospital stationed in Cairo? Alexandria? Are you going to be here long? Thanks so much for coming! Can you stay for dinner? I'm sure the officers mess would be thrilled to have you…"

"Harry!" exclaimed Burford. "Let the poor girl get a word in! And in any case, we have to meet with Colonel Berwick in about two minutes."

"Oh, uh right. Sorry." He stared at Vera. "I don't think the meeting will take long. Can… can you wait?"

Vera looked like she was trying not to laugh. "I can stay for a while, Harry. Go to your meeting. I'll wait in the shade over there."

Looking back over his shoulder at Vera, he let himself be dragged away by Burf to the headquarters building. The other officers of the battalion were already gathering and they ended up at the back of the room with more than twenty others. Colonel Berwick was at the front of the room, looking everyone over. Then he nodded and began:

"Gentlemen, that was well done out there just now. I'm sure the general was impressed. Congratulations again to those of you who were promoted and decorated. Well-earned for sure. But we have some business to attend to. First, let us all welcome back Captain Sampson." He gestured toward Burf and Harry's eyes were drawn to the third pip on his shoulder straps. He hadn't noticed them earlier. So Burf was a captain now, too. That was great—it just wouldn't be… *proper* for him to outrank Burf!

"He's still recuperating a bit from the fracas up on the Dardanelles, so he'll be on my staff for the moment. But the real reason I called for this meeting is that there is some major news that affects us Newcastles. It seems that our new prime minister, Joseph Cook, was in London last month and he made some waves about how we in the ANZAC weren't being properly supported." That brought on some murmurs of agreement and nodding heads among the officers.

"So, as incredible as it may seem, the army is doing something about it. They have been talking about and experimenting with the idea of what they are calling an 'armored division' for a while now. It would have a lot of tanks and a lot of motorized equipment and would be used primarily for offensive operations. We and a number of other ANZAC units are going to be turned into the 1st Australian Armored Division."

"We're getting tanks, sir?" exclaimed someone.

"Well, not us specifically. The division will have three tank regiments, three motorized artillery battalions, and then six battalions of so-called 'armored infantry' in those Cardigan carriers we got to use last year. We would be one of those battalions. So, we will not be going back into action for a while. They've set up a training area to the west of here and we'll be spending the next few months getting accustomed to the new equipment and training in new tactics. We'll be moving out the day after tomorrow, so get your men ready."

Berwick dismissed the formation and an excited batch of officers departed. "Sounds interesting," said Sampson. "Looks like I got back just in time."

"Yes!" said Harry. "Wait until I tell Vera!"

* * * * *

Holdfast 14-3, Cycle 597,845.7

Lutnaptinav maneuvered its travel chair into the workspace of its progenitor, Kandanginar. "You sent for me?"

Kandanginar swiveled its chair to face Lutnaptinav. "Yes, I have new orders for you."

"Indeed? And these could not be sent to me through communication channels?"

"I wished to communicate them to you directly." It extended a tendril towards Lutnaptinav and after a moment it took hold with one of its own tendril. The masses of nerve tissue in each made contact and they could communicate directly, mind to mind, rather than with the slower and less precise method of the spoken word. "I have just finished communicating with Jakruvnar. The commander was in communication with the Colonial Conclave. There is much dissatisfaction with the results of the recent campaign."

"As you predicted," said Lutnaptivav.

"Yes, the clans on the main part of Continent 1 feel that we here, and the clans from Continent 2, did not exert ourselves to the fullest."

"Have they seen the reports of the fighting along the northern waterway that barred our path?" asked Lutnaptinav with some irritation. "Our losses were huge."

"They have, and they simply sent reports of the fighting they are engaged in. Their losses are substantial, too. They are demanding we provide further assistance."

"Progenitor, a resumption of the offensive northward, without the aid of the Continent 2 forces, is impossible."

"Yes, even they admit that. But they still insist on some help and we have agreed."

"But how?"

"We and Group 13 will each send a battlegroup around the eastern side of the inland sea to the north and link up with the Continent 1 forces there."

"It is a very long distance through extremely difficult terrain," observed Lutnaptinav. "And even that way is not unguarded."

"True, but you will be supplied with fifteen extra fighting machines, which will follow in automatic mode carrying extra power cells."

"*I* will be...?"

"You will command our battlegroup."

"I do not have enough seniority for such a command, Progenitor," said Lutnaptinav.

"Yes you do. Here is the list of the others going with you." The information flowed through the neural link and Lutnaptinav absorbed it.

"Progenitor, these are all Threebo... very young."

"You were going to say '*Threeborn*', and yes, the entire force will be made up of people budded on this world."

"Then this force is... expendable. Two battlegroups will have little impact on the fighting on Continent 1."

"The force is largely symbolic, it is true," said Kandanginar. "But in any case those are your orders. You leave in two rotations so begin your preparations at once."

"I have only recently completed budding, Progenitor. The bud is not yet fully capable..."

"It will be looked after," said Kandanginar. "Now carry out your orders."

"I hear and obey," said Lutnaptinav, breaking the connection. It turned its travel chair and left the chamber. Its mind was filled with many thoughts, but one of them dominated the others:

Exile. I am being sent into exile.

Chapter Four

September 1913, Craiova, Romania

"**A**ll right, Captain, let's get aloft," said Lieutenant Colonel Erich Serno of the Imperial German Air Service.

"Yes, sir," answered Captain Franz Hoeppner, who commanded the squadron of AEG G.IV bombers lined up on the field just to the east of the Romanian town of Craiova. Hoeppner waved to the assembled air crews and they moved to man their machines. "You will be accompanying us, sir? The expression on the man's face made it plain that he was hoping for an answer in the negative, but Serno disappointed him by nodding.

"If it's not too much trouble, Captain. General von Mackensen wanted me to do a personal reconnaissance."

"No trouble at all, Colonel. If you don't mind, you can sit in the rear gunner's position of my plane. We'll be close enough that we can talk."

"Excellent. Lead on."

They headed toward the first plane of the formation. The eleven other bombers in the squadron were starting their engines and their crews were climbing aboard. "I, uh, imagine you are glad to be back with a German unit," said Hoeppner as they walked. "From what I've heard of the Turks, your experiences with them must have been rather... frustrating."

Serno clenched his teeth for a moment before answering. "It's true that the Turks lack technical training and their discipline isn't up to our standards, but..." He whirled around and placed himself directly in Hoeppner's path, the startled captain halting and stepping back so suddenly he nearly fell. Serno stepped forward until his face was only a few centimeters from the Captain's. "But, they can *die* just as bravely for their homeland as any German."

"I... I..." spluttered Hoeppner. "Colonel, I didn't mean...!"

"Before the big Martian offensive began," continued Serno, "I'd built fourteen squadrons for the Turkish Air Force. By the time we'd stopped them at the Bosporus, Captain, we had one squadron left and the Turkish pilot corps consisted of myself and four other men. In spite of the frustrations, it was an honor to serve with them. If your men prove themselves half as brave as those Turks, I'll be very pleased." He stepped back, turned around, and headed for the bomber. Hoeppner had to trot to catch up.

"You will not be disappointed, Colonel," he puffed.

They reached the AEG G.IV and Serno climbed into the rear gunner's compartment. He inspected the Parabellum machine gun and its ready ammunition exactly as if he were the regular gunner. By the time he was done, Hoeppner had finished his own inspection and the craft's two motors were running. The captain waved away the chocks blocking the wheels and a moment later the machine was rolling out onto the runway.

Serno chided himself over his outburst. It wasn't proper for an officer of his rank. But damn, he was tired of all the disparaging remarks about the people in his last command! What difference did it make that they were Turks? They were all human and that's the only thing that mattered in this fight against the aliens.

Still, there was some truth in what Hoeppner said. While there was a small part of him that regretted not being allowed to rebuild what he had created, there was a much larger part that prayed he'd never have to set foot in the Ottoman Empire again. His time there creating the fledgling air force *had* been frustrating, and the time in battle had been terrifying and heartbreaking, but they had done their job and helped defeat the southern prong of the great Martian offensive. His reward had been promotion and assignment to a regular group of German aircraft engaged in the fight against the northern prong of that same offensive.

So now he was in command of *Kampfgeschwader 4,* a formation consisting of eight squadrons, each containing twelve bombers. In terms of manpower and firepower it was bigger than the whole Ottoman Air Force had been at its height. His time with the Turks, which many of his friends had warned would be the end of his career, had instead proved to be a major stepping-stone to higher command.

Hoepper's bomber began to accelerate, bouncing down the unpaved runway, and was soon airborne, followed closely by the rest of the squadron. They formed up and slowly gained altitude as they headed east. The front line along the Olt River was less than fifty kilometers away and they needed to be above Martian heat ray range before they reached it. It was the end of summer and still quite hot on the ground, but as they reached their cruising altitude it was very brisk and Serno was glad for his leather flying jacket.

About twenty minutes went by and then Captain Hoepper turned and tapped him on the shoulder and pointed ahead. The river was visible in the distance and about three thousand meters below them. There didn't appear to be much going on today. The artillery positions to the west of the river were not firing and Serno didn't see any of the red streaks of Martian heat rays, nor the blue flashes of their artillery.

It didn't surprise him. Last spring, the Martians, after smashing through what little of the Russian Army remained in the southern Ukraine, had swept south through Moldavia between the rugged Carpathian Mountains and the Pruth River, inexorably aimed toward the Danube and Bulgaria beyond. Their ultimate goal seemed to be to link up at Constantinople with the Martians heading north through Turkey. The tiny Romanian Army, still licking its wounds from the insane fighting in the Balkans—not against Martians, but other humans—could not even slow them down.

The Great Powers, finally realizing the threat, had rushed forces to build a defense line along the Danube. Troops and tanks and guns were moved there by water, rail, and road. Mostly German and Austro-Hungarians, but some other lesser powers, like the Italians who were relatively close by. They got there just in time and in a series of titanic battles along the waterway managed to stop the Martian offensive.

But unlike the southern pincer, the northern assault did not give up.

Stymied in their attempt to smash through the most direct route to Constantinople, they spread out along the Danube looking for an easier place to cross. To the east the river made a long bend to the north through rough terrain before emptying into the Black Sea in a marshy delta. They quickly gave up on that approach. To the west, the terrain was easier, although the river was still broad and formed a formidable barrier. The defenders, still reeling from the first bloody battles, had to extend their lines farther and farther up the river, helped greatly by the fact that their reinforcements were all coming from that direction and had less distance to go.

The Martians managed to get small groups across in several locations, but they were destroyed or beaten back by the upcoming reserves. West and west the two forces went, the aliens probing for a weak spot, and the humans desperately trying to plug any holes before they were found and exploited. The Martians, much more mobile than the human forces—their three-legged war machines could move tirelessly seemingly without pause—would likely have won the race and created a bridgehead south of the river except they apparently became distracted by the cities and towns of central Romania. They lost critical time destroying Bucharest, Ploesti, Targoviste, and a dozen other places. Huge numbers of refugees streamed west, south, and north in search of safety. But the sacrifice of their homes may well have been the price to ensure there were safe places to run to.

The defenders made good use of the respite and built their lines along the Danube until they reached the spot where the Olt River joined it. The Olt flowed almost directly south from the rugged Carpathians and the defense line turned and followed it all the way to the mountains. By the time the Martians were through with their slaughters, the way west had been blocked. They made a few half-hearted attempts to punch through and then fell back and waited.

The big question on the minds of the generals was: waiting for what? The mission Serno was on today was one of many attempts to find out.

They passed over the Olt River and continued east. Their goal today was to do reconnaissance in the area of Bucharest. Or of what was left of Bucharest. As they flew on, the countryside was dotted with burned out villages and towns, some still sending up pale columns of smoke. The aliens smashed and burned anything human they encountered, killing as casually as a man swatted a fly. Except for the people they took for food. It had been suspected from the beginning, from evidence gathered after the first invasion in England, that the Martians used people for food. More recently that had been confirmed again and again. Serno looked down on the scorched landscape; the dead were probably the lucky ones.

Although there were plenty of signs the enemy had been down there, so far they had not seen any of the Martians. During daylight they usually pulled back away from the human defense lines out of artillery range. They'd learned to be wary of flying machines, too, and often hid themselves in wooded areas.

They'd been flying for nearly an hour when a burst of machine gun fire caught their attention. He and Hoeppner looked back and saw someone waving from the number seven plane. Oily black smoke was coming from one of its engines, and the pilot clearly wanted to turn around. Hoeppner glanced at him, but did not say anything. Nor did Serno; it was Hoeppner's command and his decision. The captain stood up in the cockpit and waved his assent. The smoking plane turned around and headed for home.

Neither of them had exchanged a word since their first testy exchange but Serno decided to break the ice. He leaned forward and shouted against the wind and engine noise: "Not bad, Captain. Only one plane lost to mechanical difficulties. I'd have expected more. Your people are good."

Hoeppner looked back and the ghost of a smile passed over his face. "Thank you, Colonel, they are." After a moment's pause, he added, "Bucharest is just coming into sight."

Serno looked ahead, past him and between the upper and lower wings and saw a dark patch on the horizon. As they got closer he could see it more clearly. It was constructed like a lot of cities in Europe, basically circular in shape, radiating outward from some ancient castle or fortress, he supposed. There was a small river flowing through it, the Dambovita if he recalled the map correctly. It had been dammed up at intervals to create a series of lakes in and around the city. He'd never been to Bucharest, but he'd read that it was a beautiful place, full of historic palaces, churches, and public buildings.

No more. The Martians had destroyed it as thoroughly as they had so many other places. The basic layout of the city and its roads could still be seen, and walls of many of the more heavily constructed buildings were still standing, but the city had been reduced to ruins. From three thousand meters it would have been hard to spot individual people—or individual bodies—but Serno couldn't make out either. Most of the population had no doubt fled, but there were always some who stayed, clinging to some delusion of survival as dearly as they did their homes and possessions.

There was some movement down there and getting out his binoculars, he looked closer. Machines. Not the tripod fighting machines the Martians used, nor the much smaller spider machines, but something different. They were long and relatively thin, maybe the size and shape of a city trolly car. They appeared to have multiple sets of arms and legs. Serno had seen photos of wrecked ones in his briefing materials. They were some sort of transport or work machines. These appeared to be dragging things out of the rubble and loading them into other machines which then carried them away. *They're stripping the city of anything useful to them.* The Martians had been observed doing this in other locations.

They apparently dug mines, too, but were perfectly willing to use refined metals the humans had already dug up. *Damn looters.*

"Colonel? Should we start our sweep?" Serno glanced up to see Hoeppner looking back at him.

Their mission was to do a reconnaissance search pattern around Bucharest. Intelligence reports (General von Mackensen had not bothered to tell Serno from whom) indicated that the Martians were building something in the area and they were supposed to pin-point the location and find out whatever they could about it. The intelligence was very vague about the location and the plan was to spread out and fly in an increasingly large spiral centered on the city until they found something.

Serno was about to give Hoeppner the go-ahead when his eyes were drawn groundward again. *They're building something. They'll need raw materials. These things are gathering raw materials...* The carrying machines were moving northeastward.

He looked back up at the captain and shook his head. "Follow those machines down there. They should lead us to just what we are looking for!" Hoeppner stared at him like he was crazy, but then peered over the side of the cockpit and stared down for a moment and then shrugged. He waved to the squadron and gave the *follow me* signal and turned the bomber northeast. After they were all flying the right direction the captain gave the signal to spread out into a line to either side of him. After a few minutes the bombers were in a not-terribly straight line a few miles long.

Below them the carrying machines continued on their way, apparently unmindful by the aircraft overhead. A few of the tripod fighting machines were in evidence, but they seemed equally unconcerned. In addition to the filled machines heading northwest, there were empty ones going the opposite way, back into Bucharest. "Just like a line of worker ants!" shouted Hoeppner.

Only about fifteen minutes later they saw a cloud of dust on the horizon, and as they got closer Serno became convinced this is what they were looking for. At a distance of about ten kilometers he could see a circular shape on the ground three or four kilometers in diameter. Through his binoculars he could make out machines pushing mounds of dirt and rubble into a curving wall that enclosed the ring. "They're building one of their fortresses," he called to Hoeppner. "I've seen pictures of them and this is just like them. A wall to keep us out, with heat ray towers all along it and then a base underground where they have factories and such."

"So this is to support their offensive? Right now they have to bring up supplies and reinforcements all the way from their bases in the Ukraine and farther east," replied Hoeppner. "Once they get this built, they can make the stuff right here. We should try to stop this if we can, Colonel! May I order an attack?"

"One squadron won't do much..."

"If we can wreck a few of their machines it will slow them down. Then we can report this and come back with a much bigger force. Please, Colonel!"

Reporting this to headquarters was the important thing, but he couldn't see any harm in dropping their bombs before heading back. As long as they stayed high, there shouldn't be any danger. "All right, go ahead."

With his planes all spread out, Hoeppner resorted to a flare gun to get their attention this time. A red flare streaked up signaling an attack. The other bombers closed in on the lead plane and took up a formation that would allow them to drop a nice tight bomb pattern. Each plane carried eight fifty-kilogram bombs, not terribly powerful but capable of destroying a Martian machine with a direct hit.

Bombing from a high altitude was terribly inaccurate, and without some luck the eleven bombers would probably drop all eighty-eight of their bombs in some empty piece of land, accomplishing nothing. Single-engine planes coming in low and fast had a much better chance of scoring a hit, but they could only do so by coming into range of the heat rays carried by the Martian tripods. Wood and canvas aircraft were horribly vulnerable to the heat rays and casualties were ghastly. That was what had killed the Turkish Air Force and in the early days of the fighting along the Danube it had killed scores of German pilots, too. That sort of attack was now forbidden unless approved by the high command. Bombing missions were now relegated to the larger bombers and only from a safe altitude.

The squadron headed for the construction area. Hoeppner would pick the target and the other planes would release their bombs when he did. Serno stood up in his position to get a better look forward and down. They were flying toward a concentration of the work machines; good, a denser target would be easier to hit. The gunner in the forward position was also the bombardier. He had a sight that would adjust for the forward speed of the plane. He had his right hand up in the air as he peered through the sight. They were nearly over the target when he brought his hand down and Hoeppner released the bombs. The plane lurched slightly upward when it was relieved of its load. Seno could not see the bombs falling, but he turned backwards to see the other planes dropping their bombs.

And thus he was looking right at it when the rear plane was blasted out of the sky by a heat ray. A bright red beam sliced right through the bomber, cutting it in two and sending both pieces tumbling away, burning furiously.

Their super heat ray!

During the recent fighting around the Dardanelles, the Martians had used a new type of heat ray. It was much bigger and more powerful and with a much longer range. But it was heavy and cumbersome and could not be mounted on their war machines. They had been mounted in fixed positions in tunnels dug out of hillsides overlooking waterways to be used against warships. No one thought they could be used against aircraft...

Wrong! Wrong! Wrong!

"Scatter!" he screamed, slamming Hoeppner on the back. "Have the squadron scatter! Get us out of here!"

By the time the captain turned to look, two more of his planes had been annihilated and there was no need for any order. The remaining planes were peeling off in all directions to avoid the beam of destruction that was slicing through their midst. Hoeppner banked sharply to the right and Serno had to hastily grab on and sit down to avoid being tossed out of the plane. The captain also put the machine into a dive to pick up speed. Serno would have done exactly the same thing if he'd been at the controls.

Another plane was destroyed and then another and another. The beam swung right past Serno and he could feel the heat of it, but it missed his plane to claim a different one. As he clutched the combing of his position, he was instinctively analyzing what he saw. The beam seemed to be jerking about rather than moving smoothly. Perhaps the mounting system was a jury-rigged affair and not fully perfected. But it was perfect enough to claim eight planes from the squadron before it finally cut off.

Serno slumped back in his seat, drenched in sweat despite the chill breeze. They were about ten kilometers to the east of the construction site and Hoeppner flew them another ten before they made a long swing to the right to head back to the field, giving the enemy installation a very wide berth. The other two survivors were out of sight now and presumably heading for home on their own.

He and Hoeppner didn't exchange a word on the whole flight back. When the AEG G.IV rolled to a halt at the airfield, one of the other bombers of the squadron was already there, along with the one which had turned back earlier and the remaining one was coming in just behind them. The ground crews were waiting to receive them, but except for four, the rest were standing there looking forlornly at the empty sky.

As Serno let himself down from the machine he found Captain Hoeppner staring at him with a look of restrained fury on his face. "I hope my men measured up to the standards of your Turks today, Colonel!" he snapped. Then he turned and walked away toward his surviving men.

"What the devil happened, sir?"

He turned and saw Captain Carl Wulzinger, his aide, standing there with a confused expression.

Serno let out a long sigh. "The Martians aren't stupid, Captain. Take me to von Mackensen." On the drive back to the headquarters of 9th Army, which was in an old castle to the north of Craiova, he filled Wulzinger in on the events of the flight.

"If the Martians have more of those things, we soon won't be able to use aircraft over their territory at all," said Wulzinger.

"The reports from the British say they need a lot of electrical power to operate, so they probably need some sort of permanent base," replied Serno. "In a fluid situation, we should still be fine. But once things get stalled and the Martians can dig in, you're probably right."

Von Mackensen was a white-haired and mustachioed man in his mid-sixties. He'd first served in the Franco-Prussian War in 1870 as a hussar and he still wore pieces of his old uniform at times. He took Serno's verbal report about the fortress under construction and the devastation the new heat ray had wreaked among the bombers. He shook his head over the losses and grumbled about the fortress, but the only order he issued was to forbid any additional flights into that area and then he dismissed Serno.

"So now what?" asked Wulzinger. His aide was an insatiably curious sort who'd first been assigned to him in Turkey. Before the war he'd been studying to be an archaeologist of all things and he spoke several languages. He was an efficient and hard worker, but he never seemed to know when to hold his tongue.

Serno looked at him and then shrugged. "Try to rebuild Hoeppner's squadron and wait for new orders."

And that is what they did, but the new orders arrived far quicker than Serno had expected. A breathless Wulzinger handed them to him only four days later. He opened them and read them through. "Well, the group is being relocated."

"Where are we going, sir?"

"Warsaw."

* * * * *

September, 1913, Warsaw, Poland

"Wanda! Wanda!" cried Ola Wojciech as she burst into the small office in the basement of the public library.

The woman at the desk jerked up in surprise and then glared at Ola in exasperation. Taking off her glasses, she said, "Girl, how many times have I told you not to come bursting in like that? Or shouting like a Cossack? You near frighten me to death when you do that!"

"But Wanda," said Ola, trying to rein in her excitement. "The Russians! The Russians have gone!"

"What nonsense is this?"

Ola had enormous respect for Wanda Krahelska. She was a legend in the Polish independence movements. At the age of twenty—only four years older than Ola was herself—she had tossed a dynamite bomb onto the carriage of the Russian governor-general and nearly killed him. Since then she'd become an important leader in the Union of Active Struggle, the militant wing of the Polish Socialist Party. She was one of the very few women in positions of power and one of the few willing to give a chance to young women—like Ola—to do their part. But she wasn't the easiest person in the world to work for. She was strict, meticulous, and ever so skeptical.

"Wanda, it's true," insisted Ola. "I spent nearly the whole night watching the Wschodnia Station—just as you told me to—and the trains were coming in and going out almost continuously. The outgoing ones were crammed with troops! Thousands and thousands of them. The garrison must be withdrawing."

Wanda frowned more deeply. "Perhaps they were just rotating the garrison. Bringing in new troops and taking the old ones out."

"Well, if they were, the incoming troops were being let off somewhere else. The trains that were pulling into Wschodnia were empty and the ones that left were full."

Wanda was silent for quite a while, but finally said: "You are sure of this?"

"Yes, ma'am."

She got up from her desk. "We need to go and see Kaz about this."

"Kaz? You mean Mr. Sosnkowski?" asked Ola in excitement. Kazimierz Sosnkowski was the second in command of the Union of Active Struggle. She'd never met him before—which made sense for a secret organization the Russians had outlawed.

"Yes, come with me."

They left the library through a rear, ground-level door. Dawn was just approaching and the city's new electric streetlights had not been switched off yet. The streets seemed very quiet and still. The air was chilly, a foretaste of the approaching autumn, and there was a mist over the Vistula River. But the quiet would soon end as the morning factory shifts trudged off to work and the night shift headed home. With the war, the factories worked around the clock. Warsaw was a major production center, although as a restive, subject city, the Russians permitted no arms manufacturing here. But the city produced iron and steel, railroad cars and locomotives, and dozens of other products needed both in Poland and in Russia. The gritty soot from the steel mills covered everything between rains.

Wanda led her away from the city's center into a poor neighborhood in the northwestern regions. When she turned into a small bakery, Ola's first thought was that she wanted to get something for breakfast. Her own growling stomach would not have minded a bit. But she exchanged nods with the baker and went through a curtain into the back area and then down some stairs into a basement which had been opened up to connect the basements of the two adjacent buildings. There were a number of people there busy at desks and tables piled with papers and maps. Wanda went right up to a man at one of the desks.

"Kaz," she said without preamble, "this is Ola Wojciech, one of my scouts. She says the Russian troops have pulled out during the night."

Sosnkowski was a man with a long nose, bushy eyebrows and mustache, and piercing blue eyes. He looked up from his work and a brief smile flickered across his face. "Morning, Wanda. Up bright and early, are you?"

"No earlier than you, Kaz. Did you hear what I said?"

"Yes, I did. We've been expecting this for several weeks. I just heard from my people at the telegraph office confirming it. They're gone."

"Y-you mean you already knew?" blurted Ola, her face falling.

Sosnkowski's gaze shifted to her. "Don't be disappointed, girl. A good commander always wants more than one source of information. Your efforts were not wasted and I thank you for your service to Poland."

Ola blushed and stammered: "T-thank you, sir." Sosnkowski smiled at her and then turned his attention back to Wanda.

"The Russians are pulling all their forces back to the lines around St. Petersburg—to protect the Tsar, I suppose. We've been left to our own resources, it seems."

"Y-you mean we're free?" said Ola, forgetting herself in her renewed excitement. "The Russians are gone and Poland is independent again?"

Sosnkowski snorted a sort of laugh. "For a few days anyway. We can expect new overlords very shortly."

"What?" cried Ola. "Who?"

"Yes, Kaz," said Wanda, "Who? The Germans, I'm guessing?"

Sosnkowski nodded. "The Germans—or the Martians. It might be a race to see who gets here first. I never thought I'd hear myself say it, but I'm rather hoping it's the Germans."

Chapter Five

October 1913, Warsaw, Poland

Colonel Sir George Tom Molesworth Bridges, DSO stepped off the train which had brought him from St. Petersburg to Warsaw. It was raining, but at least it wasn't snowing yet. When he'd left the Russian capital it had been sleeting and the locals said that snow would not be far behind. He was surely glad to have been ordered out of there before winter set in, but he was not at all sure that his current posting to the German headquarters in Warsaw would be much better. Everyone was saying the Martians were headed there, and he had no desire to see any more Martians.

Bridges was used to being transferred around. He was a military observer for the British War Ministry, and over the last few years he'd been in Belgium and Holland, the United States, the Near East, Russia, and now Poland. His job was to see what other nations' militaries were doing in the war against the Martians and report any interesting ideas back home. Normally he stayed well behind the lines, away from the actual fighting, but sometimes that wasn't possible.

He'd gotten dangerously close several times during his stint in America. Once with a cavalry unit out on the plains and then twice more while assigned to the American's first unit of land ironclads. He'd been in the thick of it at the pivotal Battle of Memphis, and then again during the assault on the Martian fortress to the west of that city. It was the first time one of the alien bases had ever been captured and he'd been right there to see it happen. He'd only been a major then, but the Ministry was so pleased with his report he'd been promoted to lieutenant colonel.

Then came the massive campaign around the Dardanelles, brainchild of the First Lord of the Admiralty, Winston Churchill. Bridges had been sent back to America to beg for the use of one of their squadrons of land ironclads and then he'd accompanied them into battle. That had been a near-run thing indeed and at the end of it he had found himself leading—leading!—a ragtag party of Australians, Welshmen, and US Marines into the depths of a Martian stronghold. That had been the most frightening moment of his life.

Somehow it had turned out well and he had emerged not only uninjured, but a hero. A promotion, a knighthood, and the Distinguished Service Order had followed. They'd then sent him off to St. Petersburg—as a sort of vacation, he supposed. It had been, too, almost. The denizens of the Tsar's court seemed able to ignore the dire threat poised only a few hundred miles away and make merry almost continuously. Or perhaps that was their way of coping with the danger. Whatever the case, Bridges had spent more time dancing, drinking, and dallying with the ladies than he had consulting with the Russian generals.

In truth, nothing much was going on there. The Martians, who had smashed the Russian armies in battle after battle and had driven them back thousands of miles across the Urals, across the Steppes, past Moscow, and within a few days' march for their tripod machines of St. Petersburg, had halted and turned their forces south for their great drive on Constantinople. The Russian generals had been using the unexpected respite to frantically try to put together what forces they had left into a solid defense line to protect the capital. Bridges had consulted with them, helped coordinate the delivery of the tanks and artillery England was shipping them, but had not learned much of value.

Then word had come that the Martians, stymied along the Danube, were shifting some of their forces north and striking west toward Poland and Germany beyond. The generals in London felt that this was a diversion to draw troops away from the Danube line, but they still wanted a British observer there and Bridges won the prize.

"Colonel? Colonel Bridges?" He turned at the sound of his name and saw a short young man in a German lieutenant's uniform approaching him. He had a tiny, dark mustache and piercing eyes. He was speaking heavily accented French, so Bridges answered in the same language. He had been fairly fluent in that before the war, but his time in Belgium had sharpened it and that was nearly all they spoke in St. Petersburg, so he was quite good at it now.

"Yes, that's me, lieutenant…?"

"Rommel, sir. Erwin Rommel. I am to be your guide while you are here." Rommel's French wasn't nearly as good as his own, but he could understand him.

"Ah, excellent, I was afraid I was going to have to blunder around Warsaw to find your headquarters. Oh, there's my luggage," he said, wincing as a Russian conductor tossed his belongings from the train to land heavily on the platform. The train had come here to evacuate the last few Russian officials who had missed the earlier withdrawal and the crew didn't seem to like their English passenger very much, for no reason Bridges could understand.

"I have a man to carry those, sir," said Rommel, beckoning an enlisted man forward to collect the bags. "If you'll follow me, I have a car and driver for us." He led him along the platform, crowded with people trying to board this last train north, and down a flight of steps into the station. It was even more crowded there; positively jammed with German troops getting off other trains at other platforms. They were all carrying heavy packs and bundles of other gear.

"Looks like you fellows are planning for a long stay," observed Bridges.

"Warsaw will require a considerable garrison, Colonel. When the Russians pulled out, they took all the civil administration and most of the police force. The political situation in Poland is… complicated."

"So I've heard," said Bridges, dodging around a big burly sergeant, " I hope the Poles are smart enough to realize they have much bigger problems than politics these days."

"We are all hoping that, sir."

They made their way through the throng to the street outside. It was just as crowded as the inside with troops forming up and marching off and motor lorries and horse-drawn wagons collecting stacks of gear and equipment. The rain was coming down more heavily now and Bridges turned up the collar on his overcoat. As promised, a motor car was waiting, wedged into a space between two lorries. Rommel opened the door to the rear compartment and they both got in. The enlisted man put the bags in the boot and then joined the driver in front.

The driver had to go backward and forward about five times before he could squeeze out of his parking space and get onto the street, but finally he managed it. Even then it was slow going because of all the troops in the street. The driver tooted the horn several times, but the German soldiers didn't seem particularly anxious to get out of the way. Eventually they got free from the station area and the traffic thinned out a bit and they turned south on a major boulevard.

"Where are we going, Lieutenant?" asked Bridges.

"General von Moltke has set up his headquarters in the Wilanow Palace, sir. That's in a suburb south of the city proper. It's not too far."

"So Moltke really is here? My superiors weren't too sure about that." Graf Helmuth von Moltke, often called *Moltke the Younger* to distinguish him from an earlier general of the same name, was the chief of the 'German Great General Staff', basically the top commander, subordinate only to the Kaiser himself. His usual post was in Berlin, but there had been rumors that he'd come east to personally manage the operation in Poland. Apparently the rumors were true.

"Yes, sir. No one knows how long he'll stay. I imagine what the Martians do will have a big influence on that."

"And what *are* the Martians doing, Lieutenant?"

Rommel hesitated for a moment before answering. "I, uh... I think I'll let Major Adam answer that question for you, sir. He will be your liaison with the General Staff."

"I thought you were my liaison."

"Uh, no sir, I'm just your guide while you are here. Major Adam handles all the foreign observers."

Ah, the official dispenser of information. Or perhaps 'dispenser of official information' would be more accurate. Bridges had dealt with that sort before. Some governments kept a very tight control of what foreign observers could learn, while others—like the Americans—were amazingly open-handed. So this Major Adam would tell him the things the German high command wanted him to know and Lieutenant Rommel would be his shadow, making sure he didn't wander off and learn things they didn't want him to know. He'd been under similar conditions in St. Petersburg, and oddly enough when he was in Holland. It was annoying, but he'd learned a few tricks along the way to slip his leash from time to time. He wondered if they would work with the Germans...

The car rolled south, past some public buildings, then past some rather poor-looking neighborhoods, then past smoke-belching factories where Bridges supposed the people from those poor neighborhoods worked. In the rain, everything looked sad and gray, including the people. Eventually, the factories were left behind and there was some open land with actual trees, just starting to turn color with the autumn. He spotted some large, elegant buildings behind walls and then eventually a much larger wall with iron spikes on the top and trees visible beyond. They came to a gate guarded by several dozen sentries in German uniforms. They stopped and an officer came up to the car and demanded their papers. Rommel dealt with him in a rapid German that Bridges couldn't follow. The guard officer looked closely and suspiciously at Bridges, but eventually waved them through.

The car followed a short, tree-lined driveway that opened up in a large paved area, with a very fine-looking palace at the far end. It was a two-story structure with a couple of places where a third story popped up. It was all done in pale yellow and cream colors with a green roof which Bridges found appealing even in the rain. The paved area was packed with cars, lorries, motorcycles, and their drivers. Men were scurrying in and out of the entrance doors.

"Grand place your general has picked," said Bridges.

"Part of it was actually a museum," said Rommel. "I haven't had the chance to look at the collection. Perhaps you will, Colonel."

The car stopped as near the main entrance as it could get and Bridges and Rommel got out. "Your belongings will be delivered to your quarters, Colonel," said Rommel.

"Not here?"

Rommel snorted and the first bit of a smile Bridges had seen crossed his face. "Sorry, no. This place is all filled up. You'll be staying in a hotel back up the road a bit. Don't worry, it's rather nice. I think the commander of the Russian police force lived there with some of his staff before he fled."

The German led him up to the door, where there was another check of their identities. "Rather tight security," observed Bridges. "You surely aren't worried about Martian spies, are you?"

Rommel blinked and then apparently realized it was a joke. "Uh, no. But until we're sure of how the Poles are going to react to this change in… government, we aren't taking any chances. Come on, sir, Major Adam is this way."

He led him through a grand entrance hall with crystal chandeliers, a curving staircase to the second floor, and walls covered with paintings. Then it was into side corridors which led to narrower hallways, clearly not meant to be seen by the public. The doors to some of the rooms were open and they were crammed to the ceilings with paintings and statuary that must have been removed from the museum areas. Eventually they came to a small room with a tiny window and a desk that nearly filled the space. Behind it sat a pudgy man in a major's uniform. He had a large nose, bags under his eyes and the look of someone who hadn't gotten a decent night's sleep in far too long.

Rommel stopped in front of him, snapped to attention and saluted. He said something in German, the only part of which Bridges could catch was his own name. Rommel stepped to the side and turned. "This is Major Adam, sir. He speaks French."

Bridges outranked Adam, so he felt no need to salute. He smiled and nodded and said: "Pleased to meet you, Major."

Adam leaned back in his chair, rubbed his swollen eyes and then slowly got to his feet. "Welcome to Warsaw," he said, in decent French. "Should I address you as Colonel, or Sir George? I know how touchy you English are about titles."

"Colonel will be fine, Major. Haven't really gotten used to this knight-hood business, anyway." And in fact, he had always gone by Tom rather than George, but they wouldn't let him be Sir Tom.

"Very well, Colonel," said Adam. "How was your trip? I've heard the rail line to St. Petersburg is a bit of a mess."

"There were a lot of delays. As you'd expect, there is a great deal of military traffic that has priority. But overall it wasn't bad. I've certainly been on worse in India and South Africa."

"That's right, you do get around, don't you? I glanced at your dossier yesterday and you've had the chance to spy on most of the major players. And now you are here to spy on us."

Bridges frowned and cleared his throat. "I wouldn't exactly call it spying, Major. We are allies after all."

"Ha!" said Adam, smiling—an expression his face clearly wasn't designed for. "Call it what you like, Colonel, but I was an observer a few years back—in Austria, our ally—and I was damn well a spy and so are you. But don't be offended. It's your job and it's expected and accepted. I've been ordered to accommodate you and I shall as much as I'm able. But I have to juggle the needs of you and five other observers, so don't expect me to be at your beck and call."

"Certainly, Major, I understand and I'll try not to make any trouble for you," said Bridges.

"I appreciate that. But the rules here are simple. Every morning at eight o'clock and the other observers will be allowed in our situation room for fifteen minutes to look at the maps there. At four every afternoon we will have a one hour meeting. You may bring written questions which I will answer if I am able. The rest of the day you are free to travel about with your aide so long as you follow his direction concerning where you can go and who you can talk to. Clear?"

"Perfectly. Seems entirely sensible. Thank you, Major."

Adam stared at him for a moment and then sat down. "Since you missed this morning's session in the situation room, I'll allow Rommel here to give you five minutes there and then I'll see you at four. You can spend the rest of the time in between, settling into your quarters."

"Excellent," said Bridges. "Thank you again." They exchanged nods and then he and Rommel left. "Did you catch all that, Lieutenant? He was speaking rather rapidly."

"I was able to follow it, sir," replied Rommel. "Especially since I've already been briefed on the rules and regulations. If you'll follow me, I'll take you to the situation room."

They retraced their steps and then from the entrance lobby went down a different, much grander corridor to what had clearly once been a ball room. Inside there were many desks manned by busy men. Maps were pinned up to the walls and on a huge table in the center of the room was a very large map with colored blocks sitting on it. A platform had been built near one edge where people could stand to get a better view. Rommel led Bridges to that.

The map depicted an area that stretched from the Carpathian Mountains in the south to the Baltic and Lithuania in the north. East to west it ran from Minsk to the German border. "The blue blocks represent our forces, of course," said Rommel, gesturing to the large group of them dominating the center part of the map. "The gray ones along the mountains are the Austro-Hungarian forces, and the tan ones in the north are Russian. The red ones are the Martians."

At the moment there were only a few red blocks at the southeastern edge of the map, but there was a disconcertingly large pile of unused ones sitting off the edge of the map. "So the Martians are just moving into the area?" he asked.

"We know for certain that they have taken the town of Czernowitz," said Rommel, pointing to the few red blocks. "But we are getting reports that they are spreading westward along the south bank of the Dniester River. We're expecting them to cross over to the north bank and head for Lemberg. Our Austrian allies are determined to hold Lemberg and we are moving our forces to assist." As they watched, a man came up to the map with a sheet of paper in his hand. He looked at the map, looked back at the paper, and then took one of the spare red blocks and set it on the map a little west of the ones already there.

"Makes sense," said Bridges. "You have a natural choke-point between the mountains in the south and those marshes to the north."

"Yes, the Pripet Marshes. A huge swampy region which should be very difficult for the Martian tripods from all the reports we've received."

Yes, that was one of the few vulnerabilities of the Martian war machines. They walked on three spindly legs with pointed 'feet'. While they were probably fine in the dry deserts and low gravity of Mars, they didn't work nearly so well on heavy, wet Earth. A tripod that blundered into soft ground could quickly become stuck and an easy target. Recently some new tripods had been observed with broader feet, but they would still probably want to steer clear of the Pripet. "But if they can get beyond Lemberg, they'll be past the marshes and have easier going all the way to Warsaw," observed Bridges.

"All the way to Germany," said Rommel grimly. "We are determined to stop them."

"You certainly seem to be committing a lot of forces to do that," said Bridges, pointing to the swarms of blue blocks.

"Yes. 1st, 2nd, 3rd, and 5th Armies are on their way. We've already committed the 6th through 9th armies to the Danube Front. So we are only keeping 4th

Army in reserve, although we are mobilizing more."

"What about your armored forces? I've read a bit about your new tanks and I'm rather eager to see them. Will I be allowed to do that?"

Rommel frowned. "That will be up to Major Adam. And we've used up our five minutes. If you'll come with me I'll take you to your quarters."

They went back to the entrance and peered out the door looking for their car. The rain was coming down in buckets now and neither wanted to venture out unless they were sure the car had returned to pick them up. After a few minutes they saw it coming up the drive. Rommel stepped out under the portico and waved and the vehicle managed to come nearly up to the door. Bridges and Rommel dashed out and tumbled into the car as quickly as they could, but still ended up quite wet. Rommel said something in German and the vehicle jerked into motion, leaving the palace behind.

As Rommel had promised, the hotel was only about a mile away. It was a large, three story structure built along traditional Polish lines with a stone first floor and brick upper floors except for two wings that went back which were of wood. Stone, brick, and wood were all painted in shades of yellow, similar to the palace, and the roof shingles were a faded red. Many of the widows glowed with a light which gave the place a very welcoming look on this gray, dismal day. The rain had let up a bit by this time and they managed to get inside without getting much wetter than they already were.

He didn't have to check in and was taken to a room on the third floor. It wasn't large but it was cozy with a thick-mattressed bed, an upholstered chair near the window, a dresser, and a desk with a wooden chair against the opposite wall. A single electric light hung from the ceiling and there were several oil lamps as well. A steam radiator under the window provided heat. The bathroom was down the hall. His bags were set on the floor near the closet.

"Will you be needing anything else, sir?" asked Rommel.

"No, I think I'll be fine…"

"Very good then, I'll be back to collect you before four." Rommel nodded and left, closing the door behind him.

Bridges yawned hugely and debated whether he should record what he'd learned while it was still fresh or lie down a while on that inviting-looking bed. He had *not* slept well on the train from St. Petersburg. Duty won out and after putting away his belongings, got out his journal, pen and ink, and sat at the desk and began to write.

A half hour later he was still writing when there was a tap on his door. He looked up from his work in puzzlement, it was much too early for Rommel to have come back. "Yes? What is it?" He automatically spoke in English before he could stop himself. It was unlikely whoever was on the other side of the door could understand him, but the door slowly opened anyway.

It was a young girl wearing a dark dress with an embroidered vest carrying a bundle of towels and linens in her arms. Clearly a maid. She spoke in halting and very poor French: "Excuse… sir. I here to… service you."

"Ah, all right, come in, my dear," said Bridges. He smiled, nodded and made an inviting gesture with his hands. The girl gave a ghost of a smile and made a sort of half-curtsey and then came in and started bustling around the room. She hung up the towels on a hook and then began straightening and dusting. Bridges watched her. She had a round face, longish nose, small mouth, and dark eyes. A long braid hung down from under the cloth she had tied around her head. The hair was brown with some reddish highlights. A pretty thing, if not exactly beautiful.

"What's your name?" he asked.

The girl seemed startled by the question. She stood frozen for a moment and then answered "Ola."

"Nice to meet you, Ola. My name is Tom."

"You… you are English soldier?"

"That's right. I'm here to… uh, watch the Germans."

"Watch Germans? Why?"

Bridges shrugged. "To learn. To see how they fight the war against the Martians."

"Are Ma…Mar-ti-ans coming? To Warsaw?"

"Well, I hope not. The Germans are going to try and stop them."

"You fight, too?"

Bridges laughed. "I hope not. I'm here to learn, not fight."

Ola frowned at that, looking confused. After a moment she turned and swiped her dusting rag along the top of the dresser and then said: "I go now. Come back tomorrow."

"Fine. Here, this is for you." Bridges fished a half-crown out of his pocket and handed it to her. The girl took the silver coin with a look of amazement. The Ministry kept its advisors well supplied with gold and silver money to help them in their missions. It was amazing how cooperative some people became when they saw gold.

"Thank… you, sir," said Ola. She tucked the coin away and then quickly left the room, shutting the door behind her.

Bridges smiled and turned back to his journal.

* * * * *

October, 1913, Warsaw, Poland

Ola Wojciech tapped on the door in the library basement and waited for permission to come in. When she heard a woman's voice, she opened the door and stepped into the small office. Wanda Krahelska looked up from her desk and gestured to Ola to sit in the chair opposite.

"So, how did it go?" asked Wanda.

"All right, I guess," replied Ola. "Colonel Bridges seems friendly. A lot friendlier than that American, Major McCallister."

"Did you get anything from the American today?"

Ola shook her head. "He was out almost the whole day and I was able to search his room thoroughly, but if he is keeping any written records he must have taken them with him."

"Hmmm, well, keep trying."

"The Englishman was writing in a journal when I came in. If he leaves it in the room I should be able to get a look at it when he goes out."

"And he doesn't suspect you can speak and read English?"

She shook her head. "We spoke only French."

"Good. Now remember, Ola, we need any information you can find, and sooner is better than later. But take your time! Later is better than getting caught. As far as we know, the Germans don't suspect the hotel staff is working for us. But one slip-up and we could lose the whole operation. You, the girls we have spying on the other observers, the manager, the whole thing goes up in smoke. So for God's sake be careful."

"Yes, ma'am."

Ola had been tremendously excited when Wanda had explained her new mission. The Union of Active Struggle desperately needed to know the full intentions of the Germans who were flooding into Poland to halt the Martian advance. But the Germans were very careful and getting spies into their headquarters was going to be a difficult and lengthy process. Somehow Kazimierz Sosnkowski had learned that all the foreign observers would be housed in a single location and had the brilliant idea of spying on the spies rather on the Germans. The observers would find out many things and hopefully would not be nearly as careful in guarding the information as the Germans were. Of course the sort of information the Germans would allow the observers to collect would not be everything the Union of Active Struggle wanted, but it would be a good start and all it took was a few young women pretending to be maids to get it. Ola had no doubt there were other agents working elsewhere, but naturally, she had not been told anything about them.

She and the other women had started working at the hotel a few days ago. With her knowledge of English, she'd been assigned to the American and the Englishman. Another woman was taking the French and Italian observers. She didn't envy the women assigned to the Ottoman and the Japanese observers. No one in the group knew either language, so they'd sent women with excellent handwriting in hopes that they could copy down any documents they found, even though they would just be tracing the exotic scripts, and perhaps someone could translate them later.

"Anything else to report?" asked Wanda.

"Uh, the Englishman gave me this." She handed the silver coin over to her supervisor.

Wanda took it and examined it—and did not give it back. "Well, he must like you. That's a good start."

"Uh, Wanda…" Ola hesitated. She wasn't quite sure how to say this…

"Yes?"

"Am I... am I expected to *sleep* with these men if they ask?"

Wanda was silent for a long time before answering. Her eyes seemed to be looking right into Ola. "You are on a very important mission for Poland, Ola. You must do what you think you must to carry it out."

Ola frowned. That was really no answer at all, but she hadn't expected anything different. "Yes, ma'am," she said, got up and took her leave.

* * * * *

Continent 1, Sector 184-36, Cycle 597,845.7

Lutnaptinav focused the heat ray of its fighting machine on the pile of rocks the prey-creatures were sheltering behind. It had seen them take cover there after firing their primitive and nearly useless weapons a few moments before. The ray could not hit them directly, but after only a short time the rocks were glowing red hot and the creatures, unable to stand the heat, leapt up and tried to flee. They only managed a few steps before Lutnaptinav redirected the ray against them. Their bodies exploded in a flash of flame and steam as the water in them boiled away.

It had no time to take satisfaction in their destruction because almost instantly there was a heavy impact on the armor of its machine that sent it staggering. "Beware, commander," came a warning from one of its subordinates. "They have a heavy projectile thrower mounted among the rocks ahead."

"I am aware of this," replied Lutnaptinav. "First sub-group, concentrate your fire and destroy it." This was quickly done and a brief scan revealed no further enemies in the vicinity. "All units report status."

The other members of the battlegroup quickly complied. "Commander," reported Galnatavis, "Trakmalnaza's machine has been seriously damaged. It is uninjured, but I do not believe the fighting machine can be repaired."

"Very well, transfer it to one of the spare machines, salvage the power cells, and destroy the damaged one. We cannot tarry here."

"At once, commander."

The loss of the machine was unfortunate. This latest skirmish had been more serious than most on their long journey, but this was not the first loss. Clan Patralvus, as agreed, had sent a battlegroup to rendezvous with the one being provided by Group 13. The combined force had then proceeded north toward the eastern edge of the large inland sea that separated the main landmass of Continent 1 from Subcontinent 1-4 where Clan Patralvus was located. Most of the territory was sparsely inhabited by the prey creatures and they met no opposition in the early stages. But it was a long journey of almost two thousand *telequels* just to reach the mountainous areas near the inland sea. Even without opposition, they had lost one machine to a freak mechanical failure.

Once they entered the mountainous region things became more difficult. There were several prey-creature cities in the region and the only easily traversable routes had roads made by the locals which were guarded. The fact that the defenses were designed to protect from an attack coming south out of the main part of Continent 1 rather than against an enemy heading in the opposite direction made little difference. Lutnaptinav's mission was to avoid combat and reach friendly territory intact.

Aided by detailed maps provided by the orbiting artificial satellite, they had selected two routes that appeared to be traversable, but with few if any defenses. Lutnaptinav's force attempted one while the Group 13 battlegroup, which was commanded by Nabutangula, a *Threeborn* from Clan Vinkarjan took the other. They quickly found that images taken from three hundred *telequels* above the surface could fail to reveal many important details, despite high magnification. The route taken by the Group 13 force soon proved impractical, but not before one of them was killed when its fighting machine toppled off a cliff and was sucked down to its destruction by this world's high gravity.

Clan Patralvus' route, while difficult, was not impossible. The Clan 13 group retraced its steps and followed along after them. Unfortunately, progress was slow; some days only a few *telequel* could be managed. The delays gave the prey-creatures enough time to shift some of their forces to contest the passage.

At first it was just small groups of warriors armed only with their small projectile throwers. These posed no danger and the prey would simply fire a few shots from concealed positions and then flee before they could be destroyed. But soon more serious resistance materialized. The creatures used chemical explosives to directly attack the fighting machines or sometimes to destroy parts of the path they were using. A few times they contrived to use explosions to bring down rockslides on them. Several fighting machines were wrecked in this manner. Once an explosion completely blocked their intended path and it took three full rotations to find a way around the blockage. Another time Hadramantar's machine was destroyed and it was severely injured when a bomb went off directly under it and it fell into a deep crevasse. Hadramantar was currently being carried in a rescue pod, but Lutnaptinav was doubtful it would survive to reach help.

This most recent fight over, the force formed up and resumed the march. They remained on alert because there was no guarantee there would not be more prey-creatures waiting ahead. The artificial satellite could sometimes give a warning of enemy forces, but it was only overhead for short periods and could not be depended upon. But shortly they topped a rise and ahead the land fell away in front of them and a vast plain stretched off to the north. The going steadily became easier and the chances of ambush decreased.

Lutnaptinav required only a part of its attention for piloting its machine and looking for threats so it turned the rest to contemplating its current situation. Its original conclusion that this expedition was not merely a gesture of solidarity with the clans on the main part of Continent 1, but also a means for clan Patralvus rid itself of unreliable elements was holding true. Conversation with the

Group 13 battlegroup commander indicated that it too was almost completely made up of *Threeborn*.

Lutnaptinav had searched through the memories of its short life looking for anything it had said or done which would convince the clan leaders or its progenitor that it was *unreliable* and come up with nothing. It was totally committed to the Race and its mission here. True, it sometimes asked questions which appeared to upset the older clan members, but what was the harm in that?

Obedience. It all comes down to obedience.

The central factor in the society of the Race was the instinctual obedience that each member had instilled in it during the budding process. As the bud neared maturity its progenitor would fill it with basic knowledge so it could function productively almost immediately after detaching, but it also transferred many of its own memories, and at some point the instinctive obedience would also take root.

Even after hundreds of thousands of cycles of study, no one knew exactly how the process worked. The mind-to-mind communication possible during budding or by grasping tendrils was well understood. The nervous systems could link physically and communication was possible. But the instinctive obedience was different because it was not just obedience to the progenitor, but to anyone senior to it in line of descent from the clan's most ancient ancestor. And not just up the line of descent, but sideways as well. The progenitor's siblings and the progenitor's progenitor's siblings and so on, all had to be obeyed. Anyone with seniority on the generational grid had to be obeyed unconditionally and somehow the new member instinctively knew its exact ranking within the clan and would automatically obey anyone senior to it. The prevailing theory was that in addition to the mind-to-mind link possible through physical contact there was some subconscious process occurring through what could only be called telepathy. Whatever the mechanism, it worked and worked well.

But since the Race arrived on the Target World something had gone wrong.

A newly budded member would obey its progenitor and any senior members of the clan who were on-world at the budding. But anyone who arrived in later waves of the invasion did *not* have to be obeyed, no matter what their place on the grid. If the theorized telepathic link did exist then apparently it could not reach across interplanetary distances.

The result was that instead of a rock-solid chain of command on the Target World, the Race had a multitude of separate chains, precariously tied together by a few individuals who had arrived in the first or second waves and thus present when the *Threeborn* were budded. For the most part, the *Threeborn* were obeying newly arrived senior members voluntarily because they could see the sense in doing so, but there was a huge difference in obeying because they wanted to and obeying because they *had* to.

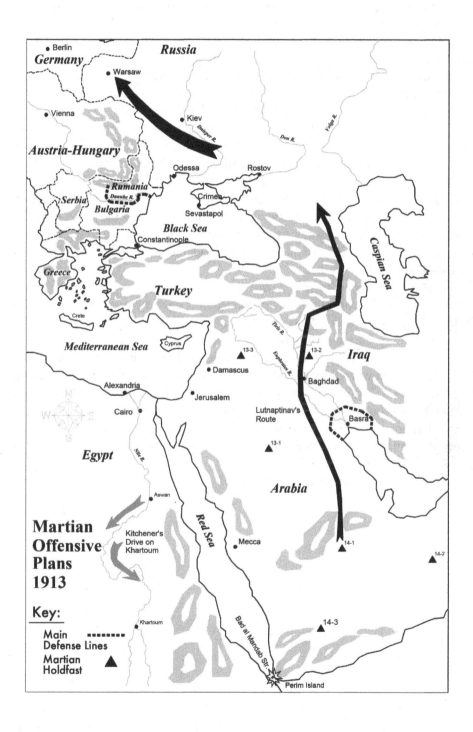

Berlin
Germany
Russia
Warsaw
Vienna
Kiev
Dnieper R.
Don R.
Volga R.
Austria-Hungary
Odessa
Rostov
Rumania
Crimea
Danube R.
Serbia
Bulgaria
Sevastapol
Black Sea
Constantinople
Greece
Caspian Sea
Crete
Turkey
Tigris R.
13-3
13-2
Iraq
Mediterranean Sea
Cyprus
Euphrates R.
Baghdad
Damascus
Alexandria
Jerusalem
Cairo
Lutnaptinav's
Route
Basra
13-1
Egypt
Nile R.
13-1
Arabia
Aswan
**Martian
Offensive
Plans
1913**
Kitchener's
Drive on
Khartoum
14-1
14-2
Mecca
Red Sea
Key:
Khartoum
14-3
Main
Defense Lines
Martian
Holdfast
Bab al Mandeb Str.
Perim Island

The situation was made worse by the casualties that were being taken during this war with the prey-creature. Key links were being killed and the chain of command was becoming fragmented. There were groups of *Threeborn* who were entirely independent of the chain of command, and many in the clan hierarchy were extremely alarmed by this and taking action. One clan had exterminated an entire group of *Threeborn* they considered untrustworthy. There had been no such trouble in Clan Patralvus so far, but the mere fact Lutnaptinav and the others were here proved that the clan leaders were concerned.

Perhaps more critically the leaders of the Race, back on the Homeworld, were so concerned by this phenomenon that it had been a critical factor in their decision not to transfer the entire population to the Target World as had been originally planned but had instead adopted a plan for those on the Target World to send critical resources back the Homeworld. Clearly, they feared arriving on a new world where much of the population would not obey them. Lutnaptinav and many other *Threeborn* felt this to be impractical, even irrational, but their progenitors had to obey those on the Homeworld and most of the *Threeborn* had no choice but to obey in turn.

There must be an answer to this...

A communication from one of the leading fighting machines interrupted its thoughts. "Commander, I have made contact with a scout from Group 10."

Checking its tactical display Lutnaptinav saw that a friendly icon had appeared on it. Group 10 had the nearest holdfast in this area, so it made sense that was who they would encounter first. Directing a signal at the newcomer, Lunaptinav said: "Attention Group 10, this is Lutnaptinav of Clan Patralvus. We are two battlegroups here at the order of the Colonial Conclave."

The answer came immediately: "This is Jadfertinel of Group 10. We were expecting you. Welcome. Please proceed to Holdfast 10-6. I am sure you need supplies and repairs."

"Yes we do. And medical assistance."

Chapter Six

November 1913, Western Desert, Egypt

Captain Harry Calloway squirmed through the rear hatch of the Raglan armored carrier and landed heavily in the sand. The damn hatch was just too small for an easy exit; it took a section nearly a minute to get out and that was just too long. They had complained about this to headquarters dozens of times, but without result. Of course, it was much easier to go out through the larger hatches on the top of the vehicle, but doing so would leave you an easy target for critical seconds. Under fire, the rear hatch was the only practical way to get out.

His headquarters section crouched behind the Raglan anxiously peering left and right as the other men of the company debarked from their own carriers. On either side, the other companies of the battalion were doing the same. Man after man squeezed out and then it appeared no more were going to emerge. "Time!" snapped Harry.

Company Sergeant Major Breslin looked at his watch and said: "Fifty-two seconds, sir."

"Still too damn slow! All right, here come the tanks, move the men out!" He waved his arm to the platoon commanders and whistles started blowing. A line of tanks stretching nearly a mile wide were rumbling up from the rear and passing through the gaps in the line of Raglan carriers. As each one passed, half a section of infantry sprinted over to get behind them and follow along. This was just an exercise—another in a seemingly endless series of them—but if it had been the real thing there probably would have been Martian heat rays blasting all around them. The infantry stayed in the cover provided by the tanks.

The tanks, mostly the Mk.V Wellingtons along with a few of the new Mk.VII Marlboroughs, advanced at a walking pace so the infantry could keep up with them—not that the vehicles could go much faster. The ground was mostly just bare, rough earth with a scattering of rocks; not too bad going. Every now and then a patch of sand would be encountered and this was not only harder going, but the tracks of the tank threw the sand up behind them showering the troops if they weren't able to bunch together behind the center of the tank away from the tracks. Even on the solid ground the tanks stirred up a lot of dust which covered the men. Most had a cloth covering their nose and mouth. A few even broke out their anti-black dust gear to cover their heads entirely. November in the Western Desert was still pretty warm, but nothing like summer, so the men could stand it. Harry made do with a cloth.

A flare shot up from one of the tanks. It was red and angled off to the right of the advance. Harry yanked down his mask and shouted: "Change of direction to the right! Heads up!"

The flare and Harry's warning were almost unnecessary. Most of the tanks had wireless sets now and would know what to do. The infantry would just follow where the tanks went, but procedures were procedures and they would be followed. The line of tanks began to swing around to the right. The ones at the far left of the line kept going at their same speed while driving in a long arc. The ones on the extreme right slowed to almost a stop. The rest of the line adjusted their speeds to keep the line straight as it swung like a door on its hinges. Or tried to, anyway; the line quickly became pretty ragged. But it was up to the tankers to straighten it out. The infantry just trudged along in the path of the tanks. Harry looked back and saw the Raglans were following along at a few hundred yards distance, ready to reembark the infantry when called upon.

The turn was completed and the line straightened out again. After a few more minutes of eating dust a loud siren began wailing from one of the command tanks and all the others came to a ragged halt. Harry and his officers and sergeants screamed: "Bombs! Bombs! Bombs! Take cover!"

They were pretending that their imaginary enemy was firing their nasty explosive bombs. Unlike the heat rays, these flew in a rather slow arc through the air and if you had sharp-eyed lookouts you might have a few seconds warning before they got to you. Troops in the open could do little but fling themselves on the ground and hope none of them would land close enough to blast them to shreds. But if you had a nice solid tank handy...

"Underneath! Get under the tanks! Move, damn you!" Most of the men quickly crawled underneath the armored behemoths they'd been following, but a few held back. Harry couldn't really blame them; a week before a man in one of the other battalions had had his arm crushed when a tank he was under turned unexpectedly. And this was just an exercise so why take chances? But if this had been a real attack, seconds could make the difference between life and death. Officers and sergeants pushed, pulled and kicked the reluctant ones into place. Harry stayed out to observe his company as best he could. When it looked like everyone was where they belonged, he joined his own half-section under the Wellington.

There was about a foot and a half of space between the ground and the bottom of the tank's hull, not enough to go on hands and knees but enough that you could wriggle forward. Harry did so until he bumped into someone. It was very dark underneath the tank after the brightness of the Egyptian day. The shade was welcome, but there was heat radiating off the tank from its petrol engine, so it was anything but comfortable.

They lay there sweating for a few minutes and then the siren gave three short blasts. "All right! Up and at 'em!" shouted Sergeant Breslin. Harry worked his way backwards, warning the men to keep their arms and legs well clear of the tank's tracks. Theoretically, they could have lain there until the tank drove away and then just stood up, but after that accident no one really wanted to. When they were clear, the tanks pulled away and they continued in their path.

After walking for about a half mile, another flare went up, a yellow one this time and the tanks came to a halt. Harry blew his whistle and waved his arm. "All right! Time for us to do what they're paying us for! Deploy!"

The men came out from behind the tanks and moved forward, weapons at the ready. The tanks with their heavy armor and big guns were there to deal with the Martian tripods. But hard experience had shown that they were ill-suited to handle the smaller spider machines. The hideous little devices were too small and too quick to be easily hit with a tank's main guns. The tanks also carried machine guns, which could hurt the spiders, but they had limited fields of fire and couldn't always stop the spiders from closing. And once the alien machines got close they could use their small heat rays to wreck a tank in surprisingly short order. They would cling to the tank and burn a hole right through the armor and set it afire. A group of tanks, caught alone in rough ground or a ruined town could be swarmed over and wiped out.

It was the job of the infantry to prevent that.

With their LCLE Rifles, LIATs, and Boys Rifles, the infantry were supposed to keep the spiders away from the tanks. Harry looked back and saw that the Raglan carriers were closing up, filling in the intervals between the tanks. The heavy machine guns mounted on them would help deal with spiders and they'd be close at hand to pick up the wounded. No one said it aloud, but they would also be extra targets for the Martian tripods, taking fire away from the tanks. For that was the key when fighting the Martians: hit them with everything you could bring to bear all at once. Give them so many targets they couldn't kill them all. To commit your forces piecemeal was just to invite their destruction. Today's exercise only involved tanks and infantry, but in real action, the Longbow, self-propelled artillery would be engaged as well. Aircraft, too, if any were available.

They plodded along through the growing heat, looking for imaginary enemies. Under the circumstances the men didn't mind since they were now out in front and away from the dust. In actual combat, however, they'd be horribly vulnerable.

Finally, they caught sight of the tiny railroad station of El Alamein in the distance, and a hint of the Mediterranean beyond, and the signal to halt was given. The tank crews clambered out of their vehicles and the infantry clustered around their carriers. As always, the first thing they did was to open up the engine access panels so they could brew their tea on the sizzling hot motors. Once they had their tea they sat in the shade of the vehicles and broke open their rations. Harry did the same and after a while his platoon commanders gathered around.

"That went well, don't you think, sir?" asked Lieutenant Boyerton.

"They've *all* been going well for weeks," said Fenwick with a frown. "The men are going to get tired of this before too much longer."

"How about you, Mr. Fenwick? Getting tired of this?" asked Harry.

Fenwick, startled, stammered: "Uh, I…I didn't mean it that way, sir. I know the training is important…"

"And you can see the men are in good spirits, Jake," said Lieutenant O'Reilly to Fenwick. "They know it's important, too."

"Yes," agreed Harry, "and I think I know why they are responding so well."

"Sir?"

"It's because these tactics we're learning are *offensive* tactics. Tactics we'll use to attack the Martians. For so long our whole strategy was to try to hang onto what we had. Defensive tactics. Those years back home defending Sydney, then that line south of Cairo. Even the drive up the Nile involved short lunges forward and then dig and defend against possible counter attacks."

"You were on the offensive up there at the Dardanelles," said Boyerton. "And that last operation we were in on the Red Sea."

"True, but the Dardanelles campaign was still basically defensive. We went up there to stop the Martians from taking Constantinople. But you're right about the last business on the Red Sea: we were taking back ground from the Martians." He looked at the young men around him. "Felt good, didn't it?"

"Yes, sir," they replied in unison.

"And now this idea of an armored division we're testing out here. It's not intended to sit still and defend ground, it's meant to go out and attack the enemy. Attack them and take ground away from them. I hear they're building three or four more of these divisions back in England. I'm no general, but I can't help but feel that maybe the tide has turned in our favor. I think the men are sensing that, too. That's why they don't mind all the training."

"I think you're right, sir," said O'Reilly.

"But will we ever get to go home?" asked Fenwick. "Take back Australia?"

Harry paused before answering. Home. Would he ever see home again? That had been on the minds of everyone. Ever since they were run out back in '11. Sometimes he could still smell the smoke of the burning city. He had nightmares of the desperate flight through Sydney to reach the last boats before the Martians. Would they ever get back? Was there anything left to get back to besides ruins covered in that damn red weed?

He realized the others were watching him, waiting for his answer. With an effort he said: "Yes. We'll go home someday. We'll take it back. The way the Americans are taking back their country. I don't know how long it will take or what road we'll have to follow to get there. But even if the road takes us through Khartoum or Moscow or Timbuktu, someday we'll get there."

His officers nodded, apparently satisfied.

After an hour or so there was a signal to get back in their vehicles and they were soon on their way to the camp that had been built for the division east of the rail station. On the way they passed a convoy of maintenance vehicles heading out to recover the tanks and carriers that had broken down during the exercise. The Raglans were pretty reliable, but the tanks were very prone to breakdowns. They'd probably left ten percent of them out there in the desert today.

Back in camp Colonel Berwick held an officers meeting to go over the day's exercise. Naturally he had some criticisms, but overall he was pleased. The inevitable question of how long they would be staying here and where they might go next came up. Usually Berwick just said that he didn't know and he would tell them when he did. But this time his answer was a little different.

"I've heard rumors of a big offensive in the works that we'll be a part of. I don't know where or how soon. If we're to join Kitchener's drive up the Nile, it could be any time. But other rumors indicate something to help out the Germans and Austrians along the Danube. Maybe a thrust into the Martian rear areas. If that's the case I wouldn't expect anything to happen until spring. At least I hope no one is planning to send us into Russia during the winter!"

"Amen to that!" said someone.

"We've all been wishing for cooler weather, sir," said Burf Sampson, "but not *that* cool!" They all got a laugh out of that.

Later, as they were walking back to their tents, Harry was talking with Sampson. "So we might see action soon, or it might be four or five months. Sure wish I knew which."

"Same as always: hurry up and wait. Well, whichever it is you can be sure we'll be in the thick of the action. They haven't created this armored division so it can sit in the rear."

He was about to answer in agreement when he saw his servant Abdo hurrying toward him. He was clutching some papers. "Ah, looks like the mail has arrived," said Sampson.

"Lord! Lord!" said Abdo. "You have a letter! A letter from Miss Vera!"

Sampson snorted and grinned. "Well, I will leave you to that, Harry." He turned off toward his own tent.

At least Sampson hadn't said anything about Vera being his girlfriend. Everyone who knew of their friendship seemed to think that was the case and some made jokes about it. He and Vera were definitely *friends*, but nothing more. Vera had been engaged to a man who had been killed fighting the Martians near the Basra oil fields and it was clear she wasn't over that yet and was not ready for another romance. He had to admit that *he* was ready, but that would have to wait.

He got to his tent and opened the letter. It was dated three weeks ago and had been sent from Cairo. So her hospital was still there. It began:

Dear Harry,

I hope you are doing well with your new division and that you are safe. We had a man in here from your division the other day who had to have his arm amputated after it was run over by a tank. So you do be careful.

Most of the page was filled with the usual pleasantries about weather and such, but then she wrote:

I attach a poem I wrote the other day. The words just came to me as they often do, so please don't attach any special significance to them. Things have actually been fairly quiet here of late.

A Military Hospital

A mass of human wreckage, drifting in
Borne on a blood-red tide,
Some never more to brave the stormy sea
Laid reverently aside,
And some with love restored to sail again
For regions far and wide.

He read the poem several times savoring the cadence. The last line especially caught his eye: *And some with love restored...* She had helped restore him after he lost his eye. With love? Maybe. But the unending labors of all the nurses was an act of love when you came down to it. Don't attach any special significance to this, she had written. Somehow he couldn't help it.

He lay down on his cot, still holding the letter, put his feet up, and sighed.

* * * * *

November 1913, New Castle-upon Tyne

"T-they're r-really c-coming along, aren't they sir?"

Frederick Lindemann glanced at his aide, Sub-lieutenant Windsor, and then back at the objects of his admiration: a line of huge, scaffolding-encased objects stretched along one whole side of the Armstrong-Whitworth construction yards. The one closest to them could be fairly easily identified for what it was: a partially completed land ironclad. The enormous caterpillar tracks, two pairs of them, formed the base for the vehicle's hull which was nearly finished. Above that the framework for the superstructure was taking shape. Large overhead cranes were lifting steel members into place. There was no sign of the weapons yet; those were being constructed elsewhere and would be moved here when ready. Sparks from welders showered down here and there. The amazingly skilled riveters were tossing red-hot rivets like they were walnuts from man to man and then into the pre-measured holes where the gunners would hammer them in. The smell of torches, furnaces, and scorched metal filled the air. Foremen shouted and men hauled materials hither and yon. The noise was just short of deafening. It seemed like chaos, but Lindemann knew that appearances were deceiving.

The next ironclad down the line wasn't quite so far advanced and many of the hull plates were yet to be installed. The next one was even less complete with the hull just rows of ribs, like the skeleton of some huge animal. The boilers and steam turbines were being fitted into place and the electrical lines ran down to the motors inside the caterpillar assemblies. At each site farther down the line the construction was progressively less, until there was nothing but a pile of materials and a space for assembly to start.

"Well, Professor, what do you think?" said a voice raised against the noise. He turned and saw the Armstrong-Whitworth engineer in charge of the project, a man named Nigel Gresley. He was a thin-haired, big-eared man in his late thirties; young for such responsibilities, Lindemann thought, but he seemed to know his job.

He hesitated a moment before responding, but finally said: "Impressive."

"Impressive?" replied Gresley. "A bloody miracle is what it is! To get this far in just five months is nothing short of a bloomin' miracle!"

"I understand you had considerable help from Metropolitan," said Lindemann.

"True," nodded Gresley. "They had already worked up a design and some of the machinery to produce the caterpillar tracks for a prior Ministry project that was stalled. They were kind enough to help us out. We'd just be laying down the first one of these but for that. But even so, to be this far along is a miracle," he said again, staring hard at Lindemann as if to dare him to deny his miracle.

"When do you estimate the first one will be complete?"

Gresley frowned. And then seemed to be ticking off things on his fingers. "April, at the earliest," he said at last.

"Unacceptable. The First Lord is planning a major spring offensive. He needs a full squadron of these and when you make allowances for the shakedown and crew training it could be mid-summer. You simply must work faster."

Gresley's face was turning red and it had nothing to do with the brisk November wind. "Impossible, Professor! That is simply impossible. There are only so many hours in the day."

"Assign additional resources and men." Lindemann spoke calmly, but firmly.

"We've already stopped work on three warships and several other army projects to divert our attention here." He waved his hand toward the construction bays. "You can only fit in a finite number of men there. Any more and they just get in each other's way and accomplish nothing additional."

"Three shifts a day? Seven days a week?"

Gresley's frown got deeper. "We give them Sunday's off. They need some rest or they start making mistakes."

"Then use some of the extra men you said you can't use to form Sunday work crews."

"They'll want extra pay…"

"Then give it to them. The Admiralty will reimburse you." He stared hard. "Mr. Gresley, I don't care how you do it, but we must have the first six of these by the end of February."

The man was angry and flustered and it seemed to Lindemann he was mustering some sort of counter-argument. He briefly considered using a threat, like to go to Andrew Noble and have him replaced. It could probably be done. As far as he knew this Gresley had no social standing at all. But after a moment he decided that the patriotism card would probably be more effective. "Mr. Gresley, I know I am asking a lot, but these machines are absolutely vital to the security of the Empire. Can I tell Mr. Churchill that we can count on you?"

The man's face grew calmer and after a moment he nodded. "Yes, Professor, you can."

"Excellent. I look forward to receiving your reports on how things are progressing. Come, Albert, we have a train to catch."

The journey back to London was uneventful. These days he made sure Albert—or 'Bertie' as he preferred to be called—packed a dinner for such trips and they ate much better than they would if they bought things from the station vendors. With the early sunsets it was dark for most of the ride and deep night before they reached London. He dismissed Sub-Lieutenant Windsor and proceeded directly to Churchill's residence. As usual the First Lord was hosting a late dinner and he managed to get there in time for the last course and the desert.

Churchill's wife, Clementine, welcomed him warmly and had a servant fit in a place for him at the table right next to her. Her husband, cigar in one fist and a glass of champagne in the other, was in the midst of a harangue against some member of Parliament but he did pause to issue a brief welcome to him before continuing. "Welcome back, Professor, do enjoy some of this dinner. We'll talk a bit later."

There were a half-dozen other diners, some of whom Lindemann had met before, but the only one of consequence was Prince Battenburg, the First Sea Lord. Churchill, as First Lord of the Admiralty, was the civilian head of the navy, while Admiral Battenburg was the military commander. Battenburg was junior to Churchill even though he was much older, but the two seemed to get along very well. Lindemann remembered the critical moment during last spring's Dardanelles campaign where the entire operation would have been derailed by the unstable Lord Fisher had it not been for Battenburg siding with Churchill and saving the day. Lindemann liked the man, not only for his loyalty and good sense, but because he, like Lindemann, had been born in Germany but was now solidly English.

"Did your trip go well, Professor?" asked Clementine. The First Lord's wife was a charming woman, one of the very few of her gender Lindemann had any respect for. She was bright and witty and played an excellent game of tennis, which he enjoyed also. But she understood her role in men's society and always used her talents to compliment those of her husband rather than compete with him. If he ever encountered another woman like her he might even be tempted into marriage. Little chance of that in these times.

"Well, enough," he answered. "Probably not well enough to please your husband, I'm afraid, but probably as well as we can hope for."

"Winston can be impossibly demanding sometimes. Don't let him brow-beat you, Professor." She had not lowered her voice and there was no doubt Churchill heard her, but he only raised an eyebrow and continued his talk. Churchill always dominated every gathering, but he could never intimidate his wife.

Eventually things wrapped up, as they always did with the men enjoying cigars and brandy and the women sipping wine in an adjacent parlor. Lindemann stood there stifling his yawns. Churchill's working day often lasted long after midnight and he was glad he'd caught some sleep on the train. But Churchill was clearly eager for a private talk with Lindemann and Battenburg and after a few not-so subtle hints the other guests took their leave. Clementine did not tarry either and bid them all a good night. Churchill immediately led the way to his map room.

When the door was shut he turned to Lindemann and said: "So, Professor, how did things go with the Armstrong people? Satisfactory progress?"

"The quality of the work appears to be entirely satisfactory. They have set up what amounts to an assembly line at their facility. They have the capacity to work on ten of the ironclads simultaneously and as each building bay is cleared a new one can be started."

"And the completion date for the first?"

"I had to do some arm-twisting, but they have promised the first by February."

Churchill frowned. "Which means we can realistically expect it by April."

"In all probability, yes, sir. Although they may surprise us."

"And then there's the whole fitting out and working up process. More time lost. Blast. There's no chance of using them in the winter anyway, but I wanted to launch our offensive in the spring."

"Spring comes late to that part of the world, Winston," said Battenburg. "Even when the snows melt, there's a month or more of everything becoming a sea of mud. Damn few paved roads there, either. Realistically we'd be looking at a May start at the earliest."

"True, true. I just hope that isn't too late," said Churchill, staring at the map hanging on the wall.

"Is the timing so critical, sir?" asked Lindemann. "Your Crimea operation ought to work just about any time, shouldn't it?"

"What?" said Churchill, spinning about. "Oh, of course, you were away when I decided to abandon that approach."

Surprised, Lindemann glanced at Battenburg, but the admiral was pointedly avoiding his gaze. In fact, he seemed to be rolling his eyes... Yes, it was true that the First Lord seemed to drop one idea in favor of another rather frequently.

"My initial thoughts were to strike into the enemy's rear areas," continued Churchill, drawing a finger across the map from the Crimea up into Ukraine. "With their forces tied up along the Danube, their fortresses ought to be lightly guarded. With some of the land ironclads we could snap them up one at a time like ripe peaches."

"And what has changed now?"

"Well, as you've heard—we talked about that at the last Admiralty conference—the Martians are now moving into Galicia and central Poland. The Germans and Austrians are rushing forces there to meet them, but it's by no means sure they can stop them. And if the Martians were to break through into Germany or even farther west and attack the great industrial centers, it could be a catastrophe. So I've decided we need to shift our efforts farther west, probably along the Dniester River and try to give some direct support to our allies."

"I see, sir."

"We do have one bit of good news, at least. The Prime Minister and I had a rather lengthy telegraphic exchange with President Roosevelt the other day and he's agreed to continue the loan of the squadron of Land Ironclads they lent us for the Dardanelles operation. They were vital to our success as you'll recall."

"I do. But two of them were lost and the rest badly damaged, weren't they, sir?" asked Lindemann.

"Yes, but we've been repairing them in our yards in Alexandria, and Roosevelt has promised to send replacements for the two that were lost."

"That's very good of him. I'd think the Americans would be wanting them for their own offensives."

"Oh, they do, they do," said Churchill. "And in fact, Roosevelt didn't just let us have them unconditionally, he insisted on a rather large concession from us for their use."

"Really? What?"

"It seems their drive to the west, to the Rocky Mountains, is being hampered by the Martians occupying central Canada. They threaten the American right flank. So, once we've completed my proposed operation in Eastern Europe, we've promised to make a major commitment of men and material to Canada to shore up that flank."

"Wouldn't that be a dangerous dispersion of our resources, sir?" asked Lindemann. Canada was almost entirely under the control of the Martians. Only the thickly populated sections along the St. Lawrence River and Great Lakes were still in human hands. To push the enemy back on an extended front would take a huge force, it seemed to him.

Churchill took a long draw on his cigar and let it out a stream of smoke before answering. "Perhaps. But at the moment the Americans are the only ones making significant headway in clearing out the invaders. If we could assist them in ejecting the Martians completely from North America, then the vast potential of our American cousins could be brought to bear anywhere we chose."

He turned to his map and touched it briefly in a number of spots. But then he shrugged and turned back to face them. "In any case, that's all for the future. Right now we need to deal with the situation developing in Poland. I just hope the Germans can hold on long enough for us to come to their aid."

Chapter Seven

November 1913, Eastern Galicia

Colonel Erich Serno looked down from the nose of the AEG G.IV Bomber as it rumbled over the Galician countryside. An icy wind nipped at the few bits of exposed flesh on his face. His leather flying helmet, goggles, and a wool scarf covered most of him, but not quite all. The November weather wasn't all that cold at ground level, but add three thousand meters of altitude and a hundred kilometer per hour wind and it was truly bitter. The wan sunlight did little to counter the cold and from the looks of the clouds building in the northwest, they wouldn't have it for long anyway.

Serno looked around at the swarms of other bombers of his *Kampf-geschwader*. His entire command was with him today and the hundred planes made a most impressive sight. And it wasn't just his group; squinting ahead into the rising sun, he could make out specks from other formations. His planes and those from half-a-dozen other airfields near Warsaw had lumbered aloft with their heavy bomb loads in the pre-dawn light. The formations got themselves sorted out and then headed east, climbing all the time. Their target was the city of Lemberg—or rather, the Martian forces that were attacking that city.

Between the Martian force moving westward out of the Ukraine and the German forces moving eastward out of Germany itself, the race for Poland had been won by the Germans—mostly. Warsaw had been secured and a fortified line was being constructed in eastern Galicia. The initial plan, or so Serno had heard, was to build the line well to the east of Lemberg following the Strypa River north from the Dniester and then linking up with the Bug River and then all the way north to the Pripet Marshes. But the Martians had not cooperated and had crossed the Strypa before significant human forces could get there. So the line had to be moved back seventy kilometers and now ran almost due north from the Dniester to Lemberg and then on to connect with the Bug as originally planned. That put the city on the front lines; not an ideal situation but fortunately, Lemberg, being the largest city in eastern Galicia, had been heavily fortified by the Austrians against a possible Russian attack in the days before the Martians arrived and made those squabbles irrelevant.

The Austrians had crammed the city's defenses with troops and also oc-cupied the line going south to the rugged Carpathian Mountains, but the line stretching northward was almost entirely held by the German Army. That line wasn't nearly as strong, but it had been strong enough—just barely—to halt the Martian advance. They had struck, taken some losses, and pulled back. Now they were bringing up reserves and it was clear that another stronger attack was coming soon. It appeared that the attack was going to go directly against Lemberg, even though that was the strongest part of the line. That might have just been a feint, of course, with the unprecedented mobility of the Martian machines they could easily shift their attack elsewhere very quickly. But for right now, their forces were massed to the east of Lemberg and so that was where the German Air Force was going to strike.

It was over a two hour flight from the airfields around Warsaw to Lemberg. If the defense lines could hold, it would make sense to shift the bases closer to the front, but until that was certain it was deemed wiser to keep them where they were. Serno hoped they would be able to move them closer. Two hours each way in the air when winter fully came was going to be hell. He scrunched down in his seat and tried to stay out of the wind.

An hour later he was trying to stop shivering when he felt a tap on his side. Twisting around he saw that it was Corporal Heineman, the radio operator. He held up a thermos flask and shouted: "Coffee?" Serno nodded and eagerly took it. He was smiling, but his scarf concealed the fact from Heineman.

The corporal started to squeeze back into the little compartment where his equipment was mounted, but Serno pulled down the scarf and asked: "Any signals from the other squadrons?" Heineman shook his head and went back into his cubby. Serno's plane, and all the other squadron command planes, had been modified to include a radio set and room for an operator. The radios were all English-made, using the amazing Martian wire that had no electrical resistance. They had far greater range than normal equipment. The British and Americans had considerable stockpiles of the wire, salvaged from the wrecks of enemy machines they'd destroyed. Until recently Germany had only had very limited amounts of the stuff, since they'd had little direct combat against the invaders except for the South American expedition. Clearly, that was changing. Hopefully Germany would be able to build things like coil guns and better radios for herself soon.

The coffee was only warm, but it still felt good going down. He examined the container. The thermos flasks were a relatively new invention, too—a German one—and had an inner and outer container with a vacuum in between to act as an insulator. He really ought to get one if he was going to do more of these winter flights. They weren't cheap, though, and he wondered how the corporal had gotten one.

He finished off the coffee and then dared the wind to look around. His formation appeared to be in good shape, but a moment later they passed through some clouds and visibility dropped to nothing for a while. When they emerged from the clouds he was concerned to notice some ice had formed on the fabric wings and a few of the bracing wires. But the wind soon blew it off and he was able to relax. He peered down over the fuselage, looking for landmarks, but there was nothing recognizable, just forests, farms, and some small villages.

Checking his watch, he saw that Lemberg couldn't be too far ahead. He twisted around and rapped the thermos against one of the aircraft's ribs to get Heineman's attention. The corporal came closer and Serno handed him the ther-

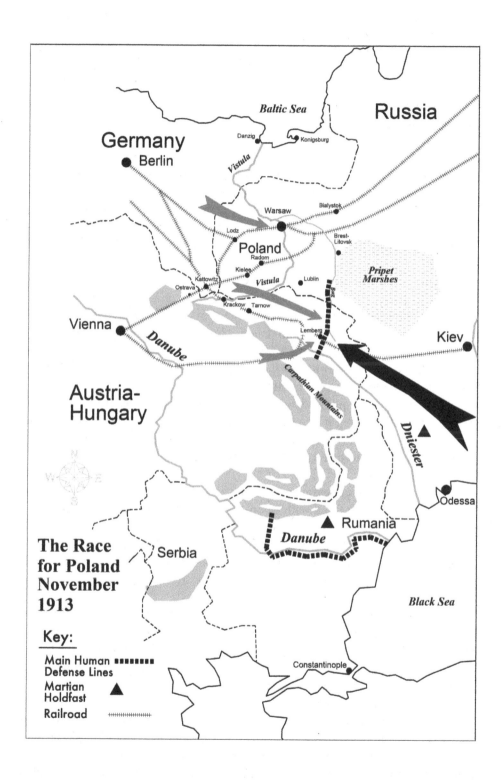

The Race
for Poland
November
1913

Key:

Main Human ▪▪▪▪▪▪▪▪
Defense Lines

Martian ▲
Holdfast

Railroad ╫╫╫╫╫╫╫╫

mos and said: "Try to contact the Lemberg headquarters. See if there's any update on the target location."

"Yes, sir!" The radio operator turned back to his equipment and began tapping a message out on the key. Serno had some familiarity with Morse, but not enough to send and receive under these conditions. A few minutes later Heineman turned back toward him and shook his head. "No sir! Our orders are unchanged. Attack the target area as planned."

Serno nodded and faced forward. Ground scouts had spotted a large concentration of tripods about fifteen kilometers east of Lemberg the previous day and requested a bombing mission. Scout planes would precede the main force and try to mark the target with colored smoke bombs, but they wouldn't know if the tempting target was still there until they arrived. If it wasn't there anymore, they had orders to split up and attack any target of opportunity they could find. He fumbled out his binoculars, hands clumsy with the heavy gloves, and looked ahead.

After a few minutes he saw a hazy gray patch in the distance, which was probably Lemberg. Below him he could now see the unmistakable collection of stuff that accumulated in the wake of a large army: roads choked with vehicles and wagons, supply dumps, hospital tents, horses and mules grazing or dead from overwork, columns of soldiers trudging toward the front—just specks from this altitude. As they got closer to the city, there were artillery parks and even closer, guns in battery firing away at distant targets.

The city was in plain view now and the leading squadrons flew toward the city's cathedral, using it as a guide point. *Course 087 from there should take us right to the target.* As each group of aircraft flew above the huge old building they adjusted course to just a fraction north of east and continued onward. The target was not far now.

A kilometer or so beyond the medieval walls, the more modern fortifications began. They were filled with troops, and beyond them the evidence of the earlier Martian attacks became evident: wrecked buildings, scorched fields, and woods reduced to charred stumps. Focusing his binoculars, Serno spotted a few wrecked Martian machines and grinned in satisfaction beneath his scarf. After the horrific fighting near Constantinople last spring, there was no sight more welcome to Serno than destroyed Martian machines.

A faint thud reached his ears, even over the steady drone of the engine. He assumed it was artillery, but it didn't sound quite right… Then there was another and another, a whole flurry of them. He looked around and then saw, straight ahead, a series of blue flashes. It wasn't lighting; wrong color, wrong time of year, and hardly any clouds. It looked more like…

"Those damn bombs!"

In the last year or so the Martians had started using an artillery weapon that could toss small bombs a half-dozen kilometers that would explode with a blinding blue flash. Fighting over Turkey, the launchers had been one of the prime targets for Serno's dwindling Ottoman Air Force. The Martians were also using them here in Poland, but these explosions weren't directed against ground targets, they were exploding high in the air! *We're the target!*

As he got closer, there was no doubt that his suspicion was correct. The planes in the group ahead of him were clearly the intended victims of the Martian weapons. A fireball erupted from inside the formation and fiery fragments tumbled down toward the ground. Another plane pulled out of formation and circled away, trailing smoke. The bombs were said to somehow work on *electricity* rather than chemical explosives. Serno had no idea how that could be, but they clearly worked. Reports said that they produced very little shrapnel, but close up the heat flash and attendant concussion could be lethal.

Through his binoculars he could see German bombs tumbling aways from the leading groups. Smoke and flames erupted from the earth far below, and the thunder of that blended with the crack of the Martian bombs and the roar of the engines to make an infernal racket. He scanned vainly for the colored smoke markers that were supposed to have been dropped as aiming points, but there was no doubt that there were Martians down there.

Serno's *Kampfgeschwader* lined itself up for the bomb run. Per their orders, it was veering slightly to the right of the lead group to hit a wider area. He hoped it might throw off the aim of the enemy gunners, but it quickly became apparent it had not. Blue flashes started to appear directly in their path, and a moment later they were in the midst of them.

Up close, the blasts were blindingly bright and Serno had to avert his eyes. Even so, there were blue after-images dancing in his vision. Concussions rattled his teeth and his aircraft and patches of his exposed skin were now hot instead of cold. A huge explosion close by had him instinctively looking for the source, despite the danger. One of his planes, just a few hundred meters away, had been hit and its bomb load had gone off. There was nothing left but an expanding cloud of smoke and debris. Another bomber, much closer to the blast, had its wings partially torn off and it spiraled down, out of control.

The enemy fire was remarkably accurate. When used against ground targets the bombs would explode just a few meters off the ground for maximum effect. Human artillerymen had been trying to perfect that technique with their shells for a century using various time fuses, but none were especially reliable. Clearly, the Martians had figured it out. Here, their bombs were exploding in the midst of the bombers without needing a direct hit to set them off. Somehow they knew exactly how to detonate them when they got close. A time fuse would require knowing the exact altitude of the planes, or perhaps there was some other method they used. Whatever, it was damned effective.

Serno's plane lurched again, but this time not from enemy fire; it had dropped its bombs, and relieved of the load had surged upward a bit. Each plane was carrying one 250 kilogram bomb and ten 100 kilogram bombs. The small ones could destroy a Martian machine with a direct hit or even a near miss. The bigger one was deadly for a larger radius. He hoped they were dropping on *something.* He dared to stand up in his cockpit and look down over the side to try and see the effect. The ground was disappearing in a huge cloud of smoke as the bombs exploded. But he couldn't really see…

A bright blue flash pierced the clouds and a moment later a shock wave rocked the plane. *Yes!* Sometimes when a Martian machine was destroyed its power storage cells would explode like a huge version of their electric bombs. When it did, the blast made the 250 kilogram bombs look like firecrackers. One of the bombs, at least, had found its target. The resulting blast could take out other enemy machines sometimes. Well, they had hurt them, at least a little.

They were leaving the target area and the Martian fire dwindled and died. Serno looked around and tried to estimate his losses. It was hard to tell, but he thought maybe eight or nine planes were missing. Less than ten percent lost. Not too bad, he told himself, but it was not insignificant. And this new development with the Martians using their bombs against aircraft was very disturbing. They had thought themselves safe at this altitude, although Serno had been wondering how long it would take the aliens to figure out a way to make their super heat rays portable enough to use outside their fortresses. But they weren't safe. The Martians kept coming up with new weapons and new ways of using old weapons. Just like the humans, he realized. In the years since the war began, Humanity had made many advancements, but now it seemed that the Martians could do that too, and stay ahead. Well, there was nothing to do except keep trying and keep fighting.

The *Kampfgeschwader* made a long turn to the north and then continued turning to head northwest back to Warsaw. But Serno's plane and four others peeled off and headed due north instead. They had one more mission to fulfill before they could head home. The generals wanted him to make a reconnaissance beyond the left end of the defense lines. He was annoyed by this extra assignment; there were scouting squadrons available, why make his bombers do this? He'd asked his superior about it, but the general had just grinned and told him that he should not have done such a good job down in Turkey. When he'd spotted the Martians massing for their drive on Constantinople and given an invaluable warning, he'd made a reputation for daring and reliability and the High Command had specifically asked for him. So, here he was.

Lemburg was left behind and following the defensive lines north, in about twenty minutes he saw the Bug River ahead. They turned slightly to the west and followed the river. There were swarms of troops working on trenches and bunkers along the western banks. To the east, he could occasionally see some Martian machines, but they were not trying to attack. Another half hour brought them to the southern edges of the Pripet Marshes.

The marshes covered a huge area stretching from Brest-Litovsk in Poland almost to Kiev in Ukraine. Nearly a quarter million square kilometers of swamps, forests, winding rivers, and mostly trackless wilderness. During the spring thaw and the fall rains, the place was usually flooded, the few roads impassable.

The Bug river and the defense lines bent a bit more to the west at that point, but Serno and his flight curved more north and a little east. They had instructions to proceed to the town of Kowel, one of the few habitations in the area bigger than a hamlet. A rail line from the east ran through there and then through the marshes all the way to Brest-Litovsk. If the Martians were going to try and move through the marshes that was probably the only possible route. Ground scouts had reported some sort of activity in the area and the generals wanted a better look.

The marshes were a dreary gray-brown at this time of year. Clumps of pines or bare-branched deciduous trees grew in forests of various sizes with wet meadows or outright swamps in between. Hundreds of small streams wandered in all directions, sometimes joining to create larger waterways. They almost missed Kowel, it being not much of a place to begin with, and apparently the Martians had burned whatever had been there. The rail line was clearly evident, running southeast to northwest. They turned to follow it toward Brest-Litovsk.

They had not seen any Martians yet, but there were plenty of trees where they could be hiding. Serno decided to risk going lower for a better view. He sent his own craft down to two thousand meters while instructing the rest to stay higher. In the event of disaster, at least someone would be able to send back a report.

Lower down, he could see that the rail line was by no means an easy road. With all the swamps and streams there were hundreds of small bridges, and nearly every one had been destroyed. Not by Martians, it seemed, but probably by the Russians before they abandoned their hold on the region.

It wasn't long before he spotted his first Martian. A glint of sunlight reflecting off metal to the right of the rail line caught his attention and he instructed the pilot to get closer. Through his binoculars he could easily make out the shape of a tripod machine. Or rather, the top half of a tripod machine, the bottom half appeared to have sunk into the mud. A few moments later, he spotted two more, one bogged down like the first and the other trying to haul it loose. Serno actually found himself laughing as the machine trying to assist sank lower and lower into the mire. Circling, they spotted several more immobilized machines.

His pilot signaled him that they were getting low on fuel and they continued on to Brest-Litovsk without spotting any more of the enemy. "Looks like they've given up on this route!" he said to himself. The generals ought to be happy about that.

He gave the order to head for home.

* * * * *

November 1913, Lemberg, Galicia

"Have you seen enough, Colonel?" asked Lieutenant Rommel.

Colonel Tom Bridges lowered his field glasses and glanced at his German 'escort'. He looked back to the east before answering, but the last of the bombers had disappeared in the distance. "Yes, I suppose so," he said. "Quite impressive. The only other place I've seen so many aircraft massed for one attack was in America."

Rommel's eyebrows went up a trifle. "Really? I wouldn't have thought them capable."

"You'd be surprised what they are capable of, Lieutenant. And the attack I witnessed was in preparation for the capture of a Martian fortress. A shame this attack of yours doesn't presage anything so important."

The German officer frowned, but then simply motioned him toward the stairs. Several other of the foreign observers had made the trip to Lemberg with their own escorts and they were chatting about what they had seen, but they also headed for the stairs. Their vantage point had been in the tower of the Lemberg cathedral and it had, indeed, been a fine place to watch the air attack from, despite the chill breeze. It had been a long climb up and an equally long descent which left Bridges' legs quivering.

The streets outside the cathedral were filled with troops and it felt much like Bridges' first day in Warsaw, except these troops were nearly all Austro-Hungarians whose blue-gray uniforms were markedly different from the green-gray uniforms of the Germans. The quality of their army was markedly different, too. Ever since the Prussians trounced Austria in 1866, the Austro-Hungarians had played second fiddle to the Germans. Their polyglot empire didn't seem to have the unity or resolve to field a first rate army. They had superb artillery, but their infantry was lackluster and as Bridges had seen, they were just now starting to produce their own tanks.

Not that the German tanks were all that impressive. He'd finally gotten to see some of them close up and he had expected the legendary German engineers to have come up with something better. Their main tanks were no better than what the Americans were using and they were decidedly inferior to the newer British tanks. On the other hand, they did seem to have a good grasp on how to use them in battle. They already had divisions which were mostly made up of tanks—something the British were still experimenting with. He hoped that he'd have a chance to see them in action—from a safe distance, of course.

The observers and escorts made their way to the train station which would take them back to Warsaw. Most of the cars were filled with wounded heading for the rear, so all the non-wounded were crammed into one car at the head of the train. No private compartments, either; it was what Bridges would have called third class back in England. No matter, he'd certainly experienced worse. He and Rommel ended up seated opposite the Japanese observer and his escort. The Japanese was named Yamamoto or something like that. He was wearing a uniform remarkably like that of a British naval officer, with three gold rings on the sleeve. Bridges had not had an opportunity to talk with the man so far but surprisingly, he spoke rather good English.

"So what did you think of the attack, Colonel?" the man asked once the train was moving.

"Well, it looked impressive," replied Bridges, shrugging. "A bloody lot of planes, for sure. But it's damn hard to do a lot of damage to tripods dropping bombs from two or three miles up. A couple of hundred planes dropping a couple of hundred tons of bombs and they'll be lucky to have destroyed more than three or four tripods."

"You speak from experience, sir?"

"I saw a number of large air attacks while I was in America. One was quite effective, because the Martians were all crowded together defending one of their fortresses, but most of the others were less effective."

"Most interesting. I shall include that in my report home," said Yamamoto. "My superiors are very interested in developing our air power. We have little beyond scouting craft at the moment."

"But you're a naval officer, aren't you?" asked Bridges.

"Yes, I first saw action at Tsushima. But I have always had an interest in aviation."

Bridges raised an eyebrow. Tsushima was the battle in 1905 where the Japanese Navy destroyed the Russian fleet. He understood that being able to claim participation in that for a Japanese was like having been at Trafalgar for an English sailor a century earlier. That probably explained why Yamamoto, who seemed quite young, was already a full commander.

They chatted amiably for the rest of the trip. Yamamoto told him about Tsushima and Bridges reciprocated by telling him about the Battle of Memphis, the capture of the Martian fortress near there, and the recent battles around the Dardanelles. They spoke mostly in English, much to the annoyance of Rommel and the other German escort. There was no dining service on the train—nor any heat—and they ended up passing around bottles and flasks and whatever food they'd brought along with them, and things actually got a bit jolly by the end of the trip, which took much of the day.

Upon reaching Warsaw, an ordinary army motor lorry delivered them back to the hotel. It seemed that they didn't rate a nice staff car anymore. He was thoroughly chilled by the time he reached his cozy room and he looked forward to sitting by the stream radiator to warm up. He put the key in the door lock but the mechanism didn't make the usual loud click that it did when the bolt moved. Had he forgotten to lock it when he left that morning? He swung the door open and there was the maid, Ola Wojciech, standing in the room. She was clutching a bundle of linens and looking very startled. "Oh, it's you, Ola," he said.

"C-colonel, Bridges, she stuttered. "Y-you are back early." She took a step backward and bumped into the desk. Her face was very pale.

"Yes, we finished up our business and came straight back. Something wrong?" he asked pleasantly, coming into the room and hanging up his overcoat. He glanced at the desk and it seemed like some of the things had been moved. Had the girl been snooping—or just dusting?

Ola quickly regained her composure and shook her head. "No, you just startled me. How did... how did things go? You went to Lemberg, yes? Do we still hold back the Martians?" The girl's French had improved remarkably in the few weeks he'd known her. She had also been hanging around his room quite a lot when he'd been there. He wasn't quite sure if she was flirting or not. He'd been tempted to reciprocate and see where things went, except Ola reminded him quite a lot of his niece and that seemed to spoil the attraction somehow.

"Yes," he said. "The line is firming up and the Germans feel that it will hold."

"The... line? Where is that? Lemberg? We... we hear so many rumors here in Warsaw, but no one tells us anything. Most of the people are very frightened." Bridges looked closely at the girl, and she did look frightened. Well, it wasn't surprising that the Germans were keeping the Poles in the dark, but extreme secrecy in this situation really didn't make sense. It wasn't like anyone could deliver information to the Martians! Taking pity on Ola, he rummaged around his desk until he found a general map of the region. He sat down, spread it out on the desk, and beckoned her over.

"Here, I'll try to explain the situation to you." She came closer and looked over his shoulder as he traced his finger from point to point. "Here is Lemberg. It is well-fortified and the Austrians hold it. They also defend a line running south into the Carpathians. That's very rough terrain so the Martians can't get around the line to the south. From Lemberg running north, the Germans are building a line. It runs behind rivers like the Bug as much as possible until it reaches the Pripet Marshes up here. The Martians dislike swamps and soft ground even more than they do mountains. They sink right down into the mud, you know. So they can't get around the left end of it either. Understand?" The girl looked at the map intently for quite a while as if taking in every detail. At last she leaned forward and put her finger on the Pripet.

"What happens when the marshes freeze?"

Bridges rocked back in his chair, a look of surprise on his face. "The... the Germans didn't say anything... no wait, they did say something, what was it? Oh yes, they said the marshes probably will freeze over in the dead of winter, but that's not for a few months yet. In the meantime they will extend their line all the way to Brest-Litovsk. They are negotiating with the Russians to see if they can take over at that point and extend it the rest of the way to the Baltic."

Ola stared at the map for a while longer and then finally said: "The winter here comes sooner than it does in Germany."

* * * * *

Subcontinent 1-1, Sector 137-14, Cycle 597,845.8

Lutnaptinav's battlegroup reached the assembly area just as the prey-creatures' air vehicles were departing. Listening in on the communications channels it did not appear that there had been any casualties from the attack, although a power cell explosion had destroyed six of the bombardment drones. The battlegroup was directed to an area where there were a number of the large plant growths which could provide concealments from aerial observation. The machines found places to halt and then powered down. Lutnaptinav contacted the local commander and was ordered to await orders.

While it waited, service machines appeared to replace depleted power cells, replenish nutrient tanks, and make minor repairs. Overall, the battlegroup's machines were in good order, although six of the spare machines had been lost to mishaps on the long journey. In this rare moment of inaction, Lutnaptinav reflected on the events of that journey.

After penetrating the mountains and entering friendly territory in Continent 1, there had been no more contact with prey-creature forces. This region had been held by the Race for several cycles and nearly all resistance had been eradicated, but the terrain itself had been so much different than anything Lutnaptinav had ever experienced. Subcontinent 1-4, where it had been budded, was a desert land which in many ways resembled the Homeworld, memories of which it had gotten from its progenitor. This new region, however, was bursting with life. There had been extensive regions covered by the tall vegetation like they were currently hiding in. Other areas were more open, but nearly every bit of land was covered by lesser green vegetation—except for places where the red *destang* plants, imported from the Homeworld, had taken hold. Broad rivers, holding vast amounts of uncontrolled water, flowed toward the seas and oceans which covered so much of the Target World. It all seemed very alien and yet... majestic somehow. Lutnaptinav and all the *Threeborn* had been brought into existence here. It seemed highly unlikely any of them would ever travel to the Homeworld...was this home now? A disturbing thought in some ways, and yet in others ways it was...

"Attention all battlegroup commanders. Attention to orders." The voice over the communicator halted Lutnaptinav's musings and it focused itself as directed.

"Prepare to receive orders for upcoming operations," continued the voice. "This is Mandapravis, commander of all forces in this sector. First, let me welcome the newly arrived forces from Group 13 and Group 14. Your arrival is fortuitous. Second, you are all aware that the purpose of our offensive was to draw prey-creature forces away from our main operations to the south, allowing a breakthrough there. Unfortunately, the enemy had more reserves than anticipated and they have succeeded in building a new defense line here.

"A direct assault might achieve a breakthrough but in all probability our losses would be so heavy that our ability to exploit the success would be severely limited. The best results can be achieved through a turning movement. Such a move to the south is blocked by the mountainous terrain in that direction. At the moment, a move to the north is also impossible due to the large region of extremely soft, water-saturated ground that lies there."

Mandapravis paused for a moment and Lutnaptinav wondered at this. Was it uncertain about the orders it was about to give? A disturbing thought.

"However," continued Mandapravis, "when temperatures fall below the freezing point, those water-saturated areas will freeze, and experience has shown that they then become traversable. Our artificial satellite and observation stations in far northern regions have seen that a mass of cold air will reach us here in three planetary rotations. This air is well below the freezing point and will endure for at least eight planetary rotations. It is estimated that after three more rotations, the ground will be able to support our fighting machines with no difficulty.

"At that point, we will send ten battlegroups with appropriate numbers of drones, through this area and around the flank of the prey-creature defenses. This should allow us to disrupt their supply lines and eventually surround and destroy the bulk of their forces in this region. Once this is done we can strike westward into their industrial zones. The following battle groups will be part of this force…"

Mandapravis listed the battlegroups and Lutnaptinav was not surprised when its own and the one from Group 13 were among the ten. This was clearly a dangerous mission and since the *Threeborn* were expendable, the logic was clear.

"At the same time, our remaining forces here will launch attacks against the prey-creatures in front of us. These attacks are intended to pin them in place but will be executed with the intention of sustaining minimum casualties. Are there any questions?" The orders were straightforward and no questions were raised.

"Very well," concluded Mandapravis, "expend your efforts prior to the attack on ensuring that all of your equipment is in perfect order. Much depends on our success." It broke the connection.

Lutnaptinav pondered the situation and then passed the orders on to the battlegroup. "We have much to do," it added.

Chapter Eight

December 1913, Warsaw, Poland

Colonel Tom Bridges was awakened out of a sound sleep by someone pounding on his door. He cracked open an eye and peered out from underneath the thick blankets. He looked to the window and did not see any light leaking through the curtains. Still night? Who would be knocking at a time like this? Granted the days were very short now and the nights very long. He muttered a curse and closed his eyes again, but the knocking persisted.

"Bloody hell," he growled. "What is it?"

"Colonel, you need to get up. Something is happening." To Bridges' surprise the voice sounded like Yamamoto, the Japanese observer. What in the world was going on? Reluctantly, he threw off the heavy blankets and shivered as the chill air touched him. An early winter storm had blown through a few days earlier and dumped a half-foot of snow on the city. This had been followed by some extremely cold weather, that not even the steam heat of the hotel could keep entirely at bay.

He dressed quickly and opened the door, but Yamamoto wasn't there. Several other of the observers were emerging from their rooms, but they looked as bewildered as he felt. Walking up to Captain Altmayer, the French observer, he asked: "Any idea what's going on?"

"No," answered the Frenchman. "Just some madman pounding on my door. What time is it?

Checking his pocket watch, Bridges said: "Just after four. Our Japanese colleague said it was something important."

"It better be. Well, I suppose we should go down to the lobby. Maybe someone there knows what this is all about." That seemed sensible and they both trooped down the stairs. The lobby was dim, but a maid was bustling about turning on some of the electric lights and lighting a few candles, too. Bridges did a quick head count and it looked as though all the observers were there... no, wait, where was Drozdovsky, the Russian? Still in bed?

He was trying to get the attention of one of the maids to see if there was any coffee, when the American observer, Major McCallister, came up to him and said: "Apparently the Martians are in Brest-Litovsk."

"What? Who told you that?"

"Drozdovsky. He got it from one of his sources, I gather."

"Where is he now?" asked Bridges, looking around the lobby again.

"Running for home, apparently. He knocked on my door, his room is right next to mine, and when I looked out, he was wearing his coat and carrying a bag. He told me the news and then was off like a shot."

"Bloody hell. If they're in Brest-Litovsk, they're only a little over a hundred miles from here. They could be here in…"

"A day if they pushed it," said McCallister.

"Damn. What do you think we ought to do?"

"Look, there's Rommel, maybe we can get some straight talk from him."

Bridges turned and indeed, the liaison officer was coming through the hotel door, brushing snow off his overcoat. The man looked like he hadn't slept for quite a while. His eyes darted around the lobby as every one of the observers present converged on him, asking questions. He stood there for a moment, weathering the multi-lingual barrage, and then held up his hands and got quiet.

"Gentlemen," he said in French, "there has been a serious development. The Martians are in Brest-Litovsk." He paused as if expecting a wave of surprised exclamations. The silence he got instead seemed to puzzle him for a moment. "You have already heard this, it seems. Very well. We received word several hours ago by telegraph that the enemy machines were emerging from the Pripet Marshes in considerable strength and approaching the city. The lines seem to be down now and we've gotten nothing further. We are trying to make radio contact with the garrison, but without success."

"How did they manage this?" demanded McCallister. "I thought the Marshes were impassible to them."

What happens when the marshes freeze? The serving girl, Ola's, words seemed to come back to Bridges. *Yes, what indeed?*

"This unseasonably cold weather appears to have frozen the marshes sufficiently to allow the Martians to pass," confirmed Rommel. "Several hundred machines at least."

"What's being done?" asked Captain Altmayer.

"The only reserves in the region, the I Cavalry Corps, consisting of two divisions, including the Guards, have been sent to delay the enemy. Additional forces are being made ready to move to the area."

"Cavalry!" snorted McCallister. "They'll be able to delay them for ten or fifteen minutes if we're lucky!"

Rommel frowned, but made no reply. Bridges had spent time in America attached to a cavalry unit. The Americans had quickly realized that while horse cavalry had its uses for scouting in areas with no roads (which made up pretty much their whole country west of the Mississippi) but to actually fight the Martian machines they needed heavier weapons than could be taken on horseback. They'd added armored cars and motorized artillery to their cavalry and given it air support where possible. The combination had proven effective at times, but they were still no match for a large force of Martians. From what Bridges had seen on his tours, the Germans hadn't caught on to this yet, and their cavalry was still primarily horsemen with a few machine guns and horse-drawn light artillery attached. Lambs to the slaughter.

"What if they can't hold?" asked Yamamoto. "A breakthrough there would outflank your whole defensive line."

"General Moltke has not seen fit to inform me of his plans," said Rommel frostily. "I am here merely to tell you of recent developments."

"So what should we do?" asked the Italian observer, Lieutenant Armellini.

"That is entirely up to you, gentlemen. You may attempt to leave if you so desire, although I cannot promise you any sort of transport. But I can assure you that the German Army has every intention of holding Warsaw. That is all I have for you… no, there is one other thing: the usual daily briefing for today has been canceled. Major Adam is quite busy." Rommel nodded, turned, and went out.

"Well, that's a fine kettle of fish," said McCallister.

"Can't argue with that," muttered Bridges. "So what do you plan to do?"

"I suppose I should telegraph Washington and see what they want me to do. If I'm lucky I might get a reply by Spring."

"Yes, I need to contact London. Let me get my overcoat and we can walk down to the telegraph station."

And so they did, most of the other observers tagging along. Not having any transport they had a long walk through the frigid night, but eventually reached the city. The streets of Warsaw, usually quiet at this hour, were very busy. Mostly with military personnel, but a good many civilians were up and about, no doubt roused by all the other activity. They reached the telegraph station only to find their trip was in vain. The facility was so overwhelmed with German military traffic, only officially sanctioned messages were going through. Grumbling, most of the observers dispersed to find breakfast. Bridges, McCallister and Yamamoto watched them go and after shivering in the wind for a while decided to go back to their lodgings.

The walk back was just as cold as the walk into town had been and they were all chilled to the bone by the time they got there. They sat down near the fire in the small dining room and called for tea, coffee, and hot food. While they waited, Yamamoto dashed up to his room and brought down a map and spread it out on the table. They used silverware, coins, and bits of bread to mark friendly and enemy positions.

"Several hundred tripods, you think?" said Bridges.

"That's what Lieutenant Rommel said," said Yamamoto.

"If there were only forty or fifty, they wouldn't be so worried," said McCallister. "So yes, I'd say several hundred, at least."

"That cavalry won't stop them long," said Bridges. "And out in the open, with no fortifications, they'll need at least a couple of corps to have any hope of stopping them."

"Yes," agreed McCallister. "Our own experience has been that a dug-in division can stop sixty or seventy tripods with its own resources. But in the open, that number drops to thirty or forty. The damn tripods can move so fast they can punch through the lines and get in among the artillery and raise havoc. With the guns gone, the infantry is nearly helpless. Tanks are just too slow to concentrate against them in a mobile situation. We found that out the hard way back in

1910."

Bridges nodded grimly. The Americans, in the early stages of the war, thought they'd penned up the Martians against the Rocky Mountains. But then the Martians had broken through their lines in a dozen places and sent small raiding parties into the rear, destroying rail lines and supply dumps. When the Americans came out of their trenches to try and deal with it, the main Martian force had attacked and slaughtered them. The Americans had been chased nine hundred miles, all the way back to the Mississippi before they could stop them.

"If the same thing happens to the Germans now, the bloody Martians will be in Paris by Spring," said Bridges.

"What sort of reserves do the Germans have?" asked Yamamoto.

"They've got maybe a dozen divisions, either newly raised ones still completing their training or badly battered ones refitting," said McCallister. "Plus maybe twenty more second-line divisions still manning the fortifications facing France."

"They're going to have to mobilize all of them if this is as bad as it looks," said Bridges.

"What of the French and the other European armies?" asked Yamamoto. "Could they send help?"

Bridges snorted. "They probably could if they really wanted to. The French have major commitments in Mexico and North Africa, but they have significant forces manning their own fortifications on the border with Germany. I bet they could whistle up twenty divisions without an effort. Another dozen from Belgium and Holland. It would be enough if they would just do it."

"Will they?"

"Who knows? Too many Europeans would be happy to see Germany taken down a notch or two. They've feared and hated them since 1870."

"Surely they will put aside such feelings in the face of a major crisis!" protested the Japanese officer.

"We can hope," said McCallister, draining the last of the coffee in his cup. "Well, I'm going to my room to try and put together some sort of report about this. Hopefully we can still get letters through to the rear even if we don't have a telegraph." He got up and headed for the stairs. Yamamoto soon followed.

As Bridges got up from the table he noticed that Ola, the Polish maid was standing a dozen feet away looking at him nervously. He went over and said good morning.

"The M-Martians," she stammered. "they…they are coming?" She seemed quite frightened. Well, why shouldn't she be?

"They're in Brest-Litovsk," he replied, seeing no reason to keep it a secret.

"They will come here? Attack Warsaw?"

"We don't know. But the Germans say they are determined to hold the city, so we ought to be safe."

"You are staying, too?"

"Probably." He hadn't made a decision yet, but perhaps saying he would stay would comfort the girl. His statement didn't seem to have that effect; she still looked worried.

He gave her a smile and said: "If it's any comfort to you, you were right about the marshes freezing. You were smarter than the Germans."

* * * * *

Subcontinent 1-1, Sector 147-22, Cycle 597,845.8

Lutnaptinav's fighting machine moved up a slight rise and finally left the low, frozen ground behind. The passage through this difficult area had taken over a full rotation and had not been without problems. The low temperatures had frozen the surface of the water-soaked ground, but only to a certain depth. In most spots it was strong enough to support a fighting machine, but there were still spots where it was too thin and a machine's leg might break through. In other places, even those areas where the ice had been strong when the first machines had crossed, the repeated impact of the legs of the following machines had weakened the ice until it broke. Lutnaptinav's battle group, one of the last in the column of advance, had encountered this problem again and again. Only two machines had become impossibly mired and had to be abandoned, but that was two too many. Fortunately, the operators had not been injured and they could be transferred to the replacement machines which trailed behind the main group on slave mode. The lighter drone machines had not encountered any serious difficulty.

Monitoring the communications on the command frequencies, it was clear that this expedition had taken the prey-creatures by surprise as had been hoped. The lead elements had encountered some small scouting parties in the night and destroyed or scattered them. Most of those who escaped had fled off to the sides of the advance, deeper into the difficult ground, and had not even been able to spread a warning. Or at least so it seemed since the stronger forces guarding a medium-sized city at the edge of the difficult area put up very little resistance.

The leading battle groups smashed through the feeble defenses and destroyed much of the city while the following groups caught up. Lutnaptinav could see huge columns of smoke ahead. As the ruins came into view, orders were received from the attack force commander, a being called Hadrampidar, a high-ranking leader of Group 10. Immediately to the west of the ruined city was a major watercourse. Despite the low temperatures, the water had not completely frozen and crossing the obstacle would have been extremely difficult, but fortunately the prey-creature bridge across it had not been destroyed. The attack force would cross and then two battle groups would split off and head due south to outflank the main enemy defense lines. The rest would continue west toward

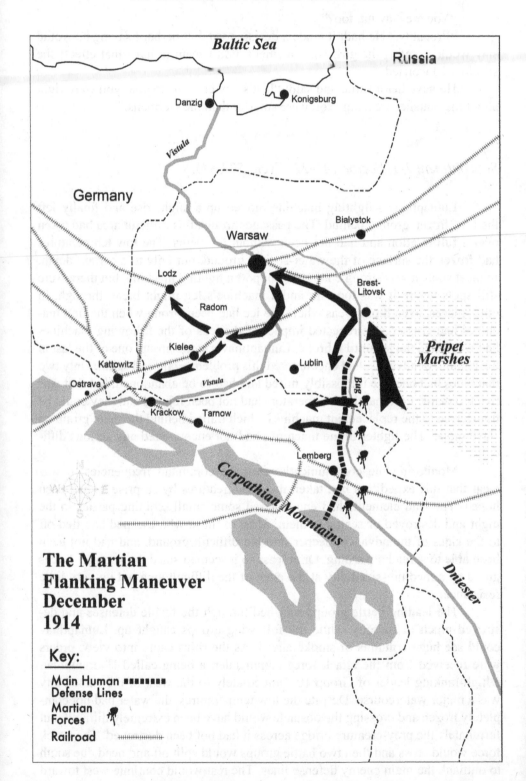

Baltic Sea

Russia

Danzig

Konigsburg

Vistula

Germany

Bialystok

Warsaw

Lodz

Brest-Litovsk

Radom

Kielce

Pripet Marshes

Kattowitz

Lublin

Ostrava

Vistula

Bug

Krackow

Tarnow

Lemberg

Carpathian Mountains

Dniester

The Martian Flanking Maneuver December 1914

Key:

Main Human ▪▪▪▪▪▪▪
Defense Lines

Martian
Forces

Railroad ┼┼┼┼┼┼┼┼┼┼

a much larger city about a hundred *telequel* away.

Most of the specific commands were to the other battle groups, but then Lutnaptinav was being addressed directly: "Battle Group 14-26, once we are across the bridge, take position on the southern end of our line and advance west, keeping contact with the Battle Group 10-39. Additional prey-creature forces are to be expected."

"Acknowledged," replied Lutnaptinav immediately. To facilitate a quick crossing, all of the drones clambered aboard the fighting machines and clung to gripping points provided for exactly that purpose. Even so, moving three hundred piloted machines, thirty spare machines, and forty of the bombardment drones across a structure that was only wide enough for a single machine took considerable time. As before, Lutnaptinav's battle group was one of the last to cross and then had to move at nearly full speed to reach its assigned position. Consulting the map of the area provided by the artificial satellite, it altered the course of its force a few degrees to the south. It could see the two detached battlegroups moving away, due south. They quickly disappeared among the tall vegetation.

As they advanced, they soon encountered prey-creatures trying to flee. Sometimes there were groups of them and other times they were individuals. They had been given orders not to slay them unless they posed some threat. At first Lutnaptivav thought that the intent of the order was to preserve the beings as food sources for later, but it was explained that past experience had shown that the fleeing creatures often congested the roads the enemy military depended on, slowing their movements. This was an interesting concept. Lutnaptinav's clan occupied a desert country where there were very few of the prey-creatures, so such a strategy had never occurred to it.

"Subcommander?" One of its subordinates was calling.

"Yes?"

"How can we determine which of these creatures are warriors and which can be safely ignored? They all look alike."

It was not an unreasonable question. Early observations by the first wave to land on the Target World had indicated that unlike members of the Race, who could perform any needed task, the prey-creatures seemed to be divided into specialized sub-castes, each of which only performed specific functions. Warriors, workers, caregivers for the young who took an absurdly long amount of time to mature, vehicle operators, givers of orders, and many others. Each had their own group which carried out the task. Among the race it was true that some members had special skills like science or engineering, but anyone could work on any project.

The situation with the prey-creatures was further complicated by the fact that they reproduced sexually with males and females. The gender which bore the offspring appeared to not be suitable for certain other tasks and were not often seen as warriors, machine operators, or in some other types of labor.

After a time, however, it was observed that this division of functions was not as strict as it had first seemed. Warriors could usually be distinguished by the sort of coverings they wore and the equipment they carried, but more and more frequently prey-creatures who did not have those coverings or equipment—even the females—had been observed carrying weapons and fighting. In some areas prey-creatures who had been harvested by gatherer machines were found to have explosives strapped to their bodies which they detonated when taken—killing themselves, but also damaging machinery and injuring or even killing their captors. Harvesting had to be done cautiously now. The situation grew more and more confusing with the passage of time.

Lutnaptinav gave the only answer it had: "If they are carrying weapons, trying to fight, or coming toward us instead of trying to flee, destroy them. Otherwise leave them be."

"Yes, Subcommander."

The formation arranged and the line of advance established, the force moved rapidly over the landscape. The frozen precipitation had turned everything white and in some areas was deep enough to hinder the drones, so they remained attached to the fighting machines, which in any case could move faster than the drones. Speed was important here. The prey-creatures' defenses had been turned and the less time they were given to react, the better. The large city ahead was a major transportation hub as well as a manufacturing center. If it could be taken it should seriously disrupt the enemy's activities.

As they advanced they began to find the bodies of dead prey-creatures. They had not been killed by any weapons as far as could be determined in a passing examination—certainly not by any weapons of the Race. Lutanptinav could only speculate that these creatures had frozen to death in the cold temperatures. Observation had confirmed that the prey-creatures were extremely sensitive to environmental conditions. Too much heat, too little heat, too little water and they died very quickly. How such flimsy creatures could have become the dominant species on this planet, Lutnaptinav could not imagine.

They did encounter small groups of fleeing warriors which they quickly destroyed. Without their large projectile throwers and armored gun vehicles they were nearly helpless and could offer little resistance. Lutnaptinav also observed creatures who wore the coverings of warriors, but who possessed no equipment or obvious weapons trying to flee along with others who were non-warriors. It was tempted to destroy them, but refrained, preferring to conserve power.

After a tenth of a rotation, with the sun well up in the sky, word came back from advanced scouts that a large body of prey-creature warriors had been spotted ahead. They were not fleeing and appeared to be seeking battle. Hadrampidar issued orders for the force to assume a linear formation, deploy the drones, and prepare to destroy the enemy. Lutanptinav quickly did so with its battle group. Each fighting machine took position thirty *quel* from the next and the drones were sent a few hundred *quel* to the front. The drones were controlled remotely by the fighting machine operators who found no difficulty doing so as well as controlling their fighting machine. At need an operator could control ten or even more, but beyond that, efficiency dropped as information overload became a factor. The bombardment drones, which had been at the rear, caught up and massed behind the middle of the line.

Lutnaptinav consulted the tactical display in the cockpit of its machine. It showed the map provided by the satellite and as the scouts reported more information on the enemy, icons began to appear on the display plotting their positions. In a short time a force estimated at twenty thousand had been detected about four *telequel* to the west. The scouts reported that there could be more prey-creatures coming up behind this force.

"There are very few of the large projectile throwers," reported the senior scout over the general communications channel, "Nor any of the armored gun vehicles. Nearly all of the enemy are riding the four-legged animals. They are not preparing defensive positions, Commander. They have definitely seen us, but they are continuing to advance."

"Excellent," said Hadrampidar. "Draw them back upon our line here. All battle groups stand ready to engage them."

Lutnaptinav's group was as ready as it could be so it simply waited and watched the icons for the enemy draw nearer. There was a low ridge about a *telequel* away that blocked vision further west so they would not be able to see the enemy until they were quite close.

The scout machines appeared atop the ridge and then continued down the near side. Several small explosions erupted near them so apparently the prey-creatures had gotten a few of their heavy weapons set up. If, upon seeing the rest of the Race's forces drawn up, the enemy decided to halt and direct the fire of these weapons, then they would have to attack instead of waiting.

But the leading elements of the prey-creature forces appeared on top of the ridge shortly after the scout machines, and they only paused a moment before coming on. Larger formations quickly followed and they began deploying into long lines paralleling the Race's. They were still out of range of the heat rays. The bombardment drones could have hit them, but they had a limited supply of ammunition and Hadrampidar must have decided not to employ them here, because they did not fire.

It took a considerable time for the prey-creatures to get their forces in order but eventually they were ready and started forward. They were deployed in several long lines, one behind the other, but there were none directly in front of Lutnaptinav's battle group; they were massed further north. No matter, they would have plenty of targets—assuming the prey-creatures weren't all annihilated by the others before they came into range of Lutnaptinav's group.

They advanced slowly at first, but then quickened their pace, the riding animals kicking up clouds of frozen precipitation as they moved. The sighting beam on Lutnaptinav's machine showed the range precisely. Hadrampidar allowed the enemy to come closer than maximum effective range before giving the command to fire, perhaps to make sure none of the enemy would be able to flee.

By the time the order came, the prey-creatures were even in range of Lutnaptinav's group and two hundred and forty heat rays stabbed out almost in unison. The leading rank of the enemy exploded into a long, nearly continuous, line of flame and steam. Even the frozen precipitation on the ground flashed to vapor under the tremendous heat of the rays. Then the rays began to sweep back and forth catching anything that had not been hit in the initial volley.

It did not seem possible that anything that lived could survive such an inferno, but amazingly some did. Here and there the four-legged creatures emerged from the clouds. Some still had their riders and some were aflame, apparently just grazed by a heat ray. Onward they came. Rays shifted to annihilate them, but this allowed even more of the second line of prey-creatures to survive and continue their charge. Most of them were carrying long poles which Lutnaptinav had been told often had explosive charges on their tips. If they got close enough they could do serious damage.

Since nothing was directly threatening its battle group, Lutnaptinav concluded it could better assist the main line by moving into a flanking position. "Battle Group 14-26, turn the line to face due north continue to…"

"Subcommander! Wait!"

Lutnaptinav was surprised by this sudden interruption of its command and for an instant a flash of indignation went through it. It instantly suppressed it; It had been Jadnarutan who had spoken and it was very reliable. Surely this must be important. "What? What is wrong?"

"Subcommander, look to the south," said Jadnarutan. "In the area of tall vegetation. There is something there."

Lutnaptinav did as directed. "I see nothing…"

"Adjust your viewer to the shorter wavelengths."

It did so and the vegetation suddenly flared brightly. Many heat sources were clearly there. A moment later they emerged into the open and there were nearly a thousand more enemies upon their riding animals. *Instead of us flanking them, they have flanked us!* They were only three hundred *quels* away and already charging.

"Shift direction to face south! Reposition the drones! Open fire immediately!"

The battle group responded at once, but the enemy was so close and moving so fast there was no way to destroy them all before they were among the fighting machines. They had the long poles like the others and it was quickly confirmed that they were indeed tipped with explosives. Despite the destructive rays that tore through their ranks they kept coming and a score of the drones were quickly blasted to pieces and then some of the fighting machines were damaged as well.

"Adjust your heat rays to wide focus," commanded Lutnaptinav. The enemy was so close it could be impossible to hit them without risking hitting friends. At the usual narrow focus this could do serious damage to a fighting machine. The wide focus dramatically reduced the effective range of the rays, but this close they would still be deadly to the prey-creatures and be far less likely to damage a fighting machine caught in the ray.

Lutnaptinav swung its ray in a wide arc, as did the others of the battle group. The drones were firing, too, as well as lashing out with their cutting blades. Some of the fighting machines were even using their manipulator arms—not intended as weapons—to seize prey-creatures or knock them from their mounts.

Something struck Lutnaptinav's machine with a heavy blow and it staggered. A quick check through the neural link did not reveal any serious damage. But almost immediately several subordinates reported more serious damage over the communications channel and then an alert that Gaglucatcar was in critical danger. It looked in that direction and saw a fighting machine crash to the ground. A cluster of prey-creatures were around it and they closed in, thrusting their poles at the crippled machine. Explosions erupted, several of them flinging the enemy away or killing their mounts.

Before Lutnaptinav could give the order, a dozen heat rays swept across Gaglucatcar's machine and the prey-creatures beleaguering it. The enemy were wreathed in flames and quickly died. It turned its attention to the other fighting around it, but discovered that the fight was over. All of the enemy, except for a few scores trying to flee, were dead or at least down.

Nearly all; a strange series of small, but repeated impacts on the lower leg of Lutnaptinav's fighting machine drew its attention. Directing the vision pickup downward it saw a single prey-creature, much of its covering burned away, swinging a metal blade against the machine's leg. It had no hope of doing any harm, but it continued until it collapsed into a mound of frozen precipitation.

"Subcommander, Gaglucatcar is dead," reported a subordinate.

Almost simultaneously came another communication, this one from Commander Hadrampidar. "Group 14-26, report your situation."

Lutnaptinav quickly scanned the status of all the machines in the group and then replied. "This is Subcommander Lutnaptinav. Group 14-26 has had one fatality and three minor injuries. Four fighting machines were destroyed or disabled, and twenty-four drones lost."

"That is more than the rest of our force combined," said Hadrampidar. "Explain this."

"An undetected force of the enemy emerged from ambush at close range and attacked before we could destroy it. It has now been destroyed."

"Why was this force not detected earlier, Subcommander?"

Lutnaptinav pondered possible replies. It had not missed the tone of reproach in Hadrampidar's question. It could make excuses such as reminding Hadrampidar that scouting duties had been given to another battle group or stating that it had been fully concerned with repulsing the enemy main attack. It doubted that any such response would be well received. So it simply stated: "I have no explanation, Commander."

There was a lengthy pause and Lutnaptinav wondered if it would be relieved of command. But then Hadrampidar ordered: "Take care of your wounded and get your group ready to move. We must press on to the prey-creature city as quickly as possible."

"Yes, Commander."

* * * * *

December 1913, Warsaw, Poland

"I want to fight," said Ola Wojciech. She was standing in front of Wanda Krahelska's desk in the library basement and trying to look stern, grown up... and brave.

Wanda removed her glasses and rubbed her eyes. She let out a long sigh. "Ola, don't be foolish."

"But the Martians are coming! They're in Brest-Litovsk! They'll be here soon!"

"Very soon," nodded Wanda, "possibly tonight. Tomorrow at the latest."

"So I want to fight for Warsaw. Please Wanda."

"With what? We don't have any rifles to spare—not that they are much use from what we hear."

Ola drew herself up. "I'm not stupid. I'll use a dynamite bomb—like you did against the Russian Governor."

Wanda tried to frown, but the tiny flicker of a smile crossed her face. "Dynamite bombs are in short supply, too, Ola. Go back to the hotel and continue your work with the foreign observers."

"But they're leaving!" Ola's frustration was bubbling to the surface.

"Are you sure?"

"The Russian's gone!"

"What about the Englishman and the American?"

"Well... I'm not sure..."

"Then until you are sure, go back to the hotel. It's important, Ola. We know the German general commanding this area is moving his headquarters out of Warsaw. But so far there's no sign the German garrison is leaving. See if you can find out if they plan to try and hold Warsaw against the Martians. If the Englishman and American do leave, then I promise you I'll save a spot for you on the barricade next to me. All right?"

"Yes, ma'am," said Ola, only partly mollified.

"Good. Now scat... oh, wait a moment."

Ola had turned to go, but now turned back. Wanda was rummaging through a desk drawer and to Ola's surprise she produced a small revolver and handed it to her. "There are a lot of frightened people out there and order is starting to break down. I have no idea if the Germans will try to maintain order, but this is in case you run into any trouble. Keep it hidden! The Germans would not be happy to find this on you."

Ola nodded and tucked the gun away inside her coat. "Thank you, Wanda."

"Good luck."

Ola left the library and made the long walk back to the hotel. There weren't any street cars running and as Wanda had said there were a lot of frightened people on the street. Most seemed to be trying to buy as much bread as they could. Others were pushing overloaded carts on the roads leading west. Abandoning Warsaw already? Some certainly were. Ola had no intention of leaving. Warsaw was her home now. Her family were mostly in Lodz, sixty kilometers to the southwest. Could the Martian get there, too? It was a frightening thought. Indeed, she found that she was growing quite scared. She'd been living with fear for years. First that the Russians would discover what she was doing, and more recently the Germans. Now she realized that what she should really have been fearing was the Martians—and they were on their way to Warsaw.

She forced herself to calm down. One thing at a time. She had a job to do. She met no trouble along the way. The other people she saw seemed completely absorbed in their own problems—just as she was. Even so, the pistol Wanda had given her was a comfort. She felt quite proud that she had been judged mature enough to carry such a weapon, although Wanda was right that if the Germans caught her with it, she could land in serious trouble. She must be very careful. No playing with it, no boasting about it, no one but Wanda should know she had it. And it must be an absolute last resort.

She reached the hotel chilled through and through as the short day drew to a close. The other maids told her that all the observers had gone off to a meeting at the German headquarters—or what had been the headquarters if what Wanda had told her was right. None of them knew when the men would be back, although presumably they would be since all their luggage—except the Russian's—was still here.

She went upstairs and briefly straightened up the American's room, finding nothing of interest there. She had just started on the Englishman's room when she heard noise downstairs and footsteps accompanied by male voices speaking in English coming up the stairs.

"Can you believe it?" said one voice that she recognized as belonging to the American, McCallister. "Can you believe that they threw away an entire corps?"

"One of their guards divisions, too," said the other, that was Colonel Bridges.

"You'd think they'd have learned something from your Charge of the Light Brigade!"

"Or at least from the experience of their own guards at St. Privat in 1870. But then these were guards, after all. Fancy units who spend years sitting around on parade and when they get a chance to actually fight, they behave like dunderheads. Not the first time, that's for sure."

Ola came out into the hallway and shut Bridges' door just as the men reached the second floor. McCallister was saying: "So are you going, or staying?"

"No instructions from London so it's up to me, I suppose. Can't say I fancy being stuck here but… oh, hello, Ola." Bridges had caught sight of her and stopped. The American did as well.

McCallister only gave her a glance and then unlocked the door to his room. "Well, I'm going to get out of here. Don't take too long to make up your mind, Bridges; the city could be surrounded by morning." He went into his room and shut the door.

Ola was left facing the Englishman. There were things she needed to know, and she should proceed carefully, but she found herself just blurting out: "The city will be surrounded? And you are leaving? Are the Germans leaving, too? The Martians will destroy Warsaw?" The fear she had been keeping in check was breaking loose and it must have shown on her face. The Englishman took on an expression of kindliness and took a few steps toward here.

"Hey, hey, I didn't say I was leaving. And the German troops are staying to hold the city. Only their commander is buggering off. Warsaw's well-fortified, you know. Come to think, I've never been in a city under siege. New experience and all that. So you calm down. Everything will be all right."

"Thank you, sir. That… that's very good to know." And it was; her fear subsided a bit. "Can… can I get you anything?"

"Oh, some hot tea would be lovely. And something to eat if your cook hasn't bolted. Maybe you could bring it up to my room. Bring enough for two, you could join me."

"I… I really shouldn't…"

"Nonsense! It will be quite all right and… and…" Bridges suddenly cut himself off and peered at her with a very odd and puzzled expression. He stared and stared.

"Sir?" she said.

"Tell me, Ola," he said slowly, still staring. "When exactly did you learn to speak English?"

Ola gave a little shriek and clapped her hands over her mouth.

Chapter Nine

January 1914, War Cabinet Offices, London

Frederick Lindemann sat in a corner of the room where Prime Minister Asquith's War Cabinet was meeting. The room was in a building next door to the Prime Minister's residence on Downing Street. For such an important gathering place it was rather plainly decorated with simple cream-colored walls and a minimum of decorative woodwork. Three narrow windows were covered by heavy burgundy drapes. Light was provided by several electric fixtures hanging from the high ceiling. Two of the walls were covered with maps showing various theaters of the war. There were about a dozen men in the room. The War Cabinet was a select body drawn from the government and military to advise Asquith on the conduct of the war. Lindemann had been to these meetings before at Churchill's invitation to provide him with scientific advice when necessary.

Aside from Asquith, the top men present were naturally Lord Kitchener, the Minister of War and de facto head of the army, and Churchill, the commander of the navy. But there was also Sir Edward Grey, the Foreign Secretary, head of the Foreign Office. He was not a member of the War Cabinet, but he'd been invited due to the nature of the current emergency. The other usual members were there: Lloyd George, Minister of Munitions, Andrew Bonar Law, Chancellor of the Exchequer, George Curzon, the House of Lords' representative on the council, and Arthur Henderson, a representative of the Labour Party. There were several other assistants and lesser ministers, but they, like Lindemann, would only speak when called upon.

There was also one other person there, seated next to Lindemann—his aide, Sub-Lieutenant Albert Windsor, the Duke of York. There was no reason for the young man to be there; indeed, from what Lindemann knew of the purpose of this meeting, there was no real reason for *him* to be there either. But apparently the King wanted his second son to attend—perhaps seasoning him for some higher position—and so there they both were. Young Bertie seemed very uncomfortable among these high-powered leaders of the Empire. Or maybe he just hadn't recovered from the New Years celebrations two days earlier.

An army colonel, one of Kitchener's men, was standing next to a large map of Poland mounted on an easel with the position of troops marked on it in gray and red. He was giving a briefing, using a wooden pointer. "Early on the 16th of last month, a large force of Martian machines emerged from the Pripet Marshes and took the city of Brest-Litovsk in a surprise assault," he said jabbing the map with his pointer. "From what little we've been able to learn, the garrison was overwhelmed in a very short time and the enemy captured the bridge over the Bug River intact. We don't know whether the speed of the attack prevented the bridge's demolition or if it had not even been prepared for destruction. Whatever the case, the enemy was across the river in short order."

There was some quiet muttering and shaking of heads in the room. Someone—it might have been Churchill—said: "So much for the legendary German efficiency." The colonel glanced at his boss, but Kitchener just made a little 'go on' gesture with his hand.

"Once across the river, the enemy force split in two. One group turned south and followed the river until it struck the northern flank of the German defensive lines. The northernmost of the units along that line were quickly broken up and forced to retreat. The Martian forces along the Bug and in front of Lemberg, which had been making demonstration attacks for several days, now began a major assault of their own. By the 19th, the German forces were mostly all falling back southward toward the Carpathian Mountains." The colonel flipped up the map and folded it behind, revealing a new one with the position of the forces changed. A large red arrow curved south and another swept west and then south as well.

"The other prong of the enemy offensive—the larger of the two, we believe—continued west, and by the 18th had reached Warsaw. The city has significant defenses, although most of them face west rather than east. The German garrison was alerted and waiting, but the Martians only made a probing attack before bypassing the city. Fortunately, the Vistula River at that point is quite wide and the only bridges in the area are inside Warsaw, so the Martians could not get across there. They were forced to head southward along the east bank. Sadly, about fifty miles south there is a railroad bridge and again, the Germans failed to destroy it." More murmurs and headshakes. "By the 20th, they were across the Vistula.

"They then struck southwest, taking the town of Radom, and then their force apparently split again into multiple columns which passed through Kielee and Lublin. Another column has been reported near Tarnow, and yet another in the area of Lodz. They are smashing everything they encounter, including supply dumps, railroad lines, and any German reserve formations they encounter. This has slowed their movements to a degree, but the Germans believe that Krackow and Kattowitz, both major rail junctions, will soon be in danger." The colonel's pointer was moving all over the map and he finally flipped it over to reveal a new sheet. This one had an awful lot of red on it.

"What is the situation now, Colonel?" asked Prime Minister Asquith.

The man took a breath and then continued. "The Austrians are still holding onto Lemberg and their line still runs back to the Carpathians as it did before this offensive; apparently they were not heavily attacked. But the German forces who were holding the line north of there, the 1st, 2nd, 3rd, and 5th Armies, have been bent back more than ninety degrees and are being pushed up against the mountains. 2nd Army, the northernmost one, has taken very heavy casualties. If Krackow and Kattowitz fall, the lot of them will be basically trapped. At this time of year most of the passes through the Carpathians are impassable and there is only one rather rickety rail line, which is totally insufficient to either supply or evacuate the German forces. If the Martians commit their whole strength against them, they could be annihilated."

Lindemann frowned. He was no strategist, but even he could see that if nearly half the German Army was destroyed, the way into the rest of Europe would be wide open. Disaster.

"So what are the Germans going to do?" asked Asquith.

The colonel gave a tiny shrug. "Our sources are better at providing factual information about things that *have* happened rather than people's future intentions, sir. But we know that the Germans are moving their strategic reserve, the 4th Army, to Kattowitz to try and form an anchor for a new line. The German border with Poland—formerly Russia—has some significant fortifications along it, but they are currently unmanned because all the troops who had been there are now in Poland. We believe the Germans are planning to strip their western defenses—those facing France—along with everything else they can scrape together and get them into those fortifications as quickly as they can."

Asquith frowned and then asked: "Do you think that will be enough to stop the Martians?"

"That will depend on a lot of factors, sir. The amount of time the Germans have to shift their forces and get dug in, how long the trapped forces can hold out, and how many Martians they can keep occupied. Much will depend on how much help the Germans can get from other powers…"

"They have asked for help, haven't they?" asked Lloyd George. "That's the rumor I'm hearing, at least."

"I believe the Foreign Minister can best answer that," said Asquith. "That is why I asked him to be here. Sir Edward?"

Sir Edward Grey straightened up in his chair. The Foreign Minister was a handsome man with dark receding hair and a large Roman nose. He was in his early fifties, but seemed quite vigorous. Lindemann recalled that earlier in his long tenure in the Foreign Office he had been a supporter of Russia and viewed Germany's expanding colonial empire with suspicion. Lindemann surely shared that suspicion. Grey picked up a stack of papers, straightened them, and then cleared his throat.

"Ah, yes, in the last three days the German government has issued a number of appeals for assistance. Initially they were aimed at the French, the Italians, and ourselves. Since then they have sent appeals to virtually every nation in Europe that has any significant military force. The first appeals they sent out were in the formal mode, but we've gotten several others since then and each one is more… how shall I say it? Insistent? Yes, more insistent than the previous ones. I'll say this: they do seem to realize the fix they are in."

"And they are expecting us to bail them out?" said Kitchener. "Sounds like they made their own problem, let them solve it!"

Emotionally, Lindemann agreed with the Field Marshal. Although born and educated in Germany, he had no love for it. He found the Germans' blatant militarism and arrogance repellant. He, like many others, wouldn't mind seeing the haughty Germans taken down a notch or two. *Except if they fall, everyone else will, too.* That was the problem, the one so hard for many people to grasp. This wasn't like past wars. Defeat didn't mean the loss of a colony or a few border provinces. Defeat meant the loss of everything—extermination. Anyone fighting the Martians had to be supported, even the Germans.

Fortunately, most of the people in the room seemed to realize that. Lloyd George was the first to respond: "Really Field Marshal, as satisfying as that might be, it might also lead to us seeing Martians on the Channel Coast of the Continent. I don't think anyone wants that, eh? So what sort of aid can we send them, and how soon? That seems to be the question we need to settle here."

There was a palpable relaxation in the room once the obvious had been stated. Churchill immediately jumped in. "Yes, David, that is the question. We simply cannot stand by and see the Germans trounced. Our Black Sea expedition isn't scheduled to begin operations until April, but in a situation like this we could well send them off early. A strike against the Martian southern flank, their soft underbelly as it were, ought to draw off forces from Poland, or at least prevent any more being sent there. But that alone won't do the job. We—and by 'we' I mean all of Western Europe—need to send everything we can directly to the German's aid in Poland."

The only force we have at hand is the XIX Corps," said Kitchener. "And that's scheduled to leave for Egypt in the next few weeks. It's headed for our Sudan operation—and we simply can't delay that *again*!"

At that, there were a number of frowns around the room. Kitchener's obsession with the Sudan and retaking Khartoum from the Martians was a recurring problem within the War Cabinet. His recapture of it from the fanatic Mahdi in 1898 had made his reputation as Britain's greatest general and it was quite obvious that he was trying to relive that triumph. It was a worthy goal, perhaps, but his fixation on it had caused problems time and again. Prime Minister Asquith, used to Kitchener's grumbling, was quick to sooth him.

"No one doubts the necessity of the Sudan campaign, Field Marshal, but surely the current emergency demands that we show some flexibility. Once we've dealt with the crisis, your operations can resume."

"Why can't we just use Mr. Churchill's Black Sea forces?" asked Kitchener, not quite ready to give up. "There's already transport assembling for them. Send them to Germany instead of Crimea or wherever he plans to send 'em now."

"Shifting them all the way to the Baltic would take several months," said Churchill. "And in any case, they aren't equipped for a Polish winter. By the time they could be, it would be far too late."

"What about the other European armies? Why can't they shoulder some of the load?"

"Well, I believe they are," said Asquith. "How about that Sir Edward? What sort of responses are the Germans getting to their appeals for aid?"

The Foreign Minister again looked at the papers in his hand. "The French have responded splendidly, sir. They have agreed to send nearly everything they have on hand, over twenty divisions, although a number of those are second line troops manning the fortifications facing Germany. The Italian response has been somewhat less enthusiastic, I'm afraid. They are refusing to send any forces to Poland or Germany, but they have promised two corps which will be sent to the Danube Front, freeing up some German divisions there which could then be shifted north." Grey shuffled through his papers. "Holland has promised two divisions... Belgium one and an unattached brigade... Denmark a brigade... Spain two divisions... Portugal has, uh, promised to send something, but they haven't specified what. There's been no response from Greece or the Balkans, but they are pretty well tied up already, I believe."

"What about Sweden and Norway?" asked Lloyd George. "They're close by, relatively speaking."

"Sweden has already committed most of her mobile forces to help out the Russians in Finland," said Kitchner, with a dismissive wave of his hand. "And Norway, well, they've only been their own country for a few years, they haven't got anything to send."

"Yes, I'm afraid that's true," said Grey.

"Still," said Asquith, "it's quite an impressive response. Assuming they can get all those troops where they are needed in time."

"Fortunately, the French and German railway systems are the best in the world," said Churchill. "And they were designed with moving large numbers of troops quickly in mind. But Prime Minister, with the other powers responding so energetically, we surely must not be seen as wavering. We must make a major commitment as soon as possible."

"I'm inclined to agree, sir," said Lloyd George.

"As am I," said Bonar Law, "in spite of the enormous costs involved." Curzon and Henderson also voiced agreement. Asquith was silent for a few moments and then nodded.

"Very well, what can we send immediately, and what else could follow on?" He looked pointedly at Kitchener and then at Churchill. The Field Marshal looked as though he had swallowed something very sour.

"As I said," he replied after a moment, "the XIX Corps is the only one we could send immediately—if you really insist upon this."

"Assuming the Germans will allow us to use their Kiel Canal—and I can't imagine they'd refuse—we could get them to... Danzig, say, in five days or less," said Churchill.

"The ships are available?" asked Asquith.

"I'll see that they are," replied Churchill. "We could send warships, too, of course, but it looks as though the Martians are going to be staying away from the water. The Germans' High Seas Fleet would be more than capable of filling any need in any case."

"Very good, please have orders for the move sent to the XIX Corps as soon as possible, Field Marshal." Kitchener looked very disgruntled, but he sent off his colonel immediately.

"I should point out," said Lloyd George, Minister of Munitions, "the German weapons are all of different sizes and calibers than our own. They will not be able to provide us with any ammunition at all. We shall have to have additional shipping to keep our men supplied."

"I will allow for that," said Churchill. "Oh, and David, those new anti-tripod bomb launchers, the LIATs, we're producing them in great numbers now, aren't we?"

"Uh, yes, a thousand launchers and ten thousand bombs a month if I recall correctly. Why do you ask?"

"From what I've read, the Germans don't have anything like them. No man-portable weapons that can hurt a tripod at all. Could we send them some? Might cheer their morale a bit if nothing else."

Lloyd George looked to prime minister Asquith who nodded. "I'll see what I can do."

"Just make sure the crates are well-labeled so the Germans know where they are coming from," said Churchill, grinning.

"All right, what else in the way of troops can we put together to send?" continued Asquith.

Kitchener chewed on his mustache for a moment before answering. "We have three new infantry divisions that are still training. We might be able to get them ready in a few months. And then there's the 1st Tank Division... maybe three months for them."

"Surely in an emergency like this we can get them ready sooner," said Lloyd George.

"Maybe," conceded Kitchener.

"What about the Territorials?" asked Churchill. "We've got, what? A hundred battalions of infantry and fifty or sixty batteries that have just been sitting around for the last six years waiting for the Martians to land in the British Isles. I'd think we can spare some of them."

Kitchener snorted. "You can't be serious. As you said, we have a hundred battalions. *Battalions*! Not brigades or divisions or corps, just individual battalions with no higher level organization, and no support units to supply them. Shipping them to Germany would just be sending lambs to the slaughter. They'd be nearly useless."

"I thought you'd been working to create those higher level organizations for some time," said Churchill.

"Working, yes. Completed, far from it."

"Well, what about the artillery? A battery of guns is a battery of guns as far as I know. They don't need a lot of higher level organization to be effective. And artillery is one of our best weapons against those tripod machines."

"How about that, Field Marshal?" asked Asquith. "Could we send some of that artillery?"

"Probably. I'll look into it." Kitchener's mood seemed to be getting blacker and blacker. He looked over at Churchill and said: "And just what is the Navy doing? When are those land ironclad contraptions going to be ready, eh?"

Churchill glanced toward Lindemann and he straightened up in his chair. "We are producing them as rapidly as we can, sir," said Churchill. "A regular assembly line. The first ones should be ready in several more months, although perhaps that can be hastened. Professor Lindemann, can you arrange to head up to Newcastle tomorrow and talk to the Armstrong people about what can be done to hurry things along?"

"Yes, sir!" said Lindemann. "I'll be on the earliest train possible." Lindemann looked to Sub-lieutenant Windsor and whispered, "Check the train schedule as soon as we're out of here." The young man nodded.

"Excellent. Let them know how urgent things have become. Still, it's not realistic to assume that we'll have them before March. But that's about the same time the Field Marshal has said we'll have those three infantry divisions and the tank division." He paused and then said. "That gives me an idea."

The other men in the room stirred and someone muttered: "Christ! Here we go again!"

Churchill probably heard, but he ignored it. Instead he got up from his chair and went to one of the maps hanging on the wall. "Now, assuming the Germans are able to shore up their defenses and keep their trapped armies intact, we shouldn't be only thinking defensively. It will take considerable forces for the Martians to keep those armies contained. More forces will end up facing the new defense line along the German border. It seems to me that this will be an opportunity for a major counterattack on our part."

"Counterattack?" said Kitchener. "Where? With what?"

"Well, with our Black Sea force driving northwestward up the Dniester River, if we were to send our new land ironclads and those other forces we were talking about down the Vistula to Warsaw and then overland southeast to link up with them, we might well bag the whole lot of them."

Kitchener snorted. "You're not being realistic, man! It's got to be over five hundred miles from the mouth of the Dniester to Warsaw…"

"About six hundred in a straight line by the scale on this map," said Churchill, using his fingers to mark off distances.

"Six hundred! A huge distance and you think you can coordinate two widely separated forces to just meet up in the middle? Poppycock! Maybe ships sailing in the open sea can behave like that, but real war doesn't work that way. If you'd ever risen above the rank of lieutenant you'd know that, sir."

An embarrassed silence filled the room. Churchill frowned and tried to take a puff from his cigar, but it had gone out. Asquith stepped into the pause to try to diffuse things. "Your northern force does seem a bit small for such an undertaking, Winston."

Churchill tore his eyes off Kitchener and seemed to shake himself. "Perhaps," he said. "Perhaps. But as we advanced, we could pick up some of the German troops along the border and they could follow along. And maybe we could reinforce this a bit." He looked back at Kitchener. "What about the Guards?"

The Field Marshal appeared taken by surprise. "The Guards? What about them?"

"I know you were working to combine the Guards regiments into a divisional formation—like you were the Territorials. Could we form them into a new division in time to take part?" He looked to Asquith and Grey. "It would be quite a statement to make to the world, too, if we let them know the Guards would be joining in."

Now Asquith was surprised. "Well… well, we'd have to get His Majesty's consent, of course…"

It was Lindemann's turn to be surprised. "The King?" he muttered under his breath. "What does the King…"

"They're his troops," whispered Bertie.

"What?"

"The… the British Army belongs to the nation, but the Guards belong to my da… er, I mean the King. They can only be used with his permission."

"Really? I didn't know that," said Lindemann. Bertie just shrugged.

In the meanwhile, the others were debating the wisdom of committing the King's troops, but finally Lloyd George stepped in. "It seems to me we are getting ahead of ourselves, gentlemen. The First Lord's proposed counterattack can only even be attempted if we help the Germans shore up their lines. I suggest we concentrate on that for now."

"Yes, quite," said Asquith. "I think we all have our tasks set out for us. Let's get on with them. Thank you, gentlemen." He rose from his chair, the meeting clearly over. Lindemann herded Bertie out of the room and down the stairs.

"We need to be on our way as soon as possible," he said.

"I'll check the schedule, sir." He paused and added: "I hope the Germans can hold out."

Lindemann nodded. "So do I."

* * * * *

January 1914, Airfield Northeast of Ostrava, Austria

Colonel Erich Serno looked over the damaged bomber and shook his head. The plane had touched down on the crude airfield and hit a patch of deeper snow and nosed over. That was the third one it had happened to today. After the second one, Serno had run around screaming at the Austrian workers who had been trying to enlarge the tiny airstrip to accommodate his bomber group. They had made a great show with their shovels, flinging snow in all directions, but apparently to little real effect. He looked up and counted a dozen more of his planes circling to land. How many more would be cracked up before they were all down?

As it turned out, the rest all made it down safely; a minor miracle. He rounded up the crews and sent them off to where some army tents had been set up for them. He walked toward the small wooden shack that was the control center for the airfield. It wasn't much, but it was out of the wind, had a small iron stove—and a telegraph.

He was shivering almost uncontrollably by the time he got to the shack. The flight here from Warsaw had been incredibly bitter even though they stayed under a thousand meters the whole way. He shut the door behind him and went and stood next to the stove, only taking off his gloves to hold his hands close to the heat radiating off the iron.

"Any word from Captain Wulzinger yet?" he asked the telegraph operator.

The man shook his head. "Nothing yet, Colonel. Oh, but the line to Tarnow has been reported down."

"Damn."

Everything was happening so fast! Just two weeks ago they'd been set up as comfortably as possible near Warsaw, bombing targets, trying to stay warm, and seeing what delicacies they could scrounge for a Christmas dinner. Serno was looking forward to when the real winter weather set in and made flying impossible for a while. He'd gotten permission to take some leave to visit his family in Darmstadt.

Then, with no warning at all, the word came that the Martians were in Brest-Litovsk and heading for Warsaw. Serno's group was sent out to bomb them and they did, maybe destroying a couple of tripods. But then the enemy didn't come on and turned south. They went up again, but the weather was lousy and they weren't able to find anything to attack. Then Martians were across the Vistula and raising havoc. Several more fruitless missions came after that and then they were told to pack up and get out. The rail connection through Lodz was being threatened and from there the Martians could turn north and overrun the airfields.

It was a mad scramble to get the equipment and ground crews packed up and on trains. Orders arrived telling them where to go, but he'd had to pour over maps for an hour just to find this Ostrava place. He'd been expecting to be sent further west, into Germany, but for some reason known only to God and the High Command, they were to go south into Austria. The planes were prepped and heartbreakingly, five planes that were down for maintenance had to be burned—not that the Martians wouldn't have burned them themselves. And then they were off, leaving Warsaw behind, and after a few hours they were here: the back of beyond, out of fuel and with no ground crews or supplies.

And the Martians might have cut the lines to Tarnow.

That was no immediate threat to Serno or his group, Tarnow was nearly two hundred kilometers to the east. But if the Martians were there it meant that the four German armies holding the defense lines north of Lemberg were cut off. Disaster.

Finally warming up a bit, he found a chair and sat down next to the stove and pestered the telegraph operator for news of Captain Wulzinger and the ground crews. If the Martians had gotten to Lodz before the trains passed, he might never see him or them again. And while that would leave his group crippled, he was more worried about the men. Wurlzinger, who had wanted to be an archeologist before everything went to hell, had been with him since Turkey, and he'd grown quite fond of him. The others were good people, too.

After an hour or so he realized he needed to check on how his air crews were making out. He got up and told the telegraph operator he'd be back in a while and if he heard anything from Wurlzinger to come find him right away. The man was clearly relieved to have the nagging colonel out of his shack.

The sun was heading down the sky toward evening and would soon be disappearing behind the peaks of the Carpathians. But the wind had fallen and it wasn't as cold as earlier. There was a crew of workers trying to right the nosed-over bomber, but they didn't seem to be having much luck. It looked like one of his men was supervising so hopefully they wouldn't damage it any more than it already was.

He reached the cluster of tents beyond the runway. They looked to be an Austrian Army issue. He was glad to see metal pipes sticking up out of them with smoke drifting away. At least his men had some heat. He poked his head inside one and was further gratified to see that there were canvas and wood cots for the men to lay on. They wouldn't have to lie on the frozen ground or the mud it would become once the stoves did their jobs.

Food was another matter. There didn't seem to be any mess tents or supply tents. He'd instructed each of his crews to bring as much food as they could carry before they left Warsaw, so they wouldn't go hungry tonight, but he had to see about getting more rations right away. *Just one thing after another...* He missed Wurlzinger—and Lieutenant Hertzeg, his commissary officer. Where in hell were they?

He went from tent to tent to make sure all his men were in good order. They seemed to be, although they all wanted to know what they were going to do next, and Serno had to admit—over and over—that he had no clue.

He was almost to the last of the tents when a gasping officer came running up. "Colonel! Colonel! They're here!"

He spun around. "Who? Who's here?"

"Captain Wurlzinger. Him and a lot of other people!"

"You mean our ground crews?"

"Them and a whole lot more! They're over there!" he pointed in the direction of the shack. The rail line was in that direction, too. He didn't quite run, but he hurried as quickly as he could as the mountains' shadows crept across the field. Arriving on the far side appeared to be a large convoy of trucks, far more than would be needed to transport all the people and gear for his group of bombers. He spotted Wurlzinger, who saw him at the same moment and waved.

"Glad you made it," said Serno once they got within talking distance. "But what's all this?" He pointed at the trucks.

"Our next mission, I guess," replied Wurlzinger. "But yes, it's good to be here, sir. Hell of a mess. I think we just made it through Lodz by the skin of our teeth. Right after we left there were explosions and big clouds of smoke. From the looks of it, Warsaw is now cut off—at least by rail.

"We made it down to Kattowitz with just the usual delays, but then the real mess began. Dozens of trains coming and going. Mostly offloading troops and guns. Looked like they were fortifying the place. I thought we'd be stuck there for days, but then some officer from the General Staff showed up out of nowhere. He cleared the way for us and attached a second train to ours and we got through the clog. And then when we reached Ostrava, there were all these trucks waiting for us, and now we're here."

"What's in the other trucks?"

"Ammunition, mostly."

"You mean bombs? For us to use?"

"No, small arms ammunition and artillery shells. But there is petrol for our planes, too, so that's a relief."

This made no sense to Serno. "What are we supposed to do with the ammunition?"

Wurlzinger rummaged in his coat and pulled out an envelope. "Maybe this explains it, sir. That staff officer gave it to me to give to you."

Serno took the envelope and opened it. There was the usual stuff at the start about sender and recipient and he scanned down to the heart of the message and read it. Twice. "Huh," he grunted.

"What is it, sir?"

"Looks like we're out of the bomber business, Captain. We'll be hauling supplies from now on."

"Where to? And who for?" asked Wurlzinger, confused.

"To our armies near Lemberg. It appears they are cut off."

* * * * *

January 1914, Western Desert, Egypt

"Come on! Come on, you lugs! Get your stuff and yourselves aboard! Move, damn your eyes!"

That cry, and a dozen variations on it, rang up and down the rail siding. Sergeants from every company and every platoon in the division were urging, pushing, and kicking their men onto the trains. Further down the siding the tanks, guns and carriers were being loaded aboard flat cars.

The 1st Australian Armored Division was on the move.

Captain Harry Calloway watched as his own company was crammed into box cars. They wanted thirty or forty men in each one and that was way too many for comfort. But they weren't going far, just back to the port at Alexandria where they would be loaded onto ships. Ships heading… where?

The word had come yesterday to prepare for a major move. There was an urgency to the orders that indicated this wasn't just the long-expected offensive finally getting under way. Something else was afoot. Rumors were rampant as to the destination, but instructions about packing their overcoats indicated they would not be heading up the Nile to join the Sudan campaign. North then.

"So what do you think?" he asked Burford Sampson as he came up beside him. "Crimea, like they've been saying for months? Or somewhere else?"

Sampson shrugged. "I've heard some rumors that the Germans have made a mess of things in Poland. We might be heading there to save their bacon."

"Poland!" exclaimed Harry. "How'd we even get there from here?"

"I guess they could send us all the way round through the Baltic, but God knows how long that would take. Or they could ship us to Italy or Marseille and by train the rest of the way. Or maybe we'd still go through the Black Sea. I guess we'll find out once we're under way."

"Every damn place on Earth except Australia," muttered Harry.

"Anywhere there are Martians to kill is fine by me," said Sampson.

"In that case, pick a direction, any direction. But it looks like the boys are aboard, we'd better, too." While the men were in box cars, the officers had a small passenger car at the rear of the train. Colonel Berwick was already aboard and he welcomed them.

"Ready for another adventure, gentlemen?" he asked.

The answers were mostly in the affirmative as the train jerked into motion.

Chapter Ten

January 1914, Warsaw, Poland

Ola Wojciech hoisted the basket of dirt and stone onto her back with a groan. It weighed almost twenty kilos and she nearly fell over before she regained her balance. Steadying herself, she trudged along the path for about a hundred meters before someone directed her where to dump it.

"You look exhausted, girl," said someone, "take a break."

She glanced up to see an old woman, probably three times her age, hauling a basket just as heavy as hers. She finished dumping and said, "I'm fine." If it had been someone her own age who had told her to take a break she probably would have, but there was no way she could stop while a grandmother kept working. Still, she wished she could. She was exhausted and it was still an hour until the midday break for lunch. She walked back to where the men were digging and put the empty basket down in the pile for them and found another full one to lug away.

When she had told Wanda she wanted to help defend the city, this wasn't exactly what she'd had in mind. Firing a rifle, throwing dynamite bombs, that's what she'd wanted to do. Instead, she was digging pit-traps and building entrenchments. It had helped a bit when Colonel Bridges had told her that pit-traps were one of the most effective defenses which could be built with simple tools. Dig a hole, maybe a meter and a half square and four or five meters deep. Cover the hole with thin planks and then hide it with a layer of dirt or snow. When a Martian tripod stepped on the cover its leg would crash through and hopefully get stuck. Even if it didn't get stuck the machine would be immobilized for a while, an easy target for artillery or even for bold people with explosives.

Unfortunately, you needed a *lot* of pit-traps.

To have any hope of actually getting the Martian machines to step in one you needed thousands of them spread across the front of your defenses. Four or five hundred per kilometer Bridges had said, usually in three or four bands. So she, and thousands more of Warsaw's citizens were out in this field on the east side of the city digging and hauling. There was about two kilometers of open ground between the outskirts of the city and where the forest began. In spring, these fields would be planted, but right now the digging hoped to raise a crop of a different kind. It was bitterly cold, but the labor kept her warm. The cold also froze the first half-meter of the soil, which made digging hard for the poor men who had to do it, although she heard someone say that it helped keep the holes from collapsing.

She dumped another load on the outer face of the trench line that was also being constructed. Not seeing the old woman around, she did stop for a short rest this time. One of the German sentries glanced at her, but said nothing. Looking west, she could see the suburbs of Warsaw a kilometer or so away. The city straddled the Vistula but the part on the east bank was newer and many of the factories were there. Dozens of tall chimneys spewed black smoke into the air, still in operation despite the presence of the enemy only a short distance away, somewhere beyond the line of trees to the east.

The Russians had never permitted any sort of armaments industries here for obvious reasons, but the factories were converting their production to simple things which could help in the defense. The ironworks were making reinforcing bars for concrete bunkers and some metal shielding that could act as armor plate. Ola had also heard they were making some sort of prefabricated hole liners to keep the pit traps from collapsing in softer ground. There was even a rumor of them making a sort of giant bear trap device to grab and hold the leg of a tripod that stepped into a pit trap. The textile mills were turning out sandbags, bandages, and even uniforms for the new Polish Army units.

Officially, there was no new Polish Army. The Germans were clearly none too pleased with the idea of armed and organized Poles in their midst, despite the current emergency. They much preferred that the Poles confine themselves to manual labor and other activities to support their garrison troops.

That wasn't stopping the Poles, of course.

New military units were being raised in spite of everything. Enthusiastic men and women were joining local companies which were being organized into battalions and regiments. Sadly, their enthusiasm was about all they had so far. They were untrained, unequipped, and mostly unarmed. A surprising number of hunting rifles and shotguns were appearing out of attics and basements, but not nearly enough for all the volunteers, and such weapons would be almost useless against the Martians anyway. Some of the companies were hanging around the German garrison units cheerfully telling them they would pick up their weapons after the Martians had killed them. One of the chemical companies in the city was converting its production to explosives, but there was fear the Germans would take it all for themselves. Ola had tried to join one of the units, but had been turned away and sent to one of the labor battalions instead. Between digging pit traps and her continued employment at the hotel where the observers stayed, she'd had little time for anything else.

She'd been surprised to still be at the hotel. She'd confessed to Wanda that she had blown her cover with Colonel Bridges, but when she'd told her that the Englishman had not been angry and in fact had no qualms about simply telling her what she'd been trying to find out secretly, Wanda had told her to stay there. So in the evenings she met him at the hotel and he briefed her on what he'd found out that day and Ola dropped off a written summary with Wanda each morning on her way to the work site. It didn't leave much time for sleep, but at least she was doing something useful.

Ola saw the grandmother coming toward her with another load and guilti-ly got back to her feet with a groan. She continued working until the noon break. Soup kitchens had been set up to feed the workers, and she was grateful to get a belly full of warm food. There wasn't much in the soup, unfortunately, just a few scraps of meat and some vegetables, but it was better than nothing. Food was being rationed in the city now. The Martians had cut all the rail lines into the city. It wasn't a close siege and people could still get in and out on foot if they wanted. A small amount of barge traffic still got in along the Vistula, but it wasn't nearly enough to feed a city the size of Warsaw. She'd heard there was enough food in the city for several months, but that wasn't very comforting.

The lunch break ended all too soon and she and the others resumed their work. It seemed endless, but little by little they worked their way along the front of the defense line as pit after pit was finished. Right now the pits seemed very obvious, but all it would take was a dusting of snow to conceal them. Still, it was boring. Ola had a keen mind and this did nothing to stimulate it.

The sun was dipping in the west, the short day coming to a close, when there was a sudden commotion. A few people started shouting and the German sentries came to the alert. Ola looked around but didn't see anything. Then there were a few shots in the distance, off toward the wood line.

"Look! Look!" shouted someone. "Martians!" A thrill of excitement and fear shot through her. *Martians!* But where? She didn't see anything...

Then she did.

Off there in the woods something was happening. There was a reddish glow and a cloud of smoke or steam billowed upward, followed by a strange sound, almost like a crack of thunder. A round metallic shape was bobbing just above the treetops. First one and then another and then what seemed a half doz-en, the leveling sunlight glinting off them. A moment later a group of horsemen, German cavalry, emerged from the trees and were galloping toward her like the devil was after them.

He is! Right there!

A tripod emerged from the forest, pushing trees aside like they were twigs, several more following it. Ola had seen pictures of the alien machines, of course, but they were nothing like this reality. She stood frozen, half in fear, half in fascination. They looked to be fifteen or twenty meters tall and even from more than a kilometer away they seemed immense and filled with menace. The leading one moved and a bright beam of red light appeared, linking the tripod to the group of fleeing horsemen. When the beam touched them, a horse and its rid-er exploded into a cloud of steam and burning fragments. The survivors turned their horses toward an abandoned farmhouse, seeking cover perhaps, but it was hopeless. The hellish ray swung to follow them and in a few seconds all had been obliterated. The ray continued to swing and the farmhouse erupted in flames.

"Run, you fool! They're coming!" Someone grabbed her arm and tugged. Only then did Ola become aware of her surroundings. More Martian machines were coming out of the woods—and heading in her direction. The other workers were fleeing toward Warsaw, more German soldiers were appearing, and it seemed like everyone was shouting or screaming. She turned and followed the others, trying to run, but slipping and sliding on the frozen ground. She scrambled along the path and then half-crawled up the side of the entrenchment and tumbled into the ditch on the other side. As she did so, a hideous red glare filled the world around her and the skin of her face felt like she was peering into a roaring furnace.

It only lasted for a moment and then moved on, but several people were shrieking in pain. Looking through watering eyes, she saw a German soldier, not more than a few meters away, thrashing on the ground, his uniform on fire. Without a thought, she crawled over to him and threw loose dirt on the flames and managed to beat them out with her gloved hands.

The man—he didn't look much older than her—was horribly burned, his face was a mass of purplish, blistering skin. His eyes looked half-melted and Ola nearly vomited at the sight of them. His helmet was gone and all his hair burned away except for a patch on the back of his head. She knelt next to him, quivering, with no idea what to do.

"H-help," she croaked, barely able to make a sound. And then stronger: "Help! I need help here!"

But if anyone heard her they were too busy or frightened to do anything. Most of the workers were heading back to the city through the communication trenches and the soldiers were crouching behind the ramparts, a few daring to pop up and fire their rifles. Ola looked around, calling for help again, but no one came. The poor boy was moaning and crying, "Bitte, bitte..." *please*. But what help could she give him? She had no bandages, no medicine... no skills.

More shouts and men around her flattened themselves to the ground and the world turned red again. Ola crouched down over the German, trying to shield him. She could feel the heat on her back, even through her coat, but again it quickly moved on. She was only a few centimeters from the boy's mouth and she could hear him gasping, "Wasser... wasser." *Water*.

She looked around but except for a few muddy puddles in the bottom of the trench there was nothing... His canteen. He still had his canteen attached to his belt and it looked to be intact. She wrenched it free and from the weight she could tell it was full. She twisted the cap off and poured a few drops into the German's mouth. His lips were black and cracked, with horribly red flesh peeking through the fissures. Again she nearly vomited. But the boy swallowed the water down and she gave him some more. "Danke... danke," he gasped and she continued to trickle it into his mouth.

Suddenly he began to cough and gasp. He thrashed his arms and legs and made a horrible sound. Was he choking on the water? In panic she dropped the canteen and tried to pull him upright, but he was jerking around with the strength of a madman and she couldn't control him. "Help! Help!" she screamed.

But then he froze and was completely rigid in her grasp. A shudder passed through his body and then he slumped down and didn't move. Didn't breathe.

She stared in horror for a few moments, and then she did vomit. The lunchtime soup surged up and out onto the ground. She twisted away not to get it on the boy. She heaved and coughed for a minute or more, the heat ray came overhead again unnoticed. Finally, the fit passed and she knelt there quivering for a while. Crying? Yes, she was definitely crying. Eventually, she picked up the canteen and used it to rinse the bitter taste out of her mouth. There was pain in her hands and she realized she had gotten some minor burns when she beat out the German's burning clothing. Her gloves were ruined. She scrubbed the tears out of her eyes and looked around.

The German soldiers in the trenches were still there on either side. Still firing from time to time. Still ducking as the red ray swept past. It was as if the world hadn't noticed this little tragedy in the mud. Anger filled her. This boy had died in agony and no one cared!

Suddenly there was a new noise. A sharp, loud crack and a moment later a deeper boom that shook the air. Another and another and then a whole flurry. Heedless of the danger, she crawled up to the lip of the trench and looked out. A half dozen tripods were out there in the open ground between the trench line and the woods. They were still a distance off and to her chagrin none of them even got close to the line of pit traps. They were firing their heat rays at the defenders, but now the defenders were firing back.

A kilometer or so to the south was one of the old forts the Russians had built. It used to have some heavy guns, but a few years earlier the Russians had stripped them all out and sent them east to battle the Martians on the steppes. Recently the Germans had moved a few field guns into the emplacements and these were now firing at the alien machines. That's what she had heard.

Puffs of smoke billowed out from the fort and moments later gouts of earth erupted close to the Martian tripods. The Martians were firing back at the fort, but it did not seem like their rays were having any effect. As she watched, there was an explosion actually on one of the machines; a bright flash and loud bang and the tripod staggered a bit, but it did not fall.

"Yes, yes," she whispered. "Hurt them. Hurt them!"

And then there was new noise. A loud whistle, like a passing express train shrieked by overhead and new explosions, much larger ones, leapt upward around the Martians. The roar of the bursting shells shook the ground and the concussion thumped against her chest. Those must be the German heavy artillery, firing from the other side of the Vistula. It was deafening, but the uproar was like music to her ears, a symphony of destruction. Her voice rose to a scream: "Yes! Yes! Kill them! Kill them!" Her fingers dug into the dirt of the parapet as she willed the enemy to die.

The Martians weren't dying, but they clearly didn't like what was happening. They started moving back toward the forest, dodging the falling shells. A near miss nearly toppled one of the tripods. It stumbled to one 'knee', but managed to get up again. The enemy were nearly to the forest when a new sound rented the air. A series of very sharp cracks, like a string of exploding fireworks, came from the south. Ola looked in that direction and saw the old fort covered with blue flashes. Each one only lasted an instant, but they were dazzlingly bright and left after-images dancing in her eyes. The fort was smothered by them, and then they started getting closer, walking along the line of trenches—right toward her.

The German infantry, who had been watching the artillery barrage just like her, suddenly dove for the bottom of the trench. Someone grabbed her and dragged her down into the mud and lay on top of her. The flashes were here. Intolerable blue light that she squeezed her eyes shut against, hammering concussions that seemed to suck the air out of her lungs, and heat that seared a patch of her skin that was exposed between her glove and the cuff of her coat.

And then they were gone, moving further along the trench line before stopping entirely. After a short time the German artillery fire ceased as well. The silence that followed seemed unnatural, hollow… strange.

She lay there gasping for a while before the person on top of her got up. It was a German soldier, naturally, and he helped her to her feet. He was saying something, but she could barely hear him, her ears were ringing so badly from the blasts. She stood there shaking until the man touched her arm. He pointed to the dead soldier and then shouted so that she could hear. Her German wasn't the best, but she got the gist of it. *I saw how you tried to help him. Thank you. But you need to go home, girl.* He pushed her gently toward the communication trench and pointed to the city.

She nodded numbly and stumbled toward the setting sun, toward home.

* * * * *

Subcontinent 1-1, Sector 147-29, Cycle 597,845.8

Lutnaptinav ordered the bombardment drones to cease fire and then guided its fighting machine deeper into the tall vegetation. The prey-creature's heavy projectile throwers soon stopped firing as well. It demanded and got status reports from the other five pilots in the force. Only some minor damage to the machines and no injuries. That was good. The battle group still had some replacement machines and some spare parts, but it was increasingly aware that they were deep in enemy territory and a very great distance from any proper repair facilities.

Lutnaptinav's battlegroup and the one from Group 13 commanded by Nabutangula had been left to seal off the large city while the rest of the attack force had moved south to engage the main prey-creature armies. It was not a very important assignment, although still necessary. It wondered if this was a deliberate slight toward the two groups of exiled *Threeborn*, or if it was just a logical task for strangers whose battle skills were unknown. In either case, the orders had been clear and Lutnaptinav would obey them.

The recent engagement had been one of several probes which had been made to test the enemy defenses and hopefully keep them off balance. The two battle groups did not have enough strength to maintain a close blockade of the city, so all that could be done was to patrol the perimeter and make these minor thrusts from time to time. Lutnaptinav did not like the fact that the two battle groups were separated by the large river. Nabutangula's force was in the more exposed position on the western shore and if there was any emergency it would take a considerable time to consolidate. But the situation was what it was and they would make the best of it.

Lutnaptinav led its force for several *telequel* back to the secure area where the battlegroup kept its spare machines and supplies. It parked its machine and powered down everything except its most basic functions. Feeling the need, Lutnaptinav pulled the nutrient tube from its holder and placed the end in its mouth and fed. The fluid which flowed down its mouth was made from the warm-blooded animals that lived on the Target World. It did not know if it came from the prey-creatures or from lesser animals, nor did it care. It was sustenance and that's all that mattered.

Lutnaptinav knew that on the Homeworld feeding was usually done directly from the food animals raised there, ingesting their blood while it was still alive. Here on the Target World that was not done. To avoid the risk of contagion—which had destroyed the first scouting expedition—the food animals were chemically liquified and sterilized to produce this nutrient solution, which was then frozen until needed. It had overheard persons who had been budded on the Homeworld complain that this method seemed unnatural, but Lutnaptinav could not understand why it mattered to them. Food was food.

Its own need for nutrition had increased slightly since it began the budding process again. The new being was now growing in the sack attached to its side and in a quarter cycle would take its place as a member of the Race. It sometimes wondered how its first bud, detached just prior to this expedition, was making out. Lutnaptinav had received no communications from it, but then why should it have? No doubt it was busy with its own tasks now.

As a matter of routine, it also tested itself for any sign of illness. Disease was almost unknown on the Homeworld and the first scouting expedition had made the fatal mistake of assuming the same conditions would prevail on the Target World. They had become ill and died in a shockingly short time. But they had transmitted valuable information home and the following main invasion was much better prepared. Still, some people did become ill and if they could not be successfully treated they would have to transfer their minds completely to a new bud before it was too late. This seemed to happen every third or fourth budding. Studies had shown that buds created on this world were significantly more resistant to the contagions. It was theorized that given time, the people would become completely immune to this planet's diseases. As it had hoped, the test results were negative and Lutnaptinav was not infected.

As it finished, Nabutangula, the Group 13 commander, contacted it. "Lutnaptinav, anything to report on your front? Did your raid go satisfactorily?"

"Yes," it replied. "The enemy is continuing construction of their fortifications. They are far from complete, but even so, formidable enough to discourage a direct assault. How do you evaluate the situation on the western shore?"

"Approximately the same, although the defenses facing west are much more extensive than those facing east. I conclude that when the prey-creatures were fighting each other, the clan holding this territory was more threatened by enemies from the west than from the east."

"I agree," said Lutnaptinav. "Unfortunate that they are not still fighting each other."

"Indeed. The only other thing of note today was a small water vessel which attempted to go past our position on the river. It was destroyed." Nabutangula paused for a moment and then said: "Have you any news from the main attack force to the south?"

"Nothing since the briefing Mandapravis gave two rotations ago. But it appears that although the attack has been generally successful and a large group of prey-creatures has been isolated, they are not disintegrating as was hoped and are continuing to fight back. No quick victory seems likely."

"That was my impression as well," said Nabutangula. "I wonder if we will be called to reinforce the main attack or if we will be left here investigating this city."

Lutnaptinav had noticed that the Group 13 leader was prone to idle speculation. It seemed pointless, but in truth there was little else to do under the circumstances.

"Only time will tell," it replied.

* * * * *

January 1914, Warsaw, Poland

Tom Bridges sat at the table in the hotel's dining room and looked at the pitiful excuse for a dinner that had been served to him. A thin potato soup, black bread, and a cup of wine that was three-quarters water. Rationing had gone into effect in the city the moment the Martians had appeared. It was a long time since he had been on reduced rations and he wondered if he had made the right decision to stay.

He still wasn't sure why he had. The official excuse he'd made to London, when he'd finally been allowed to use the German wireless, was that he wanted to observe how the Martians conducted siege operations. His superiors had accepted this, although only because by then it was too late to get out of the city any way except on foot.

About half the other foreign observers had gotten out while they could and the only one left he could really talk to was the Japanese, Yamamoto. Even Rommel had decamped along with the German headquarters. There was an infantry corps left to garrison the city, but its commander had no time or inclination to play host to the foreigners.

That left Ola.

He found that he really enjoyed talking to her. She seemed interested in everything he had to say—of course, that was her job—but she laughed at his jokes, which was not. He was coming to realize that she was actually very smart. The questions she asked were intelligent and incisive. She appeared to enjoy his company, too, although he wasn't certain if that was genuine or part of the role she was supposed to play. She was extremely tight-lipped when it came to talking about the Polish independence movement she was a part of. She wouldn't even tell him which group she belonged to—there being several from what Bridges had been told. But that didn't bother him—he had no orders to gather information on them—and he admired her loyalty.

She was cute, too. If he hadn't been over twice her age, he might have been tempted to push things and see where that led, but somehow he couldn't. He wasn't entirely sure why. But he did care for her and the thought of leaving her here in a besieged city might have been the deciding factor in his decision to stay. He didn't know how long Warsaw could hold out and if the city fell and those monsters got inside... He knew what the aliens did to the people they captured. If worse came to worse he would try to escape with her. At the very worst, he'd make sure neither of them were taken alive. Well, hopefully it would never come to that.

He heard the front door of the hotel open and a chill draft swept across the dining room. Coal was being rationed, too and the place was now damned cold. He was wearing his overcoat inside most of the time. He turned in his chair, hoping it might be Yamamoto, but was startled to see that it was Ola. She worked all day on the entrenchments and then reported in to whoever she reported to, before coming back to the hotel. She usually didn't get here until after seven, and it was only a little after five.

He started to give a greeting, but stopped dead when he really looked at her. The girl was filthy, covered in dried mud from nearly head to toe. Her hair was disheveled and her face... Her face was pale in the wavering candle light, and it was totally wiped of emotion. Just... *blank*. She usually smiled when she saw him, but not this time. He wasn't sure that she even did see him.

"Ola! What's wrong?" He was on his feet, his chair nearly falling over.

The girl blinked, took a shaking step forward, caught her shoe on the carpet, and stumbled to her knees.

"Ola!" Bridges leapt to catch her and ended up on his own knees in front of her, holding on to her arms. "What happened? Are you hurt?" He looked her up and down. No obvious injuries, except... "What happened to your hands?" There were holes in her gloves and too-pink flesh showed through the holes.

"Are you burned?"

Ola nodded numbly, but said nothing. Bridges slowly and carefully peeled the gloves off, simultaneously roaring at the kitchen staff to bring bandages and ointment. None of them spoke much English, but they quickly got the idea and ran to comply.

When he got the gloves off he saw in relief that the burns weren't too bad—not nearly bad enough to account for Ola's obvious state of shock. "Ola, what happened? Tell me what happened?" He looked right into her eyes.

She blinked again and finally seemed to actually see him. "Colonel Bridges," she whispered. She let out a long sigh and slumped against him. He picked her up and carried her to a sofa in the lobby and laid her down there. One of the other maids appeared and helped bandage her hands, while Bridges gave Ola a few sips of wine and then some hot tea. The girl's hands were like ice and he ordered blankets and more wood for the lobby's fireplace. Bit by bit, Ola seemed to come back to her senses.

"Can you tell me what happened?" asked Bridges, sitting in a chair he'd drawn up next to the sofa. She nodded and slowly replied in a small voice.

"The… the Martians attacked."

Bridges nodded. "I heard some artillery earlier…"

"They attacked right in the area where I was helping with the digging. Six of them. Six of the big metal machines. They caught some of the German cavalry with their rays. Those… those poor horses. I ran, I ran back to the trenches and hid."

"What happened to your hands, Ola?"

She stiffened and her eyes darted around the room for a moment before coming back to him. "There was a G-German soldier in the trench next to me. One of the rays must have hit him. He… he was on fire. Screaming. I put out the fire with my hands. D-didn't know I'd been burned until later. He was hurt so bad. So young. I gave him water out of his canteen. He asked me for it, but he started choking and then he… he died. I tried to help him, but he died!" Her voice was coming louder and her eyes grew wide.

"Shhh…shhhh," said Bridges, putting a hand on her cheek. "You did all you could. In a war some people die and we can't always help. You did all you could, Ola. You were very brave to stay there and try."

She turned her head away. "I… I threw up," she said, tears leaking out of her eyes, as if it was the most shameful thing in the world.

"It happens. Happened to me once. Nothing to be ashamed of. What happened then?"

"T-the German cannons started firing and the Martians stopped for a while. Then there were these bright blue flashes and more explosions. Another German soldier pushed me into the bottom of the trench and shielded me with his body. Then the flashes stopped and the Martians went away and I… I walked here." She stopped and closed her eyes and turned her head away from him.

"It's all right, Ola, it's all right. You've had a hard day. You need to sleep."

She didn't answer, but she didn't resist when he picked her up and carried her to his room. The maid helped him get her out of her filthy outer clothes and then he tucked her into his bed and covered her with blankets. The other maid seemed a bit scandalized, but made no protest. Bridges went to one of the unoccupied rooms and ruthlessly confiscated the blankets there. He went back and settled into the easy chair and draped the extra blankets on himself.

Ola stirred and peered at him. "Colonel Bridges...?"

"Call me Tom, Ola."

"T-Tom, will you stay here with me?"

"I'll be right here. Don't worry."

She stared at him for a while and then closed her eyes. He stared back at her until her breathing became steady and regular and then closed his eyes and tried to sleep.

* * * * *

January, 1914, Train to Newcastle-upon Tyne

Frederick Lindemann was annoyed when the train stopped at York. This was supposed to be an express and there had already been far too many delays on the trip to the Armstrong-Whitworth factory in Newcastle. He had planned to leave the morning after the meeting with the War Cabinet, but a flurry of last-minute chores from Churchill had forced a one-day delay. By then, it seemed as though the results of that meeting were already setting things in motion far and wide. The rail lines were clogged with trains intended for moving troops and guns and supplies, presumably to the ports for embarkation to the Continent. Every siding was filled with flat cars for guns and tanks, box cars for supplies, and passenger cars for the troops. He was amazed that the usually lethargic army could act so quickly—clearly someone was taking this all seriously.

Once the train had gotten clear of the London area, they had moved a bit faster, but it was well into the afternoon by the time they reached York, and now this unscheduled stop, with another eighty miles still to go. He looked grumpily out the window at the throngs of soldiers crowding the platform. They were obviously waiting for a train of their own, huddled in their overcoats and stamping their feet against the cold. Bertie sat quietly on the seat across from him with his eyes closed, trying to nap. The young man seemed to be one of those fortunate people who could drop off almost anywhere under almost any circumstance.

Bertie's eyes popped open and Lindemann jerked around to look as the door to their compartment opened. A man stepped through wearing a heavy tweed coat and hat. He was a distinguished-looking fellow with a large Kitchener-style mustache, bushy eyebrows, and spectacles. He looked strangely familiar but he couldn't place him. "Ahh, this is a private compartment, sir," said Lindemann.

The man looked him straight in the eyes and said: "You are Professor Lindemann, yes?"

"Yes, I am." What was this, some urgent message from Churchill? The stranger did not look like a messenger. "Are you looking for me?"

"Yes, and I'm so glad I was able to catch you here, Professor." He started taking off his coat. "My name's Kipling."

Lindemann's mouth fell open, finally recognizing him. Bertie suddenly exclaimed: "You're Kipling? Rudyard Kipling? The famous poet? I... I read some of your poems in school, sir!"

Kipling laughed. "Well, I am a poet. Not so sure about the famous part. But you must be the Duke of York. An honor to meet you, your grace."

Bertie seemed quite flustered. "I uh, I'm on duty, sir. I'm just Sub-lieutenant Windsor now, sir."

"Indeed? Well, I'm still pleased to meet you. And you, too, Professor," he said, sitting down and nodding to Lindemann. "I hope my meeting you here isn't an inconvenience."

"What?" said Lindemann. "Are you the reason the train stopped here? How did you manage that? We're on official business!"

"Yes, yes, I know," said Kipling, grinning. "You're off to meet with the Armstrong people about the land ironclads, correct? Trying to speed things up on the work so we can go pull the Germans' chestnuts out of the fire, right?"

Lindemann rocked back in his seat, stunned. While there was no secret about the construction of the ironclads, the decision by the War Cabinet to make a major effort to relieve the Germans was only a day old! "How... how did you find out about that?"

Kipling's grin grew broader. "I'm an old newspaperman, Professor. Cut my teeth on the old *Civil and Military Gazette* back in Lahore. Still do a lot of writing for the papers here in England. I've got my contacts and sources, sir. This mobilization of the Army and the Territorials is big news. I'd been meaning to write an article on the land ironclads for some time, but when I learned you were making a trip up there, I pulled a few strings to meet you here and tag along if you don't mind."

Lindemann stared. A part of him most definitely *did* mind. Not only was this a serious breach of security, it was also a shocking lapse of protocol. If it had been anyone else, he would have called the conductor and had the fellow thrown off the train.

But it wasn't anyone else, it was Rudyard Kipling. Named *Poet of the Empire*, awarded the 1907 Nobel Prize for Literature—although he couldn't collect it in person due to the Martian invasion that year—and as Bertie had said, his works were known to every English schoolboy. A famous and influential man. No, Lindemann would not have him tossed off the train.

"Ah, no, no, I don't mind," Lindemann managed to choke out the lie. "A... a pleasure to have you along, sir."

"Good! Jolly good!" exclaimed Kipling. "I was a tad worried when I learned it was you making the trip. You being German-born and all. I'm glad you didn't take that whole 'Hun' business personally."

Lindemann started, confused for a moment before he remembered. About ten years earlier Kipling had written a poem which was very critical of Germany and called them 'Huns'. It had made some people angry despite the fact that the Kaiser himself had told his own soldiers to 'behave like Huns' and take no prisoners during the Boxer Rebellion in China.

"No, no, of course not, sir," he said, making a motion with his hand in dismissal. "Just an accident of birth, I assure you. I'm a citizen of the British Empire and very proud of it."

"Ah, good. Like Prince Battenburg, eh? I assume you've met him, working for Churchill as you do."

"Yes, a very fine man."

"Indeed. I remember how when some German upstart dared to criticize him for not being in the *German* Navy, Battenburg just stared him down and said: 'Young man. I was a midshipman in the Royal Navy before the German Empire even existed!" Kipling gave a hoot of laughter and slapped his knee.

A moment later, the train lurched into motion and quickly left York and the waiting soldiers behind. Kipling proved to be a pleasant traveling companion and soon put Lindemann at ease. He asked many questions about his background and about the land ironclads, but he didn't ignore Bertie either, and the lad seemed quite taken with the older man.

As they got closer to their destination, Lindemann cleared his throat and said: "Ah, I'll be going into my meeting with the Armstrong people as soon as we arrive—we're already late—so perhaps the Sub-lieutenant can take you on a tour and show you the ironclads. They really are quite impressive to see."

Kipling frowned—the first time that expression had crossed his face. "I was rather hoping to join you in the meeting, Professor. I'd really like to take the measure of the Armstrong people."

"I'm not really sure that would be a good…"

"B-but P-professor," exclaimed Bertie, his stutter getting the best of him, "with Mr. K-kipling along, they w-would have to agree to move faster, w-wouldn't they? They won't want bad things written about them in the newspapers, w-will they?"

Kipling laughed out loud. "Ha! You understand the power of the press perfectly, young man! A shame you aren't going to be king. I wager you'd make a good one."

And so between Kipling's seemingly indomitable personality and Bertie's cajoling, all three of them strode into the Armstrong-Whitworth offices two hours later. Sir Andrew Noble, the chairman of the conglomerate, was greatly surprised by Kipling's presence, but could not bring himself to object to his being there. "Well, you represent the government, Professor," he whispered to Lindemann, "if you're willing to permit this, it's on your head." Kipling found a chair against one wall and settled into it. The other men there recognized him and seemed both awed and unsettled by his presence.

The meeting commenced and Lindemann got right down to business. "Gentlemen," he said, "I imagine most of you are aware of the crisis which has developed in Poland. Our government has decided that we must send whatever aid we can at the earliest possible moment. I am here at the direction of the War Cabinet to impress upon you the gravity of the situation and to learn what can be done to hasten the delivery of the land ironclads."

A dozen dour-faced engineers and managers looked back at him, several shaking their heads. After a long moment of silence, Sir Andrew spoke: "Professor, as you know, we are already exerting every effort to get these machines done in the least possible time. I don't see how we can…"

"Back in November, Mr. Gresley here promised you'd have six of them done by the end of February. Your recent reports indicate that the new date is late March. That simply will not do."

Sir Andrew turned to face the cringing Gresley. "He had no authority to make such a promise, Professor. Armstrong-Whitworth cannot be held to it."

"Well, I'm afraid I *am* holding you to it—and so is His Majesty's government." Lindemann hated this sort of confrontation, but knowing that Churchill was watching his back, he was able to come across forcefully and confidently.

Sir Andrew looked to the others in the room and a noisy debate erupted among the engineers and managers. Some were declaring it impossible, others were at least floating ideas about how some things could be done to speed progress. But every idea was quickly sunk by someone else. Some of the comments got heated, although it was clear that Kipling's presence was restraining everyone. The poet, himself, sat there, arms crossed and looking on with an amused expression.

Lindemann was steeling himself to step in and put an end to the bickering and demand a definite plan of action when the hapless Gresley raised a hand to get their attention. Sir Andrew called for quiet and got it. "Yes, Gresley? You have something?"

"Uh, yes, sir," said the man, looking a bit flustered. "I wanted to ask Professor Lindemann if the Navy is training crews for the ironclads?"

All eyes shifted to him and Lindemann replied: "Yes, of course. There is a facility down in Portsmouth that's being used for that. The engine room staff and the mechanics have copies of your blueprints to study, and there's an old cruiser in the anchorage with gun turrets very similar to what will be used on the ironclads. The gun crews are training on them."

"Ah, good," said Gresley, "I expected as much. But even with that, there will probably be a considerable working-up period once the crews take possession of their machines."

"Of course there will," said Lindemann, exasperated. "A month or more. That's why we need the ironclads as soon as possible!"

"Yes, sir. But I was thinking that perhaps we could bring those men here to Newcastle right now. The engineers and black gangs could take a look at the machines under construction with their skins off, so to speak. They could actually see where all the steam lines and conduits are located—far more useful than looking at blueprints. And some of the gun turrets have already been completed; the gunners could train on them."

"An interesting idea, Nigel," said Sir Andrew.

"Thank you, sir. And as the units near completion we'll be doing trial runs of the boilers and engines. To have their crews here during that process would speed things up as well."

"So it would. How about that, Professor? Can you get your people up here quickly?" asked Sir Andrew.

Impressed, Lindemann nodded. "I'll get a message off to Churchill right away. I'm sure he'll endorse the idea. If you can accelerate the completion and integrate the crew training in the process, we might have a functional squadron by late March, yes?"

"We'll certainly do our best, but there's not a moment to waste."

As Lindemann nodded in agreement, he heard a voice behind him chanting:

> *If you can fill the unforgiving minute*
> *With sixty seconds' worth of distance run—*
> *Yours is the Earth and everything that's in it,*
> *And—which is more—you'll be a Man, my son!*

To his astonishment it was Bertie speaking. The young man was blushing a beet red as every eye turned toward him.

Kipling roared out a laugh. "Well done! Well done, indeed! Couldn't have said it better myself!"

"Y-you did say it y-yourself, sir," said Bertie.

The other men in the room chuckled as well. Sir Andrew got to his feet and nodded toward Bertie. "I can't argue with that. Very well, we all have work to do. Let's get to it!"

Chapter Eleven

February 1914, Airfield Northeast of Ostrava, Austria

Serno looked up from his desk when he heard the rumble of engines overhead. He hesitated for a moment, then got to his feet and pulled on his overcoat. There was no reason whatsoever for him to go outside and watch the group return, but he'd been working on these damn reports all afternoon and was sick of them. Fuel expenditures, spare parts requests, replacement requests, maintenance schedules, and, of course, cargo reports. Cargo tonnage arrived, cargo tonnage loaded, cargo tonnage delivered, cargo tonnage lost—*cargo tonnage!* This was a bomb group, not some damn delivery service!

He stepped through the door of the tar-paper shack that served as his headquarters and let the chill February wind cool his frustration. He reminded himself—as he always did when these moods took him—that right now delivering cargo to the trapped armies was more important than dropping bombs.

Four German and one Austrian army were penned up against the Carpathian Mountains about two hundred kilometers east of here; close to half a million men. They were in desperate need of supplies and if they didn't get them, they might well be annihilated. Nearly all the passes through the mountains were blocked by snow so there could be little help or any route of escape to the south, The one small railway was being kept open by herculean efforts, but with almost no sidings to let trains pass each other, the amount that could be delivered was completely insufficient. The rest had to be made up by air.

So every day that the weather was good enough to allow flying—and there weren't nearly enough of those this time of year—his squadrons were flying dawn to dusk. On good days they could make two round trips to the airfield that had been created near Krosno, each plane carrying nearly a ton of supplies. His group wasn't the only one involved; nearly every airplane capable of carrying cargo that Germany and Austria possessed had been pressed into the effort. It wasn't nearly enough—maybe 2000 tons a day delivered, but it was better than nothing. Combined with what the railroad could deliver, they'd managed to keep the armies alive, but no one knew how long they could hold out.

Their cargoes were almost entirely ammunition, along with some medical supplies. The men needed food, of course, but without the huge quantities of ammunition delivered, the Martians would have overrun them in days. The troops were scrounging what food they could in the territory they held and so far it had been enough to keep them alive.

But it wasn't the aircraft or the railroad which had staved off total disaster, it was the mountains. If the armies had been caught out on the plains by the Martian flanking maneuver, they would have been doomed. The alien machines were so fast the retreating armies would have been cut to pieces before they could have fallen back and reorganized. Fortunately the Carpathians had provided a natural fortress to rally on. The tripods weren't nearly as mobile in the mountains and once the troops reached them and dug in, with their artillery set up in valleys behind, they had stopped the enemy advance cold.

The cost had been enormous, of course. Half a million men had reached the mountains, but there had been three-quarters of a million to start. What had happened to all the rest, no one knew for sure. Killed, scattered, or—God help them—captured? Clearly some had survived, because there was a steady stream of them stumbling into the new defense line built along the German border every day. They carried tales of Martian machines running amok through the rear areas of the army, burning everything in their path. It had been a disaster of epic proportions.

But they had bought time. The dead had bought some and the survivors along the Carpathians had bought more. And the time had been put to good use. The old fortifications along the border between Germany and Russian Poland, which had been stripped bare, were manned again—and not just by Germans.

Germany had scraped up every last man it could find and rushed them east, but they would not have been nearly enough by themselves. Alone, they would have been spread so thinly the Martians could have punched through anywhere they pleased. But the Germans were not alone. There had been an unprecedented outpouring of aid from the other European countries. French, British, Dutch, Belgian, Spanish, and troops from a half-dozen other nationalities had moved as quickly as the straining railroads could carry them to shore up the last line of defense keeping out the invaders.

Many of those soldiers had been enemies of Germany before the Martians came and uncertain allies afterwards. It was amazing. Amazing that they'd come, amazing that the Kaiser had let them cross Germany to reach where they were needed. Was everyone finally realizing that only working together could they win this war? Some people were calling it a miracle and Serno couldn't help but agree.

So the line had been manned and just in the nick of time. Once the Martians realized they couldn't quickly crush the armies trapped against the mountains, they had left enough forces to keep them contained and then sent several powerful columns west, no doubt thinking they could run rampant in Germany, burning cities, destroying factories, railroads, and bridges. But they had hit the new defenses and been stopped. Not completely; a few small groups of tripods had made it through and done some damage, but they'd been contained and driven back east or destroyed. Things seemed to have stabilized for the moment.

No one knew how long that would last, but everyone was hoping that unless the aliens brought up significant reinforcements the lines would hold until more forces from the rest of Europe could be assembled for a counterattack. Rumors were running rampant about those counterattacks. Some said that England was gathering a powerful force that included some of those amazing land ironclads like the Americans had for a landing on the Baltic coast that would drive up the Vistula, relive Warsaw, outflank the Martians, and link up with the trapped armies on the Carpathians. That seemed like a bit much to ask anyone to Serno, but who knew? The other rumor, the more likely one, was that the large international force which had fought on the Dardanelles last year—and saved Serno's bacon—was headed for the Black Sea and some sort of offensive down there. That was an awful long way away, but perhaps it would divert the enemy's attention from the Polish front.

As Serno stood in the cold pondering, the AEG G.IV bombers of his *kampfgeshwader* came in to land. He automatically started counting them. With the ones down for maintenance, they sent off seventy-three planes that morning. In ones and twos, the big aircraft set down on the frozen air strip. *Twelve, thirteen... fifteen...* As the planes landed they turned and taxied toward the long line of tents where their ground crews waited for them. There were no hangars, so the planes just stood out in the open when they weren't flying. Not good for the longevity of the equipment, but there was nothing for it. *Thirty-nine, forty, forty one...* He winced as number forty-two came down too heavily and its undercarriage collapsed, the big bomber sliding for several hundred meters before coming to a stop. Men went running out to help, but it looked pretty much intact and the crew should be all right. The bomber was another matter. It might be salvageable, but Serno was afraid it might only be good for spare parts now. Fortunately, with the air field just being a huge unpaved space, there was plenty of room for the other planes to land. He kept counting and snorted when the last one was down and his count had only reached seventy-one. Had he miscounted? Or were they just late? He started walking toward the group command bomber.

He got there just as Major Lang was lowering himself down from the cockpit. The man stretched and wiggled his shoulders. He came to attention when he saw Serno. "How'd it go?" asked Serno. "Not including the one that pancaked, you're short two planes."

Lang nodded and frowned. "One of them's still back at Krosno with engine trouble. We ought to get it back tomorrow."

"And the other?"

Lang shook his head. "Clouds closed in just as we were finishing up the landing. Visibility dropped to nothing just like that," he said, snapping his fingers. "Thank God it didn't happen fifteen minutes sooner, or we would have lost half the group. The last few planes all made it down somehow, except for Lieutenant Goering's plane in 16 Squadron. We heard the crash, but couldn't see anything. Took us an hour to find the wreck. Just plowed straight into the side of that mountain that's beyond the eastern end of the field. Didn't have a chance, Colonel. I'm sorry."

Serno nodded. The landing field they'd manage to hack out of a mountain valley wasn't easy to land on, even in good weather. They'd lost four other planes there in the past month. "Nothing you could have done, Lang. Good job getting back with the others. Get some food and some sleep. We have to do it all again tomorrow."

"Yes, sir." Lang turned and went over to his ground crew to deal with some things. There were always things to deal with and Serno hoped he would be able to get some sleep. The pace was wearing out his men faster than it was the planes.

Serno was chilled through and through by this time and walked quickly back to the headquarters shack. Captain Wulzinger was waiting for him there. He was holding a sheet of paper. "Ah, there you are Colonel. We have our orders for tomorrow."

"Back to Krosno?" he asked as he took his coat off.

"No, sir," said Wulzinger. "They are sending us off to Warsaw with some priority supplies."

"Warsaw! Where are we supposed to land? All of the airfields south of the city were overrun, weren't they?"

"Apparently they've built a new airstrip inside the defense lines. There are details here in the orders, sir." He handed the paper to Serno.

He looked them over and said, "Huh. Well, I guess we can manage it. I think I'll go along this time. I'd like to take a look at the place again."

* * * * *

February, 1914, The Dardanelles

"Didn't expect to see this place again," said Sergeant Breslin.

"Is this where it happened?" asked Lieutenant Fenwick. He and the other three platoon commanders of C Company were clustered at the rail on the upper deck of the transport *Accrington* looking eagerly to the south as their ship and over two hundred others moved into the narrow waterway separating Europe from Asia. Harry Calloway stood back, leaning against an air intake, and watched the men watching.

"The place where we fought is a bit further along, sir," said Breslin. "The Martians were holed up in a town, where the channel makes a sharp turn. You can just see the ruins of the place in the distance."

The men leaned out over the rail to peer in the direction they were moving. "Oh yes, I can see it," said Lieutenant O'Reilly. "And look, there are some wrecked ships up on the shore."

"A couple of dozen ships were sunk here, weren't they, sir?" asked Lieutenant Boyerton, turning back to look at Harry.

"About that, I guess," replied Harry. "We didn't really get to see much of that, though. They landed the army further south near that little island you can see there off in the distance. We marched overland to reach the Strait. The Martians had their super heat rays set up to cover the narrowest part of the waterway and they sank a good number of ships trying to force their way past. We were supposed to move up and take out those rays from the rear. When it got dark we could see the fires—although we had other things to worry about by then." He paused and thought back to that awful, awful night. Fighting their way into the ruined town, being ambushed by the damn spider machines at every turn, and then the Martian counterattack that sent them reeling back out of the town. If they hadn't blundered across that disabled Yank land ironclad he didn't think any of them would have made it back alive. As it was, they still lost half the battalion.

"Is… is that when you lost your eye, sir? asked Fenwick.

"No, that came later," said a new voice. Harry turned to see Burford Sampson come up and join them. "After the reinforcements arrived we pushed back into the town and started taking out the heat rays. But it was slow going and the fleet was taking a terrible pounding. Then we found a way into the Martian tunnels and Captain Calloway here managed to cut the cables to their power plant and shut down all the rays at once. That's when he lost his eye."

His lieutenants were staring at Harry with a worshipful expression that he found very uncomfortable for some reason. "I never would have had the chance if you hadn't taken out that Martian machine that attacked us, Captain," he said to Burf. "That's when *you* nearly got yourself killed. A lot of good men died giving me that chance."

"True," said Burf, smiling. "But that's war: you did the deed so you got the medal." Harry just shrugged and they all went back to looking at the shore of the Dardanelles slowly slipping past. The line of ships disappeared ahead of them as they made the sharp turns through the Narrows, and there were still a lot more who were stacked up behind, waiting to follow.

It had taken a long time to get the whole armada assembled, and there had been several weeks spent at Alexandria or in the taverns and fleshpots of Cairo before the battalion and its vehicles and supplies had been loaded up. The fleet this time was about as big as the one that had fought at the Dardanelles, but there were more transports and fewer warships. They wouldn't have to fight their way through to Constantinople this time, but they were going to need more troops when they got to wherever they were going. Vera was on one of the other ships with her hospital company. There still wasn't any definite word about where they were heading once they reached the Black Sea. Most seemed to think it would be Crimea, but others felt it would be somewhere farther west. Odessa, or maybe even the mouth of the Danube.

They reached the Narrows and could clearly see the ruined town along the southern shore. Burned and broken buildings stretched for several miles. There were a few people wandering through the rubble, but it seemed mostly deserted. What had the place's name been? Harry couldn't remember. The lieutenants looked at it very somberly. They had all seen some action on the shores of the Red Sea, but that was a thinly populated area with only a few small villages—which had been long-deserted. This was their first look at what the Martians could really do to a human town.

"I… I guess pretty much all of Australia must look like this now," said Boyerton quietly.

No one replied. Harry stared at his oh-so-young officers. They must have been fourteen or fifteen when they were evacuated and sent to New Zealand. They probably never saw their homes reduced to ashes. Harry never actually saw his house destroyed, either, but he could never forget the mad flight through the streets of Sydney to reach the boats at Botany Bay. Buildings on fire, tripods in the streets, shells from the warships exploding all around. Sometimes he could still smell the smoke, taste the bitter cordite floating in the air. Yes, home was now a pile of rubble like that town on the shore of the Dardanelles. The ruins slowly crumbling away, the Martian red weed covering what was left... He was confident that someday he—or someone—would return, but he doubted it would be home anymore.

An hour or so later they cleared the straits and entered the Sea of Marmora. They left the destruction behind and their spirits rose. The dinner call was sounded and they were soon laughing and joking again.

The *Accrington* was a new ship and it had been built with transporting troops in mind from the start. Harry had a very small, but reasonably comfortable cabin to himself. His servant Abdo kept it neat and tidy and he was soon asleep at the end of the short winter day.

Morning saw them nearing Constantinople. When they came up on deck the nearly level rays of the sun were gleaming off the gilded domes of the mosques and palaces of the city. "I can see why they call this the 'Golden Horn'," said Harry.

"Actually, it's the estuary on the other side of the city that's the Golden Horn," said Sampson, coming up beside him.

"Really?" said Harry, surprised. "But on the maps the city is shaped like a horn sticking out into the water. And with all that gold on the buildings I just thought... Why would the *water* be called a golden horn?"

Sampson shrugged. "Haven't a clue. I just know it's true."

"Huh. Well, leave it to the foreigners to do something silly like that."

The fleet formed up to pass through the Bosporus, which was even narrower than the Dardanelles. As they passed the city on their left, huge crowds of people lined the water and cheered for them, many waving flags of all the different nations that were part of the armada. This was a real surprise to Harry and the others. Most of the places they had been since leaving Australia had been deserted, or filled with refugees who had been sullen and envious of the better-fed soldiers. But the people of Constantinople were treating them like heroes.

"Well, the fleet *did* save the city, I guess," said Boyerton.

"After *we* got them past the Narrows, eh Harry?" said Sampson, smiling.

"All that matters is that the Martians were stopped and the city *was* saved," said Harry. He looked at the crowds and then used his field glasses to examine the untouched buildings behind them. The Hagia Sophia was in plain view and he had to admit it was one of the most impressive things he'd ever seen. Losing an eye to save that had been worth it—he guessed.

They were all feeling pretty good—until they entered the Bosporus.

The narrow waterway marked the farthest advance of the Martian offensive. They had made it right up to the water and had been firing across before the massed guns of the Allied fleet had turned them back. Many of the buildings on the northern shore still showed damage and there were spots where some structures had been burned to the ground. But there were a lot of people there rebuilding and many of them paused to cheer the fleet as the others had done.

The southern shore was a different matter.

It had been a densely populated area, a suburb of the great city to the north. Now it was a vast swath of charred rubble. Several hundred tripods had swarmed through the area destroying everything in their path. And then for good measure, thousands of large-caliber shells from the fleet had churned up whatever was left like a plow going through a field. Most of it was just rolling mounds of debris, but here and there a taller bit of some building poked up, like the ribs of some long-dead cow or horse. There was still a strong smell of smoke in the air despite the nine months since this had happened.

There were only a few people visible except for some military people who were salvaging what they could from wrecked Martian machines. Some of the parts—especially the aliens' special wire—were very valuable. Harry knew that in some places scavengers would try to get to the machines first, knowing they could make a pretty penny selling their finds back to the government. There was no evidence of any rebuilding on the southern shore. Perhaps the people who had lived there didn't want to risk living somewhere that the Martians might come back to…

"Blimey! What's that?" exclaimed Lieutenant Fenwick. He had his field glasses out and was scanning the southern shoreline.

"What?" asked several people.

"Along the shore. Right at the water's edge. It's all covered with white stuff."

Harry and the others pulled out their own glasses and looked where Fenwick had indicated. He focused in and as Fenwick had said the shore was covered with what looked like white stones. Or something. Staring more intently with his one eye he saw that while some of the things did look like big cobblestones, others were longer and thinner. In fact they looked like…

"Bones. They're bones," said Boyerton in a choked voice.

Sampson, who hadn't bothered with his glasses, nodded. "When the Martians broke through the Turkish and German lines to the south of here, they swept everything in front of them. There aren't any bridges over the Bosporus and all the larger boats were reserved for military traffic. The civilians… the civilians didn't have anywhere to go. I read about it in the *Times* while I was in the hospital."

"They were all massacred?" squeaked O'Reilly.

"Or drowned. A lot decided to risk the water rather than burn. Hardly any made it."

"Good God."

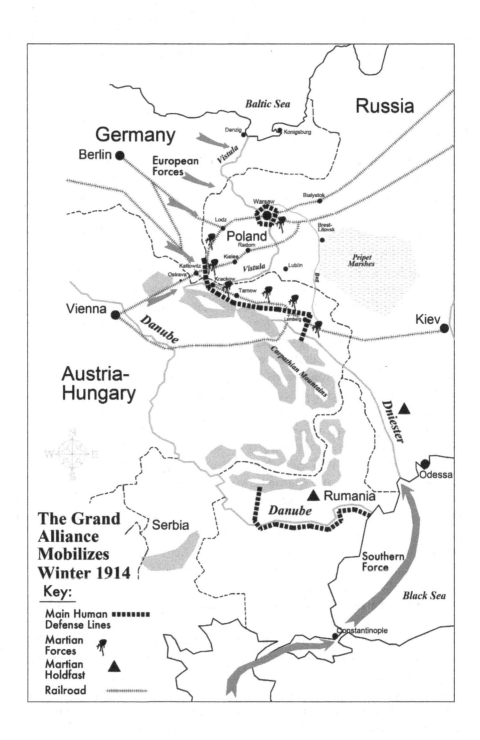

Conversation died and most either went below or went back over to the port side of the ship to look at more hopeful things. A few hours later the *Accrington* emerged into the Black Sea and turned north. There was a bitter wind blowing reminding them that it was still winter where they were heading.

And there would be Martians waiting for them.

* * * * *

February, 1914, Warsaw Poland

Ola forced her way through a snow drift and wondered why she'd been so eager to get out here. She could have been safe and warm back in Warsaw. Or as safe and warm as it was possible to be in a city under siege and with the measly rations of coal that were available. Instead, she was cold and wet and in mortal danger working with a group of Polish volunteers scouting in Martian territory on the west side of Warsaw.

She had spent two months doing manual labor on the city's defenses. But now tens of thousands of pit traps and a solid line of trenches ringed Warsaw and the demand for labor had diminished to the point that she was no longer needed for that. She'd bent Wanda's ear for a week insisting that she should now be allowed to join one of the volunteer militia companies before the woman had finally relented. The fact that there were now 50,000 Polish—many of them women—manning the trenches alongside the Germans and that she had also turned nineteen had been the deciding factors. She'd been proud to join one of the companies and sew a patch onto her coat sleeve declaring her new status.

Even so, she had to ask herself what she was doing out there right now. The scout groups were volunteers from within the volunteers. Manning the trenches at need was everyone's duty, but to venture out beyond the trenches, into the forests held by the Martians, that was not. But it was important work, it was the only way to see where the Martian machines were concentrated and hopefully get some warning of any upcoming attack. Initially her company commander, a stern fellow named Ostrowski, had been as obstinate about letting her become a scout as Wanda had been about letting her become a fighter. But when half his scouts had been wiped out on a patrol and he'd had trouble getting men willing to replace them, he'd finally relented.

Her first patrol hadn't been bad. Ostrowski had deliberately made it a short one to break in the new scouts, venturing just a kilometer or so into the forest. They'd seen nothing and returned unharmed. But two days ago the aliens had unleashed a heavy bombardment on the city with their horrible blue bombs. The German commander wanted scouts to try and find the location of the launchers so that perhaps he could hit back at them with his own artillery. As a result, today Ola and her group—and a dozen other groups from other companies—snuck out of the trenches and across the open fields and into the woods.

She felt terribly exposed in the daylight. All the experts said that the Martians could see as well in the dark as in the light, so there was no point in handicapping the scouts by sending them out in darkness. That might be so, but she still felt very conspicuous and vulnerable. The knee-deep snow and denuded trees and underbrush didn't help, either. She'd been given a white cloak to try and blend in. She hoped it would work.

Her patrol was made up of eight men and women commanded by Corporal Drozda. Two men had rifles of dubious value, several others had pistols, and they all had dynamite bombs, probably their only useful weapons. One fellow, a bespectacled youth from the university named Leslaw Gruzka carried a detailed map of the region and a small wireless set provided by the Germans. If they found the bomb launchers they were supposed to report their position. Ostrowski had informed them rather bluntly that the wireless was more valuable than they were, so make sure they brought it back.

They had crossed the open area between the trenches and the forest in the gray light before dawn as quickly as they could. They reached the cover of the trees unharmed and without seeing any sign of the Martians. From that point they advanced slowly, from tree to tree, deeper into the woods. After several hours, they had moved a few kilometers and eventually found a sheltered area in a frozen creek bed to take a break.

As they took out their rations—just some hard bread with cheese and a dried out sausage—Leslaw sat down next to her. It was clear he was smitten with her. She found his attention flattering but annoying. He was nice enough, but also a bit of a twit. "How are you doing, Ola?" he whispered.

"Shhh. We're not supposed to talk," she whispered back.

He glanced at Corporal Drozda, but he was thirty meters away, keeping watch from the lip of the gully. "He can't hear us."

"But maybe the Martians can, now shut up!" she hissed.

Leslaw just grinned, not a bit daunted, but he did stop talking. Ksenia Popek, the only other woman in the patrol, glared at both of them and put her finger to her mouth. Ola rolled her eyes at her and shrugged. She went back to eating. And thinking.

Why *was* she out here? She had no special skills in woodcraft; she was a city girl, really. Colonel Bridges—Tom—would be horrified if he knew she was doing this. She remembered how he'd taken care of her after that awful day in the trenches. He really did seem to care about her and somehow that was far more flattering than Leslaw's clumsy attention. When she first joined the volunteer company Tom found reasons to come out and visit her in the trenches. The company was allowed to give its people a half-day back in the city each week and Ola spent her time at the hotel talking with Tom.

But something had been gnawing at her. She'd behaved so disgracefully after that first encounter with the Martians: crying, shaking, it had been a day before she could even get out of bed. Was she on this patrol to prove something? To whom? Not to Tom, obviously. To herself? Who else? She had no answer.

They were just finishing up their break and getting ready to move on when they heard the low rumble of aircraft engines. They froze in place as the noise got louder and louder. "What's that?" said someone.

"All those German planes that brought in supplies yesterday afternoon," said Drozda quietly. "Guess they're heading back out now that they're unloaded."

And indeed, a few moments later they spotted the shape of one of the large planes through the bare branches of the trees. She had only caught glimpses of them the day before. The wind was out of the west and so the planes had come into the city from the east, almost invisible from the trenches on the west side where Ola was. But today, they were taking off into that west wind and their path was taking them nearly overhead. They were big biplanes with two motors and the noise they made was almost deafening as they thundered close and then turned south. The familiar German cross was painted on the underside of the lower wings.

"Damn Germans," muttered Pietr Micka, Drozda's number two man.

"Those 'damn Germans' just brought supplies so we can hold Warsaw," snapped Ola.

"Quiet, both of you," snarled Drozda. Micka glared at Ola, but she ignored him and went back to watching the planes.

In ones and twos they roared past while the patrol watched them from their gully. Ola tried to count them, but only got up to around sixty before Drozda suddenly called out: "Down! Tripods! Down!"

Ola gasped and threw herself to the bottom of the ditch. All the others did the same. "Where? Where?" cried someone.

"Over there," said Drozda, pointing toward the northwest. Ola did not dare rise up to look, but after a moment she could hear the crunching and snapping of the huge machines pushing their way through the trees.

"Have they seen us?" asked Leslaw. "Should we run?"

Drozda held out his hand, motioning the others to wait. "No... no, I don't think so, they're not coming right toward us, they're heading toward the city. Three of them. About a hundred meters away... don't move."

Ola stayed where she was, but slowly squirmed around so she could look in the direction of the noise. The bank of the gully blocked the sight line, but after a moment she could see a few of the tree tops sway violently as something hit them. A few seconds later she saw the top of a tripod through a low spot in the bank. It was moving east, sunlight glistening off its metal skin. She held her breath, but the machine did not turn, it was moving away from them. She slowly let out her breath.

But then she and all the others jerked in alarm as three red beams of light shot skyward accompanied by that hideous buzz-saw shriek that the heat rays made. They were firing! But at what?

"The planes!" said Micka, much too loudly. "They're shooting at the planes!"

Ignoring her fear—and her good sense—Ola sat up and looked. There were the tripods, perhaps three hundred meters away, barely visible through the trees, and they were firing their heat rays skyward, at the German planes taking off.

As she watched, one of the rays swung over and tore through a plane, slicing it in two from front to back. The pieces, engines still running, spun away in different directions, trailing fire and smoke. A second plane was impaled on a spike of fire and simply exploded in a cloud of flame, smoke, and debris, which rained down burning like some hideous fireworks display.

The other planes tried to scatter, some turning back toward Warsaw, others diving low to the ground and fleeing as quickly as they could. One banked so sharply it lost control, turned over, and smashed into the ground without ever being touched by the alien weapons. Another plane turned to the right to avoid a collision and then foolishly turned back to the left to head south again and that brought it almost directly over the tripods. Two heat rays converged on it and it disintegrated.

One more, staying low, looked as though it would escape when a ray sliced off about half of its right wings. The left wing swung up sharply and Ola expected it to crash like the other one that lost control, but somehow the pilot recovered. The plane was now turning sharply to the right and in a moment it was headed right for her, smoke trailing from the burning wing stumps.

"Look out!" someone cried.

Ola instinctively ducked as the crippled plane roared over, barely a hundred meters off the ground. She whipped her head around to follow and saw it clip some of the treetops and then it disappeared into a cloud of smoke and spray of snow and tumbling branches, all accompanied by a horrendous noise of shattering tree trunks, ripping fabric, and disintegrating engines.

The silence that followed seemed to ring in her ears. Except it wasn't really silent. The Martians were still firing at the few remaining planes, but the shriek of the rays and drone of the engines seemed small and far away.

"God have mercy on them," gasped Ksenia Popek.

Ola was still staring at where the plane had crashed. There hadn't been any explosion and the smoke and spray quickly dispersed. Could any of the crew have survived? Without thinking, she was on her feet and headed in that direction.

"Ola, get down!" snapped Drozda.

"Some of those men could be alive," she called back. "We have to see!"

"Are you crazy?! Get down!"

But she was running now. Leslaw called after her and then started following. Looking back she saw Ksenia was coming, too, and then nearly everyone else. Drozda cursed but then said: "Come on! All of you!" The whole patrol was moving.

She followed the creek bed until it bent away from the direction she wanted to go and then she scrambled up the bank, slipping on the icy ground. Glancing back, she saw to her relief that the tripods were now out of sight, concealed by the trees. The noise was dying down; the heat rays gave a few final blasts and then were silent. The airplane engines faded in the distance.

She forced her way through the clinging underbrush, panting as she tried to run. Several of the men caught up and then passed her on either side. Drozda was one of them and he gave her a scathing glare.

They continued along, trudging rather than running through the snow. Looking ahead she couldn't really see anything but the trees. Where was the plane? It couldn't be that far away. Then she began to see shattered branches littering the snow and then scraps of gray fabric and then broken pieces of wood and wires that must have come from the plane. "There it is," said Drozda. Yes, she could see the wreck now, maybe fifty meters away.

In the collision with the trees, the trees had mostly won it seemed. A few of the smaller ones had snapped off, but the larger ones had helped tear the airplane apart. Both wings had been sheared off and the boxy engines flung in different directions. They lay smoking and steaming in the snow. The tail was wrapped around a large pine tree and the remains of the main body of the plane was crumpled up to about half its original length with the nose buried in a deep snow bank. There was a strong odor of petrol in the air, but fortunately, it had not caught fire.

"No one could have survived this," said Leslaw.

"We don't know that. Come on, look around," she replied.

"Look quickly," ordered Drozda. "We can't stay here long."

The patrol swarmed over the wreck and tearing away the shredded fabric, quickly found the bodies of four men. They were all horribly crushed and mangled and very dead. "Wasted trip," muttered Micka, looking at Ola.

She glared back at him. "We had to try. These men came here to help us and we couldn't just..."

"Hey! What's that?" cried Leslaw. He was pointing toward the front of the plane that was embedded in the snow. Something was sticking out of the snow. It looked like... "An arm! Someone's there!"

They quickly converged on the spot and shoveled the snow away with their hands. Yes, a man was there dressed in heavy leather flying gear. Ola gently tilted his head back. The lenses in his goggles were both cracked and blood dripped down his face from under the helmet but...

"He's alive!"

They swept away more snow, exposing the upper half of his body. There weren't any obvious injuries, but the man groaned when they moved him. Leslaw pointed to an insignia on the coat. "Hell, he's a colonel."

"I don't care if he's the Kaiser," said Drozda. "We need to get him—and us—out of here. Now!"

They shoveled more snow out of the little cockpit he was in and pulled, but he seemed to be pinned by the wreckage.

"What should we do?" asked Ksenia, her voice almost a wail.

"If we can't get him loose we'll have to leave him," said Drozda.

"We can't just..." began Ola, but her words were cut off by a sudden tearing crash. Looking back the way they'd come she saw the tripod. It was less than a hundred meters away and coming right at them. How could they have not heard it?

"Down! Down!" shouted Drozda.

Ola dove into the snow next to the German flier. Others hid themselves around the wreck. But two others, Micka and a man named Kocjanek, tried to run. They didn't get far. Struggling through the snow, they covered maybe thirty meters before the Martian was upon them. The heat ray stabbed out and both men exploded into flame and steam before they could even cry out. The snow around where they'd been erupted into a white cloud of vapor. It slowly boiled upward in the still air.

Ola crouched, as frozen as the snow around her. She scarcely dared breath, let alone move. The other members of the patrol were as still as her. The tripod was now standing just on the other side of the airplane facing in the direction of the two men it had annihilated; looking for more, perhaps. Its back was to her but how long before it turned around and found everyone? Found her?

She was as frightened as she'd ever been, but somehow she felt an anger, a rage starting to fill her. Just like when she was in that trench with the dead German boy in her arms, watching the artillery exploding around the tripods. *Hurt them! Hurt them!* Suddenly the only thing in the world she wanted was to hurt these monsters. Without even thinking, her hands had fumbled out the dynamite bomb in the satchel slung over her shoulder.

It was a simple weapon. A half-dozen sticks of dynamite tied in a bundle by a long rope with the two ends loose so it could be fastened around the leg of an alien machine. A small metal ring was attached to a friction fuse. Pull the ring and you had ten seconds before it exploded.

She got it ready and then glanced at Corporal Drozda. He was staring at her with incredibly wide eyes and shaking his head. No. *No what? Stay here like trapped animals until the thing found them and killed them like the others?* "No, dammit!"

She surged up out of the snow and ran forward. The tripod's rear leg was right by the wrecked body of the plane. They'd been told to place the bombs as high up on the tripod's leg as they could reach. That normally meant up by the 'ankle' joint. But if she got up on the wreckage...

She took five long strides forward and then jumped. She was on the body of the plane and then by scrambling up on the crumpled remains she was three meters above the ground and the 'knee' joint of the tripod's leg was there—*right there!*

Her whole world focused down to just the bomb and the leg. She whipped one end of the rope around the leg, tried to catch it, missed, and nearly fell. She tried again and this time caught it. She had it! With shaking hands she tied the bomb in place.

As she reached for the fuse-ring the Martian suddenly moved. She lunged outward, caught hold of the ring, and then she was falling. She plunged into the snow with an impact that knocked the wind out of her. But she could feel the ring in her hand! She burrowed down in the snow while counting in her head. *Four... five... six...*

Boom!

An enormous blow slammed down on her, knocking out whatever wind was still in her. Everything went black for a moment and then suddenly she was out of the snow, sprawling on her back with the huge metal machine right next to her.

It too, was on its back with its legs, arms, and long thin tentacles flailing madly around as it tried to right itself. But it was tangled in the wreckage of the plane and couldn't seem to get loose. Ola just looked at it, not moving, just lying there alone, but filled with elation. She had hurt them!

And suddenly she wasn't alone.

With a cry of *Poland!* The others were swarming out of their hiding places and crawling on the tripod. They were tying their bombs to the arms, legs, and neck of the monster. Drozda was screaming at them to wait with the fuses until they were all ready. The Martian, apparently realizing what was happening, fired off its heat ray, but it could not bring it to bear on the tiny figures crawling on it and only managed to shear off some of the trees, which blazed up like torches.

The tripod lurched and twisted and Ola saw poor Leslaw go flying. Drozda shouted: "Now!" Fuse rings were pulled, and the people scattered. Drozda jumped down next to Ola and dragged her a dozen meters away before throwing himself on top of her.

Boom! Boom! Boom!

Explosions hammered at her again and then there was silence. Drozda rolled off of her and they both painfully sat up. The remains of the Martian machine were all around them. An arm here, a leg over there, the arm with the heat ray way over there. The bulbous head was cracked open and smoke billowed out of it.

The others pulled themselves to their feet. Leslaw was cradling his arm, but grinning ear to ear. Drozda drew Ola up and then said: "Come on. We need to get out of here before the others show up. Come on, move!"

Drozda was right: they could hear the crack and splinter of trees in the distance; clearly the other Martians were coming to the assistance of their fallen comrade. The scouts started moving, but then Ola noticed that in the Martian's death throes it had upended the forward part of the plane and the German flier was no longer pinned; he was lying there in the snow. One leg was badly twisted and almost certainly broken, but when they checked, he was still alive.

Drozda wanted to leave him, but under Ola's cajoling, he hoisted him onto his back and started off. "Luckiest damn German alive," he muttered.

Carrying their burden, but filled with a grim satisfaction, the patrol stumbled deeper into the forest. They still needed to get back to Warsaw, but somehow Ola was sure they would make it.

Chapter Twelve

February 1914, Warsaw, Poland

Ola Wojciech peered through the last of the trees and the bare winter under-brush at the trench line in the distance. The sun was almost touching the horizon behind her and its level rays glinted off the taller buildings in Warsaw, barely visible beyond the defense lines. She had never felt so tired; worse than the most arduous day digging pit traps. All she wanted to do was sleep, but she couldn't, not yet.

"We need to keep moving," said Corporal Drozda. "We have to get inside the lines before dark or some trigger-happy twit will kill us by mistake." The other members of the squad groaned, but they knew he was right.

After destroying the Martian tripod they had moved as quickly as they could away from the scene of the fight. The other Martians were coming and they daren't let them catch up. This had forced them deeper into the woods and farther away from safety, but there was nothing for it: the enemy was between them and Warsaw. They had had to travel in a wide arc around to the south and then back east again; probably ten kilometers all told. They had dragged the Ger-man pilot and the injured Leslaw and eventually they were dragging themselves, but now here they were: a kilometer from home.

"Anyone see anything?" asked Drozda. "Any sign of those bastards?"

Ola and the rest of the squad turned their heads from side to side looking for danger. The tripods were fairly easy to spot, but there was always the risk of their hideous spider machines. They were smaller and could hide more easily, but they were just as deadly to a person in the open as the big machines. And even though there were no Martians inside them, they could somehow commu-nicate with the aliens and give the alarm. They'd very nearly blundered into one of them a few hours earlier, but luckily they had seen it first and managed to back away and escape. But there was nothing in sight now and everyone said so.

"All right, we'll take the chance. Everyone get ready and we'll make a dash for it." They had rigged up a makeshift stretcher for the German and their two strongest men were carrying it. Ola helped the hurting and increasingly le-thargic Leslaw to his feet. They moved up to the edge of the forest and paused there, like runners waiting for the starter's gun. Drozda waved his hand and they set out.

The day of full sunlight had partially melted the snow out in the open and as they slogged across, it soaked their boots and chilled their feet and made walking difficult. Ola was gasping and stumbling before she was even a third of the way across. Leslaw nearly fell several times and she had to help him stay on his feet. The stretcher bearers were also soon in need of help and Ksenia Popek grabbed one side of the stretcher to help.

Halfway across; the trench line was close. Ola looked back at the forest, expecting to see tripods in pursuit, but there was nothing. The sun was disappearing behind the trees and the sky darkening. Three hundred meters to the trenches, two hundred... She could hear some people shouting and she looked ahead to see several men on the parapet waving to them and several more sprinting out to help. They were going to make it...

Pow! Pow! Pow!

A crackle of rifle fire off to the left pulled a yelp from her gasping throat and she nearly threw herself to the ground. The firing grew and now it was to the right and then directly ahead. She looked around frantically, but saw nothing that could be a target. Then there were shouts and cries amidst the firing, but they sounded like cries of joy rather than fear or anger. What was going on?

A man appeared beside her and helped her half-carry Leslaw, while another helped with the stretcher. They went through a gap in the wire that had been strung to hinder the spider machines and then they fell into the forward trench among a crowd who had gathered. Some helped them, but most seemed to be caught up in some wild celebration that had broken out. Men were laughing and whooping and those with rifles were firing them in the air.

"What the hell's going on?" snarled Corporal Drozda. "We need a medic. Two medics! We've got an injured German here and another of our own men is hurt!" Only a few people were paying attention, but a man nodded and forced his way through the mob, presumably in search of a medic. Ola just slumped down in the mud and leaned against the wall of the trench, too worn out to do anything more.

The cheers and cries were growing even louder and now they took on a cadence: *Poland! Poland! Poland!* Ola looked to Drozda, but the man was as confused as she was. But the Corporal had more energy than she did and he grabbed a nearby reveler and physically dragged him down and shouted in his face: "What's happening? Damn you!"

The man was startled but then laughed. "Oh, you just got back! Right! You haven't heard."

"Heard what?"

"Sosnkowski! He did it!" Ola started to hear the name. Kazimierz Sosnkowski was a leading member of the Polish Nationalist Movement here in Warsaw.

"What? What did he do?" demanded Drozda.

"He's formed a provisional government! Declared Polish independence! Just heard about it a few minutes ago! We're free, man!" The fellow pulled away and grabbed a bottle of wine someone was passing around.

Ola just sat there. She ought to have been thrilled and a part of her was, but she was too tired to feel anything but her hurts and her fatigue. Leslaw was sitting next to her with a strange grin on his face. A bottle came her way and she took a long pull on it, not even sure what it was, but it burned going down and seemed to warm her. She helped Leslaw take a drink, as he couldn't use his broken arm at all. The bottle was snatched away and disappeared in the crowd.

It was completely dark by the time the medics arrived. Two German ones, who appropriated the injured pilot and carried him off, and a Polish one who looked at Leslaw's arm, fashioned a sling and then led him away. The rest of the patrol had revived enough to drift off in search of food. Ola groaned and stood up and prepared to follow.

"Not so fast, girl!" A strong hand grabbed the back of her coat and jerked her around. It was Corporal Drozda and he didn't look at all happy. "Don't think for one minute I've forgotten what happened out there. You got two of my men killed and you are going to answer for it! Now come on!"

He dragged her into one of the communication trenches and hustled her to the rear. They were quite some distance from where their company was stationed, and Drozda pushed her through a bewildering maze of trenches. They passed through areas held by German troops and they were all eerily silent compared to the celebrating Poles. They finally arrived in their company area and all the people there were celebrating, although it had calmed down a bit from what she'd seen at first. Drozda took her to the dugout where the company commander had his headquarters, but there was just a single man sitting there.

"Where is Captain Ostrowski?" asked Drozda.

The man grinned and shrugged. "He's up at the battalion headquarters. I think. You wouldn't have anything to drink would you, Corporal?" Drozda cursed and pulled Ola into another trench heading toward the rear. She could barely walk by this point, and she was so tired that Drozda's dire threat of 'answering for it' scarcely made any impression on her. Still, the memory of the death of the two men had been nagging at the back of her mind all day. Was that her fault? She supposed that maybe it was. Maybe.

After a hundred meters or so the bottom of the trench sloped up to ground level and they were in the suburbs of the city. She was steered to a small house—headquarters, apparently. There was a sentry with a bottle at the door, but he made no effort to stop them and they walked right in. Ola blinked in the brightly lit entrance hall. There was a room to the left that looked to be an office. The battalion commander's? She was trying to remember the man's name. To the right there was a room which must have been the parlor. Four men were in there, seated on some worn and shabby furniture. There were several bottles on a table along with bread, cheese, and sausage. Ola's mouth was suddenly watering. How long since she'd last eaten?

The men looked up at their entrance. She recognized Captain Ostrowski, but the others were strangers. Ostrowski looked at them in surprise. "Drozda! Glad you made it back. But what's this? Your report could have waited until tomorrow, you know."

Drozda pushed Ola forward. "Sorry, sir. But this couldn't wait. I have a serious disciplinary problem."

"With her, Corporal?" said one of the other men. "How serious could it be?" He and the other two men laughed.

"I'm afraid so, Major," answered Drozda. "She disobeyed orders and got two of my men killed today."

The smiles vanished. "That's a very serious charge, Corporal," said the man. The major? The battalion commander?

"What happened?" asked Captain Ostrowski.

"We were out on our scouting mission today, as you know. We saw the Martians when they attacked those German planes taking off. One of them crashed near us. I ordered the patrol to stay down and hidden, but this girl insisted that we had to go look for survivors. I *ordered* her to stay put, but she ran off anyway. Several others followed and rather than have the patrol split, I went along with the rest. We found the wreck, and everyone was dead except for one German who was pinned in the wreckage. We couldn't get him loose right away and I ordered everyone to get away before the Martians came. But she wouldn't! Insisted that we try to free him. And then a tripod showed up. Just right there, before we could do anything. We tried to hide in the wreckage of the plane, but two of my men tried to run and the Martian killed them both! Just burned them up! Two good men were killed because of her!" Drozda ran out of breath and glared at her.

Ostrowski was staring at her. "This true, girl?"

"I... I, uh, I guess it is, sir." She couldn't think of anything else to say.

"This is a very serious charge. What's your name?"

"Ola, sir, Ola Wojciech."

"Well, Ola, I'm afraid you are in trouble. Corporal take her back to your company and hold her there until..."

"Just a moment, Captain," said one of the other men.

"Sir?"

"Miss Wojciech, I have a question for you."

Who was this man? Not the battalion commander. Someone higher up? "Yes, sir?"

"How did you get away? Seems like half the story is missing."

She was so tired. Her head felt like it was wrapped in wool. "Uh, well, after we destroyed the tripod we..."

"What?!" Four voices all shouted the same word, almost in unison. Ola stepped back and nearly fell.

"You destroyed the tripod?" said the same man. "How?"

Ola swayed. This was too much. "Can... can I sit down, sir?"

In a blink she was in a chair with a glass of wine in her shaking hand. She took a drink and tried to compose herself. "Do go on, Miss Wojciech," said the man.

"A-after the tripod surprised us and killed Micka and Kocjanek, it was standing there with its back to me and I..." She went on with a quivering voice to describe the fight, the rescue of the German, and the trip back to Warsaw. When she was finished she drained the glass of wine and leaned against the back of the chair, totally spent.

"Is that how it was, Corporal?" asked the man.

Drozda looked from man to man. He looked as deflated as Ola felt. Finally he said, "Pretty much, sir. But if she'd just stayed put like I said, no one would have gotten hurt!"

"Thank you, Corporal, that will be all."

"But..."

"That *will* be all, Corporal."

Drozda looked imploringly at Captain Ostrowski, but the Captain just shook his head and gestured at the Corporal to leave. Drozda gave Ola one more scathing look and then stomped out. Ostrowski looked to the other three but they were all smiling and after a moment they began to chuckle.

"He actually wanted her *punished*!" snorted the fourth man, the first time he'd spoken.

"She did disobey orders..." began Ostrowski. "She got two men killed..."

"They died for Poland, Captain," said the third man, the one who'd been questioning her. He turned to the others. "Who says God doesn't love Poland? He's already given us two miracles today: a government and a leader. And now He gives us a third! A hero!"

"I... I don't understand, sir," said Ostrowski.

I don't either! said Ola to herself.

"He's given us a hero to rally around!" The man got up from his chair and came over to Ola and held out his hand. "Come, Miss Wojciech, there are some people I want you to meet."

* * * * *

February 1914, Warsaw, Poland

Colonel Erich Serno groaned and opened his eyes and then squinted against the light. There was an incandescent bulb hanging almost directly over his bed and it was much too bright. He looked to the side and opened his eyes wider. Yes, he was still here. In a German military hospital in Warsaw. He had no memory of how he got here. The last thing he remembered was the Martians ambushing the Group as they took off... heat rays... planes exploding... his own plane getting hit... a forest rushing up to swat him. After that... nothing until he woke up here.

That was two... no, three days ago. A doctor had told him that he had a compound fracture of his left leg, a couple of cracked ribs, and a concussion. He supposed he should feel lucky to be alive, but with all the pain, it was hard to feel grateful. Inquiries about the losses to his Group had gone unanswered and questions about when he could get out of the hospital and out of Warsaw had also been deflected or ignored. The large cast encasing his leg made it pretty plain he wasn't going anywhere for a while.

He squirmed around in the bed trying to get comfortable. He usually slept lying on his side but the cast made that impossible. He was still squirming when an orderly approached leading two people. Serno's eyes widened when he realized that one of them was a young woman and the other was wearing a military overcoat and cap which were definitely not German. British he thought.

"Colonel? Colonel? Are you awake?" asked the orderly. Stupid question. If he wasn't awake how could he answer?

"Yes?" he muttered.

"I am sorry to disturb you, but these people wanted to see you."

"Why?" He'd never seen either of them before. The woman was in Polish civilian dress and the only English officer he knew was that maniac Lawrence and this man wasn't him.

"I don't know, sir," answered the orderly. "But the Englishman has a letter from Headquarters instructing the hospital staff to give him our full cooperation. He and the woman wish to speak with you."

Coming fully awake, Serno looked more closely at the pair. The Englishman looked to be in his late 30s, largish nose and the inevitable mustache. He couldn't tell his rank because of the overcoat, but he must have some pull if he had that letter ordering cooperation. The woman was young, not much more than a girl. Rather cute, but with very serious eyes. Eyes that were staring right at him.

"All right," he said. "Help me sit up so I can talk to them."

The orderly found another pillow and helped Serno up enough to cram it in behind him. Not vertical, but enough. "Do they speak German?"

"No sir, French. Do you speak it?"

"Not very well…"

"It's all right, sir, I can translate."

"Good. Ask them what they want." The orderly spoke for a moment and the Englishman replied. Serno tried to follow with his limited command of the language, but it was hopeless and he gave up. His head was starting to hurt again.

The orderly turned back to him, looking a bit surprised. "He says… uh, he says that it was the woman who rescued you from your plane crash. She wanted to find out how you were doing and the Englishman is helping her."

Serno twitched in surprise. *She* rescued him? All by herself? "Uh… how… how did she manage that?"

The orderly passed on the question and the woman suddenly became animated and spewed out a long string of French accompanied by frequent hand gestures. The orderly put out his own hands to try and slow her down. Eventually she finished and looked at Serno with a tiny smile.

"She says… as near as I can make out," said the orderly, "that she was out on a scouting mission with some other Polish volunteers and they saw your plane crash. They tried to pull you out of the wreck but you were stuck. A Martian tripod came to investigate the wreck and they destroyed it—sorry, sir, that's what she claims—and after that they got you free and carried you back to Warsaw."

"Just like that, huh?" said Serno. The orderly shrugged.

"Did she—they—find any more of my men?" The orderly asked, but she shook her head sadly.

Serno frowned. "What's he want?" he asked, nodding his head toward the Englishman.

The orderly exchanged a few words with him and then turned back to Serno. "He says he's a friend of the woman. And he confirms that a tripod was destroyed."

Serno just stared at the pair for a while, unsure what to say. He finally decided on "Thank you." The orderly passed that on, although it was hardly necessary. The woman chattered some more and then started to step away.

"She says that you are welcome and she hopes you recover quickly," translated the orderly who then led the two out.

Serno continued to stare at the space where they had been but finally said: "Well, that's damn peculiar." Then he resumed trying to find a comfortable position in the bed so he could get back to sleep.

* * * * *

February 1914, Warsaw, Poland

Tom Bridges looked at Ola as they made their way out of the sprawling German Army hospital. She had seemed very depressed when she'd come to him for help in getting in here, but now she seemed to have been perked up by her visit with the German airman. The Germans—all of them, from the headquarters where he'd gotten permission to come, to the hospital administrator, to the orderly, to the patient—had seemed rather confused by the whole thing, but if it made Ola happy, he supposed it was worth it.

He was still a bit confused himself. He had not been happy when Ola had managed to talk her way into serving with a front line volunteer company. He'd been pulling every string he could get hold of to find her a job that was important enough to satisfy her insatiable desire to serve, but that was also as safe as could be found in a besieged city. All for naught. Still, the Martians were not making any real effort to attack the city, so it had not seemed too terribly dangerous to Bridges.

But then two days ago—right in the midst of all the hullabaloo about the Polish declaring their independence—he discovered that Ola had not been tucked away in a nice deep trench. Instead, she'd been out in enemy territory on a scouting mission and not only had she rescued a German flier, but she'd destroyed a Martian tripod and was now some sort of Polish national hero!

He had not been happy.

He told himself it really wasn't any of his business what she did. She was a Pole and this was her country she was trying to defend. These days everyone had to take risks. But the thought of her being hurt or killed was an increasingly heavy weight on his heart. He liked her. He liked her a lot. And somehow he found her plain prettiness more attractive than the dazzling ladies of the Tsar's court.

He'd been married once. To a fine English girl named Molly. Married just two years when he'd been sent off to that stupid war with the Boers down in South Africa. He'd been there when the Martians dropped out of the sky onto the peaceful British countryside. Molly hadn't been killed in the fighting, but the Martians had killed her all the same. Hundreds of thousands of people had been uprooted by the first invasion and many had been crowded together in refugee camps, even in the Midlands where Molly was. Disease had inevitably broken out and Molly had died in a cholera epidemic. Bridges had come home a widower. He'd never looked seriously at another woman since then.

Until now.

Are you falling in love with this girl, you idiot?

Uh... maybe?

It was not the right time or place, he told himself. That was certainly true. But still...

"It seems like he will recover, don't you think?" asked Ola, startling him out of his reverie.

"Who?"

"The German! Colonel Serno! Who did you think I was talking about?" laughed Ola.

"Oh, him. Yes, if he doesn't come down with pneumonia lying in that bed for too long."

"I hope that doesn't happen!"

"Not after all the work you did to bring him back. That would be a shame."

A few flakes of snow were swirling down on Warsaw's streets as they walked along. They skirted around a long line of people queued up to collect their bread ration. He could hear a rumble of artillery off to the north. The German gunners were under strict orders to only fire at a good target to conserve ammunition, so he wondered what they were shooting at. "What are you going to do now?" he asked her. "I understand you won't be going back to your company."

"No. I'm sure Corporal Drozda will be relieved! I guess the new government wants to make me some sort of symbol. To help recruiting and all."

"Like that poster they have of old Kitchener back in England. 'Your Country Needs You!' and all that. Well, you're a lot prettier than him! I'll bet thousands of young lads will be flocking to the colors."

Ola laughed, but then became serious. "Tom, what do you think of this declaration of our independence? The new government and all? You've traveled all over the world and seen how a lot of governments work. Can we make this stick do you think?"

"I can't really say. But I must say that this Sosnkowski of yours is clever. By doing it here and now he's put the Germans into a real bind. They can't try to snuff it out and risk some sort of backlash. With Warsaw under siege the last thing they need is an uprising in the midst of their garrison here. That could be a disaster. So they'll probably wait and see what happens. With any luck—for you—that could turn into a fait accompli."

"Wanda, my, uh, friend, says we desperately need foreign recognition," said Ola. "Do you think England will recognize us?"

"Again, I don't know. I'm sure there are factions who want to, but they can't risk offending the Germans, either. So far, the only official recognition that we know about comes from Russia. And clearly they are just doing that to make trouble for the Germans. They probably think they will never get back control of Poland so they want to make things as difficult for the Germans as they can—assuming the Martians don't end up in control of all this anyway."

"That would be the worst possible outcome," said Ola, nodding. "Do you think we can drive the Martians out, Tom? We keep hearing rumors about a counteroffensive, but never anything definite. Will help come?"

Bridges frowned and sucked on his teeth. Communication between Warsaw and London was difficult and entirely in the hands of the Germans. His superiors were not going to put any sensitive information in a message the Germans would see, so he had no definite word on anything. There had been public declarations of support being sent from many different countries, including England and France. But no specifics. No time tables. "I wish I had a definite answer for you, Ola, but I don't. I'm sure help is coming, but all we can do is hope it gets here before... before it's too late."

"Then we will hold Warsaw until they get here," said Ola firmly. She suddenly reached over and took his hand and squeezed. "We *will* hold Warsaw! To the last!"

He squeezed back. "Yes, to the last."

* * * * *

Subcontinent 1-1, Sector 147-29, Cycle 597,845.9

Lutnaptinav activated the communicator and waited attentively for the new orders it had been informed were coming. Nabutangula, the commander of the Group 13 contingent was also tied in. Whatever was coming would affect both battlegroups. A moment later the screen came to life and they were addressed by Mandapravis, the commander of the entire region.

"There have been new developments in the strategic situation," it began without preamble. "As you know, the prey creature forces trapped against the southern mountains continue to resist our efforts to eradicate them. In addition, new enemy forces have arrived from the west, blocking our attempts to make raids against their industrial infrastructure. The current situation has devolved into a stalemate.

"Orbital observations have now detected a large water-born force moving through the inland sea to the southeast. We believe it is preparing to land in Sector 239 and drive to the northwest, perhaps attempting to cut off our forces farther to the south. Our satellite has also observed the assembly of a similar force along the coast of the large island that was the location of our initial scouting expedition. We do not know where it will be committed, but there is a distinct possibility that it will enter the small inland sea to your north. If this happens a counterattack in your area is a distinct possibility.

"If this were to happen it seems likely the enemy will attempt to link up with the prey-creature forces in the city you are observing. From there it would constitute a serious threat to our other forces in this region. It has therefore been decided that the city must be eliminated so that it cannot be used as a base against us."

"Commander," said Nabutangula, "We do not here possess the force to..."

"We are aware of that," said Mandapravis, its irritation at being interrupted plain. "Three battlegroups will be detached from our main force and sent to reinforce the effort. Ubstantinav will assume overall command when it arrives in three or four rotations. Until then you shall both increase your probes of the city's defenses. Find the weak spots so that a major attack can be launched as soon as the reinforcements arrive. Is this understood?"

"Yes, Commander," replied both in unison.

"Very well. Carry out your orders." Mandapravis cut the connection. The circuit between Lutnaptinav and Nabutangula remained open.

"What is your evaluation?" asked Nabutangula.

"Things are not going well."

"Obviously! Do you have a recommendation for our next actions?"

"Tactically or strategically?"

A lengthy silence ensued before Nabutangula replied, "For the moment, I think it wise to confine it to the tactical."

"Agreed. We should institute a series of probes around the perimeter and measure the prey-creature response. Based on those results we can launch heavier attacks at the more promising points. By the time Ubstantinav arrives we should have the data we need to plan the main attack."

"Very good. I suggest we begin tonight. Perhaps we can force the enemy to expend the bulk of its artificial illumination munitions with our probes. That would make things easier for the main assault."

"Perhaps. In any case, yes, let us begin tonight."

The connection was broken and Lutnaptinav alerted its subordinates of the new situation. They took the new instructions without comment, but it wondered if they realized how serious the situation was becoming?

Chapter Thirteen

March 1914, The Black Sea

Harry Calloway lowered his binoculars and wiped the water off the lenses. For the past two days, a cold rain had been coming down off the Ukrainian plains to the north where it was still winter. It had seemed during the voyage north from the Bosporus that the armada was bringing spring along with it. The weather had been sunny and pleasant and the men lounged on the decks watching the gulls that wheeled above the ships. Even the week they'd spent milling around off the coast of Crimea while the ships refilled their fuel bunkers from the colliers and tankers that accompanied them had been nice. But then they had turned west and followed the coast to where they were now, the mouth of the Dneister River, and with every mile spring faltered and winter reasserted itself. The winds had turned cold and the sun hid behind the clouds more and more, and often those clouds spilled a cold rain or even sleet on them. The overcoats they'd been ordered to pack and been pulled out and gratefully put on.

"What do you think, Burf?" Harry asked. "Think it will be our turn to-day?"

Burford Sampson, shrugged. "Who knows? So far they've sent gunboats and cavalry and some of those French *Tirailleurs* and *Goumiers* up the river. All light scouting forces. But if they want any real fighting done, they'll need the Yank ironclads and the heavy artillery—and us. Can't see them waiting much longer to get us on those barges—assuming they can find enough of them."

"Well, I hope it's soon. The boys are getting tired of sitting here on this boat in the rain."

"Oh, they'd rather be on a much smaller and far less comfortable boat in the rain?" asked Burf with a smirk.

"You know what I mean! They sent us here to do a job and I wish they'd let us do it!" Burf just cocked an eyebrow and went inside. Harry stayed a while longer, peering through the mist at the anchored fleet.

At least they finally knew what they were going to do. The rumors about Crimea and the Danube had turned out to be wrong. The rumors about the Germans suffering a disaster in Poland had turned out to be all too true. The bulk of their army was trapped up against the mountains west of the city of Lemburg and they were screaming for help. A surprising amount of help was coming, from a surprising number of places. Nearly every country in Europe was sending troops and ships to the fight. People were finally realizing that everyone needed to pitch in if they were going to win. The multi-national force which had saved Istanbul the previous year had been a good start, but this current outpouring far outdid it. All the signs pointed to a decisive battle in Central Europe shaping up in the next few weeks or months and it looked like the 1st Australian Armored Division—and Harry—might well end up in the thick of it.

New rumors were flying about a major British expedition through the Baltic and heading southeast. The idea was that the southern force—this force—would head northwest and meet them… somewhere. Looking at a map, it was almost eight hundred miles in a straight line from the mouth of the Dniester to the mouth of the Vistula on the Baltic and a lot longer by the paths the rivers actually followed. Harry had no idea how long it would take to link up—if such a thing was even possible. It seemed odd to him that such information was flying about so openly. Military plans were supposed to be secret, weren't they? But in this war every human was an ally of every other, at least in theory. The Martians had made no attempt to ever try and communicate with humans. Humans had made a great many attempts to communicate with the aliens but with no success—unless you believed that *other* rumor that the American had a captive Martian who they were able to talk to. Whatever the case, the high commands didn't seem worried that their plans would fall into the hands of the enemy.

Harry took up his binoculars again, only one lens of which he could use—perhaps he should get a telescope instead—and swept his gaze around to look at the fleet. Most of the ships were riding at anchor, old battleships, cruisers, and lots and lots of transports. A swarm of destroyers and torpedo boats prowled around the edges of the formation. What they were on the lookout for, Harry didn't know. Several cargo ships were moving through the narrow passage that led from the sea into the lake that lay at the mouth of the river. The lake was twenty-five miles long and about five wide and made a magnificent harbor. But with the possibility of tripods appearing along the shores, the ships were prudently staying outside unless they were unloading.

The river was only navigable to the town of Soroca about a hundred and fifty miles upriver, but a hundred and fifty miles by water was a hundred and fifty miles less wear and tear on their vehicles. Still, the river wasn't deep enough for big ships. The fleet had brought some barges that had a shallow enough draft to move up the river, but not nearly enough for the whole army. The navy had been scouring the whole Black Sea coast—even parts ostensibly under Martian control—looking for more. They were finding them, but not terribly fast. No one could say when Harry's unit would be able to go.

Swinging the glasses north, he could just catch a glimpse of the ruins of Odessa about twenty miles to the north. The Martians had taken and razed the place several years earlier. On their journey west along the Black Sea coast they had caught sight of a few Martian machines from time to time and the cavalry they had landed reported others, but they seemed to be just scouts, spying on the armada's actions. No opposition had developed yet, although the warships had fired some pot shots but with no luck. The rain, which had let up a bit, now came down again harder than ever. Harry sighed and went inside to dry out and get some tea.

Two days later the sun was out and orders had arrived. The armored division was to move inland. It took another two days to load everything onto barges and small streamers. Several ships were mounted with large cranes that swayed the tanks and Ragland carriers up out of the holds and down onto the barges. The men had seen all their stuff loaded on to the transports in Alexandria, but with proper piers and land-mounted cranes it had seemed very routine. Now, with the transports, cranes, and barges all bobbing up and down with the waves, it seemed far more precarious. Harry held his breath as his own company's vehicles were being transferred. But the men running the things knew their jobs and it was accomplished with no serious mishaps.

Harry and his men were placed on a steamer, a Greek vessel named *Hygeia* that was towing a half-dozen of the barges. It was very cramped and most of the men had to sleep on the decks. They rigged up makeshift awnings to protect them from any rain that might come along. The temperature was rising with the sun and the men's spirits were rising with it. At last they were going to get moving.

The next day they started up the river. To Harry's satisfaction, they were led by the American land ironclads. Looking through his glasses he spotted the *Yellowstone*, the ironclad which had saved the battalion during the fighting along the Dardanelles. The men wanted to give it a cheer, but it was too far ahead to hear them.

The Dniester was not terribly broad and the vessels proceeded single file against the sluggish current. The western (or was it the southern?) shore was significantly hillier than the eastern bank and sometimes tall bluffs came nearly up to the water's edge. To the east the land was mostly flat with fields and forests rolling away toward the Steppes. Except for cavalry patrols, both shores were deserted with only the blackened ruins of villages and towns to mark the spots where humans once lived. There was still some snow in shady patches, but it was clear that the spring melt was beginning. At least it was down here by the sea, they expected to find more snow as they went inland. Harry spotted a few patches of that damn red weed the Martians had brought to Earth. If something wasn't done, the bloody stuff would be everywhere.

At the slow pace the ironclads and the barges could make, along with the winding path of the river, it was going to take three days to reach Soroca and that assumed they didn't encounter any Martian opposition along the way. Harry couldn't help but think about how the Martians had stopped the Allied fleet cold at the Dardanelles the previous year. The navies couldn't get past the super heat ray positions along the narrow passage—until the army took them out from the rear. Well, if they tried that again here, the army would just deal with it again.

But during that whole first day there was neither sight nor sound of the enemy. When darkness fell, the ships anchored as best they could, the ironclads simply rolling up on the shore. They could have continued, but the cavalry and armored cars that were scouting along the shores in tandem, had to stop and rest and the ships did not want to leave them behind and risk sailing into an ambush in the dark.

They continued the next dawn which was gray and gloomy as a new wave of clouds rolled in. Soon it was raining again and the men were upset when they discovered the awnings they had rigged were by no means waterproof. Harry and the officers ruthlessly seized the few spots that were relatively dry.

"Well, this isn't much fun," he grumbled to Burford Sampson.

"Could be worse," replied Sampson.

"Really? How?"

"Could be snow."

"I don't know, I've never seen snow close up; just white patches up on mountains. I doubt any of the boys have either. They'd probably like it."

Sampson shrugged. "Maybe. But I actually meant that the rain works to our advantage. If it raises the river level we might be able to press even farther up the river before we have to get off."

"I hadn't thought of that. But snow would work for that, too, wouldn't it?"

"I guess it would. But you might get your wish, I think it's getting colder."

By late afternoon the rain turned to sleet, which was simply miserable, but a little while later it was indeed snowing. Hard. Harry, and most of the men, were delighted, at least at first. They shouted and jumped and were soon scraping it up to make snowballs which they hurled at each with great enthusiasm. But after dark their glee faded and soon they were just cold and very wet. It was more than uncomfortable, it was downright dangerous, especially for men who had never experienced this sort of thing before. They started rotating the men below to any interior space on the *Hygeia* they could find, even the engine room, to let them warm up. The men still on deck stamped their feet and huddled around the fires that had been built in empty oil drums. After a while they set details to work sweeping the snow off the decks, which had become ankle deep in spots. No one got much sleep. By dawn the snow had mostly stopped and a thin, watery sunlight started to penetrate the clouds. The shivering men grumpily tried to make breakfast, many vowing they never wanted to see snow again.

They had only been underway an hour or so when something new caught their attention. Off to the northwest there was a faint rumble. Not thunder, artillery. Their scouting forces must have run into something. Messages sent by blinker lights started coming down the line of ships from the vanguard. Harry couldn't read them, but Sampson could; the older man had a seemingly endless store of skills and abilities. "What do they say?" Harry asked.

"As near as I can make out, the scouts have found a Martian fortress, maybe ten miles north of the river, and about twenty miles upstream of where we are. There don't seem to be many tripods guarding it, but of course they can't get close enough to see what might be inside."

No, that was true. The Martians built fortresses everywhere they went to secure territory they had conquered and to act as bases of operation for future conquests. They had factories inside them to build tripods and other machines and they were all very well defended. The designs were almost always the same. They scraped a circular areas about three miles across down to a flat plain of bedrock. All the dirt and rock from that area was pushed into a rampart of sorts about forty feet high. The outward face was steep and fused solid by their heat rays. It was impassible to vehicles and very difficult to climb for infantry. They had heat ray positions all along the top of the ring. They were a very, *very* tough nut to crack. No one had ever managed to take one until the Americans, using their land ironclads, had done so in their country. They had repeated the feat a number of times as they pushed the Martians back across the Great Plains to the Rocky Mountains. But recent news said that the Martian fortresses were now mounting the super heat rays and their blue bomb launchers.

"Well, thankfully it's far enough from the river that it won't stop us from getting past," said Harry.

Sampson stared at the blinking lights a while longer before replying. "Not so sure. Says the fleet is to stop about ten miles further upriver and then all brigade and regimental commanders are to report to the flagship."

"Huh. Wonder what the general is planning now?"

"I'm sure we'll find out."

They steamed on for another couple of hours and then they saw the ships and ironclads bunched up ahead and their own slowed to a stop and dropped anchor. Through his glasses Harry saw some tents on the shore and a cluster of cavalry and armored cars—easy to spot against the snow-covered fields. Small boats were leaving ships and moving toward the camp. Some motor cars came scurrying up the river carrying more people, probably officers in the following ships, Harry supposed. The troops were lining the rails watching this and each had his own opinion about what was going on.

But nothing happened for a good long while and the men eventually went back to the business of trying to dry out their uniforms and stay warm. It wasn't until nearly dark when boats started shoving off from the shore and heading back to the ships. Even then it was another hour before Colonel Berwick climbed aboard Harry's ship. "Hello, gentlemen," he said, appearing to be in a good mood, "hope you are enjoying the lovely weather. If all the officers would join me inside, I have some information I want to share."

There was nothing like a meeting room or even an officers' mess aboard the *Hygeia*, and they ended up crowded into the galley and spilled out into the corridors beyond. The Colonel made sure all the company commanders were close to him while the lieutenants had to make do as best they could. When everyone was settled, he began.

"Well, I know you and your men have been itching for some action and we are finally going to get it. Make sure you pass on my admiration to the rank and file. As some of you may have heard, our scouts have discovered a Martian fortress not too far away. The General had decided that he doesn't want to leave such a powerful post in our rear. So…" He paused and ran his eyes over the officers. "We are going to take the place. We will start off-loading the vehicles and men first thing tomorrow morning. So, pass the word and make all your preparations tonight. I won't try to deceive you by saying this will be easy, but the General believes—and so do I—that we have the power here to do the job. All right, that's all. Get to it, and may God be with us."

* * * * *

March 1914, The North Sea

Professor Frederick Lindemann clutched the rail of *HMS Implacable* and tried not to vomit his breakfast into the roiling gray waters below him. God, but he *hated* sea travel! Cross-Channel ferries were bad enough, but the North Sea was an entirely new experience and he did not like it one bit. A strong wind was blowing from the north and whipping up waves ten or fifteen feet high. The new land ironclads, though far more seaworthy than their American counterparts, were not really meant for conditions like this. They pitched and rolled and yawed in the most alarming fashion—which did terrible things to Lindemann's stomach. The veteran seamen aboard seemed to think the outlandish amphibians were doing quite well, but Lindemann could not agree.

Looking back, he could see the other five ironclads in the squadron trailing along in a line. With the Royal Navy's love for alliterative ship names, they had been christened *Impregnable, Impulsive, Impressive, Imperial,* and *Impeccable*. This had led to the wags dubbing the whole group the 'Impossible Class'.

The name was actually quite appropriate, because it had seemed impossible that they could have gotten ready so quickly. The idea that Gresley, the Armstrong engineer, had to combine the training of the crews with the construction of the vessels had worked brilliantly and cut at least a month from the time needed to get them ready for this expedition. Not that they *were* completely ready. Construction crews were still aboard all six ships; he could see the glare of electric arc welders on several of them right now.

But the desperate plight of the Germans had spurred the Government to launch this expedition at the earliest possible moment. Looking into the distance, Lindemann saw some of the other ships carrying the troops and tanks and artillery of the army along with the supplies to keep them in action. Only a few warships were in evidence as the Germans would be providing what was needed in the Baltic.

Lindemann had been quite proud of his role in getting the ironclads ready in time and he felt that it was quite unfair that he'd been 'rewarded' by being sent off with them! It had been totally unexpected and he'd been gobsmacked when Churchill told him. It seemed that the Duke of York, young Bertie, had decided he wanted to see some action. Or perhaps it was his father, the King, who had wanted that, the story was a bit garbled. Whatever the case, Bertie was going off to war and he needed some sort of guardian to keep him out of trouble.

A serving naval officer would have made a much more logical choice (and Lindemann had argued this forcefully) but dear Bertie had apparently convinced his father that Lindemann (who he had taken quite a shine to) would be the perfect choice. Churchill had tried to convince him that this would also allow him to give a more complete report on how the ironclads performed in action. When it was clear that Lindemann wasn't buying it, Churchill had taken him aside and said that if he relented and brought Bertie home alive there could be some much more substantial reward in the offing. A title of nobility? Such things *were* done for exceptional service. Churchill wasn't saying it specifically, but that was the implication. Between the carrot and the stick, here he was.

"R-really grand, is-isn't it, Professor?"

Looking to his right, Lindemann saw that his charge was on deck beside him. Bertie's cheeks were flushed and his eyes gleaming. "The sea, the sh-ships, g-going off to smash the b-bloody M-martians. Grand!"

"Yes, grand," muttered Lindemann, looking down again.

"Buck up, Professor!" said a new voice. "Only another day or so and we'll be in the Baltic. Much calmer there, I would wager." Lindemann looked and yes, it was Kipling. Just as Bertie had done, Kipling had used his influence to come along to represent the press. *I need more influence,* thought Lindemann glumly.

"We'll be using the G-German's K-kiel -canal, won't we, sir?" asked Bertie.

"Indeed. That will cut off that whole dreary sail around Denmark and the Skagerrak. Save us a day or two. And from what we're hearing, every minute counts."

"I g-guess the G-Germans are having a hard time of it, aren't t-they?"

"They are still holding along the Carpathian Mountains, from last we've heard," replied Kipling. "And it's said that our Southern Force will be going into action very shortly in Moldavia. That might take some pressure off the Germans."

Lindemann looked up at that. This was more than he'd heard, but Kipling had many sources of information. "And w-we're heading for the Vistula R-River?" asked Bertie.

"I believe that's the plan. Sail up the river as far as we can and relieve Warsaw. From there I don't think anyone knows what will happen. Depends a great deal on how the Martians react, I expect. But for right now, Sub-lieutenant, why don't you give me a tour of this great contraption? I only got a brief look at it during our first visit to the yards and not much more since I came aboard yesterday."

"Love to, sir!" said Bertie, clearly delighted. "B-but it's *l-lieutenant* now, sir. I've been promoted."

"Jolly good!" exclaimed Kipling. "Congratulations! Well, let's be about it, shall we? See you later, Professor."

Lindemann watched them walk away, Bertie pointing out items of interest on the *Implacable*. After a few minutes he felt a bit better and his breakfast seemed like it was going to stay put. He turned and staggered down to the tiny compartment he shared with Bertie. The ironclads were unbelievably cramped and he didn't even have a bunk, just a hammock, like some common rating. He managed to climb into it without spilling himself on the deck and tried to sleep. He stayed there most of the day, missing the midday meal and only crawling out for a few bites of dinner with his two companions. Bertie had spent many days at sea during his midshipman training and Kipling had sailed all over the world and neither of them was bothered by the rolling of the ship—*lucky bastards*.

He slept fitfully through the night, but by morning the ship was far more steady and Lindemann felt much better. Coming up on deck he saw the reason for the calmer seas. They were nearing the entrance to the Kiel Canal and it was protected by the estuary of the Elbe River. It was also protected by some substantial fortresses mounting heavy guns. The Germans had built the canal ostensibly to shorten the journey for merchant traffic from the North Sea to the Baltic, but everyone knew that it was really to allow the Kaiser's High Seas Fleet to get out into the North Sea without traversing the narrow Skagerrak which was in Danish and Norwegian territorial waters and easily blocked by mines. Lindemann was certain the Kaiser never imagined his canal being used to let British forces *into* the Baltic, but the arrival of the Martians had changed everything.

The passage of the canal took ten hours and the fleet gathered around the far end to allow the other ships to catch up. There was a substantial force of German warships waiting there for them, including a dozen dreadnoughts and battlecruisers. The British naval escort was made up by a handful of old cruisers and destroyers and some gunboats and monitors with shallow drafts which could accompany them up the Vistula. They made a rather weak showing compared to the Germans.

The sun was dipping in the west when there was a sudden blast of steam whistles from the warships. Signal flags broke out on the masts and blinker lights began flashing in every direction. The German ships started weighing anchor and black smoke billowed up from funnels. "What's h-happening?" asked Bertie. "I th-thought we were going to wait here until all the s-ships were through the c-canal."

"So did I," said Lindemann. "There must have been some change in plans."

"Wonder why?" mused Kipling. "Well, let's go find out. The Commodore must surely know."

Lindemann would have waited for information to filter down to him but the newspaperman Kipling wasn't going to wait. He bulled his way through to Commodore Goodenough, commander of the ironclad squadron, in short order. Goodenough looked busy, but he spared a moment for Kipling's question.

"Orders from the Admiral to get under way at once and make our best speed."

"Why?" asked Kipling. "Has something happened?"

Goodenough nodded. "It seems that Warsaw is under attack. Heavy attack."

* * * * *

Subcontinent 1-1, Sector 147-29, Cycle 597,845.9

Lutnaptinav observed the bombardment on the defenses of the prey-creature city. The bomb-throwers' projectiles exploded just above ground with an intense blue flash. With scores of them exploding in sequence the resulting light display was really quite striking. Each bomb was a tiny power storage unit like the much larger ones that powered the fighting machines and other devices. The storage units on the fighting machines, if subjected to battle damage, could sometimes discharge themselves instantaneously, vaporizing themselves and some of the machine in a very powerful and usually catastrophic explosion. Engineers on the Homeworld had determined that the same effect could be caused deliberately and thus devised the small bombs. Lutnaptinav had pondered if an unpiloted fighting machine could be used as the delivery device for a much more powerful bomb. Perhaps it should suggest that to its progenitor.

Assuming it survived the coming battle.

After several rotations of reconnaissance, Lutnaptinav and Nabutangula, the commander of the battle group from Group 13, had determined that the most promising avenue of attack on the city was from the northeast. The defenses appeared to be the weakest in that area and the thick clusters of native vegetation would give the attackers concealment until they were quite close. When Ubstantinav, the commander of the reinforcements, arrived it had agreed with the analysis. However it had also decided that a diversionary attack should be launched against the southern area of the defenses to try and draw off the prey-creatures reserves before the main attack was launched. It had seemed a reasonable plan and Lutnaptinav was not at all surprised when its battlegroup was assigned that mission. It was clear that the expatriate *Threeborn* were not trusted with the main effort.

Checking the chronometer, it saw that the bombardment would cease shortly. It alerted the battlegroup to be prepared to move. "Make certain you adhere to the approach plan precisely to avoid the enemy snare-pits," it added. The prey-creatures had dug thousands of small pits designed to snare the legs of the fighting machines and immobilize them. They had done this many times before in other regions and the simple devices were quite effective if they could be dug and then concealed before an attacking force could arrive. But in this case, the prey-creatures had only dug the traps after they were already under observation. By taking precise measurements on the work parties from different locations and combined with images provided by the artificial satellite, it had been possible to plot the location of the pits with considerable accuracy. Not *absolute* accuracy, of course, but enough to allow the majority of the fighting machines to avoid them. The fact the enemy had continued digging them even after it was clear that they were being observed indicated they did not realize the Race had this capability.

The bombardment ceased and Lutnaptinav gave the order to advance. Twenty-five fighting machines surged forward out of their places of conceal-ment. The rest were waiting in reserve. It was about a *telequel* to the prey-crea-ture fortifications, which were covered in the smoke and dust of the bombard-ment. Had this been a serious attack instead of a diversion, it would have started moving while the bombardment was still in progress so they would reach the enemy position just before it ended, thus catching them by surprise. But in this case they *wanted* the prey-creatures to see them and react. That was also why the attack was taking place in daylight.

The land here was flat although on the left it sloped down to the river that divided the city. The surface of the ground was mostly still frozen and easily tra-versable, but the Target World had a significant axial tilt and experienced seasons just as the Homeworld did. It was now in a warming season and some areas were melting and becoming more difficult. In just the first few hundred *telequel* sever-al machines encountered such obstructing terrain and were slowed significantly. Most, however, managed a steady pace.

They had crossed almost half the distance before the enemy began to respond. At first it was just a scattering of shots from the puny weapons the in-dividual warriors carried. This was followed immediately by the more rapid fire of the automatic weapons. Lutnaptinav could hear the tiny projectiles rattling off the skin of its vehicle. These weapons were almost useless against a fighting machine, although there had been reports of damage from extremely unlikely hits on vulnerable parts of the machines. They were more effective against the drones, but there were no drones being used in this diversion, they had all been assigned to the main attack.

It was only a few moments before much heavier projectile throwers went into action. Large puffs of smoke appeared along the line of fortifications and explosions erupted from the ground near the fighting machines. "Engage any large weapons that expose themselves," Lutnaptinav commanded. "Continue the advance."

Immediately, heat rays began stabbing out and playing along the crest of the fortification. Blasts of flame, clouds of smoke, and a few small explosions were seen, but the enemy projectiles continued to fall among the fighting ma-chines. One took a glancing blow and staggered, but righted itself and went on.

Now even larger projectiles were falling. These were coming from the prey-creatures' long range throwers, which could hurl a projectile many *telequel*. Some of the throwers might even be on the other side of the river. The projectiles carried a large load of chemical explosives and even a near miss could cause serious damage. Lutnaptinav's machine shuddered from just such an explosion, but the status read-out reported no damage.

They were nearing the fortifications and passing through the area where the pit-snares were located. Almost immediately it received a signal from one of the battlegroups. "Commander, This is Tanjadacar. I am immobilized. A pit-snare not on our plot. Can you send assistance?"

Lutnaptinav looked and saw a machine three hundred *quel* to its right that had one leg in a snare. It was bent over and struggling to free the trapped limb. Before Lutnaptinav could order the nearby fighting machines to assist, several projectiles struck Tanjadacar's machine in quick succession and tore the cockpit and upper hull completely off the leg assembly, scattering pieces for fifty *quel* all directions. It ordered a subordinate to see if Tanjandacar had survived, although that seemed unlikely.

It had not stopped moving during this and was now climbing to the parapet of the fortifications along with most of the battle group. Just beyond the top was a long trench where the prey-creatures had been hiding. The appearance of the fighting machines seemed to send them into a panic. Some fired their weapons, but most only tried to flee. It turned its heat ray on the nearest group and annihilated them. All along the line the other fighting machines were doing the same. Hundreds of the enemy were slain in moments.

But others were still fighting back.

The defenders to either side of the battle group were swinging their weapons around and continuing to fire. Beyond the first line of trenches there was a second one and also separate fortified positions mounting more of the large projectile throwers. Those had been firing indirectly before, but now aimed themselves directly at the fighting machines. Some of them were beyond the effective range of the heat rays. The long range weapons had ceased firing when the battle group reached the fortifications, perhaps for fear of hitting their own kind, but after a short time the projectiles began to fall on them again.

Lutnaptinav's orders were to create a diversion, not to attempt to drive deeply into the enemy city. But now it was in a quandary: to remain here would leave them good targets and subject them to more casualties and damage. But to destroy the weapons firing at them would require a further advance. What to do? As it pondered, it saw that prey-creature reinforcements were starting to arrive, including some of their armored gun-vehicles, emerging from between the structures in the distance.

It was about to contact Commander Ubstantinav for instructions when the Commander contacted it: "Lutnaptinav, what is your situation?"

"We have reached the first line of enemy fortifications and seized a portion of them approximately one *telequel* in length, Commander," it replied. "We have inflicted considerable casualties on the enemy and taken only light losses in return. However we are still under fire from the enemy's second line and their long range weapons. Reinforcements are gathering against us."

"Excellent. Maintain your position there and continue to engage the enemy. I will begin the main attack immediately."

"I hear and obey, Commander," said Lutnaptinav and the connection was closed.

Lutnaptinav *would* obey, even though it was inevitable that losses would mount. Preventing the prey-creatures from massing all their forces against the main attack could be the difference between success and failure.

With time, the battle group destroyed most of the larger enemy weapons within reach, and eventually the large projectile throwers shifted their fire against Ubstantinav's forces. After a while, the armored gun-vehicles withdrew, presumably to move against the main attack. Even so, Lutnaptinav's force continued to be fired at. It had all of the fighting machines pull back behind the forward slope of the fortifications and lower themselves down to the loading position. This made them smaller targets and mostly protected their vulnerable legs.

Soon it could see a great deal of smoke rising off to the north. Obviously Ubstantinav's force had gone into action. More time passed with minor damage accumulating steadily and then Fradmundula, the leader of the second sub-group, contacted it. "Sub-commander, there is a prey-creature large projectile thrower in a concealed position to my right. It is causing significant damage but it is beyond range of our heat rays. Do I have your permission to detach four fighting machines to deal with it?"

Lutnaptinav considered the request but then replied: "Negative. That would require moving them a considerable distance. This might result in encountering more unengaged enemy weapons and other possible hazards. "Shift your force to the left to reduce your vulnerability."

"At once, Sub-commander," said Fradmundula. Lutnaptinav could sense that its subordinate was not pleased with the answer.

More projectiles rained down. The enemy appeared to be directing more weapons, which presumably could not be moved north to meet the main attack, against Lutnaptinav's force. Two fighting machines were badly damaged and their pilots had to be taken to the rear in rescue pods. The clouds of smoke to the north were growing larger and shifting westward toward the main part of the city. It wanted to know what was going on, but did not dare bother Ubstantinav. Instead it contacted Nabutangula, of Group 13 who was with the main attack. "How does the battle go?" it asked.

"Not easily, I fear," came the reply. "Your diversion was effective and we advanced to the prey-creatures' first line of defense easily enough, but there was a second line behind it…"

"We knew that to be the case," said Lutnaptinav.

"Yes, but there was also a second line of the snare-pits that we had not plotted. They were very densely spaced and nearly a score of our machines became entangled with them. Losses from enemy fire were considerable, especially among the drones. Even so we breached the second line and pressed into the outskirts of the city. From that point, things have gone slowly. The prey-creatures infest almost every structure. If we try to move quickly they emerge in our rear with explosive bombs. If we proceed cautiously and burn every structure, it allows them to direct their long range weapons on us. There is no room to maneuver in these narrow streets and we take more losses."

"Do you think success is possible?"

There was a delay—much too long a delay—before Nabutangula answered. "I do not know. The city is large, much larger than any we encountered on the subcontinent. Hidden enemy forces are all around us and it is impossible to secure our flanks or rear. There appear to be tunnels under the streets and buildings as well. I believe we need a larger force to succeed."

"But Ubstantinav is pressing the battle?"

"I do not know its thoughts, but it is determined to reach the bridges spanning the river. If we can seize or destroy them, then perhaps we can at least isolate and subdue the eastern half of the city. I cannot say more, we are quite busy here." Nabutangula broke the connection.

Lutnaptinav was not encouraged by Nabutangula's analysis. There were three major bridges in the city, and while two were reasonably close to each other, the third was removed by quite a distance. It would be difficult to reach all three. And if even one remained under control of the prey creatures they could shift their forces at will. In that case it was Ubstantinav's force that risked being isolated.

The day was nearly half over when the battle group was suddenly assailed from their left. Explosions erupted around them and in short order one machine was destroyed and another crippled. Lutnaptinav had to move its machine several hundred *quel* before it could see what was happening. Four small water vessels had appeared on the river to the left. Small, but each mounted at least one heavy projectile thrower. Their location allowed them to completely enfilade the battle group's position, firing right down its line. If a projectile missed one target it might well hit another further along. The vessels were beyond the range of the heat rays. Its sub-group leaders were understandably concerned by this and asked for instructions.

Options were limited. To stay here was to risk eventual destruction. To advance would force them into the inevitable second line of snare-traps that must exist. To shift left and engage the water-vessels would expose their right flank to fire from the second line of fortifications. Surely, there was little more to be gained in the way of a diversion… It sent a signal to Commander Ubstantinav.

It was a considerable time before it answered. "Yes? What is it?" came the eventual reply.

"Commander, my current position is becoming untenable. I ask permission to withdraw."

This time the reply came very quickly. "Yes, disengage, circle around to the north, and join the main attack." The connection was cut before Lutnaptinav could even acknowledge. But it wasted no time in complying. It immediately ordered the battle group to retreat and in moments they were falling back, leaving seven wrecked machines behind.

The sudden withdrawal appeared to catch the prey-creatures by surprise and very little fire followed them across the open field to the cover of the tall vegetation. Once there, they followed the concealed paths that allowed them to reach their attack position, only in reverse. They were joined by the reserve machines and two of the rescued pilots who had been carried back to the spare machines—their last two. The battle group was down to twenty-three operational machines now.

They moved north at the best speed they could manage through the vegetation and the softening ground. Eventually, they arrived in the area where the bombardment drones had gathered. They were still firing, but only at intervals. After the long bombardment ammunition must be running short—the one major drawback of the bombardment weapon. There was also an area where additional spare machines were kept and there were a number of rescue pods there as well. In fact a fighting machine arrived just then carrying two more. One of the occupants was unharmed and it was quickly transferred to a spare machine. The other was placed in another area where at least twenty other pods were sitting. A handling machine with a medical pod was attending to the injured.

The battlegroup was then guided by the other two out of the vegetation and along the path of the main attack. Much of the field was churned up by enemy projectile throwers, but only a single disabled fighting machine and the wreckage of a few drones was in evidence here—proof that the diversion had been effective. Yet even this area was not entirely safe; several explosions threw up clouds of dirt as they crossed it.

The space behind the first line of fortifications was much different. Ten or twelve fighting machines were wrecked, most caught in the snare-pits. It was impossible to get an exact count because several of the machines were torn to pieces which were intermingled. Many smashed drones were there, too. Scorched patches of ground and the remains of prey-creatures only partially caught by heat rays showed that they had paid a heavy price as well. Then they were past the second line of fortifications and into the city. Most of the structures there were still burning.

"Have caution," warned one of the guides. "From this point on we are subject to attack at any time. Those miserable creatures are everywhere!"

They proceeded about a *telequel* through the burning streets. Several wrecked fighting machines and many drones were encountered along the way. A few shots from the small weapons of individual prey creatures bounced off their machines, apparently fired from burning structures, but nothing worse. Then they encounter a small group of fighting machines heading the other way. They did not appear to be seriously damaged or carrying rescue pods. Suddenly a message arrived on the general circuit.

"This is Ubstantinav. All units are ordered to fall back to the original assembly point. Repeat, all units are to fall back to the original assembly point. Battle group commanders, acknowledge."

Lutnaptinav halted its force and acknowledged the command. It immediately turned the battle group around and headed back the way they came. It would appear that Nabutangula had been correct.

* * * * *

March 1914, Warsaw

Ola Wojciech looked anxiously as Tom Bridges emerged through the doors of the Jesuit Church on Swietojanska Street. The smell of smoke was thick in the air and the rumble of artillery echoed off the walls of the buildings. The guns had been firing almost without a pause all day. With the limited supply of ammunition in the city that alone was enough to tell her that the attack had been serious.

A part of her wanted to be out where the fighting was—across the river to the east—but another part of her was glad, very glad, that her new status as national hero kept her away from it. She didn't have any real duties other than to be seen by the people. She had a nice new uniform—they had made her a lieutenant for God's sake!—and the people cheered her when they saw her. It was sort of embarrassing, actually.

But it did allow her to rub elbows with the Polish leaders and spend time with Tom, who could rub elbows with the German military commanders. Wanda had given her a few stern warnings about not forming any emotional attachments to Tom, but Ola didn't see much of Wanda these days.

When the attack started this morning she had sought out Tom since his information on military matters was usually better than that of her own superiors. He had not known much, but as the level of artillery fire grew to a crescendo far greater than anything heard here before, he had hurried off to the German headquarters and she had tagged along. The only information available immediately was that the Martians were attacking in strength on the east side of the Vistula.

It had been a very tense day with first an attack along the southern perimeter followed by a much stronger attack in the northeast. Then word came that the enemy was inside the city and casualties were very heavy. A flood of civilians had come across the bridges to the west side, trying to get away from the Martians who were burning everything in their path. For a while the situation seemed very bad, but reinforcements were rushed from other parts of the defense and it looked like maybe they could hold.

A half hour ago the Germans had marched off to the church which had one of the tallest towers in the city. Tom and Ola had gone along. To her chagrin, Tom had been allowed to go up, but she'd been told to stay with some of the lower-ranking officers while their superiors went up. She'd paced back and forth, smelling smoke and listening to the guns.

But now here was Tom and to her relief, he gave her a smile when he saw her. "What's happening?" she demanded.

He put a hand on her shoulder and his smile grew broader. "They're falling back."

"The Martians?"

"Who else? I wouldn't be smiling if it was our forces! But yes, the bastards are pulling back. From the look of things they are going all the way back to their starting point."

"Thank God!"

"Yes, thank God, and the German and Polish armies. It was a damn near run thing from what I'm hearing."

"But they're beaten? The Martians are beaten?"

"For today, Ola. For today. But don't think for a moment that they won't be back." His smile faded and his grip on her shoulder tightened.

"This fight's barely begun."

Chapter Fourteen

April 1914, Moldavia

Captain Harry Calloway crouched at the lip of the gully and peered out at the Martian fortress in the distance. Or at least at where he knew the fortress to be. All sight of it was blocked by the dust and smoke raised by the bombardment. The shelling had begun the previous afternoon and gone on all night and was still going strong the next morning. It had taken a full day to get the troops and vehicles and guns unloaded and another to move them into position and bring up ammunition. Then the big guns had started hammering the enemy in preparation for the attack that was supposed to begin today, April 1st. *All Fools' Day. Not the most auspicious date,* thought Harry.

Initially, the firing was all from long range; the biggest guns, along with some of the navy monitors, could hit the fortress all the way from the river. The troops and vehicles stood off five or six miles and it was well that they had. The Martians had responded with a counter-barrage of their blue bombs, but they couldn't reach the heavy guns and had simply plastered the countryside, hitting any area where human forces might be concealed—fortunately empty. After hammering the fortress for a while the forces did start moving into sheltered assembly areas and drew no fire. So either the bomb launchers had been knocked out or the Martians were saving them to repel the attack which they surely knew was coming. Significantly, there had been no sign of any of the Martian tripods. Either they were also being saved, or there were few of them here.

Some scouting forces did venture in sight of the place and were quickly driven off by the many heat rays mounted on the rampart of the fortress. This was expected. What the commanders really wanted to know was whether the fortress mounted any of the super-heat rays, but if it did, they did not fire. Some scouting aircraft from the seaplane carriers that had accompanied the fleet confirmed that there was at least one of the super rays mounted to fire at aircraft. Two brave crews were lost finding that out. Observations with telescopes spotted what might be the casemates for the super rays but they couldn't be certain. Harry heard that those spots would get special attention from the heaviest guns.

Harry looked back into the gully where his company and their armored carriers had gathered. The men were lounging about, brewing tea, playing cards, and trying to pass the time. Some were trying to sleep because they hadn't gotten much last night with the guns making so much noise. The new men, in particular, had found it difficult. Fortunately, the weather had moderated and the snow all melted off. The bottom of the gully, carved out by some small tributary of the Dniester, was muddy and the men sat on their raincoats or just stayed on the carriers. They were excited and nervous and trying hard not to show it. Brave men, not quite sure how brave they really were. Terrified that they might not be brave enough.

Harry had seen a lot of combat. Sydney, the Nile, the Dardanelles, the Red Sea, but never an attack quite like this. When the signal to go came they would have to cross three or four miles of completely open ground to reach the ramparts. The conventional heat rays could kill a man in the open instantly at a range of a mile and a half and still be dangerous out to about two miles. An armored vehicle could survive at about a mile, but would quickly be in trouble closer than that. But with the super heat rays, they could punch a hole through a *battleship* at five or six miles. The Raglan carriers would burn up like a piece of crepe paper in a bonfire if hit by something like that. Harry would almost prefer to advance on foot. But it would take an hour or more to get there that way. If the Raglans could survive, they could deliver the men to the target in ten minutes—*if* they could survive. He looked in annoyance at his hand which he realized was shaking slightly. He made a fist to make it stop.

Harry spotted Burford Sampson coming down the gully from where his own company was parked. Burf had always stayed close to Harry when they were platoon commanders. At first it was to help out the green-as-grass kid who was only an officer because his father had political connections. God, he had been so stupid back then! Well, not stupid, maybe, but totally inexperienced; learning his job by trying to do it. Burf had fought in South Africa before the Martians came and knew a lot about soldiering. He'd taken Harry under his wing and helped him stay alive. They were both captains now, company commanders, but somehow Burf always seemed to turn up at the right times. Harry smiled as he came up next to him, crouching low.

"Hell of a show!" Sampson had to shout to be heard above the roar of the guns.

"Yeah," shouted Harry. "Almost like the Dardanelles. We don't have all the battleships here, though."

"Not as many guns, but all concentrated on a much smaller area."

"Sure hope they do the job. This could be bad otherwise." He lowered his voice a bit to make sure none of the men heard that—although they certainly knew it already.

"Yeah, sure wish we had a better idea of what the hell we're supposed to do once we get up there."

Harry nodded. Yes, their orders had been a bit… vague. In theory, the bombardment was supposed to knock out most of the smaller heat rays. These were mounted on short towers close to the lip of the rampart so they could shoot down the forward slopes and hit anything that got close. They were not heavily armored and could be destroyed with a close hit. In past assault attempts it had been discovered that destroyed towers could be replaced by the Martian construction machines if given time, but hopefully they couldn't get through the bombardment to do so here. The super heat rays were another matter. Dug into strong casemates they were hard to hit and harder to destroy. The bombardment probably wouldn't hurt them, but maybe their firing ports could be blocked with rubble. On the other hand, if the infantry could get right up to the walls, they wouldn't be able to hit them.

In any case, when the attack started it would be led by the Yank land ironclads. These were sure to draw the fire of any super ray still functioning. The job of the tanks and infantry was to get close and concentrate their efforts to knock out those rays. The tanks would try to get shots into the firing ports and if necessary the infantry would climb up there and knock them out with explosives. It sounded straightforward. In practice Harry doubted it would be.

"If the smaller ray towers are knocked out, we should be safe enough up there close to the ramparts," he said.

"*If* their bomb launchers are knocked out and *if* they don't have any spiders or tripods to send against us," said Sampson.

"Always looking at the bright side, aren't you, Burf? So far we haven't seen any of those."

"Just being realistic."

"Yeah. But even if we do get up there and knock out all the Martian weapons, what are we supposed to do then? I'm assuming they expect us to get inside and actually capture the place, but how? Vehicles can't get over that rampart, not even the ironclads. There's no gate, the Martian tripods just climb over the wall, so how do we get in? I'm not keen on the infantry going it alone."

"No, neither am I," said Sampson. "But I read that over in America the Yanks have dreamed up a way to punch a hole through that wall using their ironclads. Maybe they can do the same here."

Harry faintly remembered hearing something about that, but he didn't know any details. The walls were forty feet high and at least a hundred feet thick and solid stone. He couldn't see any way to get through that quickly. Were they expected to protect some sort of mining operation? He didn't like the sound of that. "I guess we'll just wait and find out," he said.

Sampson suddenly stiffened and peered outward. "Looks like we might not have too much longer to wait."

"Why? What's happening?" Harry looked toward the fortress but then followed Sampson's gaze and looked off to the left, along the army's lines. What? Oh, there! A few small vehicles had appeared and were moving quickly across the field. Using his glasses he saw that they were some of those crazy one-wheeled 'mono-tanks'. He'd seen them before during the operations along the Nile—the one where he first met Abdo, his servant. They were the craziest contraptions he'd ever seen with the operator and a gunner squeezed into a compartment *inside* a single large wheel. They could zip along at an incredible speed. But they were mechanical nightmares and weren't being made anymore; replaced with more conventional armored cars. Only a few remained in service.

These were heading toward the cloud of smoke in the distance. The bombardment was slacking off a bit and shifting its fire to the more distant parts of the fortress. Evidently the generals wanted a closer look at what the bombardment had done and how much of the enemy's defenses were still intact. Harry didn't envy the men in those vehicles; they were likely to get those answers by being burned to ashes.

The mono tanks reached the rampart in just a couple of minutes and they reached it unscathed. The concealing smoke cloud was drifting away, but no heat rays stabbed out from the walls to kill them, no tripods appeared on the ramparts, no blue bombs rained down. The vehicles split into two groups and sped along the walls in both directions. They curved around until they were nearly out of sight and then started back. They returned to where they first appeared and were lost to Harry's view.

"Well, that was too easy," he said. "I can't believe we knocked out all the defenses."

"No, I don't believe it either. The buggers held their fire. Probably trying to sucker us in before they open up," said Sampson.

Apparently the generals thought so too because the bombardment resumed and went on heavier than ever for several more hours. It was nearly noon before the word came down to get ready to move.

The men had just been getting their lunch ready, but they immediately forgot about that and excitedly grabbed their gear and got themselves ready to board their vehicles. Harry very deliberately called the company to attention and walked along the line with Sergeant Breslin looking over each group, checking their equipment and giving an encouraging word to anyone who looked uneasy and cracking jokes with those who looked confident. It was unnecessary, Harry trusted the platoon sergeants to make sure the men were ready, but it was one of the many tricks he'd learned over the years to keep the men calm. If 'the Old Man'—him for God's sake!—was looking out for them then things should be all right. If only that were true.

He had just gotten back to his command vehicle when red flares started shooting up along the line. That was the five minute signal. He blew his whistle and the engines of the Raglans roared to life and the men scrambled aboard. They still had to use those miserable small hatches at the rear. The larger upper hatches were shut and would stay that way. Between heat rays and blue bombs, the Raglans were buttoned up tight. Harry was the last one aboard and then had to push past the other men in the dark, cramped space to get to his position behind the driver where there was a small periscope that allowed him to look around. Further crowding the space was the wireless operator and his equipment, which fortunately was quite small. The new wireless sets using the special Martian wire were no larger than a bread box. Only the company commanders and higher level officers rated them. The operator, a corporal named Whelan, was wearing headphones and looked up at him. "Standing by for the execute signal, sir," he said.

Harry nodded and then checked the rack next to him that held an array of signal flags and flare pistols. If he had to pass on orders to his company, he'd have to do it the old fashioned way. There was a small hatch set into the larger folding roof panels to allow him to use them.

The seconds ticked down and Whelan shouted; "Go!" The vehicle lurched into motion. Harry had braced himself, but the sudden tilt as they clawed their way out of the gully still almost threw him backward onto the seated troops and then forward into the bulkhead as they leveled out. He sat down, telling himself there was nothing to see, but after only a few seconds, he was back up looking through the periscope. There *wasn't* anything to see; the fortress was shrouded in the smoke from the bombardment which was still going on. Every moment he expected to see red heat rays stabbing out from the cloud, but so far there was nothing.

Swiveling the periscope left and right he could see some of the other vehicles in the attack. The Raglans, full of troops, and right behind them lines of tanks, the Mk.V Wellingtons and the new Mk.VII Marlboroughs. The Wellingtons each carried two 4-inch guns and several machine guns in side-mounted sponsons. The Marlboroughs had one of the new-fangled coil guns in a rotating turret, plus a few machine guns.

Far off to his left he saw the huge shapes of the American land ironclads rumbling along. It really was amazing to see something that big moving over the land. One of the men said that they looked 'like a bloody cathedral driving down the road' and he was right. They were heavily armored and carried an array of powerful guns, but he'd seen first-hand that they were not invulnerable. One of the super heat rays had destroyed one and crippled another only a few hundred yards from where he was watching back at the Dardanelles. He hoped he wasn't going to see that again today. The fronts of the ironclads looked to be especially bulky; had they strapped sandbags or something to them for more protection?

Shifting the periscope around forward again, it didn't seem like they were getting any closer to their target. It was still just a cloud of smoke and dust in the distance with the occasional yellow flash of an exploding shell. He forced himself to sit down and look back at the men of his headquarters section looking at him. "Almost there," he said and forced a smile. Veterans like Breslin just nodded, but a few of the newer men returned nervous, almost lunatic grins.

"Bloody hell, here it comes!" shouted the driver suddenly. Harry was up in an instant and back to the periscope. Behind him he heard Sergeant Breslin growl, "For what we are about to receive may we all be truly grateful."

At first Harry saw nothing, but then a heat ray stabbed out of the smoke. It was aimed at something far down the line to his right. He swiveled the periscope, but he couldn't actually see what it was shooting at—until whatever it was exploded. Somewhere down there, the heat ray had burned through armor and men had died. The beam cut off, but then another appeared a little to his left. And another, and another.

The bombardment was lifting and the smoke thinned and suddenly the walls of the fortress were much, much closer, looming up like a low ridge silhouetted against the sky. It was less than half a mile away now and Harry could see some details. The bombardment had carved chunks out of it and it was pocked with craters. Stones and dirt littered the ground in front of it. He thought he could see the remains of some of the heat ray towers spaced along the top of the wall, but it was hard to be sure. There was a taller object there, maybe it was…

A heat ray blasted out of it.

Yes, definitely an intact tower! The ray was aimed at something to the left of him, pretty close, too. Maybe one of his company's carriers, but he couldn't be sure. His Raglan lurched and his face was slammed against the periscope housing hard enough to hurt. He was very obsessed with protecting his remaining eye and cursed both the driver and himself for not being more careful. He leaned in again to look, but wrapped both hands around the periscope to provide an extra cushion.

Several more rays were shooting, but there were explosions appearing around the towers now. The tanks were shooting at them as they rumbled forward. Accuracy from a moving tank was terrible he'd been told by some of the crews, but with enough guns firing maybe they would get lucky. *Get lucky, dammit! We're clay pigeons out here!* Suddenly the closest ray tower blew apart, pieces tumbling down the front of the rampart. *Yes!* More well-aimed shots hit other towers and the enemy fire dwindled. They might just make it after all.

Closer and closer. Five hundred yards, four hundred, they'd be at the base of the wall soon. Turning to his men, he yelled: "Get ready to dismount!" They shifted in their seats, pulled the chin straps on their helmets a bit tighter and gripped their weapons. The man next to the rear hatch took hold of the latch. Looking back to the driver, Harry said, "Get us as close as you can."

Without waiting for an answer, he made his way through the shaking vehicle to the rear. He would be the first out as was only proper. The Raglan lurched and rocked and then ground to a halt. Harry nodded to the man holding the latch and he shoved the hatch open and Harry jumped out.

He nearly twisted his ankle when he landed. The whole area had been churned up by the bombardment with rocks the size of barrels and loaves of bread tossed all over the place. Craters and smaller stones were everywhere. But he kept his footing and stood aside to let the rest of the men out. To either side of him the other carriers of his company were also disgorging their passengers. He tried to count the vehicles to make sure none had been lost, but with some parked behind others, it was impossible to get a good count. The last men of his headquarters section were dismounted now and he blew his whistle and waved his arm toward the enemy rampart which was only a few rods away. Sergeants were shouting at the men to move.

They surged across the blasted landscape and came up to the base of the wall. There was a jumbled mass of stones there and the men took cover among them. Looking to either side, Harry saw the other companies of the Newcastles doing the same. He hoped that Burf was all right. He looked up at the wall towering above them. It wasn't vertical, but the slope was at least forty-five degrees, maybe more. Its face was a mass of jagged stones, in some places looking oddly shiny—perhaps fused by heat rays? In other spots, the bombardment had gouged out craters with rock splinters jutting out. A very hard climb under any circumstances, but under fire...

Fortunately, at the moment nothing was shooting at them. He could see some heat rays to either side still firing, but all the towers along this section appeared to be wrecked. The tanks of the division were moving off to where the shooting was coming from to help silence it. One company of Wellingtons sat a few hundred yards to the rear keeping watch over the section the Newcastles were supposed to occupy. The Raglan crews were hauling up the heavy machine guns to the roofs of their vehicles and fixing them to the pintle mounts so they could shoot up the wall if necessary. Corporal Whelan, Harry's wireless operator, appeared with his device now strapped to his back. So far, everything seemed to be going according to plan.

But what was the plan now? The focus of everyone had been to reach the walls. Now that they were there—and still alive—were they to climb up? The order had implied that, but what would they find on top? A thump on his leg made him look down. It was Whelan, squatting next to him. "Order from Battalion, sir: start the ascent."

All right, one question answered. "Acknowledge the order, Corporal," he replied and then blew his whistle. He pointed up the slope. "Up we go! Get them moving!" The men stirred and began to climb. Harry waited and watched for a few moments. Yes, it was going to be as difficult as he feared. Men slipped and slid and fell back, some with bloody cuts on their hands and knees. But they kept trying, and foot by foot they were making their way up. Harry shifted to his left to what appeared an easier route and started up. After one cut on his hand, he stopped and took out the leather gloves of his anti-dust gear and put them on. That was better. Many of the men were doing the same.

They were about halfway up when there was a sudden avalanche of stone a hundred yards off to their left. Several large boulders and many smaller stones tumbled and crashed their way down the steep slope. Several unlucky men in A Company were crushed and their screams echoed off the walls. "Lucky that wasn't us," said Sergeant Breslin from a few yards to his right.

But an instant later Harry realized this wasn't just some random tragedy. At the spot the avalanche started he saw several gleaming metal tentacles showing more stones down the incline. "On your toes!" he shouted. "Martians!"

"Bastards throwing rocks at us!" snarled Breslin. He looked above them, but nothing was coming down at them. A few shots rang out from the troops of A Company, quickly joined by the machine guns on their Raglans. It seemed odd to Harry. Martians rolling rocks down on them? Was that all they had left?

An instant later the mystery was solved.

A loud hum filled the air and a moment later the awful buzz-saw shriek of a heat ray tore at his ears. But not a normal heat ray. From the place the rocks had been falling a dazzling red beam of light a yard wide erupted. *Super heat ray! It must have been buried by the bombardment!* But now the firing port was clear again and it was free to wreck destruction on the humans assailing its fortress.

Almost immediately the company of Wellingtons opened fire, but the ray had the angle to shoot back and in one long, horrifying moment it swept across them and each one exploded in turn like a string of firecrackers, leaving a dozen blazing wrecks, black smoke billowing skyward. The ray blinked off and then a few seconds later came on again, this time reaching across the field at the lumbering land ironclads.

Harry couldn't see exactly what the effect of the ray was at this distance, but almost immediately heavy shells from the ironclads started exploding around the position of the ray. The ironclads each mounted a twelve-inch gun in a forward turret along with a number of smaller guns in other turrets. They also had some sort of amazing lightning cannon, but it had a short range. The explosions from the twelve-inchers' shells hammered at Harry's senses even from a hundred yards away. *Bloody hell, what about A Company? They're right beneath the damn thing!* Part of him was angry that fellow Australians were being killed by the American shells, but the rest of him knew it was necessary. The ironclads were vital to the success of the attack and they couldn't be put at unnecessary risk for the sake of a handful of infantry. *War. It's the cost of war.*

The smoke quickly became so thick he couldn't see anything. Small rocks, thrown up by the explosions, clattered all around him or banged off his helmet. He and his men clung to the rock wall and tried to squeeze themselves into any crack or hole they could find for more cover. In the rare moments between explosions, he thought he could hear men screaming.

A minute or two went by, although it seemed like far longer, when Harry realized the super ray wasn't firing anymore. The shells continued to rain down with a few drifting off target to very near his men and then after another few minutes the fire ceased. Harry's ears were ringing and it took Sergeant Breslin grabbing him by the shoulder and pointing down the slope to realize that Colonel Berwick was shouting at him. He slid and slipped down to where he could hear.

"Harry!" screamed Berwick. "Take your company and make sure that ray is silenced for good! Understand?"

"Uh… yes sir. Understood." He looked back toward where the ray had been. Smoke was drifting away, but he remembered what had happened just minutes before. And what had happened to A Company… "They're not going to open fire again, are they, sir?"

"Who knows?" replied Berwick, looking annoyed—at him or at what had happened to A Company, he didn't know. "But get on it, Harry! Right now!" He waved his hand.

"Yes, sir!" He turned back to his men and blew his whistle. "Get up to the top and then move over to the left and check that ray position! Move!" He scrambled up to where he'd been before and then kept on climbing. Another twenty feet or so… but what would be waiting for them up there?

There was a still a huge amount of noise filling the air; the whistle of artillery shells overhead, which were hitting the furthest parts of the fortress, the ironclads blasting away at something, the sharper crack of the tank guns, the shriek of a few heat rays still in operation, and the shouts and cries of men. But Harry's ears were focused on the immediate vicinity. Some of his men were reaching the top and he was in an agony of anticipation over what they would meet. But seconds passed as he hauled himself upward and there was no sound of heat rays nearby or the screams of men caught in them. He made it to the lip of the parapet and looked over.

The top of the fortress wall had been the most heavily hit by the bombardment and it had been churned into a mass of craters and loose rock. Close at hand was the mangled remains of one of the heat ray towers. Its base was partially intact, but the rest was just twisted bits of metal scattered around for dozens of yards. About a hundred yards away to right and left were two more of them, equally smashed. Looking farther along the ring he could see the red glow of heat rays through the smoke, but there weren't any firing close by. He let out the breath he'd been holding.

The rest of his company reached the top and found cover in the craters. At his signal they started moving along the top toward where the super heat ray was located. Almost immediately men started shouting "Tripods!" in alarm and flinging themselves down. Harry stopped and crouched low himself, but when no heat rays tore through his company he looked around and seeing nothing, called: "Where?"

"Over there, sir!" shouted back a corporal. "Inside the fortress! Dozens of the blighters!"

"He's right, sir!" cried another man.

Cautiously, Harry raised up to get a better look and then, still seeing nothing, moved from hole to hole toward the inner edge of the fortress wall. *Where are they—Christ!* He instinctively ducked down. He had caught a glimpse of a mass of the alien machines just a few hundred yards beyond the wall. There had been at least a couple of dozen. Was it a counterattack? A counterattack aimed right where he and his men were?

"Get the LIATs ready!" he called. "Check your bombs!" His men got their weapons unlimbered and pointed at the edge of the wall where the enemy would appear. Harry gripped his revolver; able to fire point-blank like this, his company could probably take down a few tripods, but they could never stop a score of them! Maybe he should fall back to the front slope of the walls. Then at least the tripods would have to get right on top of the wall and make themselves good targets for the ironclads and the tanks out in front. Seconds passed while he tried to make up his mind, but then one of the men closest to the enemy called out:

"The buggers are just standing there! They ain't moving!"

Mystified, but relieved, Harry worked his way from cover to cover until he was next to the man. "Look, sir," he said. Sure enough, the tripods were still where he'd first glimpsed them. Standing motionless in three long rows, there were more than he had thought. Thirty or forty at least. But there were gaps in the neat rows. At least a dozen more tripods were toppled over, their long legs askew—or just plain missing. Looking closer, he saw that some of the still standing ones were also damaged. Clearly the initial artillery barrage had hammered this area and done the damage. And the tripods had just stood here taking it? Why? Thinking furiously he suddenly knew the answer.

"There's no one in them!"

He remembered some reports and briefing papers he'd read. The Martians could produce their machines faster than they could breed people to operate them. They would often bring spare machines along with their armies to replace destroyed or damaged machines when their operators had survived. The human armies had been specifically ordered to make sure they killed the Martian pilots when they wrecked a tripod—they were more important than the machines. The tripods here were just replacements, no more dangerous than unmanned guns sitting in an armory! Harry got out of his hole and stood up.

"Sir!" hissed Sergeant Breslin.

"It's all right. They can't hurt us. It's all right, men. They're empty. Everyone up! Get moving!"

Reluctantly, his troops got to their feet. Then with wary glances at the tripods, they started moving along the wall. Harry hastened back to the side next to the exterior slope, trying to judge just where the opening to the super heat ray mount was located. The ground was much more broken up when they got close. Large shell fragments, still sizzlingly hot, littered the area. He stopped and peered down the slope. He couldn't see any obvious opening, but there were plenty of cracks and holes that might lead to one. Well, only one way to find out...

"Carstairs, take your squad down there and reconnoiter."

Harry turned in surprise because it was Sergeant Breslin who had given the order. He stared at the Sergeant who stared back defiantly. "Not your job, sir," he said quietly. Harry bit back a reply and then nodded. Breslin was right, and they both knew it.

Corporal Carstairs, oblivious to the silent confrontation, gathered his men and started down. "If there's no way in, what do we do, sir?" asked Lieutenant O'Reilly, coming up beside him. "We could use explosives to blow our way in, sure, but that might just be doing the Martian's work for them if the ray's still working."

"True, but if we leave it be and they dig their way out, we'll have to come back and do this anyway," said Lieutenant Boyerton, joining the debate.

Harry looked around and was annoyed that the whole company was clumping up around him. One errant Yank twelve-incher could wipe out the whole lot of them. "Spread out," he ordered. "Find some cover and stay alert."

The men dispersed and set up a defensive perimeter in commendably short order. Harry squatted down and watched Carstairs and his men work their way down. The going was very rough, far worse than the climb up had been. When they were about halfway down, they stopped and began investigating the cracks. Several men disappeared altogether.

All the while, the battle along other portions of the fortress walls was proceeding. He couldn't see the ironclads anymore, they had moved off to the left, around the curve of the ramparts and a thick cloud of smoke blocked the view. He couldn't be sure, but it seemed like the firing was dying down. Fewer explosions, very long pauses between the howl of the heat rays. Was the defense being beaten down?

"What's the situation, Harry?"

He turned and saw Colonel Berwick there with his small staff. Beyond him he could see the other companies of the Newcastles digging in along the top of the wall.

"I've got some men down below trying to find a way into the heat ray position, sir," he replied. "Uh, if we can't get in, what do we do, sir?"

Berwick frowned and said: "Then I suppose we'll have to make a way in. The General wants this thing knocked out for good. Can't have it opening up again when we think our rear's secure."

"That's a job for the sappers, isn't it, sir?" asked Harry.

"Yes, but I don't see any around here, do you?" snapped Berwick. He paused, looked at Harry and then nodded. "I'll see if I can find…"

"Captain! Captain Calloway!" A shout from below caught their attention. Harry looked down and saw Corporal Carstairs waving. "We think there's a way in, but some of them damn machines are workin' on the other side!"

"They wouldn't be trying to clear the way unless the ray was still operational," said Berwick. "I'm afraid you are going to have to go in there and see to it, Harry."

"Yes, sir," sighed Harry. He thought for a moment and then decided that since Corporal Carstairs' squad was part of Lieutenant O'Reilly's platoon, he'd send them in first. He looked around and spotted O'Reilly and waved him over. "Tom, I'm afraid you win the prize. I need you to…"

A strange whistling sound caught his attention and he stopped in mid-sentence. Everyone else heard it, too. Heads turned and eyes searched for the source. "There!" shouted someone. Right overhead a long tube-shaped object was arcing toward them. An instant later it burst into an inky black cloud that fell toward them far faster than any cloud of smoke should move.

"Dust! Dust! Dust!" screamed Sergeant Breslin. "Get your masks on! Get your masks on!"

Harry froze for an instant and then he was clawing at the bag draped around his chest. He tore it open and pulled out the anti-dust mask that was inside. He'd worn that bag from the moment they'd received new gear in Egypt after leaving Australia, but never once needed it. The Martians rarely used the poisonous black dust weapon, but the horror stories about its effects had dissuaded him from getting rid of the bulky gear. Now, finally, he needed it for real.

He threw off his helmet and pulled the rubber-impregnated canvas hood over his head and twisted it around so the glass lenses were in front of his eyes—

eye—so he could see. There was a cinch cord at the bottom and he pulled that tight to seal it to keep the dust out. By good fortune he was already wearing the leather gloves that went with the gear. He quickly looked down to make sure his leggings were tight and there were no gaps in his clothing that could let the dust in. That was all he had time for before the black cloud engulfed him.

For a moment everything went dark and he could see nothing at all, not even his hand in front of his face. He stood there frozen waiting for…what? The Martian dust was horribly lethal; a man inhaling even a few grains was doomed. He would die in seconds or minutes, or the unlucky one hours, or even days. Even getting it on your skin could be fatal. The grains would burn into the flesh like sparks from a fire—except they never went out and just burned and burned. They'd been shown photographs of horribly scarred men who had survived to try and scare the troops into properly caring for their gear and never being far from it.

Seconds went by and there were no stabs of pain in his body or his mouth or lungs. The hood had a filter that allowed air to get in so he could breathe but that would –hopefully!—keep the dust out. It appeared to be working. The blackness slowly lifted as the cloud dispersed and let in the light. Shadowy shapes appeared in the gloom. There were muffled voices all around him but the hoods made it almost impossible to hear. How could he command his men under these conditions?

Then a much louder noise reached him; an inhuman howl. A shape materialized just a few feet away and staggered right into him. It was a man—one of his men—but he wore no hood or gloves. Harry could see the open carrying bag on his chest, but there were socks and a shirt spilling out of it. The damn fool had thrown his dust gear away!

The man clutched at him, nearly dragging Harry down. There were black spots all over his face and hands, each one ringed in red as they ate into him. The man's *eyes* were melting. A black-specked white foam was bubbling out of his mouth, blowing away in flecks as he screamed. Harry stood there, frozen in horror, knowing there wasn't a damn thing he could do. The man suddenly stiffened, shuddered, and then collapsed to the ground.

Harry was gasping and trying desperately not to vomit in his hood. *Bad idea, really bad idea.* He could faintly hear other cries in the distance. How many more of his men, through negligence or just bad luck, were dying like this at that very moment? He couldn't seem to get enough air. Was the filter clogged with dust? He numbly brushed at it with his gloved hands.

But then there were other sounds near at hand. Shouts, gunfire—and the shriek of heat rays! His experienced ears quickly realized that it wasn't the howl of the tripod heat rays, or the super ray, it was the sharper, higher-pitched noise of the ones carried by the…

"Spiders! Get ready! Spiders are attacking!"

The dust was settling a bit, running down the sides of the fortress wall, almost like a liquid, rather than a cloud, and Harry could see more than a few feet.

Red flashes from the direction of the fortress interior told him where the enemy was coming from. He started grabbing men and pushing them in the direction of the noise. "Form a line! Get your weapons ready!" Still dazed from the dust attack, it was hard to get the troops moving, but they eventually responded.

The gunfire was soon joined by the bangs of Mills Bombs, the chatter of Lewis guns, and the odd *ka-pong!* of the Boys Rifles. Harry and a few men stumbled forward a dozen yards and then a thin red beam appeared to his right and swung toward him. It sparkled in a strangely beautiful fashion as it burned up grains of dust still floating in the air. But he wasted no time admiring it; he grabbed the men near him and dragged them down into one of the innumerable shell craters that covered the top of the wall. The ray swept by harmlessly over his head and then winked out.

The man to his right started firing his rifle at something and he was joined by several others. Peering over the lip of the crater, Harry saw the shape of a spider machine through the dust, coming forward with that bizarre three-legged gait most of the Martian machines used. Its small heat ray stabbed out and the head of the man next to Harry exploded, the dust hood flying away in burning fragments. The headless body collapsed limply to the bottom of the crater. Harry crouched down and pulled out a Mills Bomb from his haversack. Fumbling with his gloves, he found the tab on the side and peeled off the metal cover exposing the sticky surface over the charge of gelignite. He clutched the bomb with one hand and found the arming ring with the other. He stared at the lip of the crater, expecting the spider to appear any moment.

But it didn't. Seconds went by and the firing intensified, but no spider. He inched upward and dared to look out of the crater. There it was, just a dozen feet away, but it had turned and was firing at something else off to his right.

Seeing his chance, he surged up out of the crater, pulling the arming ring as he moved. Four long strides and he was beside the hideous thing. He jammed the bomb with all his strength against the body of the spider, right next to one of its legs. The bomb stuck and he turned and dove back into the crater, banging his knees on the rocks, but scarcely noticing. He crouched down and covered his head with his hands, no longer having a helmet.

The explosion, when it came, wasn't particularly loud and the concussion minimal. For a moment Harry feared that something had gone wrong with the bomb, but an instant later, one of the spider's legs clattered down three feet away from him. He twisted around and looked out of the crater. The machine was lying on its back with a large smoking hole in one side. Its remaining legs were moving feebly like some actual crippled spider. Men in another crater beyond it were pouring fire into it and after a few seconds a shower of sparks erupted and the awful thing was still.

"That you, sir?" A man jumped down beside him and from the chevrons on his sleeve he assumed it was Sergeant Breslin. Harry was relieved that the man was still alive. As long as the first sergeant was alive, the company was, too. Officers came and went, but the sergeants were the lifeblood of the infantry.

"Yes, it's me," he replied, shouting to be heard through his mask and above the firing. "How are we doing?"

'Bloody mess, sir! A lot of the lads are down and them damn spiders are all mixed up with us!"

"Yeah, I know! We need to put together a hunter squad and take the bastards down."

Working together, Harry and Breslin rounded up about a dozen men with rifles, a Lewis gun, a few LIATS and a Boys Rifle. Then they set out to kill spiders. The dust in the air was mostly gone, although the ground was covered with it, but there was a lot of smoke now from exploding bombs and burning spiders, so visibility was still poor. Guided more by sound than sight, they crept up on one spider after another and destroyed them. At this short range the Boys Anti-Tripod Rifle was especially effective. Its high muzzle velocity and heavy projectile tore right through the machines.

They also found an awful lot of dead soldiers, too. Harry tried not to think about what sort of company he'd have left after this. It was hard, but he concentrated on the job at hand. After what seemed like hours they ran into a group of men coming the opposite way and he sighed in relief when he saw the familiar burly form of Burford Sampson leading them. B Company coming to help.

"Harry, you alright?" asked Burf when they got close.

"Just fine. Good to see you. What's the situation?"

"The attack mostly hit you, I think. Probably trying to stop you from taking out the super heat ray. Some of it spilled over into our area but we handled it without too much trouble. Just coming to help you out now."

"Well, thanks. I think things are mostly under control. Not sure how many of the damn things are left, but we killed a lot of them."

"Good! Let's finish off the rest!"

Harry attached his squad to what Burf had brought and they swept along the top of the wall, killing spiders and joining up with the scattered men of C Company. In a surprisingly short time they reached the other end of the area where the fighting was going on. Every spider in sight was dead. Looking at the more distant parts of the fortress walls it appeared that most of the other fighting was dying down, too. Harry sank to the ground, sitting on a small boulder and tried to catch his breath.

"You there!" shouted Breslin suddenly. "Get your paws off that mask! Damn your eyes, don't touch it you fool!"

Harry twisted around and saw Breslin pointing at a trooper. The man had his canteen in one hand and the other was on the cinch cord of his mask.

"But Sergeant, I'm dyin' o' thirst in this bloody mask!" protested the man.

"You'll be dyin' of the dust if you open it up! You've been warned about this! Keep the masks on until we've been properly cleaned. You hear that? All of you!"

Harry couldn't blame the thirsty soldier; he was dying for a drink himself. But Breslin was right. The black dust was all over every one of them. To open up the mask to take a drink was risking a quick and ugly death. There were cleaning units attached to the army and they were going to have to wait until one got to them.

While he was trying to sort out the company, Colonel Berwick appeared again and was directed over to him. "What's your situation, Harry?" he asked.

"We're pretty beat up, sir. Sorry, but they hit us before we could do anything about the super heat ray. I'll try and get a platoon put together to…"

"Never mind that," interrupted Berwick. "I'll have D Company see to it. You get your fellows back down to the carriers and sorted out. We'll all be heading back to the rear to get this dust off us. Understood?"

"Uh, yes sir…"

"And Harry?"

"Sir?"

"Good job." Berwick slapped him on the shoulder and then moved off before Harry could make any reply.

Slightly dazed, he found Breslin and had the word passed to fall back to the carriers. Getting painfully to his feet, he waved to Burf, who was getting his own company reorganized and then slowly made his way down the face of the Martian ramparts and back to the waiting Raglans. They'd been too close for the heat ray to hit, unlike those poor Wellingtons, and were untouched.

They stood the unhurt men to and got them into their squads and platoons and it was heartbreaking to see how small some of them were. A few squads just weren't there at all. When they took the roll that morning C Company had mustered a hundred and seventy-two men. There were barely a hundred still on their feet now. A score or so were wounded and being worked on by medics or loaded into carriers to take them back to the hospital. The rest… the rest were still up there on the wall. Lieutenant O'Reilly was one of them. Lieutenant Pinchall of 12 Platoon was among the wounded. Fenwick and Boyerton were the only other officers he had left.

Looking along the line A Company was in no better shape. They'd taken a lot of casualties from friendly artillery fire and then they'd been caught in the Martian counterattack, too. Sampson's B Company didn't appear to be too badly hurt.

After a while, there was an explosion from off to the left. D Company had finished off the super heat ray. Shortly after, they came back to the carriers and Berwick ordered everyone aboard with stern orders to keep their anti-dust gear on. They would be heading to the rear to get that taken care of.

Harry was feeling rather dizzy by then and his mouth horribly parched. He knew many of his men were in worse shape. The Raglans lurched and bounced and the ride seemed to take forever. Harry didn't have the energy to even look out the periscope. Eventually, they creaked to a halt and stumbled out the rear hatch. They found themselves near the river among a huge crowd of men and guns and vehicles, many still being unloaded from the barges. To one side were dozens of tents with hospital flags flying over them. Quite a number of men were gathered there.

Immediately in front of them were another cluster of tents with dozens of men in protective gear carrying what looked like fire hoses and scrub brushes on long poles. Several men with officers' insignia on brassards fastened to their arms began shouting instructions. 'Get in line! Get in line! Put your weapons and loose gear on that pile! Don't touch your clothing! Get in line!'

The troops obeyed and slowly shuffled along as they were directed. Harry reluctantly dumped all his loose belongings in the pile, wondering if he'd ever get anything back. It was all covered with the dust, after all. Would they just burn everything? At least his personal stuff—and all his letters from Vera—had been left back with the supply lorries. They should be all right.

Harry put himself at the head of the C Company line and led the troops through a virtual gauntlet. The first step was a series of open-ended tents, tall enough to stand in where they were attacked by men with whisk brooms who brushed away as much of the loose dust as they could. Next were more tents where they were hit with puffs of steam coming out of hoses that presumably led back to some sort of boiler. Steam was proven to lessen the danger of the dust particles. Obviously they couldn't just blast the men with a steady stream without cooking them, so the workers used short puffs to remove as much of the dust that the brushes had missed as possible. Harry guessed the tents were to keep it from blowing away and getting on someone else.

Next they were carefully and systematically stripped of all their clothing, starting with the hoods and working their way down. This was done in a slow and methodical fashion because dust particles could still be hiding in every crease and fold. Harry gasped in relief when his hood was removed. The cool air felt good on his sweaty skin and he gulped down fresh water offered to him in a bottle. Then his gloves, tunic, shirt, trousers, leggings and underclothing were removed or just cut away. He reluctantly surrendered his eye patch. Men were standing by with rags soaked in alcohol. Pure grain alcohol would actually dissolve the dust grains and allow it to be flushed or swabbed away. If any grains had been missed by the earlier processes and found bare skin, they would move in instantly. A few howls from farther back in the line showed that it was a necessary precaution. Earlier in the war a few scientists had suggested that bottles of alcohol be included with the anti-dust gear issued to the troops. Wiser heads knew that any such issue would quickly find its way into the stomachs of the men and not be available when needed.

Harry, now naked as an egg, moved on to the next tent where to his chagrin men with clippers shore off nearly all the hair on his head. "Sorry, mate," said one of the men. "If a few dust grains got caught in your hair you'd be real sorry later." The ordeal finished up with a thorough wash with soapy water and scrub brushes. A rinse and he was toweled off and ushered along to a waiting area where he was given several blankets to wrap himself in. He stood around for a bit until he spotted Burf Sampson emerging from the process. He called him over and they both sat down on a pair of crates.

"Bloody hell," growled Sampson. "Hope I never have to go through *that* again!"

"Amen!" agreed Harry. "But, God, imagine having to wear that gear in the desert!"

"Yeah, we were damn lucky the Martians never used that crap on us in Egypt or Arabia. We'd have lost as many men to heat stroke as to the dust."

A man walked by assuring the troops that they'd be issued new uniforms shortly and to just rest and be patient. Harry took the advice and leaned back against another crate, completely exhausted. A growing pain in his knees made him move the blanket aside and he was surprised to see nasty bruises on them. He had no recollection of how he'd done that and said so out loud.

"Always like that in combat," said Burf. "Your senses narrow down to sight and sound—the only ones that matter in a fight. My sense of taste and smell disappear and later I find myself covered with cuts and bruises I have no idea how I got."

"Yeah, I guess that's true," said Harry. "Never really thought about it before."

A team of men came through the gathering, handing out mugs of tea and some biscuits. Harry gratefully drank and gobbled them down, realizing he was very hungry. The sun was dropping in the west; a whole day had nearly passed since the fight started. He hoped the promised clothing would materialize before it got dark. It was only April after all, and it was going to get cold at night.

He was starting to doze off when he suddenly heard his name being called. "I say there, I'm looking for a Captain Calloway and a Captain Sampson. Are they around anywhere?"

"Bloody hell, what now," growled Sampson. When the man called out again, Burf reluctantly waved his hand and shouted: "Over here!"

A rather short fellow with a large nose, bushy mustache, and eyeglasses in black frames strode over to them. He was wearing a major's uniform. Neither Harry or Burf stood up or saluted. Just too damn tired. "Calloway? Sampson?" he asked.

"That's us," said Burf. "What can we do for you, Major?"

"Oh, I'm so glad to have found you at last. Been looking for hours, you know. Almost went right up to the front before I'd heard you'd been brought back here for dust-delousing. How'd that go, by the way?" he gestured to the processing tents. "I had a hand in designing some of that, you know. Never actually went through it myself."

"It was very… thorough," said Harry.

"Good! Good! It was supposed to be, of course."

"Why were you looking for us, Major…?" asked Sampson.

"Oh! Hobart," said the man, "Percy Hobart. Royal Engineers." The man bobbed his head and grinned. "Pleased to meet the both of you. But as to why

I was looking for you, well, the generals have decided that we must take the Martian fortress here. Can't leave it behind to threaten our supply route, y'know. We've neutralized all of their outer defenses..." He paused when there was a rumble of artillery in the distance. "Well, almost all of them. And now the Americans and their land ironclads are preparing to breach the wall. They have a fascinating system to do that, you know. Developed it back in America of course so it's been tested. The way they do it is..."

"Major," interrupted Burf. "What does that have to do with the two of us?"

"Oh, yes, of course, forgive me. Once the wall has been breached our forces will go inside and destroy any remaining defenses. But as you probably know, the main part of a Martian fortress is underground. They have factories down there and laboratories and their power supply and whole lot more. Our troops will be going down there to rout out any defenders—hopefully and take some prisoners, too—and my engineering team has been tasked with collecting any portable devices and recording everything else about the place before it's demolished."

Harry, who had been slowly relaxing back into his near doze, came suddenly wide awake. He had a horrible feeling about where this strange major was going to go next. Burf had also come to the alert. "A big job..." he said slowly.

"Yes, quite!" said Hobart. "And the thing is, not a man on my team, and from what I've been able to learn, not a man in this whole army has ever been down inside a Martian facility." The man's eyes, which had been rather vague behind his spectacles, suddenly became sharply focused. "Except for you two."

"Now wait a minute," said Sampson. "That place we were in at the Dardanelles wasn't a regular fortress. It was just some temporary base the Martians had built to power their super heat rays along the waterway! We don't..."

"Oh, yes, yes, I realize that, Captain! I'm sure there are many differences, but probably many similarities, too. In any case, your experience is far better than nothing and right now, nothing is what I have. Your experience could be very valuable. The General agrees and has given me permission to borrow you for a while. Your colonel has been informed."

"So you are saying this is an order," said Burf.

"Oh, well, yes, I suppose you could say that," replied Hobart. "But I was rather hoping that you'd volunteer."

Burford looked over at Harry. Harry shrugged. Burf rolled his eyes. "Well, since you put it that way..."

"Jolly good!" cried Hobart. "I knew I could count on you! It will take the Americans most of the night to get ready to breach the wall, so I will be by bright and early tomorrow to collect you. Should be quite an adventure! Well, good night, gentlemen, sleep well." Hobart spun on his heel and ambled off. They watched him until he was out of sight.

"Bloody hell," growled Sampson.

"Yeah," said Harry.

Chapter Fifteen

April 1914, Moldavia

Sadly, Major Hobart was as good as his word and showed up with the first light of dawn to 'collect' them. Between getting new clothes and getting the men back to their assembly area, fed, and bedded down, it had been nearly midnight before Harry and Sampson had found their own beds. They were still exhausted when they stumbled out of their tents and into the small lorry Hobart had brought. Harry's battered knees were so sore he could barely walk.

"Morning, gentlemen!" piped Hobart as he settled in beside them in the not-quite-wide-enough rear seat of the cab. A driver and a sergeant were in front and there was a squad of sappers in the back. Several other lorries were follow-ing behind. The small caravan wound its way through the maze of tents and vehicles near the river. They went past a large cluster of hospital tents and Harry wondered if his friend, Vera Brittain, was there. He'd dearly love to see her again, but there had been no opportunity since they'd left Egypt.

"Tea, sir?" asked the sergeant in the front. He had a large container and was offering a steaming mug of it. Harry looked at Hobart, but the man shook his head.

"Already had two mugs," he said, "Go ahead, gentlemen."

Harry and Sampson gratefully took the tea. The sergeant looked at him a bit oddly and he realized it was because he had lost his eye patch. His disfigured face wasn't really that hideous, but it did make people stare. Harry clasped the mug in both hands to warm them. It had been a crystal clear night and had gotten very cold. He was shivering in his new uniform. He sipped carefully as the lorry bounced and lurched over the roadless landscape. They passed masses of troops and vehicles in columns and several deployed artillery batteries. They weren't firing, but their crews were standing by ready to open up if necessary.

The sun was just peeking over the horizon as they neared the Martian fortress. The six Yank land ironclads were grouped together and with their tall observation platforms they looked like a small town all by themselves. One of them was right up against the enemy ramparts and Harry squinted to see what it was doing.

"Fascinating system they've dreamed up, the Yanks," said Hobart. "A regular bombardment would take weeks or months to blast a breach in those walls big enough to get vehicles through. The only way to do it faster would be to plant explosives—a bloody great lot of them—inside the walls. But trying to dig or bore a hole big enough with conventional methods would still probably take several weeks.

"But what the Americans have come up with are these big metal tubes packed with TNT. They're about two feet wide with very thick walls to give them strength. Each one is about thirty feet long. The first tube has a sharp point on it. They get it in position and they use the ironclad to push it into the wall. With all that weight and horsepower behind it, the tube just goes right in like a skewer into a piece of meat."

"Ingenious," said Sampson.

"Isn't it?" said Hobart, his head bobbing. "Should have thought of something like that myself. But be that as it may, once the first tube is in as far as it can go, the ironclad backs off and they attach a second tube to the first—they're designed with sockets so one fits into the other, you see—and they repeat the process. They have to be careful that they go in straight each time or they'll bend despite their thick walls. But if they do it right, they can push the tubes all the way through the wall. Then they repeat the process as many times as necessary and in just half a day they've got a hundred tons of TNT exactly where they need it. Brilliant!"

The lorries came to a halt about a quarter mile short of the ironclads and they all piled out. Hobart went forward and spoke to someone standing near a group of other lorries and then came back smiling. "Just in time!" he said. "The Americans have finished placing the last charge. As soon as their ironclads back off a bit, they'll wire it up and touch it off." Indeed, the enormous vehicles were pulling back as they watched, black smoke boiling up out of their stacks and the enormous caterpillar tracks making clanks and squeals that could be heard from where they were standing.

They were backing up directly towards them and for a few moments Harry thought their party was going to have to move, but they finally stopped a hundred yards short. Off beyond them, he could see parties of men scurrying around, apparently laying the detonator cables. It took a good half hour and the sun was fully up when one of the ironclads gave off three long blasts with its steam whistle. "Here we go," said Hobart eagerly.

They all stared toward the alien walls. Harry wished he had his field glasses, but they had been left with all his other gear and he doubted he'd ever get them back. He'd have to see about getting a new set—or maybe that telescope he'd been thinking about. Seconds ticked by and nothing happened. More seconds. He was about to turn and ask Hobart if something was wrong when it happened.

A boiling cloud of smoke and dust erupted from the base of the wall, seemingly coming directly toward him. An instant later a huge section of the wall rose up, all in one piece like a dirigible he'd once seen taking off. Then it all dissolved into more smoke and dust with millions of pieces intermixed, flying off in every direction. The roar struck them like a physical blow a heartbeat later, staggering some people backward.

The noise went on and on and the ground itself was shaking. Big chunks of rock crashed down just beyond the ironclads and smaller ones—though still dangerously large—thumped the ground alarmingly close to them. The smoke billowed up and up and eventually flattened out at the top like some misshapen mushroom. The wall was totally obscured by dust which very slowly settled or drifted away. The noise gradually subsided and Harry's ears rang like after a heavy barrage. An eerie silence settled over the watchers.

After a few minutes it was possible to see the wall again and people began to cheer when they saw the enormous gap that now existed in it. There were still piles of rubble choking the gap, but not enough to stop one of the ironclads. The whistle on one of them—Harry wondered if it was the *Yellowstone*—gave a long toot and all of them began lumbering forward.

"Good show! Oh, jolly good show!" exclaimed Hobart who was actually clapping his hands together. The little man seemed almost beside himself. "Gentlemen, gentlemen, I can't begin to tell you how it warms my heart to see an operation like this go off so perfectly! Well done! Well done, indeed!"

"It *was* pretty damn impressive," said Sampson.

"Sure was," agreed Harry. "So now we go in?"

"Well, we're going to let the ironclads and the tanks go in first," laughed Hobart. "Make sure all the Martian weapons are silenced. We'll follow on with the infantry. I imagine we'll have to wait a bit, so be patient, gentlemen."

As it turned out, they ended up waiting over two hours. The ironclads clanked their way through the gap in the wall single file, their heavy tracks flattening a path the tanks could follow. Then they could hear quite a bit of firing going on, including the big twelve-inchers on the ironclads. Some heat rays, too. The artillery joined in for a bit. Clearly, the Martians still had some fight in them. But eventually things settled down and infantry began marching in through the gap or climbing over the walls. Finally, word reached Hobart that they could come forward.

"Excellent!" he said, ushering them toward the lorries. "Let's go see what we can find!"

* * * * *

Subcontinent 1-1, Sector 147-29, Cycle 597,845.9

Lutnaptinav became aware that something important was happening while it was overseeing maintenance on its fighting machine. It was outside of the machine, directing a repair-drone which was replacing one of the main leg joints. It had taken some damage during the last attack on the city and Lutnaptinav did not want to risk going into action again with possibly faulty equipment. Especially since the likelihood of a major attack on the prey-creature city seemed high. The work was nearly complete when its communicator informed it that a high-level discussion was taking place.

It had, with only minor difficulty, tapped into the communication channels of Ubstantinav. The elders would have considered this a highly improper and downright rude thing to do, but Lutnaptinav thought it only prudent. Their hosts here clearly regarded the two battlegroups of *Threeborn* as unwelcome and totally expendable. Logic dictated that knowing what the others might have planned for them was essential for their survival. Not that their survival was of paramount importance; every member of the Race was expendable if it was for the good of the whole. But who decided what was the good? With every passing rotation, Lutnaptinav was more convinced that those in command were incapable of making that decision rationally.

It completed the repairs and then climbed into the control cabin of its machine. Making sure that its tap was still undetected, it listened in on this call between Ubstantinav, commander of the local forces and Mandapravis, commander of the whole northern offensive.

"How strong is this attack?" Ubstantinav was asking.

"Very strong," replied Mandapravis. "The fortress commander says that the outer defenses have been destroyed and the prey-creatures are preparing to breach the walls and enter. Once that happens, the fortress will fall quickly. There are too few of us there to prevent it."

"This is bad, Commander. Holdfast 10-19 is a key position in both our offensive here and the one in the south. If the enemy takes it they will be poised to disrupt both operations."

"I'm well aware of that, Sub-commander," said Mandapravis. "I was merely informing you as a courtesy as that is one of your clan's holdfasts."

"And there is no support that can be sent?" asked Ubstantinav.

"None that could reach there in time. The prey-creatures have moved much faster than we anticipated. We must proceed with our plans and reduce the besieged city."

Lutnaptinav quickly recalled the location of the holdfast in question. It lay near a river which led almost directly to the northern offensive's staging areas. Any reinforcements from farther east would normally pass through there. It was also a major supplier of parts, power cells, and replacement fighting machines. Its loss would be a serious blow. And Mandapravis said there were no reinforcements available. Had no one realized its vulnerability?

Continuing to listen to the conversation with part of its brain, Lutnaptinav attempted to tap into Holdfast 10-19's communications. It was somewhat surprised when it succeeded. The holdfast's commander was reaching out to anyone who could possibly provide assistance and the channels were all wide open. Lutnaptinav made no attempt to communicate—what could it possibly say?—but it monitored conversations between personnel in the fortress and even managed to link to some of the visual pick-ups around the holdfast. It had never attempted to do anything like this before and the results were fascinating.

Many of the images were of no use, simply views of empty corridors or sections of the fortress walls. But rapidly switching through the channels it soon found images of much greater interest. One was tilted at an angle—perhaps the pickup had been displaced by the fighting—and showed several of the prey creature's huge fighting machines moving through a gap in the fortress walls. It recalled machines of those types in the recent campaign which failed. The machines were extremely formidable. If they were inside the fortress, resistance could not last long.

Smaller vehicles followed behind the large ones and hordes of the prey-creature foot-warriors were swarming everywhere. There was no sign of any defensive fire. Had all the ray emplacements been destroyed?

Suddenly the image was blocked by something moving in front of it. Then the image jerked around wildly and Lutnaptinav found itself looking directly at one of the prey creatures from what seemed only a *quel* away! It was actually rather shocking even though it knew the creature could not see it in return. The thing had simply lifted the pick-up and was looking at it. Curiosity perhaps? Odd to think that these beings could be motivated by curiosity. After a moment the image moved again and then there was nothing but blackness. Lutnaptinav switched to another pick-up.

After a score of random images it was then looking at what had to be the main power generating chamber of the holdfast. The hemisphere of metal holding the reactor was clearly visible. A number of people in travel chairs with manipulator arms were moving around the reactor doing… what? Lutnaptinav looked closer and suddenly it was clear exactly what they were doing. *This should be interesting...*

* * * * *

April 1914, The Martian Fortress, Moldavia

The land ironclads and fifty or sixty tanks had gone through the gap in the wall before them. The heavy machines had tamped down most of the loose rubble, but the path was hardly *smooth*. The lorry carrying Harry, Sampson, and Major Hobart leaped and jerked like a bucking bronco. Harry clung to the seat in front of him and tried to avoid being smashed against the roof of the cab. *They'll be lucky not to break an axle!*

As they made their way through, Harry marveled at what the explosives had done. The amount of rock they had displaced was almost unbelievable. Boulders the size of autocars had been tossed around like a child's toy blocks. He'd often felt a sense of awe—and fear—when he saw what the Martian machines could do. Had the aliens felt something similar when they saw what mere humans were able to do to their mighty fortress? He hoped so.

At last they made it through and the bouncing ordeal was over as they reached reasonably level ground. Still not terribly smooth, the interior of the fortress was a mass of craters from the bombardment, but passable. Looking through the lorry's windscreen or side doors Harry could see the land ironclads spaced more or less evenly around the three-mile wide circle of the fortress. The tanks were similarly scattered and swarms of infantry were poking around here and there.

"I say, that's unusual," said Hobart, pointing to some sort of structure at the center of the ring. "Driver, head over that way." The man complied and the small caravan of vehicles slowly worked its way over to the structure, dodging craters, tanks, and ironclads. "The drawings and photographs of other Martian fortresses I've seen have a relatively featureless interior," said Hobart. "All sorts of hatches and ramps leading down, of course, but nothing built up like that."

It took about five minutes to reach the thing and then everyone piled out of the vehicles and looked it over. It was made of metal and was a cylinder about thirty feet in diameter. It appeared to have originally been fifty or sixty feet high, but the top was a twisted wreck, obviously smashed by the bombardment, or maybe by the big guns on the ironclads. Pieces of metal, large and small, were scattered all over the place. Some were the shiny silver-gray color of the Martian metal and others were clearly fragments from artillery shells.

"What do you suppose it was?" asked Hobart, squinting through his thick glasses. "A communications antenna perhaps?"

Harry was still looking at the debris on the ground and suddenly spotted something that looked familiar. He went over and squatted down. It was a long rod with strange crystal-like disks positioned along it. The rod was bent and many of the crystals cracked or smashed, but it looked just like what he'd seen in that tunnel at the Dardanelles. He looked up and said: "Major? Major Hobart?"

The man turned to face him. "What is it, Captain?"

"This bit here looks just like some of the wreckage I saw in a super heat ray position. Could there have been one mounted on this tower?"

Hobart came closer and looked at the pieces Harry indicated. He slowly nodded his head. "Yes, I've seen some photographs of them and you certainly could be right." He looked up at the tower. "By George, you *are* right! We knew the Martians had mounted super heat rays to shoot at aircraft, this must be one of them! Of course! Put it on a tower so it will have the best field of fire. Well done, Calloway! Well done!" He turned to some of his men and directed them to start taking measurements and photos.

Sampson came over to Harry. "Damn good thing the artillery knocked this out before we attacked. Mounted up on this tower, the bloody thing could have swept the entire top of the walls. We all would have been burned to a crisp."

Harry looked at the ramparts ringing the fortress and realized Burf was right. It would have had a perfect shot at anything trying to cross the walls. He shivered at the thought of what might have been.

While Hobart and his men were working, Harry and Sampson had nothing to do but watch and look around. The ironclads were sitting motionless except for their turrets swinging back and forth occasionally and thin columns of black smoke coming out of their stacks. The tanks had taken up positions to cover every inch of the flat plain. Groups of infantry were mostly standing around, although some were poking or prying at metal doors or hatches that seemed to be in random locations. A few parties of sappers were placing explosives in hopes of blowing some of them open. After a while Harry noticed one such group hastily scurrying away from where they had been working. Another minute or so went by and then there was an eruption of smoke from the ground and a circular object flew up into the air. The concussion reached them a second or two before the object—a hatch presumably—slammed to the earth. When the smoke cleared, the sappers went to inspect their work. After a moment one of them waved to a nearby infantry company. The officer there blew his whistle and the men started moving toward the sappers.

"Looks like they've made a way in," said Sampson.

"I suppose once they've cleared out any resistance, Hobart and the rest of us will be going in, too," said Harry. "I'll tell you, Burf, I'm not looking forward to that."

"Neither am I. But orders are orders."

"Yeah, but I don't see why…"

Harry stopped in mid-sentence; interrupted by a loud screeching sound, like an enormous rusty hinge. Everyone stopped what they were doing and looked around, trying to find the source of the noise. "Over there!" shouted one of Hobart's men.

Harry looked the way the man was pointing and saw a large hole opening up in the plain, maybe four hundred yards away. One of the big hatches was grinding open and almost immediately the bulbous heads of tripods appeared, moving up a hidden ramp. "Bloody hell!" snarled Sampson.

Frozen, Harry watched as a dozen of the alien machines marched up out of the ground. They were accompanied by a swarm of spider machines. Heat rays started stabbing out in all directions. At the same time blue bombs began exploding all over the place. Infantry and sappers scattered for cover and Burf grabbed Harry's arm and dragged him around the side of the big cylinder to get out of sight of the tripods. Harry crouched down behind some wreckage and peered around, trying to see. He was acutely aware that he was completely unarmed. His trusty Webley revolver had been left with all of his black dust-covered gear the day before and he hadn't found a replacement. He didn't even have a Mills Bomb. At least he did have a dust protection kit. He clutched it and was ready to tear it open if another black cloud appeared.

For a few moments confusion reigned inside the fortress, but then the tanks and ironclads, positioned to deal with just this sort of situation, opened fire. The Martians found themselves in a deadly crossfire. Tripods started going down with legs shot off or heads blown open. One of the ironclads, the closest one to the ramp, cut loose with its amazing lightning cannon and an eye-searing bolt of blue-white energy leapt from the cannon to touch a tripod. The bolt then jumped to one of the spiders and then hopped from spider to spider until a dozen of them were all linked by this man-made chain lightning. After a few seconds the bolt cut off and every one of the enemy machines it had hit collapsed to the ground. An ear-splitting thunderclap shook the air. "Wow!" gasped Harry.

The Martians seemed stunned by what had happened and fire tore through them from all sides. In an amazingly short time all of the tripods were down. The spiders took longer and unfortunately a number of them made it in among the infantry and did their usual bloody work before they could be destroyed. The blue bombs continued to rain down for a while before their hidden launchers could be located and destroyed. Finally, the firing and explosions faded away and silence filled the circle—except for the inevitable cries of the wounded.

Harry and Sampson got up and dusted themselves off. None of the spiders had gotten near them but a stray heat ray had set fire to one of Hobart's lorries and the man was clearly very irritated about that. Several tanks and a few other vehicles were on fire, too, but they had paid very lightly to destroy a dozen tripods.

Infantry began gathering around the newly exposed ramp. Some of the sappers went to work, apparently to jam it open so it couldn't be closed again. A squadron of tanks rolled up to the edge of the ramp and after a while they started down, followed by infantry. The earth seemed to swallow them up. Harry expected to hear firing, but there wasn't any. "Maybe that was their last gasp," he said.

"We can hope," said Sampson. He sat down with his back against the tower, Harry followed his example and tried to relax. It wasn't easy. The sun was well up now and the nighttime chill was gone, but he had no idea what time it was. His watch was lost, too. Hobart's men went back to work and eventually they finished up and the Major, as Harry had feared, directed them toward the ramp. Some of the men had to walk, their lorry being destroyed.

By the time they got there a lot of troops had already preceded them so there shouldn't be much danger left down there—or so Harry hoped. Hobart got out of the lorry and conferred with another officer standing at the top of the ramp. After a bit of gesticulating by both parties Hobart returned and directed his little convoy to go on and drive down the ramp. Harry had assumed they'd be proceeding on foot and was surprised. Burf just shrugged and said, "If we do have to beat a hasty retreat at least we can drive."

The lorry scraped its bottom a bit as it transitioned from flat to slope—something the Martian machines didn't need to worry about—and started down. The angle was fairly steep, but not excessive, and it was as smooth as a billiards table—a welcome relief from what they had been driving on. They went down and down and then they were underground with the roof far above their heads; tall enough to accommodate a tripod. The place seemed dim compared to the bright sunshine outside, but it wasn't completely dark. A faint illumination came from above, although Harry couldn't determine what was creating it.

The ramp ended and they were on level ground again and a huge space opened out before them. There were thick columns holding up the roof that marched away at intervals into the distance to meet barely seen walls. Ahead of them were tanks, men and… "Bloody hell," said Sampson.

Toward the far wall were a couple of dozen tripods. They had their legs bent to lower the heads as far down as they could in a rather obscene squatting position. None of them were moving and Harry quickly realized they were empty like the ones he'd seen during the attack yesterday. There were infantry swarming all over them, but they were clearly harmless.

"According to the plans I have from the fortresses the Yanks captured," said Hobart, "the far wall there must be nearly under the outer ramparts. We ought to find passageways into the main sections of the installation there." He directed the driver to continue on until they reached the far side of the space. By the time they got there and unloaded Harry's eye was fully adjusted to the dim light and he could see without problem.

As Hobart had said, there were doorways in the wall opening into corridors. The engineers got out and shouldered their equipment; cameras, transits, measuring tapes and lots and lots of paper and clipboards. Burford Sampson stood there with his hands on his hips, scowling and chewing his lip. "Major," he said, "this place is enormous. You could spend *months* down here and not see everything. I don't know if you have months, but Captain Calloway and I surely don't. What are the top things on your list you want to see?"

Hobart seemed taken aback. The look on his face was like that of a child wandering into some enormous toy store. He probably couldn't understand how anyone would not want to explore it all. "Oh... uh, I see," he stammered. "Well, I suppose I'd most like to find the power generator. The Americans haven't been as forthcoming as we'd like with their analysis of the ones they've captured. After that, perhaps the command center. And then some of their manufacturing facilities and..."

"Let's look for the power generator," said Sampson, ruthlessly interrupting. Harry could see that Burf was nearing the end of his patience.

"Yes!" said Harry, trying to head off Burf from saying anything inappropriate to a superior officer. "At least we've seen one of those. We, uh, we found it by following the power conduits leading from their super heat rays. Perhaps we could look for something like that here."

Hobart's eyes widened behind his spectacles. Then he smiled. "Jolly good idea, Captain! Yes, let's go look!"

They went through the nearest door and found themselves in a large corridor that was sort of tube-shaped, although the floor was flat and perhaps twenty feet wide. It stretched away into the distance in both directions, but since there was a gentle curve—following the shape of the walls above, perhaps—they couldn't see more than thirty or forty yards before it curved out of sight. They looked up and there were indeed bundles of pipes fastened to the ceiling. Unfortunately, they ran in both directions with no indication which way might lead to the generator.

"Which way do you think?" asked Hobart.

"To the right," said Sampson instantly. "At the Dardanelles place we went right and found it."

"Really?" replied Hobart. "Very well, right it is." He got the party moving in that direction.

"Burf," whispered Harry. "We got into that tunnel from the end! There wasn't any right or left!"

"I know, but did you want to spend a half hour arguing over it? The damn place is a circle, isn't it? Right or left, we'll eventually cover it all." Harry snorted and then smiled.

They walked along for a few hundred yards and then Hobart exclaimed in satisfaction. "Look! More conduits coming out of the walls and joining the main bundle! You were right, Captain, this must be the way to the generator!" Sampson looked at Harry and winked.

After about a quarter mile they came to a larger chamber. There was an opening on the left that went into a new corridor which paralleled the first except the way to the right sloped down while to the left it sloped up. The cables mostly followed the down ramp. That was the way they went. The slope wasn't too steep and the floor of the corridor was made of some substance that gave very good footing. Not slippery at all. The place had a very clean, almost clinical look to it, much different from the hastily carved tunnels they'd been in at the Dardanelles. Harry brushed his hand on the wall and it seemed like it was made of some sort of ceramic tile, slick, smooth and very hard. In spite of that, there were several spots where water was oozing out of the joints between the tile and trickling down the slope.

They'd seen small groups of soldiers here and there as they walked. Some were poking into chambers that opened off the corridors and others didn't seem to have a particular goal, they were just marching along, headed somewhere. Harry was glad to see them. He was tempted to commandeer a rifle or Mills Bomb from one of them just to have some weapon, but whatever poor sod he chose would probably get in trouble from his sergeant, so he refrained. A couple of serious-looking troopers pelted past them, running at top speed; clearly messengers with something important to tell someone.

They descended quite a way, maybe forty or fifty feet as far as Harry could guess, when the corridor leveled out again. It was still curving and the bundles of pipes overhead continued to increase. Then from ahead they caught sight of a group of soldiers heading their way. A large group it seemed, a whole company, maybe more. The first ones who reached them had grim, even angry, expressions on their faces and more than one had tears on their cheeks. A few were cursing out loud with an amazing collection of profanity. "Oh the bastards!" snarled a sergeant. "Those miserable bastards!"

"I say," began Hobart, "what's hap..." But his words died on his lips when he saw the faces of the men. The first of the troops pushed on by the engineers and then Harry saw what was following.

People... men... women... children...

Harry sucked in his breath and his hands involuntarily clenched into fists as he saw what was coming. They were nearly all stark naked, although a few had soldiers' tunics or blankets draped on them. They were clutching each other, or being helped along by soldiers. Children clung to the adults and sobbed. Indeed, most of them were crying, although some were clearly crying tears of joy. A few were babbling away in some language Harry didn't understand, but he could tell they were thanking their rescuers.

They were filthy and even Harry, no stranger to the smell of unwashed soldiers, wrinkled his nose at the stench that accompanied them. *Food animals! We're just food animals to them!* He involuntarily found himself muttering "Bastards! Bastards!" just like that sergeant who had passed.

The column took four or five minutes to shuffle by them and they all stood there in silence for at least a minute after the wretched mass had gone before they moved again. Hardly a word was spoken as they walked, following the conduits.

After a few hundred yards they came to the entrance to the place the human prisoners had been kept. There was still a cluster of soldiers there along with some medics who were tending to some people who were too weak—or too overcome—to walk. Hobart stuck his head into the room to look around, but even his curiosity was satisfied after only a few seconds. They moved on.

Harry was beginning to think they were going to end up circling the whole fortress like Burf had said when they finally reached their goal. Up ahead they saw a large group of soldiers clustered in the corridor. There were several of the smaller, open-topped Martian tripod-vehicles standing there, and one that seemed to have tipped over.

"Oh! By Jove! They've caught some of the blighters!" exclaimed Hobart.

And indeed they had. Five of the Martians were sprawled on the floor with soldiers with fixed bayonets surrounding each one. Harry reflected that this group of troops must not have witnessed the horrid scene of a few minutes before or not one of the aliens would still be alive. As it was, a few of the engineers had to be ordered to keep their hands off their pistols. Hobart went up to a captain who seemed to be in charge of the troops and talked for a bit. They had captured this lot trying to come out of a large chamber just off the corridor to the right. Hobart took a look and then excitedly waved his group forward. "It's in here! Come on!"

They moved forward, edging around the Martians, who except for a few waving tendrils appeared completely inert, and entered the compartment Hobart had already disappeared into. The chamber was large, not as big as the place at the base of the ramp when they entered, but still quite large. In the center was an immense metal hemisphere that looked very familiar to Harry. It was five times the size, but it looked just like the generator they'd seen at the Dardanelles.

"Well, that's it," confirmed Sampson.

"You're sure?" asked Hobart, overhearing him.

"Sure as we can be."

"Excellent!" exclaimed the engineer. He seemed to be nearly dancing with excitement. He began calling to his men and giving them instructions on how to begin recording their find. Harry and Burf just stood near the door watching. There wasn't a thing either of them could add now. A drop of sweat rolled down Harry's cheek and he moved to wipe it away but then paused.

"Burf? It's like a bloody oven in here. Was the one we found giving off heat like this one is?"

Sampson scowled and then shook his head. "No... it wasn't."

* * * * *

Subcontinent 1 1, Sector 147-29, Cycle 597,845.9

Lutnaptinav was watching every detail of what the Holdfast 10-19 power technicians were doing when there was a sudden commotion. The people hurried to finish up and then turned their travel chairs and moved out of range of the visual pick-up. It tried to find another that would show where they were going, but could not before there were suddenly prey-creature foot-warriors swarming into the chamber.

They cut that too close. I doubt any of them escaped.

But they *had* finished what they were doing. They had shut down the reactor cooling system and disabled the normal safety features which would have shut it down automatically. The reactor was going to melt down, destroying itself and probably rendering most of the holdfast uninhabitable.

It wondered how long it would be before the prey-creatures realized what was happening?

* * * * *

April 1914, Martian Fortress, Moldavia

"Major? Major Hobart?" Harry came up behind the engineer who was busily giving out instruction to his men. He had to actually tap Hobart on the shoulder to get his attention.

"Yes, yes, what is it?" Hobart had generally been very polite, but he was now clearly wrapped up in his work and obviously didn't want any distractions. But Harry was damn well going to distract him!

"Major, I think something is wrong here. That machine is putting off heat like a bloody furnace. The one we saw at the Dardanelles was not. It was completely cool on the outside."

"Well, this one is a lot bigger, isn't it?" said Hobart. "Maybe this is normal for a unit this size."

"I don't think so, sir..."

"Look, Captain, I appreciate your help here, but I have a job to do and I'd appreciate it if you just keep out of the way and..."

"Major? Major!" One of Hobart's men, standing quite close to the big machine, was calling to him.

"What is it, Hansley?" Hobart was getting annoyed.

"This thing is so hot I can't get close to it. I think something is wrong here, sir." The man was shielding his face with his hand.

Hobart stood motionless for a moment and then walked toward the machine. When he was about fifteen feet away he stopped and shielded his face like the other one was doing. "No… no, you are correct. This can't be right."

"Is there any way to just switch it off?" called Sampson.

Everyone looked around, but all Harry could see in the way of controls were the short rods that seemed to be what made all of the Martian machines work. They'd found many a wrecked tripod with dead Martians still in the cockpits with their smaller tendrils wrapped around those rods. There weren't any switches or levers or dials or gauges or anything like you'd find with a human machine. The big generator was just like that. No convenient red switch with an 'off' sign anywhere.

"Major, we better get out of here—*now*!" said Sampson.

Hobart still hesitated. He stood there shaking his head. "The buggers must have done something to it…"

"*Now*, Major! Come on! All of you, we're getting out." Sampson started giving orders to Hobart's men and they didn't look inclined to argue. One of them took the major by the arm and pulled him away from the machine which was becoming unbearably hot. They moved out into the corridor to find that the Martians and most of the men guarding them had left. They ordered the few remaining men to get out and sent a squad running down the corridor to give the warning to anyone they found. Harry and Sampson and the rest went back the way they had come at a brisk pace. Harry's knees, which had eased a bit during the morning, were really aching now, but he didn't slow down.

They ordered anyone they encountered to leave. Most of them were glad to obey, but when they reached the holding area for the prisoners they encountered a colonel with the Medical Corps who insisted his patients shouldn't be moved. "On whose authority are you ordering this evacuation, Major?" he demanded.

"Uh, well, no one's really…" began Hobart, but Sampson pushed him aside.

"Colonel, have you ever seen the results of a ship's boiler explosion?"

"Actually, yes, I have," replied the man, frowning. "The survivors were horribly burned…"

"Well, that's exactly what's going to happen here! The Martians have set their boiler to explode and we have no way to stop it. Now get these people out of here!" He turned to Hobart's people. "Come on! You men, drop your gear and help with these people!"

"But… but my equipment…" mumbled Hobart. But his men were already dropping their loads and helping pick up the stretchers the people had been placed on. Within seconds the whole mob of them were heading up the ramp toward the exits.

"Nice work, Burf," said Harry. "You really think the whole place is going to explode?"

"Who knows? But it got them moving and that's all that matters."

"I... I don't know how bad it could be," said Hobart, puffing along beside them. "Rutherford is convinced the Martian power comes from atomic sources and I tend to agree. That... that American, William Rollins, has been warning people for years about the danger from X-Rays and other kinds of particles. I just don't know. But... but I suppose better safe than sorry."

"Damn right," gasped Harry.

They went up the ramp and made it back to the huge space they had first come through. By then the word to evacuate had already set off a bit of a panic and there was a large exodus of people and vehicles up and out. They saw the stretcher-bound people onto ambulances and then boarded their own lorries, the extra men clinging to the outside, and motored up and followed the crowd.

They made it outside and drove back to the central column they'd first examined and stopped there. "You think it's safe stopping here, Major?" Sampson asked Hobart.

"I... I don't know. I suppose I need to inform headquarters what's going on and ask for instructions." He turned away and took out a pad of paper.

Sampson shook his head. "Come on, Harry. We've done everything we can do here. Let's get back to our battalion."

Harry hesitated. They'd been ordered to assist Hobart. But Burf was right. It was time to go. He turned and followed Sampson. It was a long walk to the hole in the wall and a lot longer back to the battalion by the riverside and he was limping badly now. Maybe they could hitch a ride with someone...

A faint thump that seemed to come up through the ground and into the soles of their feet made them stop and look around. At first there was nothing they could see to account for it, but after a moment a small cloud of smoke, or maybe it was steam started drifting lazily out of the opening over the big ramp. Harry and Sampson exchanged glances and walked briskly toward the exit.

* * * * *

Subcontinent 1-1, Sector 147-29, Cycle 597,845.9

Lutnaptinav kept watching on various video pick-ups until the power failed. It had been disappointed when the prey-creatures appeared to realize their peril and fled. It wondered how many of them got out in time.

It considered the situation. A vital holdfast destroyed and little or nothing between the enemy which had destroyed it and the rear of the offensive. Surely it was time to fall back and regroup and make new plans. The question was: would the commanders see the obvious? At the moment they were still focused on taking the besieged prey-creature city. More forces were arriving and the attack was imminent.

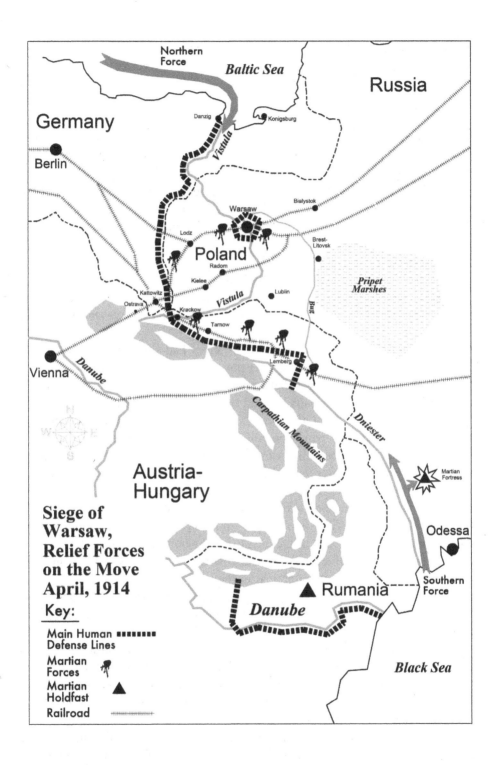

Northern
Force

Baltic Sea

Russia

Germany

Danzig
Konigsburg

Vistula

Berlin

Bialystok

Warsaw

Lodz

Poland

Brest-Litovsk

Radom

Kielce

Pripet Marshes

Kattowitz

Ostrava

Krackow

Vistula

Lublin

Bug

Tarnow

Lemberg

Vienna

Danube

Carpathian Mountains

Dniester

Martian Fortress

Austria-Hungary

Odessa

Siege of Warsaw, Relief Forces on the Move April, 1914

Rumania

Southern Force

Danube

Key:

Main Human Defense Lines

Martian Forces

Martian Holdfast

Railroad

Black Sea

Chapter Sixteen

April 1914, Warsaw

Ola Wojciech clutched one of the window sills in the tower of the Jesuit Church and watched Warsaw burn. It was the middle of the night and the flames lit up the whole eastern horizon like some awful doomsday dawn. The smell of smoke was thick in the air. Explosions rumbled from every direction, intermixed with the ringing of church bells. The bells of the Jesuit's had been ringing when she first got there, but someone had made them stop because it was annoying the commanders—and surely no one needed the bells to tell them something was wrong anymore!

Like during the last attack Ola had tagged along with Tom Bridges and once again been forbidden to ascend with the generals. But then they had left and Tom had escorted her up to get a view. One look told her this was *not* like the last attack.

The initial jubilation at the earlier victory had slowly ebbed away as the damage was assessed and the defenses put back in order. The information from the defenders had made it clear that somehow the Martians had known where all of the laboriously dug pit-traps beyond the outer line of trenches were located and been able to avoid them. Ola, who had helped dig those traps, had been very annoyed at that. All that work for nothing! On the other hand, the enemy had *not* known where the second line of traps, the ones dug between the outer trench line and the inner one, were and they had been very effective. So after considerable debate among the German and Polish commanders, the outer line had been abandoned, except for a token force, and the troops pulled back to the inner line, behind all of the still—hopefully!—hidden pit-traps. A new inner line was constructed right at the edge of the city, using the building there as strong points. This reduced the overall length of the defense lines and that was good since they had fewer people to man them now after their losses.

It had been a huge amount of work and there had been a lot of grumbling. Ola had been sent out to visit the work crews and try to encourage them. Quite a few times she'd picked up a shovel and worked alongside them for a while. They seemed to appreciate it, but she wasn't really sure. The grumbling grew louder when the authorities began forcing the civilians from the east side of the city to evacuate across the bridges to the west side of the Vistula. No one wanted to abandon their homes—not when winter had barely passed—and move to some camp or into some stranger's crowded home.

But the word was spread that the enemy was gathering for another attack and that it would be much worse than the last one. At first Ola had hoped that the authorities were saying that to simply scare the people into moving, but Tom soon confirmed that the threat was real.

"We've won a big victory down south," he explained. "Captured one of their fortresses and that seems to have thrown them into a bit of a panic."

"I heard about that," said Ola, "but that's a long way off, isn't it?"

"Yes, but our boys are moving northwest now, along the Dniester, into the enemy rear. And what you haven't heard is that our other expeditionary force, the one coming directly from England, has landed at Danzig and they'll be on their way here any time now."

"Really? Well that's good news, isn't it?"

"For certain, but the Martians can't just sit and wait for our two forces to link up. They need to do something and fast." Tom had paused and chewed on his lip and stared at Ola.

"What?" she had demanded.

"Well, our reconnaissance is indicating that they are assembling their forces, stripping what's facing the German border and also what's keeping the German army penned up in the Carpathians and massing it... here."

"Here? You mean Warsaw?" A chill had gone through Olas when she realized what that must mean.

"So it would seem," said Tom, his face grim. "The sensible thing would be for them to give this up as a bad job and withdraw east. But we're guessing that instead they are going to mass everything they can here and take Warsaw—so we can't use it as a base. Then they will probably try to beat the force coming from Danzig and then turn and defeat the southern force. Unless they have a lot of uncommitted forces we don't know about, they are probably biting off way more than they can chew, but..." He'd paused and looked away.

"They *do* have enough forces to take Warsaw," Ola had finished.

"Maybe," Tom had conceded.

That had been a week ago and day by day the evidence that the Martians were going to make an all-out attempt to take Warsaw had grown. German reconnaissance planes were seen frequently overhead and once Ola had even spotted one of their Zeppelin airships far above, glittering in the sun like a silver cigar. She never saw any of their reports, but Tom kept her informed. The Martians were massing to the east in large numbers. They still had a cordon around the west side of the city to prevent supplies from getting in, but it seemed clear that the main attack would hit the east side of the city again. There was a frantic rush to improve the defenses there and a sweep through the buildings to find and move any civilians who had not left. A shocking number had been found and Ola had to believe that there were probably still more in hiding.

The Polish leaders had sent her on tours of the defense lines and through the refugee camps to try and keep morale up. The city's orchestra had set up a tent and the musicians played lively and patriotic tunes all day long. The people seemed glad to see her and she told lots of comforting lies and half-lies to encourage them, but she felt it was a hollow gesture. She started carrying a rifle and some dynamite bombs; her superiors thought they were just props, but she had every intention of using them if—when—the time came. Tom realized that immediately, but he didn't try to dissuade her.

Word came that the British force at Danzig was on the move and had reached Grudziadz. That cheered everyone, but Grudziadz was still nearly three hundred kilometers away along the winding Vistula. A lot could happen before they got to Warsaw.

Then, yesterday, Tom had found her and taken her aside. "We think the attack will begin tomorrow, probably tomorrow night. The blighters seem to like the dark," he had said. "The Martians have assembled nearly three hundred tripods and swarms of their spider machines." She had choked back a gasp and simply nodded. *Three hundred!* Tom stared at her for a moment before continuing.

"The Germans are going to try and evacuate their wounded down river in barges tonight. I don't give much for their chances, but they won't have any chance at all if they stay here and the Martians get in. But..."

"I won't go with them," she'd blurted suddenly. "So don't ask."

Tom had looked surprised. "No, no, I wasn't going to suggest that. But..."

"But what?"

He'd taken a deep breath. "The Germans have scouted out what seems to be a safe route through the Martian cordon on the west side of the city. Not suitable for wounded in lorries, but good enough for small groups on horseback. They are planning to send out some of their higher ranking staff people and a few others not vital to the defense. They will go tonight as well. They... They're allowing any of the remaining foreign observers to go with them if they want."

"Are you going?" A strange feeling had passed through her then. Of course he would go. He wasn't Polish. He had no stake here. His mission was to observe and report back to his own people. He had observed and now it was time for him to go.

The tall Englishman had stared at her even more intently. "I'll go if you'll come with me. I can get a horse for you."

Ola sucked in her breath. This was not at all what she'd expected him to say. It had taken a minute or more before she was able to answer. But when she did, there weren't any doubts in her. "Tom, I can't. Warsaw is my home. Poland is my home. How can I abandon them?"

"It would only be temporary," he'd said. "As soon as the relief force arrives we'd be able to come back." She had seen in his eyes that the argument didn't even convince him.

"Come back? To what? A destroyed city full of the dead? I can't do that, Tom," she'd said. "You know what I've been doing. Trying to give confidence to the people. Tell them we can win. Don't worry, help is coming. How could I ever look at myself in the mirror again if I ran away and left them?"

He'd nodded and said: "You couldn't. Neither could I." He took a deep breath. "All right, we'll both stay."

A thrill had gone through her, but her mouth had mechanically said, "Tom, you aren't Polish! This isn't your country. There's no need for you to…"

"Maybe not," he'd said. "But then I always was a damn fool." And he'd smiled.

Ola had looked at him for a long time and then stepped closer, stood up on tip-toe and kissed him. After a moment he'd kissed back. But that was all. People were around them and they both had duties. That night she'd found a tall building with a view to the northwest, the direction the Vistula flowed. Sometime after midnight there had been flashes of light from that direction and some low rumbles. Clearly the barges had run into trouble. Due west, things remained dark and quiet. She wondered if maybe she and Tom should have taken their chance that way. But no, she'd made her decision and she knew it was the right one. In the deep dark before dawn, she'd gone into a church and said prayers for Tom and for herself.

The next day had been as tense as anything she'd ever experienced. There were noises off to the east and scouting parties couldn't even get out of sight of the city's defenses before they ran into Martian tripods and spider machines. Several scouting aircraft sent from airfields off to the west were shot down. The attack was coming and everyone knew it. Ola had slept very little but she made her rounds of the trenches and the camps as she always did, trying to soften peoples' fears. The orchestra played on. She doubted she was successful, and Tom was off somewhere so she had no one to soften hers. She'd sought out Wanda and a few other people from her resistance days, just to… just to see them one last time. But the one she most wanted to see was Tom.

He'd found her just before dark and they'd shared a meager dinner. He tried to make some joke about them not needing to conserve food anymore, but it had fallen flat. She liked Tom a lot, but his jokes were terrible. Finally, they'd ended up on Swietojanska Street near the Jesuit Church, the copper roof of its tower catching the last bit of light from the west. They'd gone up the tower and looked, joining the pair of German observers with field telephones who were already up there, until a chill breeze drove them down to the main floor. Several hundred evacuees were there, huddled in groups, clutching whatever belongings they'd been able to bring with them. A few, seeing Tom's uniform, had come over to ask questions, but even with Ola translating there wasn't much he could tell them and they eventually gave up.

The attack began about nine o'clock.

Unlike the previous attack, there was no preliminary bombardment. The first warning anyone had was when the tripods materialized out of the dark along the eastern trench lines. Only seconds later waves of the spider machines swarmed over the defenders. Heat rays lit up the night along with exploding buildings and vehicles. These were quickly joined by flares and star shells bursting into blinding life above the fields, revealing the enemy hordes advancing against the city.

Ola had wanted to climb back up into the tower to see, but Tom held her back. Within minutes several German staff cars arrived and officers pushed past the clamoring refugees to go up the stairs to see the attack for themselves. "We'll go up after they're done," he'd assured her.

Soon the German artillery was replying in earnest, clearly not holding anything back. If this attack wasn't repelled, it wouldn't matter if they had any ammunition left or not. They'd waited for perhaps a half hour and then the Germans, or most of them anyway, came back down and departed. Tom and Ola had wasted no time in going up.

And so here they were, watching Warsaw's death throes. Or so it seemed. About half an hour after the assault began, the Martian bombardment weapons began falling. Not against the front defense lines like in the previous attack, but all over the city. Tom said that they were probably intended to hinder the movement of reserves or maybe to knock out the defending artillery. To Ola it seemed random, but she was no expert. A few bombs exploded near the church and many of the old stained glass windows had been shattered. Dozens of fires had sprung up around the city, even on the western side of the Vistula.

"How long do you think we can hold?" she asked Tom.

He shrugged. "We've already held, what? Three hours? That's better than I was expecting, to tell the truth. We haven't seen a single tripod near the river yet and that's good. Very good. All three bridges are wired for demolition and none of them have been blown yet. If we can keep even a toehold on the far bank it will be quite an accomplishment."

Ola puzzled over the word 'toehold' for a moment but eventually realized what he meant. "But if we blow up the bridges they won't be able to get across, right?"

"Maybe, but it would also mean that every man we still have fighting on the east side will be doomed."

"Oh, that's true, of course."

"And if they secure the whole eastern shore, they could shift their forces across the river—they've built some sort of bridge or ferry upstream of the city—and hit our western defenses which aren't nearly as strong anymore."

"So we need to hold them there," she pointed across the river, "as long as we can."

"Yes, keep them tied up, hurt them as badly as we can. If they're still tangled in the city when the relief force arrives, we could really smash them up."

A series of flashes from explosions across the river, including a bright blue one, caught their attention. Tom started counting seconds aloud. He got to ten when a strong rumble shook the church. "About two miles. That blue flash was a Martian tripod blowing up."

"Really? So we are hurting them?"

"The mere fact they're still two miles away shows we are hurting them. You can feel proud of your people, Ola. Without the help of the Poles the Germans never would have been able to hold out."

"German and Poles fighting together side by side," she said in wonder. She glanced up at him. "And Englishmen, too, of course."

"And a whole lot of other folks, Ola. I've traveled a lot and seen Americans and Russians, French and Italians, Turks and Australians fighting these bastards. And now Germans and Poles. Back in '08, I think it was, President Roosevelt called for a grand alliance against the Martians. It took a long time, but I think maybe it's finally happening."

"Don't forget the Japanese. We've fired a shot or two."

They turned and Ola recognized the Japanese observer coming up the stairs. She'd seen him a number of times when she was still working at the hotel and obviously he had not decided to leave when he had the chance. He spoke very good English—better than Ola. "Ah, there you are, Yamamoto," said Tom. "Wondered where you'd gotten to."

"Just snooping around, as you'd say."

"Find anything out?"

"Our German hosts are as tight-lipped as ever, but I did learn a few things. Ammunition for their heavy guns is going to run out within the hour. They have enough for the lighter guns until morning—maybe."

"Not good."

"No. And they just sent their last reserve battalion over to the east side, along with every tank that can still move. They had kept a lot of stuff on the west shore in case the Martians used their mobility to suddenly shift their attack to that side of the city, but they are clearly committed now, so all our reserves are being sent in."

"Worse and worse. Any word on the relief force from Danzig?"

"Nothing new that I've heard, but they were only about sixty kilometers away yesterday so theoretically they could show up at any time."

Tom snorted. "Only if everything has gone perfectly for them, and when does that ever happen?"

"Pretty much never in my experience," said the Japanese.

"Exactly," replied Tom. He paused and looked at Ola. "But everyone is doing a hell of a job. We'll hold on as long as we have to."

"Yes, but…"

Yamamoto was interrupted by a bright flash of light and after a few seconds a huge explosion that shook the church more strongly than the blue explosion had done. Ola leaned out the window and looked to the north. A cloud of smoke, flickering in the firelight, was boiling upward above the river. "That was the railroad bridge!" she exclaimed.

"Yes, I expect so," said Tom leaning out above her. "The northernmost bridge. Still two more left, though."

Ola looked to the Alexander Bridge, only a few hundred meters away to the east. Thankfully, nothing seemed to be happening there. The last bridge, the

Poniatowski, was out of sight, well to the south.

They were holding out, but for how much longer? She looked to the eastern sky glowing red. The real dawn was still hours away and what hope would it bring?

* * * * *

Subcontinent 1-1, Sector 147-29, Cycle 597,845.9

Lutnaptinav maneuvered its fighting machine along the open spaces between the rows of burning structures. It eyed them warily as they had a tendency to collapse—even when the prey creatures were not deliberately doing it to trap or destroy the machines. The flames from the buildings lit up the entire area, negating the usual advantage of attacking at night. In open country, the prey-creatures had to use illuminating munitions to fight effectively at night, but here, in this city, there was no need.

The attack appeared to going well, although Lutnaptinav had been held in reserve with its battlegroup and was among the last to enter the city. The attack force had been truly impressive, twelve battlegroups and over four hundred drones and that didn't include the sixty bombardment drones. Still it had taken far too long, in Lutnaptinav's opinion, to assemble the force. It had been nine planetary rotations since the disastrous loss of the holdfast in the southeast and seven since the artificial satellite detected the other main prey-creature force moving from the north along the river that led to this city. Overcast weather had prevented any further observations, but it could be drawing near even now. With that threat and the advance of the other enemy force from the southeast it was clear that time was of the essence and yet rotation after rotation went by while reinforcements were assembled. It had dared to suggest to the commander that a smaller attack launched quickly might serve better than a larger one later, but its advice had not been received well.

It reached an intersection where several thoroughfares met. There had clearly been serious fighting here and the wrecks of three fighting machines and a score of drones were scattered about along with a number of prey-creature vehicles. It consulted its tactical display and turned to follow the road leading west. As it did so there was a large explosion in the distance to the right. It was much larger than ordinary enemy munitions would make and the wrong color for an exploding fighting machine. After a moment a message arrived from the command group. "The northern bridge has been destroyed. Forces in Sector 23-9 redirect your advance to the south. Battlegroups 23, 34, and 19 continue toward the southern bridge. Reserve forces move against the middle bridge and engage at once. Capturing a bridge intact is a priority."

Lutnaptinav consulted the display again and saw that it was already on the best route to that bridge and continued. Another battle group had already passed that way and was half a *telequel* ahead. Hopefully, it had destroyed any major resistance along the route. As it moved it received a message from Nabutangula, the commander of the Group 13 battlegroup, which was following along behind. "Lutnaptinav," it said, "Things appear to be progressing nicely. Do you agree?"

Nabutangula tended to talk too much, but as the other exiled *Threeborn* commander it had become a confidant of Lutnaptinav during this expedition. "So far. But reports indicate considerable losses. Almost twenty percent of the fighting machines and nearly a third of the drones. We have hurt the prey creatures, but they are not fleeing as they often do when things go against them. They are contesting every *quel* and we cannot sustain this sort of losses forever."

"But we should be able to secure the other two bridges soon," said Nabutangula. "Once we have complete control of the eastern side of the city we will be in a much better situation."

"Perhaps. But Mandapravis wants to move our forces to the west bank of the river and complete the city's destruction. If we cannot capture a bridge intact, we will have to move to the crossing point we built south of the city and then attack it from the outside. We cannot take too heavy losses here and still do that before the new enemy force arrives."

"Always the pessimist, Lutnaptinav."

"Just realistic. But I am occupied. We will talk later." It broke the connection.

While it had been talking it had reached a section of the city which was not on fire. This was concerning. If the battlegroup ahead of it had come this way, why had it not set fire to the buildings? That was the surest way to drive out defenders and keep them from returning. Had it taken a wrong turn? The maps of the city created from images taken by the artificial satellite were not completely accurate. The structures were clustered so close together it was often difficult to determine where passible routes existed. It double-checked the position of the leading battlegroup and compared the map to what it was seeing. After a moment of indecision it led its force onto a new street which seemed to be a better route.

It had only advanced a few hundred *quel* when there was a large explosion to its rear. It turned in time to see several structures on either side of the road collapse right on top of two fighting machines, burying them almost completely in an instant—and cutting off Lutnaptinav and four other machines from the rest of the battlegroup trailing behind. As the dust began to settle it saw that the head of one of the buried machines could still be seen. Perhaps, Habdatnajan, the pilot, could be rescued. Telemetry from the other machine was inconclusive about its condition. Uncovering it would take far too long. If the pilot still lived it could be rescued later. "Attempt to free Habdatnajan," it commanded the machines on its side of the debris. "The remainder of the battlegroup will attempt to find an alternate route and rejoin me here."

But before anything could be done one of the pilots gave a warning: "Sub-commander! Beware! The prey-creatures are…"

A heavy blow struck Lutnaptinav's machine and then there were prey-creatures everywhere. They came boiling out of the remaining structures on either side and some were even leaping *off* the roofs of the structure to land on top of the fighting machines! Lutnaptinav immediately set its heat ray to wide-angle, low power mode and swept the ray in an arc to catch as many of the awful creatures as it could. The low-power mode was still enough to slay unprotected creatures, but too weak to damage a fighting machine with a short exposure. Enemy warriors burst into flames but not nearly fast enough. They were planting their explosives, tying them to legs, draping them on limbs, or just stuffing them into joints.

One blast after another ripped through the fighting machines. Two crashed to the ground with legs damaged or destroyed and another staggered and collided with a structure, smoke pouring out of its cockpit. Lutnaptinav's own machine suddenly lurched and tilted sideways and despite every effort, slid down the side of a building to the ground.

The one upright machine remaining swept its own ray across Lutnaptinav's machine, hopefully eradicating any unseen enemies clinging to it. But then it, too, staggered backwards as something hit the arm holding its heat ray, snapping off the weapon and sending it spinning.

Lutnaptinav had not seen any prey-creatures attacking that machine. Were there additional foes nearby? Assessing the condition of its machine, it used its remaining limbs to roll it over so it was facing the opposite direction. Yes, there was the enemy! One of the prey-creatures' armored gun vehicles had come around a corner and was now firing. With every one of its machines on this side of the collapsed buildings damaged, this enemy vehicle might well destroy them all. It wished it had some drones, but those had all been allocated to the first wave of the attack. It had no resources but its own.

Shifting its machine again, it managed to free its heat ray and bring it to bear on the enemy vehicle. Resetting it to full power and narrow focus it fired. The beam caught the target in the middle of its boxy shape. At this range the metal immediately began to glow. Orange, red and then white, the ray sliced into it. One of its guns got off one more shot, which dealt a ringing blow to Lutnaptinav's machine, but then the enemy exploded and was left a burning wreck.

Shifting its view it looked for more enemies but found none. Apparently they had struck their blow and then died or fled. The weaponless fighting machine strode along the street, its manipulators plucking up a few dead or injured enemy creatures and flinging them away.

"Sub-commander Lutnaptinav! Are you all right?"

It managed to turn the head of its machine enough to see several of the members of its battlegroup hauling themselves over the wrecked buildings. A short while later more appeared from the other direction, having found a route around the blockage. As quickly as it could, it transferred to an undamaged machine, leaving its pilot in a rescue pod. With the damage sustained it only had eighteen serviceable machines left. Five pilots could be saved and given new machines in time, but for right now it would have to proceed with what it had. Nabutangula contacted it to learn its situation, concerned by the halt in the advance. "We are resuming our movement," Lutnaptinav told it.

"What happened?"

"The prey-creatures are not giving up. You should proceed with caution. We still have a serious fight ahead of us."

* * * * *

April 1914, Location unknown

Colonel Erich Serno of the Imperial German Air Service felt something grab him. He could barely feel anything, the icy water of the Vistula had nearly frozen him solid, but he felt the hands on his arms.

There were voices, too, but he couldn't understand them. Not German. Not Polish. English maybe? He was too dazed to be sure. He was being lifted up and a searing pain in his leg cut through the fog in his brain and he came more alert.

Where the hell was he? Why was he so cold? And wet? His eyes fluttered open but it was dark. Only a few flickering lights could be seen. More movement, more pain and then he was swaying through the air and bumping against something solid. More light, but still too dark to see anything. Then he was set down on something solid. Solid, but moving a bit. A ship?

Yes, a ship, that sparked a memory. He'd been on a ship. A barge. Yes, that was it, he was on a barge trying to slip out of Warsaw. His shattered leg had healed a bit in the time since he'd been shot down, but he still couldn't walk or do much of anything useful and he'd been told he was being evacuated.

That hadn't worked out so well.

The last thing he remembered was shouting and explosions and the shriek of Martian heat rays. Then somehow he'd ended up in the water, clinging to a bit of wreckage. Cold, it had been so cold. And now he was here, wherever "here" was.

People were clustered around him and one of them had a lantern. A yellow glow lit up a ring of faces, all strangers. They were jabbering at him, but he couldn't understand them and he tried to tell them that in a mumbling voice. Then he was carried inside, out of the cold and put on a soft bed and wrapped in blessedly warm and dry blankets. Someone held a hot cup of something, tea? Yes tea and dribbled a few drops into his mouth. Oh, lovely, lovely…

Several people were fussing over him, getting him out of his sodden clothing, trying to ease his leg. His vision was improving and he briefly saw the cracked and broken plaster cast that had been the bane of his existence since the crash. They were trying to remove what was left of it. Probably to put another one on, damn it.

And then there was a naval officer there, talking to him. English probably, although so many countries' naval uniforms looked alike. The man looked frustrated and then called another man up next to the bed. He wasn't in uniform. Amazingly, he addressed him in accented German. "Hello, there. I'm Professor Frederick Lindemann, can you tell me your name, sir?"

"S-Serno. Erich Serno. I'm a c-colonel in the Air Service."

The man turned to the officer and said something and the man brightened and seemed excited. He said some things back and then the Lindemann fellow spoke again. "That's excellent, Colonel. Tell me, were you in Warsaw?"

"Yes, until they evacuated me."

"How did you end up in the river?"

"I was on a barge. They were evacuating the wounded. But we ran into Martians."

"When did this happen?"

"I... I don't know. Last night? Earlier tonight? I don't know how long I've been in the water. Where am I?"

Lindemann spoke for a while with the officer and then turned to him again. "You are on board His Majesty's Land Ironclad *Implacable*. We are about twenty miles downstream from Warsaw. I'm sorry to say you are the first survivor we've encountered. It's a shame you didn't stay where you were."

Serno tried to absorb this. Only survivor? There had to have been four or five hundred men on those barges. "Where...? Where are we going?"

Lindemann's eyebrows quirked. "Why, back to Warsaw, of course. I hope you don't mind."

* * * * *

Subcontinent 1-1, Sector 147-29, Cycle 597,845.9

Lutnaptinav's battlegroup had been forced to shift its route of march due to heavy fighting and destruction and ended up reaching the river about a quarter *telequel* to the south of the middle bridge. Just as it reached the river bank there was a large explosion to the south. The southern bridge had been destroyed. Only the middle bridge remained.

Hadrampidar, who it had dealt with before, was the local commander. It was massing its forces to launch the attack on the bridge and Lutnaptinav's depleted battle group was added to it. During the march, Lutnaptinav had observed large numbers of prey-creature forces clustered around the approaches to the bridge or retreating back toward it. The prey-creatures clearly had all the bridges rigged for destruction and success here seemed unlikely.

From its position it could just see the bridge. It examined the river flowing by, but it was very wide and filled with floating chunks of ice. Lutnaptinav had had little experience with rivers. There were none on the homeworld, of course, and the original landing site for its clan was in an arid country with little open water. It had encountered more since then, but had never made an assault across a defended waterway. Information from groups who had attempted such a thing made it clear that a large river like this one was very dangerous to try and traverse in a fighting machine. The bottoms were treacherous and it was all too easy to become stuck or to be swept away by the current. The fighting machines had no significant buoyancy in this world's heavy gravity and if they could not regain their footing they could well be destroyed. It did not think it wanted to attempt a crossing of this river, so that left only the bridge.

Hadrampidar was organizing a mass assault on the position. Over a hundred fighting machines and several hundred drones were assembling in areas that could not be fired upon directly by the prey creatures. The total volume of fire that the enemy was expending had dropped off significantly and Lutnaptinav wondered if that was due to lack of munitions, or the loss of heavy weapons—or if they were simply holding their fire until a good target materialized.

It studied the tactical display and concluded that the attack had a good chance of smashing through the prey-creature defenders and reaching the bridge, but the probability of capturing it intact seemed far less good. The other two bridges were destroyed as soon as the attackers got close. Why would this be any different? *How do they detonate the explosives?* The question rose to the forefront of its thought-processes and it realized that it did not know the answer to this straightforward question.

The Race, in such a situation, would have receivers attached to each explosive charge and a simple communications signal would detonate them. But the prey-creature's knowledge of electromagnetic communications appeared to be primitive. Captured equipment had proved bulky, weak, and inefficient. A large amount of their communications was transmitted through physical metallic wires strung on poles above the ground. If the explosives on the bridges were controlled in that same manner, the wires were the weak link. If they could be cut...

It trained its video pickup on the bridge and used maximum magnification. The image did not reveal much. Perhaps some objects attached to the bridge that did not appear to be part of the structure and possibly some wires, but nothing definite. Could firing heat rays from this distance sever any wires? Or would they just detonate the explosives instead? Would even the attempt cause the prey-creatures to detonate them themselves? Too many unknowns. The only way to be certain of preventing the demolition would be to seize the bridge and do the job at the site.

Or was it?

A loud noise made Lutnaptinav turn and look upstream. Mixed in with the floating ice slabs was a mass of wreckage, perhaps from the recently destroyed southern bridge. It was grinding its way along, bumping into the near shoreline from time to time. It would come abreast of its position shortly. From there, presumably it would be carried on downstream until...

Lutnaptinav looked at the wreckage… looked at the ice… looked at the mass of waiting drones… looked at the bridge…

"Commander Hadrampidar!" it said in its communicator. "Respond at once! Urgent!"

It was a moment before Hadrampidar responded and when it did so its irritation was evident. "Subcommander Lutnaptinav, I am extremely busy and have no time for…"

"Pardons, Commander, but I have an idea!"

* * * * *

April 1914, Warsaw

Colonel Tom Bridges stood shivering in the church tower with Ola, watching the battle. Most of Warsaw east of the Vistula was either burning or already reduced to ashes. The smell of smoke was thick in the air even though a brisk west wind was carrying most of it away from him. A few fires were burning on the west side, although not as many as before. Apparently the city still had some sort of fire brigade. He was afraid it would be overwhelmed before long.

The Martians had reached the river both upstream and downstream of the remaining Alexander Bridge a quarter mile to his east and the Poniatowski Bridge had been destroyed a short time earlier. The Vistula was wide, but not so wide that the enemy could not fire across it with their heat rays. It was probably only the remaining pockets of resistance on the eastern shore that had diverted their attention from doing so already. He could see some flashes and explosions in various locations to the east, but most of the resistance was centered nearby. That last rear guard was in an ever-shrinking pocket holding the eastern end of the bridge. Bridges didn't think they'd be able to hold out much longer. From the tower he could see the Martian tripods gathering for a final attack. With most of the ammunition for the German artillery expended, it seemed certain to succeed. One of the German staff officers who came and went from the tower periodically told him that everything they had left would be used to put down a barrage to let the rear guard escape across the bridge before it was blown up. Privately, Bridges thought they should tell the men on the eastern shore to make a run for it right now and just blow the damn bridge as soon as they were across rather than waiting for the Martians attack, but the Germans were probably hoping to catch the enemy in a killing zone short of the bridge and hurt them as much as possible before pulling out. A risky plan.

"Will they be able to get away, do you think?" asked Ola. The girl had stayed right next to him through the whole fight, eyes glued to the battle raging through her home. He could scarcely imagine what she was feeling. Bridges had been in South Africa fighting the Boers when the Martians had attacked London. He'd gotten home months later and seen some of the devastation, but it was nothing like this. Come morning there probably wouldn't be a building standing on the east side.

"Evacuating a bridgehead under fire is one of the trickiest military operations there is," he answered truthfully. "We can't let them get the bridge, so it will have to be blown as soon as there's any danger of the Martians getting to it and removing the explosives or cutting the detonating wires. Once the men holding over there get the order to fall back it will be a race to see if they can get across before the officer at the detonator decides he can't wait any longer."

"A race? But the Martians' legs are so much longer."

"Yes, that's true. It's going to be a hard thing." He wished he could get her down from the tower so she wouldn't have to see what he knew was coming. But he also knew wild horses couldn't drag her away. Sometimes Ola seemed like she was made of iron.

"God help them," said Ola. "How long until... until it happens?"

"I don't know, but probably not long. The Martians have overrun pretty much everything on the east side. They can concentrate almost everything they have left against the bridge." He paused for a moment and then added: "Once this bridge is destroyed, the enemy will probably start firing on the buildings on the west side. We'll be in easy range here, Ola. We need to be ready to get out—quickly."

She nodded, but said nothing. She went back to staring at the inferno on the east shore. Bridges watched for a few minutes, but then turned his field glasses northward. Where was the damn relief force? Yamamoto kept coming and going on a circuit between the church and German headquarters. Each time he showed up he said the Germans were claiming that it was only a matter of hours before it arrived. Hours? That could mean anything. How *many* hours? Surely the Martians must have left at least a few forces watching in that direction and when the relief force bumped into them there would be firing. But the northern horizon remained dark.

And what would the Martians do once the last bridge was gone? Would they be satisfied with just holding the eastern shore? Or would they shift forces across the river somehow and continue the assault? The western defenses were substantial, but there were no reserves left to shore them up. It probably depended on how badly the Martians had been hurt in the fighting on the east side. They had certainly been hurt; Bridges had seen at least three of the big blue explosions from tripods whose power supplies had discharged and there must have been a lot of others destroyed which hadn't exploded. The fight over there had been going on for almost eight hours and it would be dawn in...

"Tom! Tom!" cried Ola suddenly. "Something's happening! Something's happening on the bridge!"

He turned to look and saw that there was shooting and flickers of light on and around the bridge. He trained his field glasses on the span and sucked in his breath. The bridge was swarming with spider machines! How had they...? Looking closer he could see that there was a mass of ice and debris piled up around the bridge abutments and they were covered with the spiders and they were climbing up the sides or even clinging to the underside. The men on the bridge were fight-ing, but they were being overwhelmed by this surprise attack. At the same time a new roar of firing rose up from the rear guard as a mass of tripods emerged from the streets leading to the bridge.

"Oh my God!" he hissed. "Blow it! Blow it now, you fools!"

As if in answer, there was an explosion, a blast of smoke and flame erupt-ed, but it wasn't large and it was only from the western end. When the breeze blew the smoke away, the bridge was still standing.

"The rest of the charges didn't go off!"

"Oh, no!" cried Ola. "Look! Look at what's happening!"

Bridges could see it all too clearly. When the cry of Martians in their rear reached the last defenders, they had panicked and tried to make a run for the bridge. The defense had collapsed almost instantly and then the enemy was on them. Heat rays swept over the masses of fleeing men, incinerating them in moments. It was a slaughter.

Those who weren't killed immediately were herded toward the bridge, but they met a mass of spiders and were cut down in droves. Others, seeing that they couldn't get across the bridge, headed for the river. Some of them made it and flung themselves into the icy water and tried to swim for it. More heat rays followed them and the horror was soon hidden by clouds of steam.

Bridges, like Ola, had stood frozen, watching the disaster but now he re-alized they had to move. Tripods had reached the far end of the bridge and were starting across. Far too late the German covering barrage began falling, but that wasn't going to stop the enemy. They would get across—and they would only be a few hundred yards away when they did. He grabbed Ola and dragged her toward the stairs.

"Come on! We have to get out of here!"

Chapter Seventeen

April 1914, Warsaw

Ola Wojciech stumbled down the last few steps from the church steeple and would have fallen except for Tom's strong hand on her arm. They emerged from the stair into the entrance vestibule and Tom steered her toward the door. She twisted around to look back at the mass of people huddled in the nave and shouted as loudly as she could: "Get out! Get out! The Martians are crossing the river! Run for your lives!"

Tom roughly pulled her away and out onto the street ahead of the now-screaming mob behind them. "They're going to panic," he gasped.

"I couldn't just leave them for the Martians!" Ola gasped back at him.

"I guess not. But let's move!" He started to turn south along Swietojanska Street, but she yanked him back the other way.

"This goes to the main street leading to the bridge! We'll run right into them!"

"Oh, good thinking!" said Tom, turning about. "This way, then. We want to go north in any case." They ran up the street just ahead of the mob erupting through the doors of the church. Their cries were now louder than the roar of the German bombardment, which was dying away—their last shells probably spent. But another noise was growing louder—the shriek of Martian heat rays.

An explosion from behind her made her look back in time to see one of those rays slice off the top of the church's steeple. Burning, it toppled over, bounced off the main roof, and crashed onto the street—right on top of some of the crowd. She was horrified, but there was nothing she could do. They kept running and she shouted at the houses on either side warning people to flee. She doubted anyone could hear her, but people were emerging from the buildings, so maybe she was doing some good.

They reached the end of the street and turned left to head west. She had no particular plan of where to go, but any direction away from the Alexander Bridge seemed a good one right now. Tom said something about heading north and she supposed he hoped to meet the relief force that was supposedly coming. If nothing else, there would be organized defenders manning the fortifications guarding that side of the city. She couldn't think of any better idea.

Right turn, left turn, they zig-zagged north then west, and north again. Or at least as best they could; the old part of Warsaw didn't have a nice grid of streets in many areas. The noise of the heat rays faded a bit as they put distance between themselves and the Martians. The artillery had almost stopped although a few shells continued to fall. But there was another noise and it was growing: the babble and cries of people. Some church bells were ringing in the distance.

When they'd first bolted from the church, the streets had been nearly empty, but now they were encountering more and more, despite the early hour. Ola doubted that many people had been able to sleep through the battle and there were probably a lot of them watching through their eastern windows. They'd have seen the flames and explosions creeping closer and closer to the river. Now they were seeing the flames on the western shore and many were taking that as a signal to flee.

More and more people were emerging from the buildings on either side of them. They were mostly women and children and men too old or infirm to join the defense battalions. Some were carrying absurdly large bundles of possessions on their backs, or suitcases in either hand. She and Tom dodged around them as best they could and kept watch for less crowded streets going the way they wanted. Ola kept glancing back, trying to judge the progress of the Martians by where the flames were. At one point where the buildings were lower and she could get a better view she was momentarily startled by what appeared to be the whole sky turned crimson. Then she realized that what she was seeing was the coming dawn, blood red and smeared with columns of black smoke. The night had seemed to last forever, but the world turned on, not caring what little things were happening on its surface.

They rounded a corner and Tom pulled her over against a brick wall and stopped. They were both gasping for breath by now and Ola was sweating, despite the chilly air. They had come two or three kilometers from the church, although much less in a straight line. She looked around and was not sure where they were or how much farther it was to the northern defense lines. "H-how much further, do you think?" asked Tom.

She shook her head. "Don't know. Still a couple of kilometers, I guess."

"Damn. And we haven't seen a single armed party so far."

"I guess most of the Polish troops were defending the eastern side," she replied automatically. But then the reality of that simple sentence sent a chill through her. Most of the people she'd known and served with were probably dead now. Burned to ashes or crushed under toppled buildings; dead trying to help Warsaw live. She choked and nearly vomited, doubling over and gripping her knees.

"And any Germans left on this side, except for the artillery and supply troops, are probably manning the western trenches," said Tom, seemingly oblivious to her distress. "We need to get there."

Ola just nodded, unable to squeeze any words out. They started moving again, not quite as fast as before. Her arms and legs were quivering with the effort. They found the crowds getting worse as more and more people joined the flight. Most of them were trying to go west and at one point they were carried along for a block before they could break free into a smaller street heading north. The sky was getting lighter and at last a few rays of sunshine escaped the smoke clouds and touched the tops of some of the buildings, the patinated copper roof of one church glowing oddly green against the still-dark western sky.

They stumbled on and the houses were getting smaller and more widely spaced and at last they emerged into a park where they found a German artillery battery. Or they found the equipment of a battery. There wasn't a soldier to be seen, just a scattering of dazed civilians wandering around. The park was a dreary place. All the trees had been cut down, first to clear the fields of fire for the guns, but later for firewood in the besieged city. The ground was all torn up and there was trash and debris piled everywhere. Empty shell casings had been tossed into piles taller than a man's head. The sharp smell of gunpowder was thick in the air.

"Where… where are the soldiers?" gasped Ola.

"Probably heading for the outer defense lines. They ran out of ammunition so they just abandoned the guns. But come on, the trenches can't be far now." Tom led them across the park and into a street on the far side. They went about a block and then a squad of men in German uniforms emerged from a side street and ran past them. One looked back and, seeing Tom's military overcoat, shouted at him in German and they hurried on.

"You catch any of that?" asked Tom.

"Just something about Martians… and telling us to hurry," said Ola.

"Good advice," sneered Tom. "I think those buggers are getting closer." She looked back and saw that the clouds of smoke had completely obscured the sunrise. Were they closer? Catching up? Maybe. She tried to move faster. Finally, they cleared the last of the houses and saw the defense line up ahead. The defenses on the western side of Warsaw were actually more impressive than those on the east. During the long years of the occupation, the Russians had seen the main threat as coming from the west—from Germany, which was only about a hundred kilometers to the west. A number of forts had been built facing that way. They had strong, underground concrete bunkers and before the Martian invasion, had mounted heavy guns. All those weapons had been stripped out and sent east to fight the Martians in the early years after the invasion. The weapons were gone, but the bunkers remained. Those were now garrisoned, and the forts were linked by new trenches, which held more troops. Smaller artillery pieces— which couldn't reach the eastern part of the city—were here and presumably still had some ammunition.

Right now Ola could see some of those guns being turned around to face the threat of a Martian attack from the rear. There were crowds of troops making similar preparations. There were also growing crowds of civilians milling around aimlessly. German soldiers were screaming at them to get out of the way, but where were they supposed to go? She and Tom walked through the Germans toward the nearest fort, their uniforms allowing them to pass unquestioned.

"Where are we going?" asked Ola.

"Inside, I guess," answered Tom. "Safest place to be and maybe there's someone inside who knows what's happening." She followed him down a ramp to a set of metal doors in a thick concrete wall. Two nervous sentries stood there, but Tom simply glared at them and marched past and neither one had the nerve to say anything. Inside was a bewildering labyrinth of corridors and chambers, most of which appeared to be empty. A few electric lights were hung at intervals, but only provided poor illumination. "There must be a command post of some sort down here," muttered Tom, "But I can't find it."

"We could ask," said Ola. They had seen a number of Germans in the corridors.

"My German isn't up to it, and if you tried, I'm sure they would want to know why we're here." Ola had to agree he was probably right.

After a while, Ola said, "Tom, there is so much empty space down here. Couldn't we try to get some of the people outside to safety?"

Tom looked around and frowned. "I guess all of these rooms were for supplies in case of a siege. The Russians must have cleared everything out before they left. But I don't know if the people would be safe down here..."

"Surely safer than outside!"

"I suppose you're right. Let's see what we can do."

They retraced their path and made it back to the surface. Despite the clouds and smoke, it seemed dazzlingly bright after the dark fortress. The smoke appeared a lot closer and a few of the guns they'd seen being turned around were firing now. Squads of soldiers were rounding up the civilians but they didn't seem to know where to send them. Tom snorted and stood up straighter. "Well, we managed to bluff *our* way in, maybe we can bluff for everyone else, too." He looked at Ola. "What's the German for 'get them inside'?"

"Uh... *hol sie rein*. I think."

"Well, let's try it out and see if it works."

It did.

Tom strode out into the midst of the Germans and started shouting the phrase and waving toward the entrance to the fort. The soldiers stared at him for a moment and then did as he told them. They herded the civilians down the ramp and inside. Ola shouted encouraging things to them and she and Tom parceled them out into the various storerooms they had found earlier. She told them to stay put and wait for help. She had no idea if any help would come, but the people seemed glad to have put many feet of concrete—and some German soldiers—between themselves and the Martians. The two of them went back to the entrance and saw the soldiers were now directing any civilians who showed up down into the fort.

"Military discipline. Ain't it grand?" said Tom, grinning.

Ola looked to the south and saw that the fires which had consumed Warsaw east of the Vistula were now at work destroying the western part of the city. Some of the flames were quite close now and at times she could see heat rays. Explosions rumbled at intervals and the civilians who appeared were running and nearly all had abandoned anything they might have been carrying. "They're getting close," she said.

"Yeah," said Tom. "Come on, we better get inside, too."

They followed the others back into the fortress. The rooms and hallways were now getting crowded. Tom then led them into a part of the fortress they had not explored yet and finally found what had to be the command center. It was full of Germans, mostly officers. Many were on field telephones, while others poured over maps. It seemed like everyone was talking at once and Ola couldn't see how anyone could actually be communicating.

No one paid the slightest attention to them and they wandered around at will. Eventually, they found where some armored cupolas extended above ground level with vision slits so they could look out. Most were already occupied, but they did find one that was empty and squeezing up the ladder, they were able to get a view. What Ola saw was terrifying.

The whole city was in flames as far as she could see. And emerging from the smoke a quarter kilometer away was a line of Martian tripods, coming straight toward her.

"Here they come, "said Tom.

* * * * *

Subcontinent 1-1, Sector 147-29, Cycle 597,845.9

Lutnaptinav's appraisal of the battle was significantly more optimistic than it had been only a short time ago. Its plan to seize the bridge had worked amazingly well. And while it doubted anyone would give it any credit, the sudden shift in the momentum of the battle was reward enough. The drones, carried to the bridge on floating ice and wreckage, had swarmed over the defenses and cut most of the detonating cables to the explosives the prey-creatures had planted. Only one small blast had gone off, doing minor damage to the structure.

Simultaneously the massed fighting machines had moved forward, smashing through the enemy defenses. As so often happened, when the prey-creatures were faced with a surprising situation, all cohesion was lost and they dissolved into an easily destroyed mob. Nearly all of them had been annihilated as they fled toward the bridge. The fighting machines were through them and across the bridge in a matter of moments. They then began spreading out into the western part of the city.

Lutnaptinav, and the remainder of its battlegroup, had followed behind the main force. Mandapravis had issued new orders to the entire force, directing the various components into an expanding arc which would ultimately take them against the prey-creature defensive lines which enclosed the western part of the city. Presumably, whatever enemy military forces that still survived would be assembling there—where they could be destroyed. Lutnaptinav was sent in a northwesterly direction with orders to destroy as much of the city and its inhabitants as it could without slowing its progress.

At first the passageways between the structures were mostly empty, but as the heat rays systematically set fire to the buildings, creatures began to spill out of them and then from others further away that were not yet afire. Slow, and confined between the structures, they were easy targets and swiftly destroyed. Still, Lutnaptinav, remembering the earlier ambush, maintained a cautious and methodical advance to be sure nothing was waiting to strike. They advanced several *telequel* without meeting any resistance, leaving a burning swath out through the city behind them. But it was a large city and even with all the battlegroups working on it, there were still considerable parts that had not been touched. Lutnaptinav supposed there would be time later to complete the destruction.

Or at least it assumed that was what Mandapravis was thinking. The commander had issued no orders concerning the enemy force that was said to be approaching from the north. There was frustratingly little information on its size, composition, or likely time of arrival. This unknown variable could significantly affect all future plans. The artificial satellite would be overhead soon, perhaps it could provide more information.

After a time Lutnaptinav called a halt and the battle group assembled and replaced their power cells with spares that had been carried along. The prolonged use of the heat rays had expended power at a high rate and it did not want to risk going into a new battle with depleted cells. Just as they were finishing there was a priority message from Mandapravis to the entire force.

"Attention. All groups are to converge in sector 24-375. New enemy forces have been detected approaching from the north. All groups acknowledge immediately and proceed at maximum speed."

Lutnaptinav acknowledged and put its battlegroup in motion, turning slightly more to the north. It ordered its subordinates to cease using power on destruction of buildings or fleeing prey-creatures. It suspected every bit of power would be needed for more dangerous targets.

* * * * *

April 1914, HMS Implacable, *North of Warsaw*

"G-good G-God!" exclaimed Lieutenant Albert Windsor. "L-look at that!"

Professor Frederick Lindemann standing next to him said nothing, but felt exactly the way the young Bertie must feel. They stared at the southern horizon in awe. Or more precisely they looked at where the southern horizon *ought* to be. A vast cloud of black smoke obscured a quarter of the sky, roiling upward and slowly drifting eastward. Flickers of red flame could be seen near the bottoms of the clouds. Most of the rest of the sky was tinted a strange pink color that was unlike any sunrise or sunset sky Lindemann had ever seen. The spectacle was at least a dozen miles away, but there was still a strong odor of smoke in the air.

"T-the whole city must be burning," said Bertie.

"It would appear so," said Lindemann. He couldn't think of anything else to say.

"Lo, all our pomp of yesterday, Is one with Nineveh and Tyre, Lord God of Hosts, be with us yet, Lest we forget—lest we forget," said a voice. Lindemann turned and saw Kipling there. The man's eyes were fixed on the horizon.

Lindemann almost asked the man what he meant and then realized he was just quoting himself again. He seemed to do that a lot. Before anyone said anything else an alarm bell began to ring. A naval officer approached and said, "Sorry gentlemen, we are clearing for action and we're going to be very busy up here shortly. I have to ask you to go below."

They were in the big observation platform atop a tripod of large pipes that towered high above the rest of the ironclad. In battle it was one of the main fire control centers for the vessel. There would be no room for sightseers. They made their way down a ladder and onto the flag bridge. Commodore William Goodenough was there. He nodded toward them. "We just received a wireless signal from the German headquarters," he said. "They are still holding out. We are not too late."

"Thank God for that!" said Bertie.

"So what are our plans now, Commodore?" asked Lindemann.

The Commodore, a tall, lanky man with a long nose and amazingly large ears, turned to face him. "Well, now that we know that the garrison is still fighting and we won't be facing the entire Martian force ready and waiting for us, we can begin our deployment. The barges carrying the tanks and vehicles will begin unloading immediately. The gunboats—and us—will proceed at top speed and cover them and make contact with the garrison. Excuse me, Professor, I must be about things." He began issuing orders and the bridge got very busy. The trio moved to one of the vision ports in the heavily armored compartment and tried to stay out of the way.

In spite of the imminent battle, Lindemann actually felt himself relaxing a bit. The last day, ever since they fished that German officer out of the river, had been very tense. They had no real idea what they were heading into. From the time they'd gotten the word that Warsaw was under attack, they'd been rushing to get here in time. The whole force had become badly strung out along the winding Vistula and Lindemann had had a growing feeling that they might be sticking their heads into a trap. But so far they had not run into any Martian forces. The enemy scouting forces which had been watching the Germans along the border had all vanished and as they progressed southward, the convoy had picked up an escort of mobile troops from the border fortifications. The Vistula, swollen with the spring rains and melt, had stayed deep enough that the ironclads and most of the shallower draft vessels could proceed by water. And now here they were, only a dozen miles from their goal and seemingly in time.

The *Implacable* chugged along, batting aside the chunks of ice floating in the river and periodically lurching as it reached a shallower section and had to run on its caterpillar tracks for a while before finding deeper water again, and the distance to Warsaw grew less and less. Looking back, Lindemann could see

barges run up along the banks disgorging vehicles and troops, but they were being left behind. He didn't know how long it would take for them to get organized
and follow along.

There had been a steady rumble from the south, from Warsaw, all
through the night and into the dawn, but now there was the sound of firing
from much closer. All eyes turned forward trying to see what it was. Lindemann
could not see anything except for the river and the surrounding countryside, but
the Commodore was conferring with some of his people and he briefly turned
to face them. "The scouting gunboats have run into some tripods up ahead," he
said. "They destroyed one and lost a boat, but the others have retreated. We're
getting close."

They turned a bend in the river and saw the scene of the skirmish. A
wrecked tripod was crumpled on the eastern bank and the burning gunboat was
swept past them by the current. "All right," said Goodenough. "I think it's time.
"Turner, signal to squadron: deploy ashore on the right and form a line of battle
facing south."

"Very good, sir," said Goodenough's flag lieutenant, who hurried off.
The Commodore looked back at them.

"Brace yourselves, gentlemen, this could get a little rough."

A few moments later *Implacable* turned to its right, directly toward the
western riverbank. Suddenly the tracks touched bottom and then the whole vessel lurched upward and clawed its way up the bank and onto level ground. Lindemann, Bertie, and Kipling all clung to the combing of the viewport and managed
to stay upright. Goodenough was peering through another port and nodded his
head, smiling.

"All made it. I was certain at least one of us would throw a track. Good!
Now let's go get those bastards!"

* * * * *

April 1914, Warsaw

Tom Bridges stared at the line of approaching tripods and then glanced
at Ola. "We better go down," he said. "When they open up with their heat rays,
we could get burned right through these vision slits." Ola took one last look and
then nodded and they made their way down to the corridor below.

The underground bunker was insulated pretty well from exterior noise,
by the many feet of earth and concrete, but it echoed and magnified the noise
from within. He could hear tromping boots and many German voices coming
seemingly from every direction. This was now joined by the chattering of machine guns. In addition to observation cupolas, there were also many that were
designed to mount machine guns or small cannons.

He stood there with Ola for a minute or two and then with no better idea
they went back to the command center. He watched the frantic activity for a

while, noticing that the highest ranking officer there was only a major. Clearly, he was just in command of the fortress and perhaps the supporting troops outside. There were eight such fortresses in the western defense line and it appeared that the general in command of the whole Warsaw garrison had made his headquarters in one of the other ones—assuming he was still alive.

When some of the Germans started staring at them suspiciously, they left and Ola dragged him through the maze of corridors checking up on the groups of civilians they had brought in. They were huddled in frightened groups and he noted that there were now German soldiers preventing them from leaving the rooms they were in. One of the guards looked as though he wanted to add Ola to the others, but Tom stared him down. The fact that Ola was still carrying a rifle and several dynamite bombs may have also helped dissuade him.

All the while, he kept his ears cocked to catch any new sounds from the battle. Anything that might indicate the Martians were blasting their way in. So far there had been nothing and he supposed that was a good thing. But what would happen if they did get in? Experimentation had shown that concrete was an excellent deterrent to the Martian heat rays. If it was properly cured, it could stand up to the searing heat for hours with only minor cracking. So it was doubtful they could simply blast their way in with the rays alone. But the fortress had metal doors which could be melted. And then those damn spider machines could get in. All he had was a revolver, which would be useless against even a spider. He managed to persuade Ola to give him one of her bombs, but it wasn't much reassurance—and setting one off in the close confines of the fortress might prove more deadly to the user than the target. Still they could make a fight of it. There was no way they would let themselves be taken alive by the Martians.

They were heading back to the command center when he nearly collided with a short man with no hat or helmet and whose clothes were singed and smoldering. In an instant they recognized each other.

"Yamamoto!"

"Bridges!"

"Glad to see you alive, old man," said Tom, gripping the Japanese by the arms.

"Just barely," gasped Yamamoto. "Damn near run thing, as you Brits would say."

"You mean you just arrived? How'd you get past the Martians? They're all over the place out there, aren't they?"

Yamamoto muttered something in Japanese and then added in English, "Yes, they are rooting out all the troops manning the trenches. Poor blighters are being slaughtered like rats in a trap. Nowhere for them to run. I made the mistake of hanging around the German headquarters in the city too long and then when things went to hell there weren't enough vehicles to carry everyone and the bastards left me behind." He paused for breath and bent over, grasping his knees for a moment. "So I ran. Martians everywhere, but I managed to avoid them somehow. Whole bloody city is on fire now. But I headed north and got here just *behind* the Martians. When they attacked, I watched for a while, but a second wave was coming up and they were sure to spot me, so I made a run for it. Lucky for me, some of the troops in the trenches can still fight and they knocked out a tripod and I made it through the gap in their lines. Found a doorway and a more gentlemanly German than the ones who abandoned me let me in. Heat ray passed over just as I slipped through but all I lost was my hat and my greatcoat." The man ran out of breath and fell silent.

"Not just your coat, sir, you've got some burns there," said Ola, touching the smoking clothing.

"Ah, the charming Miss Wojciech, too," said Yamamoto. "Yes, a few here and there. Not too bad, really."

"Here, old man," said Tom, pulling his flask out of his coat. "You could use a nip of this, I expect." The man took it and Tom grimaced as he drained the whole thing. It had been a third full.

"Did you learn anything at the German HQ about the relief force?" asked Tom.

Yamamoto shook his head. "They made wireless contact with it just before they pulled out. I didn't get any details, sadly. Thank you for that," he said, handing back the flask.

They waited while Yamamoto caught his breath and then slowly walked back to the command center. The noise and confusion had, if anything, increased and they could not get any useful information. But as they stood there a low thud reached their ears and the whole room shook slightly, bringing down some dust from the ceiling. That brought everything to a dead stop and everyone looked nervously at the ceiling. Several more thuds, fainter then the first, came and then everyone seemed to be talking at once.

"What was that?" asked Ola, nearly shouting.

"Artillery?" ventured Tom. "Maybe guns from one of the other forts trying to help out here?"

"Maybe," said Yamamoto. "Is there any place we can look out?"

"Yeah, there are a few places, let's give it a try."

They went out and followed a corridor toward where they knew there were some observation points. They were just passing a ladder that led up to one of the machine gun positions when there was a red flash from the top of the ladder that briefly lit up the corridor. At the same moment the machine gun stopped firing and there were several horrible screams. They stopped in their tracks and looked up. One scream kept going and an instant later a German soldier, wrapped in flames, fell down the ladder into a heap at their feet. They beat out the flames but the man was clearly dead. The stink of burned flesh filled Tom's nostrils and he nearly choked.

Tom and Ola stood there, stunned, but Yamamoto crept up the ladder and peered into the chamber it led to. "Two more dead up here," he said. "Looks like the gun might still work though." He looked down at them and grinned. "You game, old man? I'd rather go down fighting if I was given a choice."

Tom hesitated but then Ola said: "Yes. Me, too."

That shook him out of his funk. "All right. Yes. But you stay here, Ola!" He turned and went up the ladder.

Naturally, Ola did *not* stay there.

When he reached the top he saw that there was a small compartment with a firing port, a machine gun, boxes of ammunition, and two more dead Germans. The ray that had killed them must have just swept over the position and through the firing port. It hadn't done much other damage, but had lingered long enough to kill. Yamamoto had already dragged the bodies out of the way and was fiddling with the gun, a Spandau machine gun, if he wasn't mistaken. Tom pushed right up and grabbed the handles before Yamamoto could and said "I'll fire and you feed, all right?" The handles were almost too hot to touch, but he didn't let go of them. Without waiting for the Japanese's reply, he fired off a burst. The gun bucked on its mount and barked and the vibrations were strangely satisfying.

Yamamoto took his position on the side of the gun to feed the belt of cartridges and then Ola was there, too, lugging a box of ammunition. Tom gritted his teeth and peered out through the port, looking for targets.

There were plenty.

Even with his narrow field of vision, he could make out three of the big tripods, striding around, firing heat rays at unseen victims nearby. He swung the gun to aim at one of them when he spotted a much better target. One of the spider machines crawled into view only a few dozen yards away. It was passing in front, moving from left to right. He immediately shifted the Spandau to point at it and pressed the trigger.

The gun roared and bullets slammed into the alien machine, raising sparks where they skipped off its metal body. The spider stopped, hesitated a moment, and then turned toward him. Tom kept firing even though he knew short bursts were best. "Die you bastard!" he screamed. The spider was just raising its small heat ray when a bullet punched through. A larger shower of sparks and a puff of smoke came from it and then the horrid thing leaned over to the left and rolled on its back. Its legs waved feebly for a moment and then went still.

"Good shot!" said Yamamoto.

"You got it, Tom!" added Ola.

"Yeah! Yeah!" cried Tom, a feeling of enormous satisfaction surged through him. *Yes!* He'd hurt the bastards! He wanted to do it again and again and…

"Oh shit…"

One of the tripods was turning to face him. His small victory had not gone unnoticed. He adjusted his aim and started firing again, this time at the more distant tripod. He could see his bullets sparking off the machine, but the tripod was far more heavily armored. He knew that sometimes small arms fire did bring down a tripod, but it was a million-to-one shot. "Ola! Ola get out of here!" he shouted as he kept firing. He heard no answer, but he knew she wouldn't leave.

He kept firing.

The tripod fired its ray, a brilliant red beam of destruction. It was aimed at something off to his right, but it swung quickly in his direction. The Spandau stopped firing. The belt was empty and there was no time to load another. The ray was nearly on him, he could feel the heat…

The tripod exploded.

One moment it was there, spewing death, and the next a cloud of smoke and flame tore it apart, throwing arms and legs and bits of head in all directions. The concussion slammed into him and Tom rocked backwards, stunned. Yama-moto and Ola were crouching on the floor of the chamber, looking cautiously out the port.

"Wha… what happened," squeaked Ola. "Did… did you get it?"

"I… I don't think so… the gun was empty…"

"Look out," said Yamamoto. "There's another one out there." He pointed to where another tripod was coming through the cloud left by the destruction of the first.

It exploded, too.

Another blast shook the air as the Martian machine was blown to bits. The trio just gaped, unable to understand what was happening. More explosions shook the compartment and gouts of dirt were thrown up off toward the Martian lines. In between the explosions Tom thought he could hear men's voices. Men cheering.

"The relief force,' he whispered. "It's got to be the relief force!"

* * * * *

April, 1913, Warsaw

"All units commence firing!"

Frederick Lindemann braced himself as the crew of *HMS Implacable* obeyed their commodore's orders. The pair of eight-inch guns in the forward turret belched flame and a huge black cloud of cordite smoke. The concussion and recoil shook the whole ship. A moment later the four six-inchers mounted in single wing turrets followed suit and the ship shook again. Someone on the flag bridge gave a cheer, but he could barely hear it. His ears were ringing from the blasts.

He would have preferred to have been someplace more secure. Good God, he would have preferred to be back in England! What in Creation was he doing here, driving headlong into battle? But the answer to that question was standing right beside him. Young Bertie was staring through a pair of field glass-es at the spectacle. Lindemann thought it was probably him who had cheered. He had been sent along on this expedition to watch out for the King's son, but what could he possibly do to watch out for him in a situation like this? He had no command authority, he could not make the Commodore pull a sixth of his force out of action. And only pulling out of action could keep Bertie out of danger. If *Implacable* fought the Martians then one lucky heat ray could blow it, Bertie, and Frederick Lindemann to Kingdom Come.

And *Implacable was* fighting the Martians. It along with *Impregnable, Impulsive, Impressive, Imperial,* and *Impeccable.* The *Impossibles* were going to war! And from the hoots and hurrahs on the flag bridge, they must be doing a pretty good job of it, too. Lindemann knew the specifications of the ships by heart, of course. Firing forward, the squadron could hurl twelve eight-inch and twenty-four six-inch shells at the enemy several times each minute. When they got a little closer another twenty-four four-inchers would join in. The only thing missing were the Tesla lightning cannons; the rush to completion had prevented the American inventions from arriving in time. They were probably sitting in crates on the Liverpool dock right now.

Frustratingly, Lindemann could not see what all that firepower was doing. All the bridge windows had had their armored shutters closed and there were only narrow view slits fitted with thick quartz blocks to see through and every one of them had someone looking through them right now. Bertie's special status had rated him with one and he and Kipling were hogging it, but Lindemann had lost out.

"What's happening?" he shouted in Bertie's ear. The noise of the guns was downright deafening.

"We're blowing the shi—er, we're really giving them a pasting Professor! I've seen five or six tripods go down already!" Lindemann grinned in spite of the situation. When Bertie got excited his stammer disappeared almost completely.

That sounded like good news, but there were surely a lot more than six tripods to deal with. Lindemann turned and went to one of the rearward facing viewports—the only ones unoccupied—and looked back. Most of the view was blocked by the ironclad's funnel, but he could see a bit and he wasn't happy with the fact that he was seeing almost nothing. The six ironclads had deployed out of the river and then proceeded directly toward the beleaguered city, not waiting for any of the other forces. All Lindemann could see were a few armored cars. All the tanks and artillery had been left behind. The Ironclads could do about eight miles an hour on open ground and their support must be miles behind them now. The ironclads represented a fearsome amount of firepower, but they were all alone. Would it be enough?

He returned to Bertie's side and the young man was kind enough to relinquish his spot for a while and even gave Lindemann his field glasses. Moving up to the view slit he looked through it and the glasses and tried to see something. It wasn't easy. The quartz in the view slit wasn't perfectly transparent and there was smoke from the guns, the ironclad was shaking as it moved over the ground, and the things they were shooting at were still several miles away. He finally thought he could make out a low hill with tall shapes moving on it. It was almost a shock to realize they were Martian tripods. He'd been studying the things for years, even had an actual one in a laboratory to work on before he'd become Churchill's science advisor, but he had never seen one moving around before.

The ironclads were closing on the enemy so the image in his field glasses was growing larger by the second. The smoke cleared for a moment and he got a better view. The strange motion they made while walking was mesmerizing. He'd seen a few grainy motion pictures that daring photographers had captured on other battlefields, but seeing it here, in real life, was fascinating... One of the nearest tripods shifted and suddenly the whole world turned red.

Lindemann felt a brief moment of searing heat and then he instinctively flinched away from the view port. Several men cried out and everyone ducked as the heat ray washed over the outside of the flag bridge. Some of the quartz blocks shattered into pieces and a red glare filled the compartment for a moment before the ray moved on.

"I think we got their attention," said Kipling.

"We're in their range now, sir," said Lieutenant Turner. The remark was quite unnecessary in Lindemann's opinion. His eyes were watering and he rubbed them as a rating with heavy gloves went around replacing the quartz blocks in the view slits. They'd been designed to be easily swapped out for new ones. Bertie retrieved the field glasses from Lindemann and as soon as the quartz was replaced he went back to looking at the battle.

The battle; how was the battle going? The roar of the ironclads' guns was incessant, but what were they doing to the enemy? Bertie had said they were beating the shit out of them, but was that really true? He took a look out of the rear port and the fields behind them were still empty of any real support.

The red glare which had filled the compartment before returned again. Men flinched and quartz cracked. But this time the glare did not go away. It stayed, and small shafts of red came through the ports and started burning the paint off the wall they touched. Kipling had to dodge aside to avoid one. The air was getting hotter by the moment.

"They're concentrating on us, sir!" cried Lieutenant Turner.

"The others should know what to do," replied the Commodore, "but send out the signal for Plan Baker-two anyway, William."

"I'll try, sir," said Turner, who began shouting into a speaking tube.

Concentrating. Did that mean all the Martians in range were focusing their fire on *Implacable*? How long could they hold out under such a Hellish concentration? The ironclad lurched slightly and he put out a hand to brace himself but then he snatched it away. The metal wall was too hot to touch! The air was getting horribly hot, too. He looked toward the forward bulkhead and gasped when he saw it was turning a dull red.

* * * * *

Subcontinent 1-1, Sector 147-29, Cycle 597,845.9

Lutnaptinav's battle group reached the designated sector just after the enemy reinforcements arrived. There was some sort of underground fortress there and the fighting machines and drones had been working to destroy the defenders when six of the prey-creatures' huge war vehicles appeared several *telequel* away. Almost immediately they commenced a very effective fire which destroyed seven fighting machines in just a few moments.

The enemy was beyond effective range of the heat rays so the fighting machines responded by making evasive maneuvers to throw off the enemy aim. This helped to some extent, but the prey-creature machines continued to advance and their aim grew more and more accurate. Fighting machines continued to fall.

Finally, the enemy drew close enough and the Race could fire back. Scores of heat rays stabbed out, but as Lutnaptinav had feared, the vehicles were as heavily armored as the ones they'd faced before and no noticeable damage was done.

Mandapravis arrived on the scene and commanded the nearby machines to concentrate all their fire on just one of the enemy and this was done, although some of the prey-creatures who had been hiding in the fortress were now emerging and attacking at close range and had to be dealt with, lessening the fire on the vehicle.

"Sub-commander Lutnaptinav," said Mandapravis, suddenly on the communicator. "You have encountered these vehicles before, have you not? During the failed southern offensive?"

"That is true, Commander," it replied. "These appear to be a slightly different design from the ones we fought, but are similar in most respects."

"What is your evaluation of their capabilities?"

"They are extremely dangerous. Powerfully armed and heavily armored. A heavy heat ray could deal with them, but we have none here. Normal heat rays have little effect."

"Even if we concentrate as we are now?" The enemy vehicle it had selected was turning a dazzling red.

"Given time, I have no doubt we could destroy it, but look, even now the other vehicles are moving to shield it from our fire. Doing this could prevent us from ever concentrating for long enough."

The targeted vehicle disappeared behind two others and all the rest were continuing to fire. One fighting machine after another was blown apart. With the losses taken in the earlier fighting scarcely more than a hundred remained in the entire force.

At that moment the artificial satellite passed overhead and the information it gathered was added to the tactical display. It showed scores of water vessels on the river to the north unloading hundreds of vehicles which were moving in their direction rapidly. The prey-creatures' long range projectile throwers were starting to fire already and shells were falling among the fighting machines.

"Commander Mandapravis," said Lutnaptinav, "We could, perhaps, destroy these six vehicles with an all-out attack, but only at the cost of the destruction of our entire force." As if to emphasize its statement, one fighting machine's power cells exploded in a huge blue flash which destroyed it and four other machines standing close to it.

A long moment went by before Mandapravis replied. When it did so, it was on the general circuit: "All forces, all forces fall back to sector 24-361. Make preparation for a general retreat. Collect all rescue pods and wounded, all spare power cells and the bombardment drones. Begin at once."

A few of the other sub-commanders, perhaps surprised by this sudden change in orders, asked for confirmation from Mandapravis, but Lutnaptinav immediately complied and its battlegroup quickly retreated into the dubious shelter of some buildings. Soon all the other fighting machines were retreating as well. They made use of their speed and quickly broke contact with the enemy. Shells still fell around them, but they were clearly firing blindly in hopes of a random hit. Still, it had no doubt the huge machines were following.

"We are giving up on the attack?" asked Nabutangula over a private circuit. "After all we have expended to get this far?"

"It is the only logical course," said Lutnaptinav to the other *Threeborn*. "Losing everything over some point of honor is madness. I am thankful Mandapravis saw the truth of this."

Nabutangula made no reply.

They had traveled south several *telequel* when Mandapravis contacted it again. "Sub-commander Lutnaptinav, Sub-commander Nabutangula, respond." Lutnaptinav did so as did the commander of the Group 13 force. "I have a special mission for your two battlegroups."

"Yes, Commander?" said Lutnaptinav. Mandapravis had selected the two groups of *Threeborn* exiles. It had little doubt what this mission was.

"We will be retreating to join the forces we still have containing the prey-creature armies along the southern mountains. It is vital that we divert at least some of this pursuing force. You two will take your battlegroups west and cause as much destruction as possible. This should force the enemy to turn at least some of its forces against you."

To Lutnaptinav it was instantly clear that it and its forces were expected to sacrifice themselves to save the others. But Nabutangula had apparently not yet reached that conclusion. It asked: "How far west should we go, Commander?"

"As far as you can," replied Mandapravis. "Is this clear?"

"Entirely clear, Commander," said Lutnaptinav. "We will comply."

* * * * *

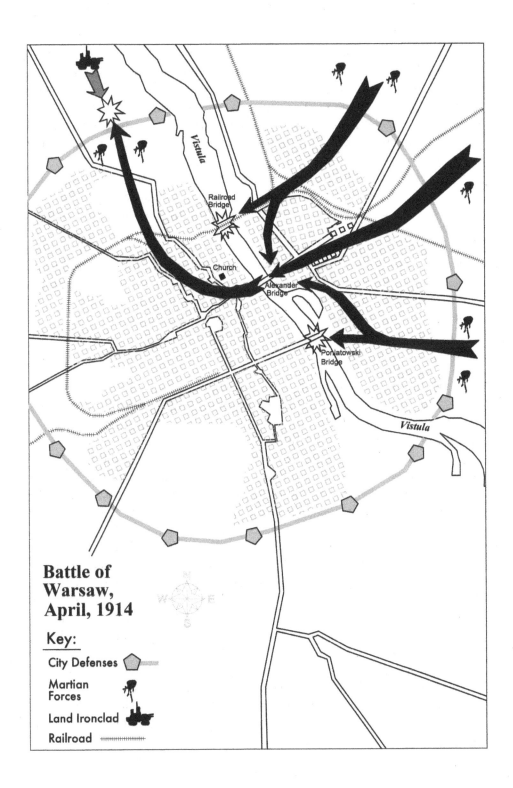

Battle of Warsaw, April, 1914

Key:

City Defenses

Martian Forces

Land Ironclad

Railroad

April, 1913, Warsaw

The metal, which had been glowing red, slowly faded back to a dull, but strangely colored shade. The paint had all melted off and the steel had that strange blue-brown whorl of colors that it got when subjected to extreme temperatures. The rating with the heavy gloves went around throwing open the armored shutters to let in cooler air and Lindemann sucked it in greedily. Bertie and Kipling and the other men on the flag bridge pulled themselves together and tried to go about their business.

"Worked, sir!' said Lieutenant Turner. "The other ships are shielding us!"

"Well, thank God for that," replied Goodenough. "Tell the Captain that as soon as we're cooled off enough, get us back into action."

"Right, sir!"

Minutes went by while things cooled. All the while the guns of the other ironclads kept firing. A bright blue flash in the distance was followed by a heavy concussion, so clearly the fire was having its effect. Just as *Implacable* started to move back into line, Lieutenant Turner, his ear to a speaking tube, suddenly shouted: "Sir! Signal from *Impressive*! The enemy is retreating!"

"Jolly good!" said Goodenough. "Make a signal to the squadron: General Pursuit."

"Yes, sir!"

The firing died down, although there were now shells whistling overhead, probably artillery from the main force. Someone threw open the hatch at the rear of the flag bridge and Lindemann gladly went out to find more cool air. He was soaked with sweat. Bertie and Kipling followed along.

They looked around and saw that *Implacable* had suffered quite a bit of damage from its ordeal under the heat rays. Smaller pieces of metal were bent and twisted, there were several holes in the funnel, the main observation platform seemed to be a bit tilted, and every bit of exposed paint had been burned away. But the ironclad resumed its place in the fighting line and the six of them rumbled up to the line of trenches defending the city. Ahead of them, much of Warsaw seemed to have burned or was still burning, although some buildings had survived. Of the Martians, there was nothing to be seen except the wreckage of their tripods.

"God of our fathers, known of old, Lord of our far-flung battle-line, Beneath whose awful Hand we hold, Dominion over palm and pine—" chanted Kipling.

Men were emerging from holes in the ground and they were cheering. Throwing helmets and rifles in the air and waving their arms. Commodore Goodenough joined Lindemann and Bertie and Kipling along with his flag lieutenant and looked at the cheering throng. He glanced upward and then turned to his lieutenant.

"William, talk to the captain and see about getting some new lines in place and run up the battle ensign, please. In fact, send a signal to the squadron and have them all raised." He gestured to the men. "Let's let these chaps know who saved their bacon."

Lieutenant Turner grinned and gave a snappy salute and said: "Right away, sir!"

* * * * *

April, 1913, Warsaw

Ola stumbled out into the sunlight, clutching Tom's arm. She jerked to a halt at the sight of half a dozen enormous gray machines rumbling by on either side of the fort. They were incredibly huge. Shaped like boats, but moving on two pairs of gigantic caterpillar tracks like the Germans' tanks. Guns stuck out of them at almost every point and tall masts supported blocky lookout towers. Black smoke poured from their stacks. The ground was actually trembling from their passage—or maybe it was just her that was shaking.

"What...? Who...?"

But even as she spoke, great flags were being pulled up and they billowed out in the breeze. They must have been ten or fifteen meters long and they were red and blue and whiter than new-fallen snow. British flags, she thought. The soldiers all around them were cheering and now cheered even louder. Several of the machines responded with toots from their steam whistles.

"About time you buggers showed up!" shouted Tom loudly, shaking a fist and laughing at the same time.

"I say, those really are impressive," said Yamamoto coming up behind. "We *really* need to get some of them."

They climbed up on top of the fort and collapsed on a small hillock which had had all the grass burned off. There was a wrecked Martian tripod only a few dozen meters away, but that somehow seemed normal now. She helped the Japanese out of his tunic and looked over his burns, which were worse than he had let on, but she didn't think he was in any danger—if he could get medical care. She hoped this relief force brought some doctors.

"Hell of a day," said Tom, "hell of a day." He looked exhausted and Ola could feel her own arms and legs quivering. It seems like weeks since they had fled out of the church, but looking at the position of the sun she realized it was probably only four or five hours.

"But we beat the bastards," he added.

Ola looked out at the remains of her city. Much of it was still in flames. Most of it was charred rubble. How many people were dead? How many hurt? How long would it take to rebuild? Victory? She supposed it was. Some of the city had survived. Some of the people, too. And the Martians were gone. They would rebuild. She leaned against Tom's arm.

"I guess we did," she said.

Chapter Eighteen

April 1914, Western Moldavia

"Can you fix it?" asked Captain Harry Calloway.

The mechanic backed out of the maintenance hatch of the Raglan carrier and shook his head. "No sir. At least no time soon. Needs a full repair facility, I'm thinkin'—like half o' the Raglans in the battalion."

"In the whole division," muttered Harry.

"God's truth, sir," agreed the mechanic.

Harry sighed and looked to Sergeant Breslin. He tugged his new eyepatch back into place. The damn thing didn't sit as well as the old one. "How many spares do we have left now?"

"Just two, sir," answered the company's first sergeant. "I'll have one of them brought up and we can transfer the gear."

"Very well." Breslin sent off a runner and then gave orders to the headquarters squad to get their gear out of the disabled carrier. The men grumbled, but complied. Corporal Gearing pulled out Harry's kit. Most of his stuff was back with the supply trains under Abdo's care, so it wasn't much.

As they waited for the replacement vehicle, Colonel Berwick's carrier came to a stop beside them. "Another breakdown, Harry?" asked the Colonel.

"Yes, sir. We're bringing up a spare. Only one more of those left in the company, sir."

"Yes, yes, it's the same story in the whole battalion," said Berwick.

"If they don't give us a chance to rest and fix things up, half our men are going to be walking soon, sir."

"Well, there might be some good news on that score soon," said Berwick.

"Sir?"

"Just got informed that the northern force has relieved Warsaw. The Martians appear to be pulling back. So perhaps they won't be in such an all-fired hurry to get us up there."

"Thank God for that!"

"Yes, but no one's changed our orders for today. We've still got to get to, uh… Czernowitz before we halt," said Berwick.

"We'll catch up, sir," said Harry.

"See that you do. Good luck." Berwick thumped the roof of his Raglan and the vehicle lurched into motion, its engine sounding just about like the one in Harry's Raglan had before it died.

They waited for the replacement to show up and the men brewed tea and offered Harry a mug. He sipped it, watching the army stream by. After they captured the Martian fortress, they had continued up the Dniester in boats and barges until they had reached the head of navigation at a town named Soroka. Then they had debarked and continued to follow the river on both shores along with a few very shallow-draft vessels which could still use the river. It had seemed a bit risky to Harry to have the army divided in two like that, but they had a pontoon bridge train with them so they could shift forces from bank to bank relatively quickly. They had scouts out in all directions to a good distance, as well, including some scout planes, so hopefully they would spot any enemy forces early enough to give warning.

And so far they hadn't seen much in the way of Martians. The scouts had caught sight of a few tripods, singly or in small groups, but none had attempted to get close to the army. The information they'd had was that Warsaw was under assault and their orders said to move as fast as they possibly could. And they had, even though Warsaw seemed an impossible distance away. The motorized forces moved ahead and the foot and horse drawn forces tried to keep up. But the roads were poor, or non-existent, and the rains turned what roads there were into axle-deep mud. The pace was hard on men and animals and harder still on vehicles. They had left a trail of broken-down tanks, lorries, carriers, and two land ironclads for a hundred miles behind them. Harry hated to think about it, but if they hadn't lost a third of the battalion's men back at the fortress, they'd have run out of working carriers days ago.

Now it seemed that their rush had not been needed. Warsaw was saved by the northern force, much of which had come all the way from England. Harry had only a vague idea why Warsaw had been so important to anyone other than the Poles. But it was a human city and apparently the Martians had wanted it pretty badly, and that was reason enough to keep them from getting it.

He leaned against the broken carrier and watched the troops still on the road. The mix of nationalities was amazing—and heartening. There were British and Australians, of course, but there were also Italians and French, Greeks and Egyptians, even a few token Turks, although most of them were still home trying to shore up the defense line against the Martians down in Arabia. From what he'd heard, the northern force that had saved Warsaw had Germans, more French, Dutch, Belgians, Spanish, Norwegians, and Swedes in it. The whole world was getting involved—and that was a good thing.

As he finished off his tea, a troop of cavalry trotted past and halted near a little creek flowing into the Dniester. They dismounted and let their horses drink. From the looks of them—dark-skinned, light-colored loose-fitting clothing, and turbans or fez-things on their heads—Harry guessed they were some sort of North African French colonial troops. His guess was confirmed when he spotted the officer who was wearing the typical blue coat and outrageous red trousers of the French Army. The man—he looked no older than himself—turned his horse over to an aide, lit a cigarette and puffed on it for a moment, and then he spotted Harry and walked over to him, smiling.

Harry knew no French at all. The school he'd attended in Sydney had one instructor who taught the language, but it wasn't required and Harry had seen no point in learning the language of a country half a world away. So as the man approached all he could do was nod and smile in return. But the Frenchman did seem to have a small bit of English and spoke to him, "British, eh?"

"Australian, actually," he replied.

The man frowned in puzzlement and then his eyebrows shot up. "Ah! Aw-stray-lia! Certainement! You are very far from home, sir, no?"

"Very far, yes. Very far."

"Vraiment! But now you here. Fighting the…" he said some word Harry couldn't make out at all, but it was obviously some epithet for the Martians. "I far from home also. Not as far as you, but I also fight them." He waved his hand at the passing troops. "We all fight them! C'est bon! C'est bon!"

"Yes, yes, it is. Bloody wonderful, really. My name is Calloway. You?"

"Ah! Oliva-Roget, Lieutenante Oliva-Roget, Premier Cavalerie Algerienne!" He stuck out his hand and Harry shook it. He gestured toward Harry's face—his eyepatch, he realized—and said something incomprehensible. What did he want to know? How he got it? It wasn't a story that could be told in a few words, or one he wanted to tell at all.

He was saved from coming up with an answer by the arrival of the replacement Raglan carrier. He held up his hands and said, "I must go. A pleasure meeting you, sir." Sergeant Breslin was already herding the headquarters squad into the vehicle. Harry took a quick look around to make sure nothing and no one was left behind and then climbed aboard. The engine roared and they moved out.

"What did the Froggie want, sir?" asked Breslin.

"Just saying hello."

"So, the colonel said that Warsaw's been relieved, right, sir? Where we headed now?"

"For now, the same place, Czernowitz, as before. After that, who knows? Somewhere there's Martians to fight, I imagine."

* * * * *

April 1914, Warsaw

Frederick Lindemann stepped out onto the bridge wing of *HMS Implacable* and stared back at the smoldering ruins of Warsaw, dwindling in the distance. Over half the city had been reduced to blackened rubble in the recent fighting. No one had any idea how many of the citizens had been killed, but surely a lot. Still, the Poles were a resilient people. Their country had been fought over again and again over the centuries and somehow they had always endured. If they were left alone, he was sure they would rebuild the city and go on.

It was two days since the battle and the army was now unloaded and ready to move. They were heading southeast along the left bank of the Vistula, but Lindemann didn't know their destination.

He turned as Bertie came up beside him. "It… it's a sh-shame we couldn't have gotten here even a day s-sooner," he said, pointing toward the devastated city. "We m-might have p-prevented a lot of th-this."

"It seems like war is always a matter of time. Days, hours, minutes, even, can make a huge difference. So, what did you think of it? Your first battle?"

"N-not like anything I've ever seen, P-Professor. We were so close to the M-Martians. When I was aboard *Collingwood* our g-gunnery practice w-was against targets t-ten or even fifteen thousand yards away. Here, you c-could almost reach out and t-touch them!"

"Indeed. And they could reach out and touch us."

"Yes! I was certain for a moment that we were g-going to fry for sure!"

"So did I," said Lindemann, trying not to shudder at the memory. The image of the steel bulkhead turning red wouldn't leave his mind. He looked at the young man next to him. "You certainly held up well, Bertie. I'll make sure the First Lord knows that."

"T-thank you, sir. But... I *was* scared."

"So was I. But you carried on and that's what counts."

"I was w-watching the commodore. *He* wasn't scared! J-just gave the right orders and it all worked out."

Lindemann was quite certain that Commodore Goodenough was just as scared as anyone else. Or at least he certainly hoped so. The thought of being under the command of some fearless maniac was almost as unsettling as the danger itself. He wasn't about to say that to Bertie so he just said, "Military discipline can be wonderful sometimes."

They both turned as the commodore himself, along with Kipling, came onto the bridge. "Ah, there you are gentlemen," he said with a disarming smile. "I've just received news from the General. Thought you might be interested."

"Indeed, sir?" said Lindemann.

"Yes, well first of all, we've gotten a wireless signal from London. A message of congratulations on the victory here from the Prime Minister, the First Lord of the Admiralty, the Minister of War, and from the King. A hearty well-done and all that. I'm having printed copies sent to the squadron. You can read it in Officers' Mess. Rather wordy thing, I expect Churchill composed most of it." He smiled to let them know it was a joke.

"He does get carried away sometimes," said Kipling.

"Yes, but of more concern to us, our orders are to head southeast along the Vistula toward Lemberg. We're to pursue the Martians and link up with the German armies along the Carpathian Mountains and relieve them from their siege."

"Once w-we link up with all of them, we sh-should have quite l-large force, won't we sir?" asked Bertie.

"In theory, yes, in practice, no, I'm afraid. From the information we have on those forces, they'll be in no condition to do any serious fighting for a while. The men have been on half rations for a month, they are very low on ammunition, and they've been forced to slaughter and eat nearly all their horses, so they are immobilized. Once we open things up, they can be resupplied, but it will probably be several months before they are ready to do anything. Still, we are picking up quite an escort to our force. All those troops that the Germans and the other European countries rushed to the German border can follow along now. Well, some of them, anyway. And our southern force will be waiting for us to arrive. Once we are all together we ought to be able to handle anything the Martians have left."

"Do we know how much they have left?" asked Lindemann. "The Martians, I mean."

Goodenough shook his head. "German scout planes and Zeppelins have spotted a hundred or so tripods retreating ahead of us. As fast as they are, we'll never catch them if they keep running. The Germans are guessing another hundred are watching their armies along the Carpathians. The Southern force hasn't seen any significant enemy force in their area since they captured that fortress. The only other large force that we know of is the one along the Danube line. Three or four hundred tripods down there, but there's no sign they are pulling out."

"So unless they have some unsuspected reserve out on the Russian Steppes, we seem to have the upper hand on the blighters," said Kipling.

"We can hope," said the commodore. "Oh, and the Germans are a bit worried about the report of a force heading west toward their territory."

"West, sir?" said Bertie.

"Yes. Not a big force, twenty or thirty tripods, but they were spotted yesterday. No one's seen them since, but even a small force could do a lot of damage if it gets loose in their rear area. Still, that is not our problem. The Germans can worry about it. Our business is south and east." Goodenough nodded to them and took his leave. Kipling remained. The man stared back at the remains of Warsaw, just as they had been doing minutes before.

"I guess... I guess you'll have a lot to write about for the newspapers now, sir," said Bertie.

Kipling stayed silent for a while and then spoke: "Y'know, I've flitted around the edges of war nearly all my life. Watching soldiers, talking to soldiers, even to generals. India, the Northwest Frontier, South Africa. Wrote about them a lot. But this was my first battle. Not quite what I expected... death just a few inches away... but I'm glad I came."

Lindemann shivered. It had been his first battle, too. But then Bertie's word about arriving sooner and saving more lives came back to him and he thought about what might have been if they had come a day *later*—or not come at all. "Yes," he said at last. "It was a terrible thing, but worth the trip."

Kipling nodded, sucked on his lower lip for a moment, and then said:

"From our towns in far lands we came,
To save our honor and a world aflame.
By foreign towns in a far land we sleep;
And trust that world we won for you to keep!"

* * * * *

April 1914, Warsaw

Tom Bridges sat at his desk and tried to finish the blasted report. He'd been working on it on and off for nearly a week. Trying to put the experience of the past months into some coherent order that the War Ministry would want to see was proving far more difficult than he'd expected. He'd done dozens of these things in the past. Several of them had even been reports on battles he'd been personally involved with. The skirmish with that Yank, Captain Dolfen, in the American west, the battle of Memphis and the assault on the Martian fortress afterward, and that nightmare in the tunnels along the Dardanelles—none of them had been as hard to describe as the siege and battle of Warsaw. He wasn't sure why.

At least he could do this in relative comfort. The hotel where the foreign observers were housed, being in the far south of the city, had escaped destruction. The spring weather had turned beautiful and the windows were open and a west wind was bringing in the scent of flowers and blowing the smell of smoke and death away. Even the view from his window was unremarkable; flowers budding, trees in leaf, and every building he could see was untouched. There were even birds singing outside as if there was not a care in the world. But his window faced south. If he looked out a north-facing window, the view was entirely different.

When he wasn't working on the report, he escorted Ola around the city. She still had the job of inspiring and cheering the people. He could tell that she would far rather be helping the wounded and injured, or clearing away the rubble, or helping to rebuild. Or killing Martians. He told her there were plenty of other people to do that and that her job was important too. He wasn't sure if she believed him. But the story of how she'd been manning a machine gun to the very last, before the relief forces arrived, had spread through the population and almost everyone was glad to see her, cheer her, shake her hand, or plant a kiss on her cheek. Bridges wasn't about to spoil the image by telling anyone that *he* was firing the gun while Ola lugged ammunition.

Even so, he was rather surprised—and secretly pleased—that he was often cheered as well. The people had seen those enormous flags on the land ironclads and the British were very popular in the city now, too. And since the relief force had moved on, pursuing the Martians, he was almost the only Englishman left in Warsaw.

Fortunately, there were plenty of other visitors in the city who were doing more than cheering people up. The relief force had left behind a lot of medical people and there were now French, Danish, Swedish, and Belgian field hospitals seeing to the injured. Convoys of German lorries were bringing in food and medical supplies and German engineers were repairing the railroads from the west to bring in more. A lot of people were suffering, but it was spring and help was coming and there was time to build or repair the houses before the next winter. Warsaw would survive.

He sighed and picked up his pen again, but was immediately interrupted by a knock on the door. "Come in," he said, hoping it was Ola.

But it was Yamamoto instead. The Japanese had mostly recovered from his burns, but still bore a few bandages. He stuck his head into the room and said, "I don't know if you are interested, old man, but that Rommel character is back. He's down in the lobby."

Bridges started in surprise. He'd completely forgotten about the German liaison officer who had buggered off with the general staff weeks ago. He really didn't give a damn about whatever the man might have to say, but it would allow him to escape the report for a while. He pushed away from the desk and stood up. "I'll come," he said.

"Oh, and the American, McCallister, came with him," said Yamamoto, leading the way down the hall to the stairs. As he'd said, Lieutenant Rommel was there in the lobby with Major McCallister beside him. They both turned as they descended the stairs to join them.

"Ah, there you both are," said Rommel in French. "You gentlemen are the only foreign observers still in Warsaw now, and I wanted to inform you that General von Moltke will not be returning his headquarters to Warsaw. The city is too badly damaged and it appears that the front lines are going to be moving east very shortly, so he will be moving his headquarters to follow. You are welcome to stay here if you wish, but there will be very little for you to observe."

"Where is the general's new headquarters?" asked Yamamoto.

"Krakow for the moment, but he hopes to push on to Lemberg as soon as possible."

"Are you heading there now? Can we get transport with you?"

"Ah, I'm afraid not. I am heading back to Germany. I've been promoted captain and I will be taking command of a new panzer company that's being formed. There will be a new liaison with the general's staff. I haven't been informed who. And you can talk to the garrison commander here about transport."

"Congratulations," said Bridges. "So you came all the way here just to tell us this? Very kind of you."

Rommel shrugged. "General von Moltke insisted. He's very meticulous about tying up... loose ends." He looked from man to man and then smiled. "And that concludes my duty, gentlemen. I will now leave you to your own devices and be on my way." He saluted and then faced about and walked out of the hotel.

"Huh," said McCallister. "German manners combined with German indifference. So, what are you two going to do? I suppose my orders demand that I follow Moltke."

"Mine as well," said Yamamoto. "What about you, Colonel?"

Bridges thought for a moment. "My orders were to come to Warsaw and observe the situation here, not to follow von Moltke, or any other German general, hither and yon. I think I shall stay here, finish my report, and wait for new orders."

"Ah, lucky you," said Yamamoto. "A cozy hotel, beautiful weather... and the charming Miss Wojciech for company." The man didn't quite leer.

Bridges chopped off a snappish reply and simply scowled. McCallister seemed oblivious to the exchange and only said, "I better go see the garrison commander about transport."

"How did *you* get here today in the first place?" asked Bridges.

"Came with Rommel—I left a few things here I want to get, assuming no one's stolen them. By train to just south of Lodz, and then by car the rest of the way. The tracks from Lodz to here are all torn up. But I understand the line running west from Warsaw to Bromberg will be repaired in a day or two. That's probably how Rommel will be going. If I can't get a car or truck back to Lodz, I suppose I'll have to go west and then curve back east further south."

"I'll come with you," said Yamamoto. The pair walked out into the spring sunshine, leaving Bridges behind. He looked out through the door and almost went out, almost went out to look for Ola. But he restrained himself and went back to his report.

He worked for most of the afternoon and was actually making some progress when he heard footsteps on the stairs. Ola, perhaps? He really hoped it was her; he missed her. But no, the steps were too heavy and yes, there were two sets. A moment later there was a rap on his door and before he could say anything the door swung open and there were Yamamoto and McCallister. Neither looked happy.

"Back again?" said Bridges. "No luck with transport, eh? I guess you'll have to wait for the rail line to be repaired."

"No, no luck at all. The headquarters is in a tizzy and the rail line might not be repaired for quite a while!" said the American grumpily.

"What? Why the tizzy? What's going on?"

Yamamoto stepped in and said, "It seems that rumor about a Martian force heading west was true. They hit the line to Bromberg about a hundred kilometers from here yesterday. Destroyed several trains and tore up a few kilometers of track. No one knows where they are now." He sat down on the edge of Bridges bed. "It seems we're all stuck here for the time being."

* * * * *

April, 1913, Thorn, Germany

Colonel Erich Serno sighed in relief as he was loaded aboard the train. He was so glad to get out of Thorn, so glad to get out of that miserable excuse for a hospital, so glad to get away from those incompetent doctors! The idiots wanted to take his leg off! He'd refused to let the doctors in Warsaw do it and he'd be damned if he'd let these morons do it either. Yes, it had been badly broken in the crash, and yes it had been further abused when the Martians sank the barge he'd been evacuated on, and the British hadn't been careful when they'd fished him out of the water and then dumped him on a boat headed back downstream. Those had been a bad couple of days.

When they offloaded him at the town of Thorn, he thought the worst was over. But no, the doctors said the breaks in the bone were too bad to mend and there was some infection there, too. It needed to come off. He'd argued with them, but they were adamant.

So he'd pulled rank. He was a colonel, damn it! He'd forced them to send a few messages to people he knew in Berlin and quickly orders arrived to ship him there so some experts could take a look. Serno was relieved—and it was clear the doctors in Thorn were glad to have him off their hands.

The train whistle blew and then they jerked into motion. The car he was aboard was made for stretcher cases like him and had racks on either side of a central aisle where stretchers could be secured. There were only two other patients in the car; Thorn was too far north from the fighting to have any large numbers of wounded passing through. He looked out a window as they chugged across the high bridge spanning the Vistula and then rolled across the flat plains of East Prussia. Spring had finally arrived and the low, marshy land was amazingly green in the sunlight. Farmers were plowing fields or leading cows out to pasture. This part of Germany had little industry and the bucolic scene was like a balm on Serno's raw nerves. Bit by bit he was able to relax and he eventually fell asleep.

When he woke he was surprised to see the late afternoon sun streaming redly through the windows. He'd slept the whole day? Apparently so. Well, he'd needed it. He'd been on edge for months. The bombing raids, the supply missions, the slow but steady loss of men and machines. The crash and the aftermath, all had been wearing him away.

But that was done. He'd get to Berlin, and the doctors would save his leg. He realized that there would be a long recovery period and it would be a long time before he could fly again. But that was all right. He was sure he could get himself sent to one of the good hospitals in Frankfurt and his home in Darmstadt was only a short distance from there. He'd really like to see his parents and his sister again…

He'd gotten one brief note from Wurlzinger, his aide, assuring him that the *Kampfgeswader* was still hauling supplies and that the man now in command hadn't succeeded in destroying it yet. Well, it wasn't going to be his worry for quite a while. He slowly let himself unwind.

The sun set and darkness gathered outside the train windows. An orderly walked by and said, "We'll be in Poznan in about an hour, Colonel. We'll be stopping there for a while and we'll have dinner brought aboard."

"That would be wonderful, thank you," he replied. He stared at the window, but aside from an occasional passing light all he could see in it now was his own reflection lit by a few electric lamps inside the car. He scarcely recognized the man staring back at him. Gaunt, hollow-eyed, hair thinning... Well, his mother would fatten him up, he was sure. He looked forward to her good cooking. He started to doze off...

A squeal of brakes and the sudden pressure of rapid deceleration snapped him awake. The train's whistle was howling like a damned soul and the car was shaking like a plane in a thunderstorm. Serno gripped the rails of his stretcher and tried to see out. What was wrong? Some sort of mishap on the tracks?

The answer came with that familiar and oh, so horrible shriek of a Martian heat ray. A red glare poured through the window, tinting the whole inside of the car like blood.

No! How can they be here? We're two hundred kilometers from the front! Not here! Not again...

The car lurched like it had been struck by a giant fist and the inside lights went out. Serno's stretcher came loose and he tumbled to the floor of the car as pain shot through his leg and then all the rest of him. He tried to grab something solid but the car was tilting. He slid up against the side wall as the car tilted further and further and then it was rolling. He was tossed about like a pea inside a can and his whole world devolved into pain and the red glare.

The car suddenly stopped and he was slammed into a wall. The pain and the light fled into darkness.

* * * * *

Subcontinent 1-1, Sector 197-35, Cycle 597,845.9

The heat ray sliced through the steam-powered machine that was pulling the long line of conveyance vehicles. The boiler exploded in an expanding ball of hot water vapor and molten metal. More rays incinerated some of the other vehicles or destroyed the metal rails they were riding on. Even those vehicles that were untouched by the rays tumbled from the rails and were smashed by their own momentum.

The entire destruction had only taken moments and Lutnaptinav and Nabutangula immediately ordered their shrunken battle groups to reform and continue on their way. Only a short distance ahead there was another river with a bridge crossing it. There did not appear to be any significant forces guarding it, so they would use it to cross the river and then destroy it behind them. A large habitation zone lay beyond.

So far the hopeless mission ordered by Commander Mandapravis had gone far better than Lutnaptinav had expected. After they had been given their orders, the two small battlegroups had broken off from the main force and headed west at the best speed the terrain would allow. They had quickly outdistanced any possible pursuit by the prey-creatures near the city. The lands to the west were mostly empty, their inhabitants had fled soon after the city had been put under siege.

They had continued west, circling south of a region that was heavily overgrown. From there they had encountered one of the prey-creatures' railed transport lines. Since their orders was to attract as much of the prey-creatures' attention as possible, they had slowed their pace and destroyed ten *telequel* of the rails along with two of the linked transport vehicles they had met. There had been no immediate response from the enemy, so they continued west toward where they knew a significant line of defensive works existed.

Lutnaptinav, who had become the effective commander of the combined group, decided there was little to be gained by an all-out attack on this line and instead ordered an attempt to pierce the line and continue toward the industrial centers they knew lay further west. Nabutangula, who appeared fully willing to cede leadership to Lutnaptinav, had agreed.

The attack was made at night when the prey creatures were least danger-ous and was successful, although three fighting machines were lost to pit-traps and two more to fire from the heavy projectile throwers emplaced among the de-fenses. A sixth machine was lost when it attempted to destroy a large collection of supplies only to discover some of the containers held significant amounts of chemical explosives.

There had been only minimal pursuit by prey-creatures riding on animals. The animals could not maintain the pace necessary to keep up and were left behind after a rotation. From that point they had encountered almost nothing in the way of military forces and far more non-combatant prey-creatures. It seemed they had penetrated into the vulnerable rear areas. Cognizant of their mission to draw the enemy away from Mandapravis' retreating force, they had slain any prey-creatures they encountered and destroyed any structures they came across. These had usually been in tiny groups of only two or three buildings or clusters of a score or so. They had been completely undefended.

But now a significant city was in their path. Not as large as the one they had hoped to capture, but many times larger than the small groups of structures they had found recently. Destroying it would take time and a considerable expen-diture of their energy supplies. There were only twenty-seven fighting machines left in the two groups and the time spent destroying the city would allow the prey creatures to gather their forces. Lutnaptinav wondered just how long they could continue. But their orders were to advance as far to the west as they could.

They reached the bridge, a large metal structure. A group of prey-crea-tures were gathered there, attracted, perhaps, by the flames from the destroyed rail vehicle. They began to scatter as soon as they saw the fighting machines approach, but scores were incinerated before they could escape.

The machines advanced across the bridge single-file. Some of the cross-bracing in the structure had to be scrambled over or under in an awkward fashion, but it was soon done. Once across, they lined up on the river bank and opened fire on the bridge. The main supports were stone and it would not be profitable to waste fire on them. But the main metal members of the bridge were soon glowing red and then white hot. With a groaning shriek, like some dying animal, the bridge collapsed into the water, the hot metal hissing and producing clouds of steam where it struck the cold water.

Lutnaptinav opened the general communications circuit. "Attention. We will attack the city to the west of us. We will form a single line with one hundred *quel* between machines. Advance at the standard speed. Our objective is maximum damage in minimum time with minimum risk to ourselves. Proceed through the city without stopping. If you meet any serious opposition, go around it. Assist anyone who runs into trouble. We will regroup on the other side of the city. Questions?"

There were none.

"Very well. Proceed."

Chapter Nineteen

May 1914, Western Moldavia

"**G**et down! Here they come!" screamed Harry as a heat ray swept by just a few feet over his head. He ducked further down into the ditch he was crouching in until the beam was gone. He dared to poke his head up to take a look, but his eye was assailed by such an array of images that it was hard to make much sense out of it.

It was sometime after midnight, he guessed, but the darkness was being ripped away almost continuously. A half-dozen star shells drifted down on their parachutes, each one a dazzlingly bright pinpoint, bathing the ground with a pure white glare. From behind him and off to his left and then circling half the horizon back to his front there was the near-constant flash of the artillery. Closer at hand were the abrupt sparks of the tank guns and smaller field pieces, the flickering of the machine guns, and the individual winks of rifles. Across the smoke-shrouded expanse in front came the red lances of the Martian heat rays, stabbing out in all directions. A few searing flashes of the blue bombs lit up the landscape from time to time, but thankfully only a few.

And every one of those light sources had a noise associated with it. The night was filled with a rattling, roaring, thundering, sizzling sound that assaulted his ears as intensely as the light assaulted his eye. Looking to either side, he saw that some of his men were being overwhelmed by it all; they were flat on the ground or curled into balls with their eyes squeezed shut and their hands over their ears.

But he didn't have that luxury. He was in command and he had responsibilities. He had to look and listen and try to make sense of the situation so he could keep his men—and possibly himself—alive.

Peering out from the ditch he could see the shapes of the Martian tripods striding through the clouds of dust and smoke thrown up by the artillery. Some were just dim outlines, while others came into sharp focus, the light of the star shells glittering off their metal skins. They were moving fast, their long legs eating up the distance with their strange alien gaits. Moving fast, but not toward him. They were heading east, moving from right to left across his front.

It had been almost two weeks since they'd been given a few days' rest at the town of Czernowitz. The pause in the advance was much needed to rest the men and repair equipment. But then orders came to continue the trek up the Dniester. They were heading toward the city of Lemberg where the Austrian Army was still holding out. If they could link up with them they might just trap the retreating Martians between themselves and the pursuing force coming down from Warsaw.

But then two days ago the word came that the enemy were moving much faster than expected. They had abandoned their siege of the Germans along the northern slopes of the Carpathians and they were collecting themselves and heading east as fast as their metal legs could carry them. There would be no chance of reaching Lemberg before the Martians were past it—assuming they intended to bypass it—and no chance that the northern force could catch up with them before they did so. That put the southern force—Harry's force—squarely in the enemy's path—and all by itself.

General Legge had halted the advance and set up a defensive line about forty miles west of Chernowitz where the Dniester bent south toward the mountains and the smaller Prut River. To the north was a tributary of the Dniester, the Zbrucz, creating a natural choke point. It was the best position they were likely to find.

At that time the Martians were following the north bank of the Dniester, but the river was low enough that the aliens would have no trouble fording it almost anywhere. The General put his least mobile forces, the Italians, French, and Greek troops, to the south of the Dniester and had them dig in. He kept his more mobile and most powerful units on the north side. They'd have the best chance in a straight-up fight, and if the Martians did shift to the south bank, they could be redeployed the most quickly to meet them.

So, they spent a day digging in and four pontoon bridges were thrown across the Dniester. The 1st Australian Armored Division—and Harry—didn't dig in too deeply; they would be part of the army reserve, ready to shift to wherever needed. Two very tense days followed receiving periodic reports from aircraft confirming that the Martians were moving around Lemberg's northern perimeter and continuing to head east and south along the Dniester.

Yesterday morning scouts made contact with the enemy vanguard and the army went to full alert. They were only about sixty miles away and the tripods could cover that in less than a day. By afternoon they could hear some faint firing off to the west and he had his men stand close by their carriers. If the order to move came, he wanted there to be no delays.

Then… nothing.

The firing died away and the scouts reported the Martians had pulled back. The weather was lousy and they had no aerial reconnaissance that day, so they didn't know what the enemy was planning. Theoretically they could shift their direction to the northeast and just fade off into the endless Russian Steppes and not come this way at all. But if they were trying to link up with the Martian forces along the Danube, the straightest route was right through them. The day wore on and darkness fell. No one relaxed—the Martians liked to attack at night.

And they did. About ten o'clock, the sky lit up with the flashes of artillery. But it was the sky to the south, on the other side of the Dniester. The Martians had crossed the river, side-stepping the main human force, and were hitting the weaker line to the south. Word quickly came for the 1st Armored to cross the bridges and reinforce the troops there.

They moved as quickly as they could, but not fast enough. As they reached the other side, they learned that the Martians had punched a hole through the defenses, overrun an Italian division, and were now moving through into the rear areas. There was no time to get in front of the enemy, no way to reinforce or back up a defense line that no longer existed, all they could do was hit the Martians in the flank and hope for the best.

Hit them they did and here they were. The division's tanks, the Wellingtons and Marlboroughs, led the way with the Raglan carriers and the Longbow artillery close behind. Roaring through the rear area of the French division closest to the river, scattering the supply troops like a flock of partridges, they advanced, spreading out at the same time, until they found the Martians. They found a lot of them.

Cresting a low ridge, they halted on the lip of a broad valley, a valley filled with fleeing Italians and their Martian pursuers. The valley was also filled with exploding artillery shells. As soon as the enemy point of attack was determined, every long range gun the army possessed was directed against it. British four-point-five inch howitzers and eighteen pounders, French seventy-five and one hundred and twenty millimeter guns and even the 12" guns from the American Land Ironclads rained down. The ironclads were on their way, but they were so slow it would be quite a while before they could arrive—but that didn't stop them from throwing shells all the same. The valley was turned into a boiling cauldron. No doubt many of those shells were killing friends, but this war had long since shown that killing Martians was more important—no matter the price.

The tanks had deployed and opened fire, the Raglans halted just behind them, and further to the rear the Longbows had gone into battery and added their shells to the mix. The nearest Martians had fired back and the troops, not wanting to burn up inside their carriers, had spilled out to find cover. Harry and the 15th Newcastles were among them.

In the rush to get here, command and control had become muddled. Harry had no specific orders, so he fell back on what they'd been trained to do during those long months in Egypt: the tanks were engaged in a long-range firefight, but not advancing, so deploy to protect them from enemy spider machines. He got his company sorted out and found some cover—a sunken road, he thought—and set up a firing line. He had no idea where Colonel Berwick was; he wasn't even sure where the other companies of the battalion were, but he was here and here he would hold until someone gave him new orders.

Sergeant Breslin appeared next to him, his craggy face lit by the blazing star shells. "The lads are all in position, sir!" he screamed above the din. "I got one man in each squad keeping a lookout and the rest are keeping their fool heads down!"

"Good! Anyone seen any of the spiders?"

"Not that I know. Haven't seen any myself."

Harry dared to take a look again. No, nothing to be seen but explosions and tripods. But the spiders were so small they could easily be sneaking up to attack. Spotting them before they got close was vital. Once they got in among the men it would be a bloodbath. He stared until another heat ray swept by and he was forced to duck down. The brush and bushes on the edge of the sunken road burst into flames, and it was some time before he could look out again. He crouched down and coughed from the smoke, his eye watering. He prayed that the Martians didn't use their black dust weapon now; they'd never see it coming until it was too late. All the while the guns roared. The four-point-five-inchers on the Wellingtons barked, the concussion from each shot hammered at him. The coil guns on the Marlboroughs made much less noise, just a weird *whoosh-crack*, like a miniature thunderbolt.

A few of the tanks were burning now, but not many. The number of heat rays coming their way seemed to be diminishing, too. When the burning brush died down he looked out again, and while the valley was still an inferno of bursting shells, he didn't see nearly as many tripods and those he did were scurrying eastward and south, getting further and further away. Some of the artillery fire was following them, and one clearly found its mark when a dazzling blue flash illuminated everything for a moment and then long seconds later a huge roar washed over them. *Got at least one of the bastards!*

"Looks like the blighters are running, sir!" said Breslin.

"Yes, it does. We should get after them."

But nothing happened immediately and the tanks, lacking targets, stopped firing. Some of the artillery was still shooting at something, but the noise was dying down. Harry looked around and saw Corporal Whelan with his wireless set. Harry waved him over. "Eric, anything coming through? Any new orders?"

Whelan shook his head. "Lots of folks sending messages, but nothing for us that I can make out, sir."

"Bloody hell," said Breslin, frowning fiercely. "They're getting away!"

And so they were. It was nearly dawn before they got orders to get moving. It was very quiet by then, although everyone's ears were still ringing. They mounted up and followed the tanks down into the valley. It was a scene of devastation. Craters everywhere, shattered trees, splintered fences, burned out farmhouses, wrecked supply lorries, smashed tripods... and bodies, lots of bodies.

"The Valley of Death," muttered Harry.

"Yeah," said Breslin. "That Tennyson guy ought to see *this*!"

The remains of the Italian division were sobering, but Harry and the other men in his carrier were cheered by the number of wrecked tripods they spotted. It was hard to count them considering how torn up they were, but Harry thought he could see at least thirty, and there had to be more he couldn't see.

"I don't see any of those bloody damn spiders," said Breslin.

"No, but they could be so torn to bits we wouldn't recognize them. Still I didn't see any during the fight, either."

"Maybe they used 'em all up against the Jerries, up north," said one of the men in the carrier. One of the new men, named Perkins, "Maybe we won't have to worry about 'em no more."

"Oh don't you worry about that, Perkins," said Breslin. "They're makin' more just for you."

"Thanks, Sarge, thanks very much."

As the sun came up they finally regained contact with Colonel Berwick. He confirmed that the Martians had only wanted to break through their lines so they could continue retreating. They were miles ahead of them now. Their orders were to pursue.

"So we're turning around and heading back the way we came?" asked Private Perkins. "All this way and we just turn around and go back?"

Harry smiled grimly and said: "Welcome to the army, private."

* * * * *

May, 1914, Lemberg, Austria-Hungary

Professor Frederick Lindemann stiffly lowered himself down the last few rungs of the metal ladder and jumped down to the ground. This was the first time he'd been off the land ironclad *HMS Implacable* since they had left Warsaw over two weeks ago. It felt good to be released from that rolling, shaking, smelly, overcrowded prison. Young Bertie had preceded him down the ladder and he was stretching and looking around. Kipling thumped down just behind him.

"Ah," said the writer. "Good to be out of there." He looked around and added, "Pity this place is such a dump."

They had reached the city of Lemberg in what could not really be called a pursuit of the Martians. The aliens were vastly faster and had left them far behind after the first day. They had followed anyway. The Northern Task Force as it was being called now, had orders to sweep along the northern edge of the Carpathian Mountains to make sure all of the enemy forces which had been besieging the four German armies trapped there were gone. Other German forces were rushing to reestablish contact with them and bring in the supplies they needed to become operational again and it was the Northern Task Force's job to make sure nothing interfered with that.

They had found no trace of the enemy. The Martian force retreating from Warsaw had gathered them all up ahead of them. The combined force had retreated as fast as it could, swinging around the heavily fortified Lemberg to the north, and a few days ago it had punched through the Southern Task Force and was now heading… no one was quite sure where, but scouting planes reported it was still retreating.

The Northern Task Force—or what was left of it—reached Lemberg and halted. Their losses at Warsaw had been light and they had not lost anything to the enemy during the long pursuit, but fully a third of their vehicles—including two of the land ironclads—had broken down and were scattered in a two hundred mile line stretching almost back to Warsaw. The professionals Lindemann had spoken with told him that they had been lucky not to have lost half or more.

But the vehicles which had made it to Lemberg were in such a decrepit state that there was no possibility of advancing further until some serious repairs and maintenance work could be done. Lindemann was looking forward to some time off. He just wished he could spend that time somewhere else. Surveying his surroundings, he had to agree with Kipling: Lemberg really was a dump.

He supposed it wasn't the fault of the city. He found a lot of Eastern European architecture drab, but there were usually some really splendid churches and other public buildings. But Lemberg had been under siege for almost six months and it looked it. Even though it had not come under direct attack, every tree had been chopped down for firewood and he could see a number of buildings which had also been dismantled for that purpose. There were piles of refuse everywhere and despite the mild spring weather, there was hardly a green growing thing in sight. The unpaved areas were just a sea of mud, churned up by all the military traffic. A crowd of civilians had turned out to gawk at the enormous land ironclads and they all seemed dirty, tattered, and malnourished. Indeed, many of them were begging for food from the newly arrived Britishers. He could see some of the crew tossing food down from *Implacable*. He hoped they were saving some for themselves—and him. A few of the Austrian defenders looked as though they wanted to do some begging too. The rail lines from the west were still being repaired and it would probably be weeks before any significant aid could reach the city.

Lindemann had been planning to take a stroll around the city—anything to get away from *Implacable* for a while—but now he was having second thoughts. He was afraid that the sight of his well-clad and well-fed form would soon have him surrounded by a mob of hungry peasants. He really despised the lower classes and a mob of lower class *Slavs* would be intolerable. No, he would not go walking—except in a large and well-armed group. Kipling and Bertie didn't seem to have such inhibitions and they were wandering off to sight-see. Lindemann supposed Bertie would be safe enough under Kipling's wing.

As he stamped around in the mud, stretching his legs, he began to realize that he'd been harboring unrealistic expectations for this stop in Lemberg. His subconscious had been making plans for sleeping in a bed instead of a hammock, and eating food prepared in a proper kitchen instead of a the tiny galley on *Implacable*, and dining off fine China on a linen-covered table. None of that was going to happen here. He could see some of the crew lowering down bundles of canvas and wooden poles that were tents. So he could probably sleep on a cot instead of a hammock if he wished, but that was the only luxury he was going to find in Lemberg.

After he'd gotten all the leg-stretching he wanted, he wandered over to where the tents were going up. He found *Implacable's* first officer there overseeing the activities. The man saw him and waved. "Will you and Lieutenant Windsor be wanting a tent for tonight, Professor?" he asked.

"Uh, yes, yes, I think so," he replied. Not luxury, but any change would be welcome.

"Very good, sir, we'll have it set up for you in a bit."

As he turned away, he saw Bertie returning alone. "Where's Kipling?" asked Lindemann.

"Oh, h-he wanted to explore s-some more. I t-thought I ought t-to be getting back. N-not really m-much to see."

"Well, I told Commander Burling that we'd be sleeping in one of the tents tonight. Thought it would be a good change. I suppose we should get our things organized and brought down, eh?"

"G-good idea, Professor," said Bertie, grinning. "Yes, let's go." They went back to the ladder and climbed back up. At the top they were met by Commodore Goodenough's flag lieutenant William Turner.

"Ah, there you both are!" he said. "The Commodore just sent me to find you."

"Oh, what about?" asked Lindemann.

"He didn't say, but we just received a number of wireless messages so I suppose there must be something that concerns you. Come, let's go."

They made their way past bustling crewmen and up to *Implacable's* flag bridge. Goodenough was there, talking with the captain. He smiled when he caught sight of them. "Excellent! I have some news for you gentlemen."

"Sir?" said Lindemann.

"Yes, the people back In London seem to think this campaign is all wrapped up. Can't say I actually agree with them, but no matter. We've gotten orders from the Admiralty for you and Lieutenant Windsor to return to London by the quickest means possible."

"Really?" said Bertie. The expression on his face was half excitement and half disappointment.

"Yes, it seems that our victory at Warsaw is all the talk back home. Wouldn't be surprised if there are some rewards waiting for both of you there—but that's just speculation. In any case, orders are orders. I'm making arrangements for a fast scout car with proper escort to take you back to the head of navigation on the Vistula and then a courier boat to get you back to Danzig. I imagine there will be a cruiser waiting for you there. Oh, do you suppose that Kipling will be wanting to go back with you? I can fit him in."

"No idea. He's off in the city, I believe."

"Well, you'll be leaving in an hour or so. If he's not back, you'll leave without him."

Lindemann nodded. "Well, sir, it's certainly been an interesting time, you've shown us. Thank you for your hospitality."

"It's been an honor having you," said Goodenough. He looked at Bertie. "Both of you." He stuck out his hand and shook with each of them. "But you better get your things together. I'll have a man come and collect you when your transport is ready."

They thanked him again and went down to their tiny cabin and began stuffing their meager belongings into bags. Kipling still had not returned when they were escorted down the ladder to three waiting armored cars.

"D-d'you think we should make them wait for Mr. K-Kipling, sir?" asked Bertie.

"Doubt they'd agree. They've got orders. Anyway, Kipling has more experience knocking around the world than all the rest of us combined. He'll make his own way." Lindemann looked at the young man next to him and put a hand on his shoulder. "Come on, Bertie, let's go home."

* * * * *

Subcontinent 1-1, Sector 205-72, Cycle 597,845.9

Lutnaptinav attempted to raise the fighting machine to an upright position, but it toppled over again, jarring it considerably. He used the neural control link and explored the circuits of the machine. The exploration told him what he already knew: the machine was severely damaged. The heat ray was unserviceable, one manipulator tendril was inoperable, some of the sensors had been destroyed and most important, leg number 3 had been severed between the second and third joint.

What sensors that remained indicated that there were no prey-creatures in the immediate vicinity, but that probably would not remain the case for long. Still it was early in the planet's night cycle and the inhabitants did not function well in darkness. They might not find it until daylight.

But they surely would find it eventually and that would mean death.

The rampage through the prey-creatures' rear area had come to an end. It had gone on longer than Lutnaptinav had expected, but the conclusion had been inevitable. After devastating the one city, the prey-creatures had brought their forces against them quickly. Large projectile throwers, armored gun vehicles, foot warriors with explosives, and flying vehicles had converged from every direction. They had used their greater speed to elude them time and again, but they had lost machines at every encounter. The force had shrunk and shrunk as they continued moving west. They had destroyed bridges and the rail transport systems when they could, but they did not dare linger long anywhere. They encountered several other cities, but the defenses were too strong to attempt an attack, so they bypassed them and moved on. Nabutangula had urged that they attack, but Lutnaptinav had overruled it and it had accepted that decision.

After their first successes, Lutnaptinav had wondered if the main force, instead of fleeing, could have done vast amounts of damage in the enemy industrial zones if they had broken into ten or twelve small groups. But the areas that they passed through were densely populated, far more so than any they had seen before. Their wire-carried communication network was dense and the enemy was constantly being informed of their whereabouts. That combined with their rail transport system the prey-creatures could concentrate against them far quicker than they could in open country. No, if the main force had split up, each part would just be hunted down and destroyed.

But even avoiding hopeless battles, Lutnaptinav's force had quickly run out of options. Whatever direction they chose, they ran into serious opposition. Flying machines followed them almost continuously in daylight and scouting forces riding animals maintained contact in the dark periods. They were down to only ten fighting machines, every one of them damaged to some extent and burdened with occupied survival pods. Only a few spare power units remained.

Finally, Lutnaptinav, using maps provided by the artificial satellite, attempted to break contact, at least for a while, by turning east and moving through an area heavily overgrown with vegetation. At first it seemed like a wise move, but they quickly found that the terrain was very rough, with numerous ridges and steep gullies. Two machines were lost to mishaps. They were also seriously slowed down and the enemy, knowing where they had entered the area, were given the time to assemble forces at all the likely exit points.

Like this one.

Early in the current night cycle they had been suddenly attacked by a powerful prey-creature force waiting in ambush near the edge of the overgrown area. Three machines were destroyed in the first moments. Lutnaptinav tried to push through, hoping the enemy defenses were thin enough to allow escape. The loss of four more machines convinced it that this would not be possible. It, along with Nabutangula and one other, attempted to retreat. They nearly managed it when the third machine suffered a catastrophic hit which discharged its power cells. The blast had thrown Lutnaptivav's machine down a steep ravine—where it now lay.

It again attempted to pull itself upright and again it failed. It evaluated its situation and concluded it was not good. Without a replacement leg there was no hope of regaining normal mobility. It was theoretically possible to remove the lower parts of the remaining legs and attempt to walk on the stumps. In flat terrain this might be possible, but here in this rough area it would likely prove impossible. And even if it succeeded, its speed would be so reduced that it would quickly be caught. No, there was little hope that...

"Lutnaptivav? Is that you?"

The voice on the communicator came as a considerable surprise. But a welcome one. "Yes," it replied. "So you have survived as well, Nabutangula? What is your condition?"

"Yes, I am about one hundred *quel* to your east. I can just see your machine through the vegetation. My machine is severely damaged and immobilized. I assume you are damaged as well?"

"Yes. Not too badly, but I have no weapon and one leg is wrecked."

"Just one? Two of mine are ruined."

"What of the third?"

"Only slightly damaged, but of no use without the others."

"One plus two equals three, Nabutangula."

"Are you suggesting that we can produce one working machine by salvaging parts from the other?"

"It seems the only option. Unless you would prefer to lie here until the prey-creatures find us."

"I am open to this. Can you drag your machine in my direction? I will try to move in yours."

By using the remaining limbs, Lutnaptinav was able to drag and lurch its way toward Nabutangula's machine. The other was barely able to move, but eventually they were in reach of each other.

"We do not have much time before they find us," said Nabutangula.

"The vegetation is all burning in the direction toward the enemy. That may hold them off for some time. But you are right. Let us hurry."

Fortunately, the fighting machines were designed for quick and easy replacement of damaged parts. Working in concert with their remaining manipulators, they were able to remove the damaged leg on Lutnaptinav's machine at the second joint and then replace it with the lower part of Nabutangula's remaining leg. Nothing arrived to interfere.

"We have no survival pod," observed Nabutangula.

"We can fit you into my machine."

"Truly?"

"I will not leave you behind."

"It will be very crowded."

"Truly."

And it was. But they managed it. The two of them squeezed their bodies into the control area only meant for one. Then Lutnaptinav pulled the machine upright and tested its mobility. Not perfect, but it would suffice.

"And where shall we go now?" asked Nabutangula.

"I judge that we have fulfilled our mission and have advanced west 'as far as we can'."

"I concur," said Nabutangula.

"Very well. Then let us head east."

* * * * *

May, 1914, Warsaw, Poland

"You have to go? Really?" asked Ola Wojciech. She stared into Tom Bridges' eyes. The tall Englishman nodded.

"Yes. My orders just arrived. I can probably stay another few days while I arrange for transport but... I can't disobey my orders, Ola. I have to go. I'm... really sorry."

She believed him. She did. But he had to go and it felt like her heart had just dropped into her stomach. It was still beating but it felt... *wrong*. Everything felt wrong. Tears started in her eyes and she bit her tongue—hard—to stop them. She couldn't think of a thing to say.

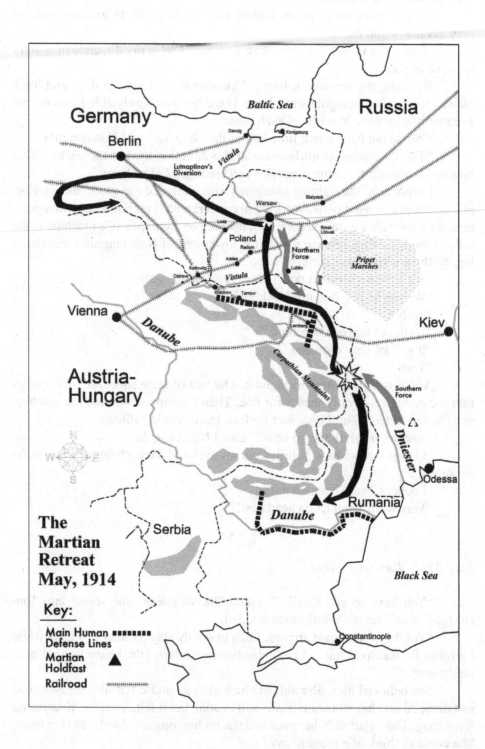

The Martian Retreat May, 1914

Key:
- Main Human Defense Lines
- Martian Holdfast
- Railroad

"I… uh, I… could… maybe I could figure a way to… you know… to take you with me. If you wanted…" Tom was turning a bright red, and his stumbling speech was almost enough to make Ola laugh. Almost.

Instead, she reached out and took his hands. "Thank you, Tom. Thank you. But I can't. You know that. You've seen Warsaw, seen the mess it is. How could I leave? Leave all the people here trying to rebuild. Trying to survive. I have to stay and help. You know I can't leave."

"I know," he said, nodding. "I knew that would be your answer. But I had to ask. Ola, I don't want to leave, but I have no choice. But… but when this is all over, I'll come back. I'll come back to you. If… if you want me."

Now she nodded. "Yes, I want you. I want you very much. But…"

"But what?"

"You said you could stay for a few more days?" She gave him a tiny smile.

He smiled back. A much bigger smile. "Yes. I can certainly do that."

She moved in to hug him. He hugged back and then bent to kiss her.

Chapter Twenty

May 1914, Southern Moldavia

The breeze was warm and filled with the fragrance of flowers. The sun was dipping into the west, turning the puffy clouds a fine shade of pink. It was a beautiful, perfect day. But Harry's eyes were not on the sunset. Instead, he was looking at the lovely young woman walking beside him.: Vera Brittain, Voluntary Aid Detachment nurse, poet, and... his friend.

"It's really grand to see you again, Vera," said Harry. "It's been what? Three months since the last time?"

"Yes, about that, I think, back in Egypt," she replied.

"I... I've missed you."

She turned her head and looked right at him. "I've missed you, too, Harry." Harry felt his face flushing, and his breath coming faster. But he smiled, and mustering every bit as much courage as it took to charge a Martian spider machine, he reached out and took her hand. When she did not pull it away, his smile grew broader. She rewarded him with a smile of her own.

But then her smile faded and she looked away—but did not withdraw her hand. "I've been worried about you, too. Every time there is fighting and the wounded start coming in I'm in terror that I'll see you on one of those bloody stretchers."

Harry's smile faltered, too, but he gave her hand a little squeeze. "At... at least there hasn't been too much fighting so far. We lost some men at the Martian fortress, but that was about all."

"Except for the Italians."

"Oh... well, yeah, right, they got hit pretty hard. Did... did any of their wounded come your way?"

"Some," she said, her eyes falling. "The Italian medical detachments got overrun along with the rest of their troops. They had to send their wounded to everyone else. We got a few dozen. But, no, you're right, things haven't been too bad. Certainly not compared to what it was like at the Dardanelles. But even when there's no fighting, we still get the usual portion of sick and injured."

"Yes, I guess that's true. I guess the men still get sick no matter what we're doing."

Vera was silent for a moment and then said, "Some of the doctors are worried. We've gotten a batch of men who are sick with something they've never seen before. It's a whole group of engineers—all from the same unit. They said they went down into the Martian fortress. They're all weak, run fevers, and they throw up what we feed them and some of them have their hair falling out. One of them has died. The doctors are afraid there was some sort of contagion down there. Except a lot of other men went in there and it's only this one batch who are sick."

Harry's blood ran cold. He and Burf had been down there! But he felt fine and Burf wasn't sick either. But wait a minute... a group of engineers? "Vera, is the commander of those engineers a funny little man named Hobart?"

"Why, yes it is. Do you know him?"

"Burf and I were attached to his unit for a half a day. We... we went down into the fortress with him."

"Harry!" Vera's face turned pale and she clutched his hand.

"I'm fine! I'm fine! Fit as a fiddle, really. So's Burf."

She stared at him intently, reached up and felt his forehead and took his pulse. "You seem all right... no symptoms of any sort?"

"None. I'm fine, Vera."

"Well, I'm glad. But if you start feeling bad, you come right to the hospital."

"All right."

"I mean it! Harry, promise me!"

He was really touched by her concern. "I promise," he said. Then a thought struck him and he suddenly blurted out: *"Idiot!"*

Vera stepped back, surprise on her face. "I beg your pardon?"

"Hobart! That damn fool must have gone back in after the generator burst!"

"What?"

"The Martians set their electrical generator machine to blow up. We realized it and only got out just in time. But then Burf and I left Hobart and came back to our unit. Hobart must have gone back down after we left. The fool was so eager to get his hands on the Martian machines he couldn't resist. He knew it was dangerous but he went in—and took his men in—anyway. Damn the man!" He saw that Vera was staring at him and he was embarrassed by his outburst. "Is... is he going to make it?"

It took a moment for her to reply. "Probably. Nearly all of them have been showing some improvement in the last few days."

"Well, that's good."

She looked toward the west. The sun was disappearing behind a line of hills. "We better be getting back." she said. "I have duty tonight."

Reluctantly, Harry agreed and they started walking back toward the camps. It was quite a ways because as soon as they'd started their walk they had headed away from the huge collection of men, tents, vehicles and supply dumps which had surrounded her hospital. They were both sick of the clamor and filth. It was nearly dark by the time they reached the hospital.

They stood there a while, holding hands in silence. Harry did not want this day to end and it seemed like Vera didn't either. He became extremely aware of how close she was to him and he caught his breath when she actually leaned into him, her left shoulder pressing into his right arm. Dare he put his arm around her? They had been friends for several years and she clearly enjoyed his company, but had never given any sign that it went farther than that—until now.

There were people all around, some lighting lanterns and others tending cook fires, but no one was paying any attention to them. He raised his arm and slowly put his hand on her right shoulder...

Harry froze and Vera yelped when a star shell suddenly burst to life half a mile to the west. Rifles and machine guns started firing from off in that direction and then some heavier guns joined in.

"What's happening, Harry?" asked Vera. "You said there weren't any Martians close by."

"That's what we were told! I don't know..."

"Look!" Vera pointed.

Out of the dark a Martian tripod had materialized, the glare of the star shell reflecting off its metal skin. It was only a few hundred yards away and appeared to be heading right toward them at a terrible speed!

"Get down!" cried Harry. He dragged Vera behind a stack of wooden crates. He fumbled out his revolver, not that it would be useful. But before he could form any plan of action, the tripod ran—the bloody thing was *running*!—right past them not thirty yards off. It was not firing its heat ray and after only a few moments it disappeared into the darkness to the east. More star shells burst to life and the firing went on for another ten minutes before slowly dying away.

Harry and Vera got to their feet and dusted themselves off. "Well, what do you suppose that was all about?" she asked.

"Not a clue. But it seemed to be in quite a hurry!"

* * * * *

Subcontinent 1-1, Sector 67-43, Cycle 597,845.9

"It would appear that you were correct in your evaluation," said Nabutangula. "A sudden dash did take them by surprise."

"Random chance has acted in our favor," replied Lutnaptinav as it maneuvered the fighting machine away from the areas lit up by the prey-creatures' illumination munitions. A few of the enemy projectiles, apparently fired at random, continued to explode here and there, but none of them came close. A short while later they stopped completely.

"What now?" asked Nabutangula.

"We must find a safe spot to cross the river. Once south of that, we should encounter friendly forces sooner or later."

"Our course would be much safer if we downloaded data from the artificial satellite. Or contacted any friendly forces that might be in the area."

Lutnaptinav refused to be drawn into this debate again and did not reply. Of course, Nabutangula was correct: data from the satellite or communications with friendly forces would make this last stage of their journey much easier. But it would also alert the commanders that they were still alive and that could invite new orders that could once more see them being sacrificed.

It had no intention of being sacrificed.

The discourtesy and outright contempt it had encountered from the commanders of the Continent 1 forces had erased any feelings of loyalty it might have had at the start of this venture. Were it possible, it would have simply headed back directly to its home holdfast on Subcontinent 1-3.

But it was not possible. The power levels in the fighting machine's cells were dangerously low. Indeed, they would have been exhausted several rotations ago if they had not managed to salvage a partially charged cell from a wrecked machine they had found along the way. And even if they had enough power, the machine was in great need of maintenance. Several non-essential systems had ceased to function and some of the vital ones were in danger. No, they had no choice but to go to the newly constructed holdfast near the southern front of the offensive. There they could get new machines—and Lutnaptinav could be freed from the close company of Nabutangula. It also hoped to find those members of its battle group who had been wounded in earlier fighting. It had been promised they would be taken care of.

A ray of light appeared suddenly off to the right and Lutnaptinav slowed the machine and steered it into a patch of tall vegetation. "What is it?" asked Nabutangula.

"It appears to be coming from one of the water vessels on the river. Yes, look, there is another one. The prey-creatures have spread an alarm about our passing, I would conclude."

"What do you intend?"

"We shall not take unnecessary risks. Not now, after making it so far. We will move farther to the north and then east again. We will search for an unguarded spot to cross the river," said Lutnaptinav.

"That might take a while," said Nabutangula. "The enemy uses this river for its supply vessels. The traffic might be heavy."

"We have spent almost thirty rotations making it this far. Traveling by night, hiding by day. I have no intention of making some foolish move now out of impatience to be done."

"As you say," said Nabutangula, subsiding.

In the end, it took two more rotations to find a safe time and place to cross the river. But it was done and then they headed south at their best speed. Another rotation passed before they encountered a patrolling fighting machine. Lutnaptinav created the fiction that their long-range communicator was inoperable (and before they reached their destination it would make the fiction fact) and the one they encountered accepted it. It seemed quite surprised by their appearance, but let them pass and directed them to the holdfast where they could find help. It was several rotations' journey, but with no danger of enemy interference, Lutnaptinav was confident they would make it.

* * * * *

May, 1914, Frankfurt, Germany

"Desk duty won't be so bad, Erich."

Erich Serno looked at his sister, Matilde, sitting next to his hospital bed and forced himself not to shout at her. He'd forced himself not to shout at his mother when she said the same thing to him at least a dozen times a day, but a shout nearly broke loose from him now. Desk duty... desk duty... it was all he was fit for now. He looked down at the flat place in the sheet where his leg should have been.

He'd been sure that the doctors could save his leg, and maybe they could have if his train hadn't been wrecked by the Martians on the trip home. But after that nightmare he'd spent weeks in a delirium of pain and fever and drugs until his head had finally cleared and he found himself a cripple.

"Mama said the doctors say they will have a wooden leg ready for you soon, Erich," continued Matilde. "Then you'll be able to get out of bed and get around." She seemed oblivious to the reality of what she was saying. Yes, he could stump around on a wooden leg. But he couldn't fly a plane. Ever. And while it was true that once he had been given command of a *kampfgeswader*, he spent more time at a desk than he did in a cockpit, he did so love to fly. To never be able to do that again...

The Air Service would no doubt find some sort of job for him. There was a war and everyone had to do their part. But he'd probably end up a supply or personnel officer, directing men and equipment to the units who would do the actual fighting, while he stayed behind.

"Papa is very proud of your new medal," said his sister, pointing to the small flat box sitting on the bedside table. Inside was a small blue and gold medal called the *Pour le Merite*. Frederick the Great had invented it back in the 1700s and it had been for the Prussian Army. Since 1871, it could be awarded to any German soldier. It was quite an honor, he supposed, but he'd gladly trade a hundred of them to get his leg back. "Papa is going to talk to the mayor of Darmstadt about a welcome home ceremony."

"What?" snapped Serno. That was the last thing he wanted!

"After you get your new leg, I mean," burbled Mathilde. "You'll look so fine there in the square in your uniform, with your new medal."

Serno snorted. Yes, that was another job they could find for him: parade him in front of the people looking so fine with his pretty medal! See? The war isn't so bad. Not every one of your sons will come back as a pile of ashes. Some will only come back missing an arm or a leg or a face. But we'll give him a pretty medal and find work for him. No, it's not so bad at all, is it? He looked away from his sister, out the window and said nothing.

"Oh, and your old friend, Hannah, was asking about you the other day."

"Who? Oh, right. Why?"

"Why? Because she wanted to know how you are! She said she was so sorry you had been wounded."

"Oh."

"She was sweet on you once, wasn't she?" Mathilde gave him an odd smile.

"Back in school! That was years ago. Anyway, she's married, isn't she?"

"Not anymore! Her poor husband was killed in Bulgaria or some such place last year. I wrote you about that! Didn't you get my letter?"

"I guess not." He tried to remember any such letter, but could not. Hannah, eh? She had been a pretty little thing back then. He wondered what she looked like now?

"She said she would come by and see you when you get home. That would be all right, wouldn't it?"

"I suppose."

His sister finally left. He had been glad to see her, but she could chatter so. Just like Mother. He settled back in the bed and forced himself to think about the future. He couldn't lie here feeling sorry for himself forever. A desk job. He could do a desk job if he had too. And he wouldn't be moving around so much the way he'd been the last few years. It would be nice to stay in one spot for a while.

Hannah, eh?

* * * * *

May, 1914, London

Professor Frederick Lindemann brushed a tiny speck of lint off the coat of his best suit and then returned his attention to the ceremony taking place on the Horse Guards Parade. This open area in central London bordered St. James Park and was surrounded on the other three sides by government buildings. The Prime Minister's residence was to the south, Whitehall and the War offices to the east, and the Admiralty to the north. At the moment it was, well, not filled, but occupied by a group of military personnel, a small band provided by the Horse Guards, and a modest gathering of spectators.

The ceremony was centered around a few high-ranking military officers. Prince Battenburg, First Sea Lord, was there, along with an Army general, who's name Lindemann had forgotten, who was standing in for Field Marshal Kitchener, who was busy elsewhere, and a few lower ranking aides. Among the spectators, standing beside Lindemann, was Winston Churchill.

"Shouldn't you be up there, sir?" whispered Lindemann. "You are head of the Navy, after all."

"No, no," replied Churchill. "This is a strictly military matter, you know. Heaven forbid civilians be a part of it."

Lined up in front of the commanders were a few dozen men from the Army and Navy. They were mostly officers, but a few enlisted men were there, too. They were all to receive medals for things they had done in the line of duty. Normally, Lindemann understood, medals were just sent off to the recipients, wherever they happened to be stationed, but every so often a ceremony like this was held for men who were in the London area. The British loved this sort of thing.

Today, however, Lindemann suspected that the ceremony was for the benefit of one specific recipient. From his vantage point he could just see where Bertie, Lieutenant Albert Windsor, RN, was standing with the others. The young man seemed a bit nervous, but clearly proud.

"I'm surprised that the King isn't here to see his son get his medal," said Lindemann.

"Oh, he is," said Churchill. He jerked his head toward the Admiralty building. "His Majesty is watching from one of the windows. He didn't want to distract people from the ceremony. But he's quite proud of young Bertie. From your report—and Goodenough's—it's clear he behaved admirably during the battle."

"Yes, sir, he never flinched, even when the walls of our compartment were glowing cherry red from the Martian heat rays." Lindemann suppressed a shudder at the memory of that awful moment.

One by one the men were called up to receive their medals. A few words were said, the medals pinned on, salutes exchanged, and the men returned to the ranks. Lindemann could not discern any pattern to the order the medals were given out, but finally it was Bertie's turn.

Battenburg's voice, which was already quite loud, got a bit louder. "For commendable actions during the Battle of Warsaw, Lieutenant Commander Albert Windsor is awarded the Distinguished Service Order."

"He's been promoted, too?" asked Lindemann.

"Oh yes," said Churchill. "It's expected."

Bertie returned to the ranks and the ceremony went on. Churchill shifted his feet and his hand went up to his face, probably reaching for the cigar that wasn't there. He cleared his throat and said, "I didn't want to ruin the surprise, but I thought I should mention that you have not been forgotten in all this Professor."

Lindemann's eyebrows went up. "Sir?"

"Yes, your actions in flogging the Armstrong people to finish the ironclads in time and, of course, bringing young Bertie home alive has been noticed at the highest levels. So, when the next Honor's List is published, you will find yourself Viscount Cherwell."

Lindemann's mouth dropped open and he could not think of a word to say. A peerage! A title of nobility! It was something he dreamed of receiving someday—many years from now—in recognition of his scientific accomplishments. But to receive it now—and for military accomplishments was something he could never have expected. Churchill was grinning at him now. He could imagine what his face must look like. He managed to pull himself together and blurt out, "Thank you, sir." After a few seconds he said, "Cherwell?"

"Little place up north," said Churchill, flipping his hand. "Not like the old days of course. You aren't going to own Cherwell or anything like that, the name is meaningless. But the title is real enough. You could even take a seat in the House of Lords if you wanted."

Lindemann blinked. He supposed he could, but in the last few decades the upper house of Parliament had been stripped of almost all its powers except for a few ceremonial ones. Lindemann couldn't see any real reason for wasting his time there. "I... I'll have to think about that."

"Do so," said Churchill. It looked like he was going to say something else, but just then the band struck up a lively march and they realized the ceremony was over. The men were dispersing and the spectators began to wander off. Bertie came over to meet them. His new medal hung from his chest and Lindemann noticed the new, narrow gold ring on each sleeve.

"Congratulations!" said Churchill and Lindemann echoed him. They shook hands and Bertie's face was beaming.

"T-thank you, sir, P-Professor. I-I'm sure you b-both had a hand in this. I r-really didn't d-do m-much except stand t-there."

Lindemann was impressed by the boy's humility. "Nonsense!" he said automatically. "You were a great help to me, and you stood your ground when a lot of men might have run. I know *I* surely wanted to!"

"Yes," agreed Churchill. "I've been shot at on more than one occasion, and while it's quite thrilling when they miss, I can scarcely imagine what it's like to be nearly roasted alive. The award was well-given, Commander, don't you worry about that!"

"T-thank you, sir. B-but am I.... am I still the Professor's aide? I over-heard my f-father saying s-something about a n-new assignment?"

"Nothing's been decided yet. But speaking of your father, he's up there in the Nelson Room waiting for you. Why don't you nip up there and say hello?"

Bertie's face lit up again. "He's here? Watching? Yes, sir! I'll go right way!" He spun about and nearly ran toward the Admiralty Building.

"*Will* he still be my aide, sir?" asked Lindemann.

"I doubt it," replied Churchill. "I think his father will want him around him for a while. Probably send him off on recruiting tours or something like that."

"I'll miss him," said Lindemann truthfully. "And what about me, sir? Am I still your science advisor?"

"Of course!" said Churchill. "As long as you want. Unless you want some assignment that takes you closer to the fighting. I know that a taste of combat can lead some men to want more."

"Uh, well, I'm not one of them, sir! One taste was more than enough for me!"

Churchill chuckled. "All right then. Come by and see me tomorrow and we'll find something for you to do."

* * * * *

Subcontinent 1-1, Holdfast 10-22, Cycle 597,845.9

The war machine was making some truly ominous creaks and groans by the time they reached the holdfast. It had gone far too long without maintenance and more than once Lutnaptinav had feared that it would break down short of their goal, forcing them to call for assistance. That would not be a bad thing in itself, but it would destroy the fiction that their long range communicator was damaged. It had not wanted to risk getting some new order from the area commander that might have sent it off somewhere else to be destroyed.

But with the holdfast in sight, it now had Nabutangula wreck the device in a convincing manner. It doubted anyone would check the story, but there was no point in taking chances. They soon encountered the local patrol and were passed on to the holdfast. "Take note," the sentry said, "the Northern Force has been here for a number of rotations refitting. It is scheduled to depart almost immediately and you will probably encounter considerable congestions in the hangar and repair facilities."

Acknowledging the warning, they proceeded to the holdfast. "Leaving?" said Nabutangula. "Where are they going, do you suppose?"

"Without more information on the situation, speculation is difficult, but I would assume they are going back north to create a defensive line in the rear to cover the withdrawal of the southern force."

"Withdrawal?"

"Surely, with the convergence of prey-creature forces we can soon expect from the north this position will become untenable," said Lutnaptinav. "A complete withdrawal to the east is the only logical choice."

"I'm not sure our superiors will see things that way," said Nabutangula.

As they approached the walls of the holdfast, there was the sudden appearance of scores of fighting machines climbing over the walls in the opposite direction. Maneuvering around them, Lutnaptinav reached the top and they saw many more on the central plain and still more coming up the ramp from the underground hangar. They halted by one of the defense towers and let them pass.

After a few moments a message was directed at them. "Fighting machine at 147-29-8, identify yourself."

"Lutnaptinav of Clan Patralvus. Nabutangula of Clan Vinkarjan is also aboard," it replied. A considerable length of time went by before another message arrived, it was from Mandapravis, commander of the Northern Force.

"Lutnaptinav, explain your presence."

"We have completed the last orders you gave us. Being in critical need of repairs we have come here, the closest base."

"Completed? How so?" demanded Mandapravis.

"We advanced west, doing what damage we could, until all the fighting machines in our two battlegroups had been destroyed or rendered inoperable. Salvaging parts from two damaged machines, we were able to create one mobile, though unarmed, machine. We were then able to return here."

"Were you? I look forward to a full report from you, Lutnaptinav."

"You will have it," Lutnaptinav replied curtly. "Are the other surviving members of our clans here? I was promised they would be taken care of."

There was another lengthy pause and then Mandapravis replied. "They are. Now that a... *reliable* chain of obedience is restored, you are ordered to assemble your people, reequip them, and join this force in the defense of the holdfast."

"For how long?"

"Until you are given new orders! The Colonial Conclave has ordered this holdfast and this area to be held at all costs. You have your orders."

"Commander, during our journey here we observed very powerful prey-creatures forces moving in this direction. I doubt..."

"They have already been noted by the artificial satellite. Now obey your orders!"

It could see that no further discussion would be productive, so it merely said, "As you command," and broke the connection. "It would appear that you are correct, Nabutangula. Our superiors are insane."

"That is not what I said!" said Nabutangula in alarm. Lutnaptinav made no reply.

By this time the mass of the fighting machines had departed and there was no problem entering the main hangar. It parked the machine and lowered it to the loading position. The hatch opened and they transferred themselves to two travel chairs. The holdfast seemed nearly deserted, just a few people tending the production machinery and main control area. But they were able to find where their clanmates were being housed and quickly rejoined them. The eight members of Clan Paltravus and seven others from Clan Vinkarjan, were surprised and elated to see their commanders arrive. A few moments were spent sharing information on what had befallen each of them since they parted. Lutnaptinav noted that the fifteen survivors had spent nearly all of their time doing little or nothing.

"You were assigned no duties?" asked Lutnaptinav.

"They did not appear to trust us," said Galjintaram, the senior most of the Paltravus survivors. "With you and Subcommander Nabutangula presumed dead, there was no chain of obedience in place and they seem to think that any *Threeborn* in that situation will simply run amok!" Several others echoed those sentiments and Lutnaptinav could feel the discontent in all of them.

"What shall we do now, Subcommander?" asked Galjintaram.

"Our orders from Mandapravis are to equip ourselves with fighting machines, reorganize our battlegroups, and join the Northern Force in the defense of this holdfast," said Lutnaptinav.

"With the losses that have been taken, is there any hope of success?" asked Galjintaram.

"Unless there are significant reinforcements coming from the east—and none were mentioned—I see no hope of defeating the forces being arrayed against us," replied Lutnaptinav.

"So we are to be sacrificed... again."

"So it would seem."

"But it is not just we *Threeborn*," said Nabutangula. "It is everyone in this entire region, well over five hundred of the Race."

"Cannot the Colonial Conclave be made to see reason?" asked Galjintaram.

"Reason from us? *Threeborn*? I think not," said Lutnaptinav. "They have little respect for our opinions."

"The Conclave must place great value on this holdfast," said Nabutangula. "Perhaps they have reasons we do not know of."

"It is the only source of fighting machines and replacement parts in this area. Also the reactor here is the only place our power cells can be recharged," said Lutnaptinav. "Without it, any sustained operation here would be... impossible." It paused as a sudden thought occurred to it.

"So then we have no choice but to do as Mandapravis has commanded?" asked Galjintaram.

"Perhaps..." replied Lutnaptinav. Its thoughts went back to when it had tied into the vision pick-ups of the doomed holdfast to the north. That holdfast had been constructed by the same clan who had built this one. The design should be identical...

"Commander?" Everyone in the chamber was looking at it. The plan that had materialized was very dangerous and would be the death of every one of them if it failed—perhaps even if it succeeded. Could it trust them to follow? It believed that it could. The anger radiating from them was almost palpable.

"Without the reactor here, defense of this area would be impossible. The reactor is the key."

Chapter Twenty-One

Subcontinent 1-1, Holdfast 10-22, Cycle 597,845.9

Lutnaptinav's plan proved to be absurdly easy to carry out.

The holdfast had a garrison of less than two score and they were all occupied with production of fighting machines, drones, ammunition for the bombardment drones, spare parts, energy cells, or food. Only three were assigned to the reactor. The first step was to disable the vision pick-ups in the reactor area and the corridors leading to it. This could be done remotely and was quickly done. It would be noticed given time, but Lutnaptinav was not going to give anyone that time. The experience it had gained watching the activities in the other doomed holdfast was invaluable here.

As soon as the pick-ups were disabled, the seventeen members of Clan Paltravus and Clan Vinkarjan went into action. Five went to ready the fighting machines they would need to escape. The rest descended on the reactor chamber to take control. Unfortunately, this meant slaying the three people there—they could leave no witnesses—but the deaths of these three would mean saving the lives of five hundred more, so it had no trouble in convincing the others of the necessity.

The reactor crew had suspected nothing, so it was easy to get close enough to them to use electric shock devices to terminate them. The next step was to disable all of the telemetry from the reactor to the main control center and substitute false data so no alarm would be sounded. This took a small amount of time, but was easily done.

"Why are there no safeguards to prevent something like this?" asked Nabutangula as they worked.

"Because our seniors cannot conceive that anyone would ever try to do this," replied Lutnaptinav. "Their rigid thinking is why we are losing this war against creatures who are so far inferior to us."

"But *we* can conceive of it. Perhaps they are right in fearing the *Threeborn*."

"Perhaps," conceded Lutnaptinav. "But it will be for the good of the Race in the long run." Nabutangula did not reply but continued working. Once the telemetry was disabled they set the reactor to overload and melt down. This required a number of manual adjustments to the hardware itself and then actions from the command stations, but again, its earlier observations had revealed all those steps. Finally all was in readiness. A single additional command would set everything in motion.

"Everyone into your travel chairs," Lutnaptinav ordered. "When I finish with this, we will all move to the main hangar by the predetermined routes. Understood?" Everyone answered in the affirmative. It wrapped a tendril around one of the control rods and initiated the destruct sequence. "Very well. Go."

The twelve of them quickly exited the chamber and set out on several different routes so as not to arouse suspicion by traveling in one large group. Lutnaptinav paused to seal the chamber doors and jam them and then followed. It encountered no one on the way to the hangar except for a person tending the holding cells for the prey-creature food animals. Lutnaptinav doubted there would be any attempt to remove the creatures once the disaster unfolded. They would die from radiation or eventually lack of food and water. It was of no concern, they were to die in any case. It reached the hangar and was pleased to see all of the others already there when it arrived. No alarm had been sounded yet and only a short while longer would be required for the reactor to reach a point where no countermeasures could save it. They mounted their fighting machines and all seventeen moved up the ramp, followed by six other machines on automatic mode carrying spare power cells.

They reached the central space of the holdfast and Lutnaptinav contacted the main control center. "This is Lutnaptinav of Clan Paltravus. We and Clan Vinkarjan are proceeding to join the Northern Force as commanded by Mandapravis."

"Acknowledged," came the reply. There was not the slightest indication of anything wrong.

"Excellent," it said to the others. "Let us make the best possible speed." It turned its machine and headed north; the others followed.

"I hope you know what you are doing, Lutnaptinav," said Nabutangula on a private circuit.

"It is far too late to do anything but carry on," it replied.

* * * * *

May 1914, Moldavia

"God damn it! They're getting away—again!"

Harry wasn't sure who among his men had made the exclamation, but the words exactly expressed his own feelings. Through the field glasses pressed to his good eye he could see the huge swarm of Martian tripods moving rapidly off toward the northeast, pursued by artillery rounds, a few squadrons of armored cars, and a couple of gunboats on the Dniester River. The sight of the dozens of wrecked tripods on either bank of the river softened his irritation, but only slightly. Two days! If the Martians had delayed their attack for just another two days, the Northern Force could have arrived in time to bag the lot of them. But the Martians hadn't waited and the Northern Force hadn't arrived and the Southern Force by itself simply wasn't strong enough to withstand an attack by nearly five hundred tripods.

The sudden approach—it couldn't exactly be called an *attack*—of that large a force had come as a surprise. All the generals seemed to think that the Martians were determined to hold on to their positions along the Danube and continue the fight. The force that had invaded Poland had fallen back and, rather than continue east into Ukraine, had crossed the Dniester to join the forces in Romania. That would only make sense if the Martians planned to hold the place. But then a few days ago the enemy forces along the Danube line had suddenly retreated and headed to the northeast—toward the Dniester. Pursuing forces from the south reported that the Martian fortress near the remains of Bucharest had been destroyed in a manner similar to the one Harry had helped capture. So this wasn't just a redeployment. The Martians would only have done that unless they were planning to abandon the whole region.

Scouting aircraft had then spotted the entire Martian force gathering a day's march south of the Dniester, with scouts pushed forward to the river. The Southern Force had taken up a position along the river, stretching forty or fifty miles, awaiting the arrival of the Northern Force and whatever Germans and Austrians from their armies that were fit to march. The plan was that when they arrived, the combined force would cross the river and head south into Rumania to attack the enemy from the rear and hopefully destroy them all.

But without those reinforcements, the Southern Force could not hope to take on a Martian force of that size by itself. So the order had gone out to concentrate and shift everyone to the northwest. They had done so and taken up a strong position on the edge of the likely route of the Martians. If the aliens came right at them, they could hold out long enough to allow the Northern Force to arrive, and if they were only trying to escape they would be in position to hit their flank as they moved past and do as much damage as possible. The 1st Australian Armored Division had been kept in reserve, ready to rush to any threatened spot on short notice.

The Martians had only been interested in escaping—for which Harry was secretly grateful. He'd already been in one desperate fight waiting for rescuing forces to arrive and he had no wish to do it again. But the enemy had paid a considerable price to escape. The heavy artillery, tanks, gunboats, and land ironclads had pitched into the Martian flank and probably destroyed fifty or more tripods as they crossed the river. Other ships, from further down river, had harried the other flank, doing more damage. Harry and the 15th Newcastle Battalion had joined in, but only fired a few long range shots.

So they'd hurt them, but they had been unable to stop them. The bulk of their forces had made it across and were now heading toward Ukraine at a speed that no human force could match. Fortunately, losses had been light on the human side; the enemy being intent on escape, not destruction.

Harry lowered his field glasses as the last of the tripods disappeared in the distance, and sighed. An opportunity had been missed, but he reminded himself that this was still a great victory. When they had set out from Alexandria the Martians were driving into Poland, knocking at the gates of the rest of Europe.

Now they were fleeing back into the vast reaches of Russia. And it had been a combined force of nearly every country in the world who had pushed them back. Truly a grand alliance. In the long run that might be more important than the casualties inflicted or the ground won. Harry hoped so.

"So what do you think we'll do now, sir?" asked Sergeant Breslin, coming up beside him.

"Chase them, I guess," replied Harry.

Now Breslin sighed. "From the maps I've seen, there's a bloody lot o' land in that direction. Goes on forever and ever. We could have the Devil's own time catchin' the bastards."

"God's truth, Sergeant. But for now I guess we just wait for orders."

So they did, but when the orders came they weren't what any of them expected. The Martians would be pursued. But they would be pursued by the Germans and Austrians and French and Belgians and Dutch and even the Russians coming down from the north. The British and Australians and Americans in the Southern Force—and their attached medical services, Harry was pleased to learn—were to join their brethren in the Northern Force and reorganize for a new assignment—what, no one seemed to know.

"Where do you suppose they'll send us now?" he asked Burford Sampson.

Sampson shrugged and then said, "I don't know, but you can be sure there will be Martians there to fight."

* * * * *

Subcontinent 1-1, Sector 84-21, Cycle 597,845.9

Lutnaptinav checked the status of the combined battlegroup with satisfaction. They had crossed the river and broken contact with the prey-creature forces with only the loss of a single fighting machine and that was one of the unpiloted ones carrying only spare power cells.

"What now?" asked Nabutangula on a private circuit. "So far your plan has worked and there seems to be no suspicion that we were responsible for the destruction of the holdfast reactor."

This was true. The sudden loss of the holdfast as a supply base had thrown the high command into what could only be called a panic. As Lutnaptinav had hoped, the loss of the base and the convergence of powerful enemy forces had finally convinced their leaders that continued resistance in this region was hopeless and could only lead to the destruction of their entire force—something which simply could not be afforded at this time. An immediate withdrawal was essential and any investigation into the cause of the reactor meltdown would have to wait.

"Given time, their suspicion will grow," it replied. "While any physical evidence has been destroyed or lost with the holdfast, the fact remains that we were there when it happened. And we are *Threeborn*. Their distrust of us will only be strengthened and I have no doubt they will come up with some new plan that will lead to our destruction."

"So what shall we do?"

"Go home. I see no other option."

"Home?"

"Back to rejoin our clans. We have sufficient spare power cells to reach there if we avoid any serious combat."

"But our orders are to accompany the others to a position to the northeast," protested Nabutangula. "We can hardly leave without it being noticed."

"True, but if we plan our departure well, they will have great difficulty in stopping us. Far more difficulty than it will be worth bothering with."

"You hope."

"In any case, I will attempt it with my people. You are welcome to come with us or stay here. Or you could betray our plans to Mandapravis and see us destroyed—and perhaps gain its thanks and trust."

Nabutangula was silent for a moment, but then it said, "I think not. Mandapravis' gratitude would be short-lived and it would no doubt find some way of disposing of me and my people quickly. And…"

"Yes?"

"After all we have experienced together, I find the thought of such a betrayal… distasteful. You have led us well through many difficult situations. I will continue to follow your lead, Lutnaptinav."

Lutnaptinav did not reply immediately. Nabutangula's profession of loyalty to it—a being from an entirely different clan—produced an odd feeling in it for which it had no words. Odd. But enough of that. "Here is what I propose."

For the next two rotations, they followed the force northeast, but they slowly worked their way to the eastern edge of the formation and dropped gradually toward the rear. Then, it informed Mandapravis they would be stopping briefly to change power cells—something that was not yet necessary.

Upon receiving its routine acknowledgement, they disabled their locational transponders, shut down long range communications, and immediately set out almost due east at the maximum possible speed. It was nearly a sixth of a rotation before anyone noticed their absence and they were over two hundred *telequel* away by then. It was another half a rotation before the artificial satellite passed overhead and they made sure they were well concealed by thick vegetation when it did. Numerous messages were directed at them, which they ignored, and they proceeded east and south without being detected by any forces of the Race, although they surprised and ignored many small groups of prey-creatures who somehow managed to subsist in the region.

They traveled almost all the way to the rugged territory between the inland seas before encountering anyone. When they did it was only a small group of scouting machines. They demanded to know their identity and purpose, of course, but they were too weak to attempt to stop them when Lutnaptinav failed to respond. They shadowed them for a full rotation but were left behind when they entered the mountains.

"Nothing but prey-creatures lie between us and friendly territory," said Nabutangula.

"Yes," replied Lutnaptinav. Privately it wondered just how friendly that territory would actually be.

* * * * *

June, 1914, Warsaw, Poland

Ola Wojciech strained to hold the wooden post in place while another man secured it with a half-dozen nails. When he was done, two other men arrived with another post. It was far too big and heavy for Ola to move herself, but they set it into the right position and left Ola to hold it while they went for another one. This went on for an hour or more until Ola's arms and legs were quivering with the effort. Finally, they reached the end of the row and the men called for a halt. She slumped to the ground and wiped the sweat off her face. It was quite warm for early June, but she was glad she wasn't trying to do this in the middle of winter.

She sat and looked at the wall she had helped build. One wall of one building. She gazed around at the ruins of Warsaw and how little difference her efforts had made to the devastated landscape. Square kilometer after square kilometer of shattered and gutted buildings. Some were just piles of scorched rubble while others had a few stone or brick walls still standing, chimneys or beams reaching skyward like skeletal fingers. The smell of burning still clung to the place and she doubted that the rain would ever completely wash it clean.

But looking closer, she saw that her little band of workers were not alone. Thousands of people were laboring to clear away the rubble and repair or construct new shelters. Winter was still half a year away, but this was a job that could not wait. She grimaced when she saw one work party halt and then start waving to the ever-present burial groups. While the Martian heat rays usually left little of a person to bury, it seemed like most of Warsaw's dead had been trapped in collapsing buildings. She was glad she was in a construction party rather than one clearing the rubble—or collecting the dead. She'd seen plenty of dead, but she wished to see no more. Her status as a 'war hero' could have gotten her a different—and cleaner—job if she'd asked, but somehow she couldn't bring herself to do so.

The team leader called them back to work and they started on another wall. Some of the timbers being used had been salvaged from the rubble, while others were new cut, brought in from the surrounding forests where the lumberjacks labored. Other material was coming in from outside, too, on the newly repaired railway lines. Building materials, and more importantly food. No one was sure how many people remained to be fed in Warsaw. Wanda had told Ola that before the battle, the city held nearly 700,000 people. There weren't nearly that many left now. But they all would need shelter before the first snow fell.

Warsaw's population was actually continuing to fall. Most of the young men had gone to join the army. The New Polish Army. Not the local volunteers who had helped to defend the city, but the actual *Polish* Army. When Kazimierz Sosnkowski had declared Polish independence and formed a provisional government, no one knew if the Great Powers would let him get away with it. German troops were garrisoning the city and holding large parts of the country. Once the Martians were pushed out, if the Germans had wanted to, they could have done whatever they wanted. But then England had recognized Poland's independence and they were soon followed by France, the United States, and a dozen other countries. Germany, still very much in debt to those countries for the help they'd given in repelling the Martians, had been forced to go along. While there were still German troops all over the country, the new Polish government was taking control and raising a real army. The Germans might not be happy, but they weren't making any trouble—so far.

Ola would have much rather been with the new army, but despite the very large part women had played in the city's defense, old habits had reasserted themselves now that the immediate danger had passed and women were not allowed in the ranks of the *real* army. She felt rather bitter about that, but there were rumors that a woman's auxiliary was going to be raised and if so, she was determined to be a part of it. In the meantime, she would help build houses.

The long day came to an end with them not quite finished with the fourth wall of what was going to be a very ugly house. They trudged back to the tent complex that housed their labor detachment. The tents had been supplied by the Danish Army if she was reading the stamps on them correctly. The cots appeared to be French. There was a cook tent and after a hot, filling, but very bland meal she found her own cot in one of the women's tents and stretched out on it and tried to rest. She could hear some music being played outside and she hoped it wasn't going to be a noisy night. How people could work all day and still have the energy for merriment she couldn't understand. Still, it was better than some sullen silence, she supposed.

She had nearly drifted off to sleep when a sudden shout jolted her awake: "Ola! Hey Ola! You have a letter!"

She sat up on the cot and saw Aniela Dabrowski, a woman about her age, standing in the tent opening waving an envelope. "A real letter!" she said. "How do you get a letter, Ola? *Nobody* gets letters these days!"

It was true that the postal system, which the Russians had kept a tight control of, had yet to be rebuilt, but if she was getting a letter, there was only one person she could think of who could have sent it—and gotten it through to her. *Tom!* She sprang from the cot, but Aniela's cry had attracted the attention of a half-dozen other women, who clustered around.

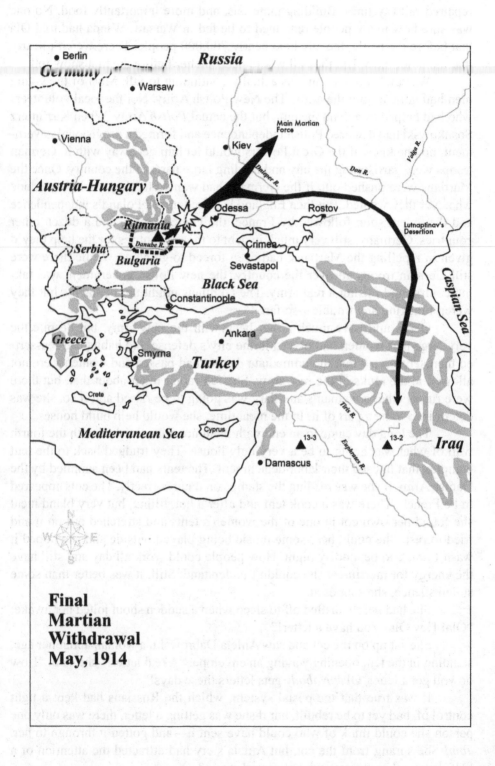

Berlin

Russia

Germany

Warsaw

Vienna

Kiev

Main Martian Force

Dnieper R.

Don R.

Volga R.

Austria-Hungary

Odessa

Rostov

Lutnaptinav's Desertion

Rumania

Danube R.

Crimea

Serbia

Bulgaria

Sevastapol

Black Sea

Constantinople

Caspian Sea

Ankara

Greece

Smyrna

Turkey

Crete

Mediterranean Sea

Cyprus

13-3

Tigris R.

13-2

Iraq

Damascus

Euphrates R.

N
W   E
S

**Final
Martian
Withdrawal
May, 1914**

"Where's it from?" "Look at the man on that postage stamp—is that the Tsar?" "No, I think it's the British king!" "Look, it's from London!" "Who do you know in London, Ola?"

"Give me that!" she cried, snatching it out of Aniela's hand.

The woman laughed. "All right! All right! No need to get angry! But who do you know in London, Ola?"

She looked at it and by the return address she saw it really was from Tom Bridges! Her heart seemed to swell inside her. *Tom!* He'd sent her a letter! "Just someone I met during the siege," she said to Aniela, knowing she had to give some sort of answer, or they'd never leave her alone. She pushed past the others out of the tent and she nearly ran until she was alone. There was still enough daylight to read, so she stopped to open it. The envelope was creased and wrinkled and smudged by many different hands. She could barely imagine what route it had taken to reach her. It was addressed to her, but also had *'Care of the garrison commander, Warsaw, Poland'* written in English and some rather bad Polish. She supposed that his military rank and the fact that many people still remembered her from her *'Hero of Poland'* persona during the siege had allowed the letter to finally find her.

She carefully opened it, noting that it clearly had been opened at least once and resealed, and found inside a letter along with a smaller envelope addressed to Tom, with several stamps already on it. *He wants me to write back!* The letter was in his own handwriting that she'd learned to recognize when she was spying on him back at the hotel. Those days seemed years ago now. It wasn't very long and contained such ordinary pleasantries about his trip home and the weather and his health and inquiries about hers that it nearly made her laugh. Such ordinary things were from another time. Another world. But they were such precious things nonetheless that they brought tears to her eyes.

But the closing was anything but ordinary: *I miss you very much Ola. Very much. I will try to get back to you somehow, God and the war allowing. Stay safe. Be safe. All my love, Tom.*

She sat down in the dirt and reread the letter. Four times. And then the ending. Six times. She pressed the paper to her chest, closed her eyes, and breathed deeply. She remembered those last two days before he left and her heart beat faster. She missed him so much. Would she ever see him again?

God and the war allowing.

She was certain God would have no objections, but what about the war? The war had been going on for seven years, although only the last one had directly affected her. But the war could only end in total victory—or total defeat. No negotiated settlements. No trifling exchanges of territory. Victory or death.

Victory. Warsaw had been a victory. From the news they heard, there were other victories, too. The Martians were being pushed back on many fronts. Perhaps they would be beaten. Perhaps they would be beaten before she was an old woman.

And perhaps Tom would come back to her.

* * * * *

Holdfast 14-1, Cycle 597,846,0

"I must admit that I am surprised to see you again, Lutnaptinav," said Kandanginar. "I did not expect it."

"Nor did I, in truth," said Lutnaptinav, looking at its progenitor. They were alone in a small chamber in the holdfast where it had first achieved consciousness. The trip through the mountainous territory had been harrowing, but only a single person had been lost to the prey-creatures and that had been from Nabutangula's people. Once in friendly territory, they had reactivated their long-range communicators and reported in. Nabutangula had been ordered back to its own clan territory and Lutnaptinav had been ordered here. It would not have been surprised if it had been terminated upon arrival, but it had not. Reprieved? Or merely deferred?

"We have received communications from the Continent 1 commanders," continued Kandanginar. "They have some serious questions about the destruction of the power reactor in Holdfast 4-19. It seems you and your people were there at the time this happened." Kandanginar extended a tendril toward Lutnaptinav. If it reciprocated, a neural link would be created allowing them to share their thoughts. Lutnaptinav kept its tendrils where they were.

"I would prefer not to lie to you," it said.

"Meaning if allowed, you *would* lie to me." It was not a question so Lutnaptinav did not answer.

A lengthy silence followed before Kandanginar spoke again. "If the situation were not so serious, I would order your termination."

"A logical choice. Why have you not?"

"Aside from the… questionable actions which you refuse to discuss, your actions as a combat commander during the recent operations were very impressive. We will need every person in the coming times and especially those with combat skills and experience."

"You imply that new and important operations are in the offing," said Lutnaptinav.

"Yes. While you were detached there has been a change in policy on the Homeworld."

"Again? This… vacillation in their directives is most disturbing."

"That is not something that you or I should question," said Kandanginar tersely.

"Nevertheless."

"I caution you, Lutnaptinav. Control these thoughts or I will reconsider termination."

"Very well."

"As I was saying, a new and major effort is being undertaken to bring a successful end to this war. You, and everyone, will be needed."

"Interesting," said Lutnaptinav. "I look forward to learning the details."

Kandanginar again extended a tendril and after a moment, Lutnaptinav took it in its own.

Epilogue

Excerpt from "The First Interplanetary War, Volume 3", by Winston Spencer Churchill, 1930. Reprinted with permission.

The victory at Warsaw and the eviction of Martian forces from eastern Europe can be seen as a major turning point in the war. Forging a strong European and American alliance was critical if victory was to be won. Despite many promises and a few encouraging examples of cooperation previously, it was the great crisis along the Dardanelles, Danube, and Vistula that finally shook the slumbering power of Germany awake and made that alliance a reality. That, along with a number of key technological developments like the land ironclads, saw the true turning of the tide.

Throughout the summer and fall of 1914, the rejuvenated armies of Germany, along with major forces from France and eventually Russia, drove the enemy ever eastward. A half-dozen Martian fortresses were taken and they were compelled to fall back all the way to the Volga. In Africa, Field Marshal Kitchener's long-held dream of retaking Khartoum was realized. And in America, the aliens were driven all the way back to the Rocky Mountains and the immense bounty of the farms in the Great Plains began to flow out to a hungry world yet again. The outlook at the end of that year was bright.

But the enemy was not yet beaten. On their dry, distant planet they were drawing new plans against us. Plans which would unleash destruction upon Mankind unlike anything we had experienced before.

1915 would begin with disaster. But in the end, it would surely be our finest hour.

The End

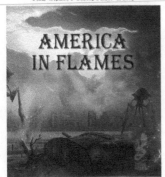

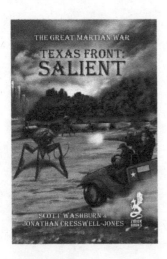